Isaac ASIMOV's
WONDERS OF THE WORLD

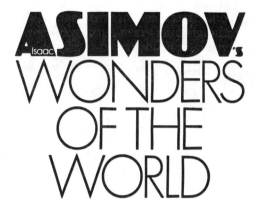

Isaac ASIMOV's
WONDERS
OF THE
WORLD

Edited by
Kathleen Moloney & Shawna McCarthy

The Dial Press

Davis Publications, Inc.
380 Lexington Avenue
New York, N.Y. 10017

FIRST PRINTING

(Copyright & acknowledgments page for
Isaac Asimov's SF Anthology, Vol. 6.
Hardcover title: Isaac Asimov's
WONDERS OF THE WORLD)

SF/sc
Asi

COPYRIGHT NOTICES AND ACKNOWLEDGMENTS

Grateful acknowledgment is hereby made for permission to reprint the following:
Lirios: A Tale of the Quintana Roo by James Tiptree, Jr.; © 1981 by Davis Publications, Inc.;
reprinted by permission of Robert P. Mills, Ltd.
Exposures by Gregory Benford; © 1981 by Davis Publications, Inc.; reprinted by permission of
Richard Curtis Associates, Inc.
For the Birds by Isaac Asimov; © 1980 by Davis Publications, Inc.; reprinted by permission of
the author.
The Woman the Unicorn Loved by Gene Wolfe; © 1981 by Davis Publications, Inc.; reprinted by
permission of Virginia Kidd, Agent.
Death in Vesunna by Eric G. Iverson and Elaine O'Byrne; © 1981 by Davis Publications, Inc.;
reprinted by permission of the authors.
I Dream of a Fish, I Dream of a Bird by Elizabeth A. Lynn; © 1977 by Elizabeth A. Lynn; reprinted
by permission of the author.
Fire Watch by Connie Willis; © 1982 by Davis Publications, Inc.; reprinted by permission of
the author.
Full Fathom Five My Father Lies by Rand B. Lee; © 1981 by Davis Publications, Inc.; reprinted by
permission of the author.
The Moon and the Moth by Peter Payack; © 1982 by Davis Publications, Inc.; reprinted by
permission of the author.
Trial Sample by Ted Reynolds; © 1981 by Davis Publications, Inc.; reprinted by permission of
the author.
Elementary Decision by Don Anderson; © 1982 by Davis Publications, Inc.; reprinted by
permission of the author.
The Storm King by Joan D. Vinge; © 1980 by Davis Publications, Inc.; reprinted by permission
of the author.
The Regulars by Robert Silverberg; © 1981 by Davis Publications, Inc.; reprinted by permission
of Scott Meredith Literary Agency, Inc.
Memo by Frank Ward; © 1982 by Davis Publications, Inc.; reprinted by permission of the author.
Enemy Mine by Barry B. Longyear; © 1979 by Davis Publications, Inc.; reprinted by permission
of the author.

CONTENTS

EDITOR'S NOTE

Wonders of the World is the sixth collection of stories compiled from the award winning *Isaac Asimov's Science Fiction Magazine*. In keeping with tradition, this anthology offers the reader some of the best science fiction and fantasy by many of the field's most honored writers.

For instance, we are thrilled to include James Tiptree, Jr.'s haunting "Lirios: A Tale of the Quintana Roo." It's hard to keep up with Tiptree's awards but at last count we believe it was four Nebulas and two Hugos. Two-time Hugo winner Joan D. Vinge brings her special combination of exciting adventure and lush description to a tale of a prince's fierce battle with an ancient dragon. Gene Wolfe, who in the past two years has cornered the 1981 World Fantasy Award, the 1982 British Science Fiction Award, and the 1982 Nebula, tells us the story of a modern romance between a woman and a unicorn. In "The Regulars," multi-award winner Robert Silverberg reveals some of the strange going-ons in a rather unusual bar called Charlie Sullivan's Place. Of course this collection also offers a breath-taking, technical science fiction tale by the master himself, Isaac Asimov. In his story, "For the Birds," the reader will soar along with the main character in his attempt to defy gravity on the Moon.

All these masters and such fiery new authors as Rand B. Lee, Connie Willis, and Ted Reynolds add up to a truly wondrous collection of captivating stories. So turn the page and step into some of the wonders of the world of science fiction.

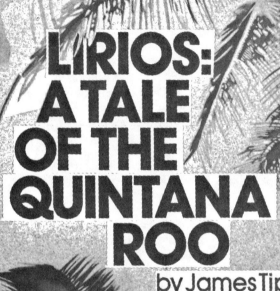

LIRIOS: A TALE OF THE QUINTANA ROO

by James Tiptree, Jr.

art: Artifact

The author, a retired experimental
psychologist, resides in Virginia,
and would like readers to know that
Quintana Roo is pronounced Keen'Tahnah Row.

The tourists throw spent Polaroid
Where Spaniards threw spent slaves:
And now and then a tourist joins
Four thousand years of graves;
For loves it's wiser to avoid
Smiles from those brilliant waves.

The old coco-ranch foreman saw him first.

It was a day of roaring hot south wind. The beach smoked under the thrashing coco-palms, and the Caribbean raved by like a billion white devils headed for Cuba, four hundred miles north. When I went down to see what *Don* Pa'o Camool was peering at, I could barely hold one eye open against the glaring, flying sand.

The beach stretched empty to the hazed horizon: dazzling white coral marked only by faint hieroglyphs of tar and wrack.

"¿Qué?" I howled above the wind-shriek.

"Caminante."

Interested, I peered harder. I'd heard of the *caminantes,* the Walking Men of old days, who passed their lives drifting up and down this long, wild shore. One of the dark streaks was, perhaps, moving.

"¿Maya caminante?"

The old man—he was a decade younger than I—spat down hard at a ghost-crab blowing by. *"Gringo."* He took a hard sideways squint up at me, as he always did when he used that word.

Then he screwed his face into one of his wilder Maya grimaces, which might mean anything or nothing, and stumped back up the bluff to his lunch, slapping his big old-fashioned *machete* as he went.

My eyes were caked with salt and sand. I too retired up to my wind-eroded patio to wait.

What finally came plodding into view along the tide-line was a black skeleton, a stick-figure with fuzz blowing around the head. When he halted by the compass-palm and turned to look up at the *rancho* I half-expected the sea-glare to shine through his ribs.

The *rancho* was a straggling line of five small pole-and-thatch huts, three smoky copra-drying racks, and a well with a winch-bucket. At the end was a two-room owner's *casita,* on whose rented patio I sat.

The apparition started straight up toward me.

Nearer, I saw he was indeed a *gringo:* the hair and beard whipping his sun-blackened face was a crusted pinkish grey. His emaciated body was charred black, with a few white scar-lines on his legs, and he was naked save for a pair of frayed shorts and his heavy leather sandals. A meagre roll of *serape* and a canteen were slung on his shoulders. He could have been sixty or thirty.

"Can I have some water, please?"

The English came out a bit rusty, but it was the voice that startled me: —a clear young voice right out of Midwest suburbia.

"Of course."

The sun glittered on a shark-knife hanging from the stranger's belt, showing its well-honed edge. I gestured to a shady spot on the patio curb and saw him slumped down where I could keep an eye on him before I went in. Incongruous young voices like his aren't unknown even here; they come from the scraps of human flotsam that drifts down the tropic latitudes hoping that tomorrow, or next year, they will get their heads in order. Some are heart-breaking; a few are dangerous, while they last. I knew that slant eyes were watching from the *rancho*—but no one could see into the *casa* and only a fool would rely on a Maya to protect one old *gringo* from another.

But when I came out he was sitting where I'd left him, gazing out at the blazing mill-race of the sea.

"Thank you . . . very much."

He took one slow, shaky sip, and then two more, and sat up straighter. Then he uncapped his canteen, rinsed, and filled it carefully from my pitcher before drinking more. The rinse-water he poured on my struggling casuarina seedling. I saw that the canteen under its cooler-rag was a sturdy anodised Sealite. The knife was a first-rate old Puma. His worn sandals were in repair, too; and wearing them was a mark both of status and sense. When he lifted the glass again, the eyes that glanced at me out of his sun-ravaged face shone a steady, clear, light hazel.

I picked up my own mug of cold tea and leaned back.

"Buut ka'an," the young stranger said, giving it the Maya click. "The Stuffer." He jerked his wild beard at the brilliant gale around us, and explained, between slow sips, "They call it that . . . because it blows until it stuffs the north full, see . . . and then it all comes blasting back in a Northeaster."

A scrap of my typing paper from the local dump came flittering by. He slapped a sandal on it, smoothed it, and folded it into his pack. As he moved, a nearby palm-root suddenly reared up and became a big iguana. The creature stared at us over its wattles with the pompous wariness which had carried it from the Jurassic, gave two ludicrous intention-bobs, and streaked off at a flying waddle, tail high.

We both grinned.

"More water?"

"Please. You have good water here." He stated it as a known fact, which it was.

"Where did you fill your canteen?"

"Pajaros. *Punta* Pajaros. Ffah!"

I refilled the pitcher, more than a little appalled. All ground-water quits at the lagoon-mouth a kilometer south. Even considering that he was walking north, with the wind, had this man, or boy, really come the thirty miles of burning, bone-dry sand-bar between here and the Pajaros lighthouse on that canteen? Moreover, Pajaros itself has no water; the fishermen who camp there occasionally bring in an oil-drum full, but were otherwise believed to subsist on beer, tequila, and other liquids not usually considered potable. No wonder he had rinsed the canteen, I thought, hunting out my pack of sodium-K tabs. Even without the Stuffer blowing, people can desiccate to congestive heart-failure without feeling it, on this windy shore.

But he refused them, rather absently, still staring at the sea.

"All the electrolyte you need, right there. If you're careful. Our blood is really modified sea-water . . . isn't that right?"

He roused and turned round to look at me directly, almost appraisingly. I saw his gaze take in the corner of the room behind us, where my driftwood bookshelves were dimly visible through the glass sliding doors that had long ceased to slide. He nodded. "I heard you had a lot of books. *Muy pesados*—heavy books. *Libros sicologicos.* Right?"

"Um."

This chance visitation was changing character unwelcomely. It wasn't odd that he should have known much about me—gossip has flowed ceaselessly up and down this coast for three thousand years. Now I had the impression that something about those "heavy psychological books" had drawn him here, and it made me uneasy. Like many experimental psychologists, I have had harrowing difficulties trying to explain to some distressed stranger that an extensive knowledge of, say, the cognitive behavior of rats, has no clinical applications.

But his own radar was in excellent shape. He was already wrapping his canteen and slinging on his roll.

"Look, I don't mean to interrupt you. The breeze is easing off. It'll be nice later on. If you don't mind, I'll just go down by that big driftlog there and rest awhile before I move on. Thanks for the water."

The "breeze" was doing a roaring 30 knots, and the huge mahogany timber down on the beach could hardly be seen for flying sand. If this was a ploy, it was ridiculous.

"No. You're not interrupting anything. If you want to wait, stay here in the shade."

"I've snoozed by that log before." He grinned down at me from his skeletal height. His tone wasn't brash, just gentle and resolute; and his teeth were very white and clean.

"At least let me pass you a couple of spare grapefruit; I've more than I can eat."

"Oh, well, great . . . "

Looking back, it's hard to say when and why it began to seem important that he stop and not go on. Certainly my sense of him had changed radically about that time. I now saw him as competent to this country, and to his strange life, whatever it might be; doubtless more competent than I. Not flotsam. And not in need of any ordinary help. But as time went on, something—maybe a projection of my own, maybe the unrelenting wind-scream that day—perhaps merely the oddness of the sea-light reflected in his pale eyes—made me sense him as being, well, *marked*. Not at all "doomed"—which isn't uncommon in this land, particularly if one neglects to contribute to the proper officials. And not "scarred" as by some trauma. Or watched by an enemy. I had merely an unquieting sense that my visitor was at this time in some special relation to a force obscure and powerful, that he was significantly vulnerable to—I knew not what, only that it waited ahead of him, along the lonely sand.

But his talk, at first, couldn't have been less ominous. Stowing the wizened grapefruit, he told me that he came down every year to walk this coast. "Sometimes I get as far as Bélizé, before I have to start back. You weren't here when I passed going south."

"So you're on your way home now. Did you make Bélizé?"

"No. The business went on too late." He jerked his beard in the general direction of Yankeedom.

"May I ask what the business is?"

He grinned, a whimsical black skeleton. "I design swimming pools in Des Moines. My partner does most of the installation, but he needs my designs for the custom jobs. We started in college, five years back. It really took off; it got so heavy I had to get away. So I found this place."

I poured myself some more stale tea to let that sink in. Would my scrap of paper end as a sketch for some good citizen's Iowa patio?

"Do you ever run into any of the old *caminantes?*"

"Only a few left, old men now. Hidden Star Smith—Estrella Escondida Camal. Camol, Camool, it's like Smith here, you know. He stays pretty close to Pajaros these days. And Don't Point at Rainbows."

"I beg your pardon?"

"Another old *caminante,* I don't know his name. We were watching this storm pass at sunset, see? Maybe you've noticed—they can throw this fantastic double, triple *arc iris.* Rainbows. First one I'd seen. I pointed at it and he got excited and clouted my arm down." He rubbed his elbow reminiscently. "He doesn't speak much Spanish, but he got it to me that something bad would jump out of the rainbow and run down my arm right into my ear. So whenever I meet him I tell him *'No puncto,'* and we have a laugh."

My visitor seemed to be enjoying talking to someone who knew a little of this shore, as his Des Moines clients would not. But his gaze still roved to the gale-torn sea, and he had not unslung his blanket-roll.

"How do you get across those two monster bays between here and Bélizé? Surely you can't hike around? Or have they finally cut back there too?"

"Not yet. No way. What isn't under water is tribal treaty land. I saw an air photo with three unnamed villages on it. I know where a couple of *sac bés* come out though—you know, the old Maya roads. They're nothing but limestone ridges now. There was this man on one of them one night, he wasn't wearing pants. He disappeared like—whht! . . . I wanted to walk back in a ways this trip, but—" His gaze turned away again, he frowned at the wind. "I hated to get so far . . . inland."

"So, how do you cross?"

"Oh, I work my way on a fishing boat, fixing stuff. It's unreal, what this climate does to engines. They keep them going on string and beer. I have a couple of guys who watch for me every year. If I could only leave a set of tools, but—"

We both knew the answer to that one.

"Sometimes they take me all the way, or they drop me at Punta Rosa and I walk down and catch another ride over Espiritu Sanctu."

I asked him about the rather mysterious stretch of coast between the two huge bays.

"The beach is mostly rocks; you have to watch the tide. But there's an old jeep track up on the bluff. Five, no, let's see—six coco plantings. And the Pickle Palace, you know about that?"

"You mean it really exists?"

"Oh yes. This incredible *rico-rico* politico from Mexico. The pickles were just a sideline. I guess he wanted a private paradise. Turrets, stained glass windows, at least a dozen guest-houses, everything tiled. An airstrip. And every damn bit brought in by lighter, through the reef. They say he went down a couple of times but his mistresses didn't like it. Of course it's all overgrown now. There's an old caretaker who chops it out and grows corn by the fountain. The thing is, the whole place is in exquisite taste. I mean really lovely. Nineteen-thirties art deco, top grade."

The incongruous words from this wild naked stranger—like the Pickle Palace itself—were eroding my sense of reality. This is not unusual in the Quintana Roo.

"And nobody seems to have looted the inside. I went in the kitchens, he had what has to be the first microwave oven in the world. Didn't stay long—there was a live tiger asleep in the living-room."

"You mean a jaguar?"

"No. A real tiger-tiger from India, with stripes. And huge. He must have had a zoo, see—there's birds that don't belong here, too. This tiger was on a white velvet couch, fast asleep on his back with his paws crossed on his chest, the most beautiful sight I ever saw. . . . " He blinked and then added quietly, "Almost."

"What happened?"

"He woke up and took off right over my head out the door." My guest grinned up, as if still seeing the great beast sail over. "Of course I was down, crawling like a madman out the other way. I never told anybody. But when I came by a couple years later there was his skull speared up on the wall. Pity."

"That's a lovely story."

"It's true."

His tone made me say quickly, "I know it is. That's why it's good; made-up yarns don't count. . . . Look, this wind isn't going to quit soon. Maybe you'd like to come in and wash up or whatever while I scare us up a snack. Tea suit you, or would a coke or some *cerveza* go better?"

"That's really good of you. Tea's fine."

As he followed me in he caught sight of his reflection in the sandy glass, and gave a whistle. Then I heard a clank: he had quickly unstrapped the knife and laid it down inside the sill.

"You really are *bueno gentes,* you know?"

I pointed out the old gravity-feed shower. "Don't get too clean, it'll draw the *chiquistas.*"

He laughed—the first carefree young sound I'd heard from him—and started turning out his pockets, clearly intending to walk straight under, shorts and all.

I put the kettle on my gas one-burner and started loading a tray with cheeses and ham. He came out just as I was pouring, and I nearly dropped the kettle on us both.

His skin was still burnt black, showing several more scars where he had apparently tangled with a coral-reef. The wet shorts were still basically khaki, but now visibly enlivened by sturdy Mexican floral-print patches, and edged top and bottom by pink lines of less-burnt skin. The effect was literally and figuratively topped off by his damp, slicked-down hair and beard: relieved of its crust, it shone and flamed bright strawberry red, such as I've seldom seen in nature—or anywhere else.

He seemed totally unconscious of the change in his appearance, and was looking carefully around the kitchen corner and my wall of books.

"You like stories?" he inquired.

"Yes."

"For a taste of that real maple syrup up there I'll swap you a good one. I mean, true. I want to ask you a question about it."

I was too occupied reassembling the tray and my perceptions to indulge in any more suspicions, and answered simply, "With pleasure."

He watched appreciatively as I poured a generous dollop into a baggie and secured it in a sea-scoured *detergente* jar. "You scrounge the beach, too. . . ."

"My *supermercado,*" I told him.

"That's right." His gravity was returning. "Everything you need . . . it sends."

When we'd got ourselves settled I saw that the Stuffer really was subsiding slightly. The coco-palms swept the sand in a wind which had lost a decibel or two; and the sea beyond was regaining some of its wondrous Carib turquoise, shot with piercing lime-green in the coral shallows. The white lemmings of the bay raced northward still; but the far reef was now visible as a great seething tumbling snow-bank, lit with the diamonds of the afternoon sun. It might be

JAMES TIPTREE, JR.

a nice night.

"It began right out there by your north point, as a matter of fact," my guest pointed left with his piece of cheese, and took a small bite. "This particular evening was fantastic—dead calm, full moon. You could see colors. It was like looking at a sunny day through a dark cloth, if you know what I mean."

I nodded; it was a perfect description.

"I was going along, watching the sea like I always do. You know there's an old pass through the reef out there? You can't see it now." He peered out to our left, absently laying down the cheese. "Well, yes, you can if you know. Anyway, that's where I noticed this pole sticking up. I mean, first I saw it, and then I didn't, and then it bobbed up again, shining in the moonlight. I figured some idiot had tried to stick a channel-marker there. And then I saw it was loose, and wobbling along in the current. I guess you know there's about a three-knot current to the north all along here."

"I do. But look, eat first, story later. That cheese will die of old age."

I passed him some ham on a tortilla. He thanked me, took one big bite and laid it on his knee, his eyes still frowning at the reef, as though to recapture every detail.

"I slowed down to keep pace with it. Every big swell would wash it in closer. It kept almost disappearing, and then it'd come up again, bigger than before. For awhile I thought it might be some huge fluorescent tube—you know how they come in, waving—but when it got inside the reef I saw no bulb could possibly be that big, and it had some sort of—something—on it. By this time it was free of the reef, and going along north at a pretty good clip. Just this big pole in the sea, swaying vertically along getting shorter and taller—maybe two metres at times. I stayed with it, puzzled as hell. By this time I figured it might be the spar of some buoy, maybe dragging a chain that kept it upright."

He broke off and said in a different tone, "That lad in the blue hat. He your boy?"

I peered. A familiar battered bright-blue captain's hat was disappearing over the dune beside the *rancho*.

"That's Ek. Our local *niño*." I tapped my temple in the universal gesture that means here, child of God. "He's somebody's wife's sister's son by somebody's cousin. Sort of a self-appointed guard."

"He chased me off your well with a *machete* when I came by last year."

"I think he's harmless really. But strong."

"Yeah . . . Well, anyway, this thing, whatever it was, had me sort of fascinated. When it got hung up I'd sit down and wait until it went on again. I wanted it, see. If it was an instrumented buoy maybe there'd be valuable stuff on it. I've heard of people getting return rewards— Aaah, no. That's just what I told myself. The truth is, I just *wanted* it. I had a feeling—maybe this sounds crazy—like it was meant for me. I don't tell this well. You know, something coming in from the sea all by itself, and you're all alone—"

"I know exactly what you mean. This tea-tray came in like that. I spent half a morning getting it, in a Noreaster."

He nodded his amazing-colored head and gently touched the fine wood of the tray, as if I had passed some test.

"Yeah. Anything you need . . . Well, by this time what tide there was was going out, and I saw that the thing wasn't coming any closer for awhile. But we were about half-way to that point where there's a back-flow. What they call a point around here is about as flat as your hand, but this one really does shift the current. About ten miles down. Some crazy Yank tried to build a resort there. *Lirios.*"

"Yes. The Lilies. I came here the year the government had chased him out. Misuse of agricultural land, they called it. He seems to have left owing everybody. I imagine they cleaned him out pretty well first; he had great plans. Is anything left?"

"Just some foundations with nice tiling, and part of a construction trailer. Fellow called Pedro Angel from Tres Cenotes has his family there; he runs a one-bottle *cantina*. Among other things. The *poso* is still fairly good. I was going to get my water there if you weren't here."

I shook my head, thinking of those extra miles. "Ek shouldn't have done that to you. I'll talk to Don Pa'o."

He glanced at me, Maya-wise. "Don't bother. I mean, it won't help. Thanks anyway. Look—are you sure you want to hear all this?"

"Very sure. But I wish you'd put that ham out of its misery; you've picked it up six times. Is there anything you'd rather eat?"

"Oh no, this is great." Obediently, he took two small bites and drank some tea, looking for the moment like a much younger man, a boy. His eyes were still on the calming reef, where even I could now see the zig-zag of darker water that was the old pass. The tide was running out. A solitary cloud cast a rosy reflection on the glittering horizon, and the palms were quieting. It would be a beautiful night indeed—with, I now recalled, a fine full moon. I had long since planned to bed my visitor down on a hammock in my "study." Maya hospitality is no problem; every corner has its hammock-hooks, and most commercial travellers even carry their own nets.

"Anyway, there I was, with this thing making long, slow bounces, getting taller and shorter, and me following right along. This beach in the moonlight . . . " His voice softened; the face in its flaming frame was still a boy's—but shadowed now by deeper feeling.

"The moon had started down inshore, so that it really lit up the pole, and just about the time we got to Lirios I saw that the markings were something wrapped around it. When it came up high I could see sort of white bulges, and then some dark stuff started to drift loose and blow. At first I thought it was seaweed, and then I decided it was an old flag. And I hadn't seen it before because the chain, or whatever was weighting it, held it down in deep water. But now it was dragging on the shallows, riding much higher out. And then it stuck on the Lirios sandbar; and I saw it was a long thin bundle, wrapped or tied on the pole. It stuck there until a swell turned it around and carried it right toward me.

"And I saw the face."

His own face had turned seaward now, so that I had to lean toward him to catch the blowing words.

"It was a person, see, or a—a body. Tied to that spar, with long black hair floating and a sort of white dress flapping out between the ropes, starting to dry whenever it stayed out of the sea. . . . The person had to be dead, of course. But I didn't stop to think much, after I saw the face. . . . It . . . the . . . " He swallowed. "Anyway, there's a rotten back-flow there. Even if they say there's no such thing as an undertow, it feels like one. A sea-puss. I was wading and stumbling out, see. It's steep, and rough gravel. Not like here. But I swim a lot."

I repressed a protest. The Yank who built Lirios lost four customers before he would believe the locals: the surf there is no place to swim, even on the calmest days.

"The first wave that lifted me up, I saw the thing wasn't a buoy at all; there was more stuff surfacing beside the spar. Next time I got a look, I saw gunwales, and the top of a cabin astern. A fancy long-boat, see, maybe eight or ten metres. And polished—I could see the moon on wood and brass. The—the person was tied on the broken-off mast."

He took another mouthful of cold tea, his eyes on an inner vision. He seemed to be making an effort to recount this very carefully and undramatically.

"Polished . . . " He nodded to himself, yes. "Wet wood might look shiny, but not those oarlock things. Hell, I *felt* it, too! I'd got there, see, not even thinking. I mean, I'd never touched any dead people. Not really *dead*-dead. Just my grandfather's funeral, and his casket had glass. This was a lot different. I thought about what really dead fish were like, and I almost turned back. And then the next wave showed me the face close, and the eyes—her eyes were open. By then I was sure it was a woman. Her eyes seemed to be looking right at me in the bright moonlight. Shining—not dead. So huge . . . and her arm moved, or floated, like it was pulling at the ropes. So I kept on."

His hand instinctively moved to touch the knife he'd laid beside him.

"My leg hit something on the side of the boat beside her—that's where I got that one." He indicated a long grey scar. "And I started cutting ropes, all in among this silky stuff. The boat rolled as under water. I remember thinking, 'Oh God, I'm cutting into dead meat; maybe she'll come all apart.' And the boat rolled worse; it was hung up on its keel, trying to go turtle." He drew a long breath. "But then her arm hit me and it felt firm. So I got a good grip on it and took another lungful of air, and cut the footropes way down under, and kicked us both out of there just before the whole thing rolled." He sucked in another lungful, remembering.

"After that it was just a battle. All that damn silk, and I can still see the moon going round and round through it; and I couldn't get any decent air at all, until a lucky wave rolled us up on that sliding gravel stuff. It isn't like here. I knew I had to get us farther up fast before the backwash. I caught one good look at this face, with the dark hair streaming over it. Her eyes were closed then. I sort of passed out for a minute; but I couldn't quite, because I knew I had to do something about the water in her. But all I could do was grab her waist—it was tiny, I could almost touch both hands around and kind of jolt her face-down as I crawled up the shingle on my knees. A gush of water came out. And then we both fell into the trash-line, and there was my canteen. So I managed to pour some fresh water more or less at her mouth through the hair, and I thought her eyes were opening again just as I passed out for good. . . . Funny," he added in a different tone, and frowned.

"What?" I was frowning too, wondering how strong those skeleton tendons could be. A formidable feat, if true. But he was not, after all, much thinner than Cousteau, and a lot younger. And the Quintana Roo is peopled with survivors of harrowing ordeals.

"The trash-line was different," he said slowly. "No *basura*, no

JAMES TIPTREE, JR.

kipple at all—just a little natural tar, and weed and sea-fans, you know. I can see it." He screwed up his eyes, remembering hard for a moment.

"Anyway," he went on, "I was out cold, I don't know how long. The next thing I remember is hearing that voice." His lips twitched in a dreamy grin.

"It was a perfectly beautiful voice, soft and rough-low—contralto, d'you call it?—going on and on. I just lay still awhile, listening. She was standing up somewhere behind my head. This incredible emotion! And complicated too. Controlled. I couldn't make out the language, although I heard *'Dios'* a few times. And then I caught the lisp: *ththth. Thetheo,* what they call Castilian. I'd heard it once on a tape, but never like this. At first I thought she was thanking God for saving her." His grin flickered again.

"She was cursing. Swearing. Not like a *puta,* no simple stuff, but this long-cadence, complex, hissing fury. So intense—I tell you it was so savage it could scorch you if you didn't know a word. Among everything else, she was letting God know what she thought of him, too.

"You know they say down here the Spanish is five hundred words, and four hundred are curses. She used up the ones I knew in a minute or so and went on from there. I began to understand better—a lot about *oro, poso dorado,* fountain of gold; and about her crew. She was pacing then, every so often I could hear her stamp. I pieced together that they'd found something, gold or treasure maybe—and her crew had deserted and left her tied on the boat. Or maybe they'd hit a rock in a storm—it was all pretty confusing. There was a lot about fighting, very violent. Maybe she'd tied herself on when she was alone in the storm. It sounded unreal, but real, too—I mean, I'd cut those ropes. And now she was asking—no, she was *telling* God exactly how to punish everybody. I think she was partly talking to the Devil, too. All in the most graphic detail, you couldn't imagine—talk about bloody-minded—"

His lips still smiled, but his eyes were wide and sober, staring north up the beach.

"I lay listening to her, and picturing her in my mind. Like a woman out of Goya, you know?—Someone I'd never believed existed. Then I got my eyes open—it was bright, blazing moonlight, everything glittered—and I rolled over to see. Oh, God.

"I was looking up straight into this beautiful furious face—big black eyes actually flashing; scornful, utterly sensuous curled lips and nostrils—talk about aristocratic. She'd pulled her hair back and tied it. But then I saw the rest of her. It was all wrong. My woman was gone. The person was a man."

He shook his head slowly from side to side, eyes closed as if to shut out some intolerable sight, and went on in a flat, controlled tone.

"Yeah. He was younger than me, no beard. What I'd thought was a dress was this great white silk shirt, he was stuffing it back in his pants while he cursed and paced. Shiny tight black britches, with this horrible great fly, cod-piece, whatever, right in my face. He had loose soft black boots, with heels, and tiny feet. Ah, Christ, if I had the strength I'd have dragged him right back into the Caribbean and left him on that boat, I wanted my woman back so bad. . . .

"Then he noticed I was awake. His only response was to wind up one terrifying curse, and say 'Vino' at me. Not Hello or what—just 'Vino,' without hardly looking at me. Like I was some kind of a wine-machine. And paced off again. When he turned back and saw I hadn't moved he glanced at me sharper and repeated 'Vino!' quite loud. I still wasn't moving. So he came a step nearer and said, 'Entonces. Agua.'

"I just stared up at him. So he snapped his fingers, like he was talking to a dog or an idiot, and said very clearly, '¡A-gua! Agua para tomar.'

"You never saw arrogance like that. To get his point over, he flipped the empty canteen over in the sand toward me with the toe of his boot. That really pissed me off, getting sand on the screw-threads. I had him figured for some zillionaire general's spoiled brat, playing games. I started getting up, not really sure whether I was going to murder him or just walk away. But I found I was so weak that standing up was about it for me then. So I remembered this thing a lady had put me down with, and wrestled it into my best Spanish.

" 'The word you're groping for, man, is thank you.'

"It must have sounded like some weird dialect to him, but he got the point of that 'hombre.' Oh, wow! Did you actually ever see anyone's nostrils flare with rage? And the mad eyes—you wouldn't believe. His right hand whipped around and hit a scabbard I hadn't noticed—lucky for me it was empty. I could see the gold jewel-work on it glitter in the moonlight. That gave him a minute to look me over hard.

"I guess I puzzled him a little, when he came to look. I was a lot huskier then, too, and my gear was in better shape. Anyway, he stayed real still in a sort of cat-crouch, and said abruptly, 'Ingles.'

" 'No,' I told him. '*Estados Unidos del Norteamerica.*'

"He just shrugged, but the edge was off his rage. He repeated more calmly, extra-clear, 'I desire more water. Water to drink.'

"I was still mad enough to say, 'More water—*please.*'

"Man, that nearly sent him off again; but he was still studying me. I was bigger than him, see, and he didn't know I was about to fall down if he pushed. I saw his eyes flicking from my hair to my knife to this big flashy diver's watch I wore. By luck the thing did one of its beeps just then, and his fantastic eyebrows curled up and met, in the moonlight. Next second he gave a chuckle that'd curl your hair, and suddenly bent and swept me an elaborate bow, rattling off the most flowery sarcastic speech you ever heard—I could only get parts, like 'Your most gracious excellency, lord of the exalted land of hell-haired lunatics,' and so on, ending with a rococo request for water. The word 'please' was of course nowhere in it. No way.

"Would you believe, I started to like the little son-of-a-bitch?"

My visitor turned to look straight at me for a moment. The blaze of the calming sea behind him made a curly fire of that beard and hair, and there was a different look in his hazel eyes. I recognised it. It's the look you see in the eyes of men from Crooked Tree, Montana, or Tulsa, or Duluth, when you meet them sailing the Tasman sea, or scrambling up some nameless mountain at the world's end. The dream—faintly self-mocking, deadly serious dream of the world. *Farther*, it says. *Somewhere farther on is a place beyond all you know, and I shall find it.* It had carried this boy from Iowa to the wild shore of Yucatán, and it would carry him farther if he could find the way.

"—maybe it was just his *macho*," my visitor was saying. "I mean, the little bastard had to be half-dead. And his crazy get-up, and the *poso dorado* business. For some reason I figured he might be from Peru; there's some pretty exotic super-rich types down there. But it was more than that. More like he'd found a key to some life way out, free—something neat. I mean really far off, far away, *lejos* . . . "

His own voice had become far-off too, and his eyes had gone back to the sea. Then he blinked a couple of times and went on in his normal tone.

"He misunderstood my standing there, I guess. 'I will pay you,' he told me. '*Pagare.* Gift. *Te regalera.* ¡*Mira!*'

And before I could find words he had reached down and slapped one boot-heel, and his hand came up with this wicked little three-inch stiletto on his thumb. His other hand was yanking up his shirt.

LIRIOS: A TALE OF THE QUINTANA ROO

The next thing, he was sticking this blade right in by his lowest rib.

" 'Hey, man—No!' I sort of lurched to get his arm, but then I saw he was just slicing skin. Two big gouts came welling out. They fell on the sand, with only a little blood—and they rolled! One of them flashed deep green in the moonlight, deep green like the sea. He picked them up, with that thumb-sticker pointed straight at me, and looked them over critically. The green one he dropped into his boot somewhere, and the other one he held out to me. It was dark, about as big as a small marble, lying on this slender, pointy-fingered hand.

" 'A token of my estimation for your timely assistance.'

"When I didn't move, the palm began gracefully to tilt, to spill the stone on the ground. So I took it. Anybody would. Not meaning to keep it, you know, just out of curiosity, to see it close.

"It wasn't gem-cut, only polished-off cabochon, but when I held it up the moonlight showed through dark blood-red, like there was a fire inside. It had to be a ruby. If it wasn't too badly flawed, it must have been worth God knows what. I figured it was good, too; obviously he had chosen his best stuff to sew into his hide.

"My Spanish was drying up. I was trying to make up a suitably polite refusal and get the thing back into his hand, when I saw his eyelids sliding down, and his whole body sagged. He got himself straightened up again, but I could see him swaying, fighting to stay on his feet. Jesus, I got scared he was going to die in front of my face after what he'd been through.

" 'Rest. I will bring water.'

"I had the sense not to touch him, even then. I just picked up the canteen, nearly falling over myself, and smoothed off a clean spot for him to settle onto. He sank down gracefully, resting his chin and arms on one knee, the knife still in his hand. The moon was starting down behind us, into the inland jungle, and its pitch-black shadow was spreading from the bluff to the beach where we were. I couldn't spot the trail up to Lirios. It's all low there, though, and I knew it had to be close, so I just started straight up the nearest gully.

"I needed both hands to haul myself up, so I stuck the ruby in my pocket." My visitor's hand went to his shorts. "The left back one, with the button." He nodded his head. Again I had the impression he was trying to recall every detail. "I remember I had a hell of a time securing it, but I knew I shouldn't lose *that*. And then I went on up to the top of the rise. Wait—" He clenched his eyes, saying almost to himself, "Coco-palms. Did I see cocos there? . . . I don't know. But there aren't very many; it's never been farmed. Just wild ones.

JAMES TIPTREE, JR.

"When I hit the top, I found I'd made it wrong. There wasn't any clearing, just a trail. But Lirios's damn radio goes twenty-four hours a day; I knew I'd hear it soon. The night was dead calm now, see; every so often I could hear a wave flop on the beach below. So I staggered along north, stopping every few steps to listen. I was feeling pretty low. If Pedro's radio was off, there was no use looking for a light—he shuts up tight. All I heard was a couple of owl hoots, and the moon getting lower all the time. And dry—I tried to chew a palm-leaf, but it only made me worse.

"I'd just about decided that I should have gone south—this was only my second trip in there, see—when I saw a clearing right ahead and there was this funny slurping sound. The moon was shining on a kind of *ruina* by one side. I wondered if maybe this was a secret *poso*—people don't tell you everything, you know. When I got about ten steps into the moonlight a peccary exploded out and tore off like a pint-size buffalo. It about scared the pants off me, but I knew that slurping had to mean water. So I went over to the stone blocks and stepped in a wet place. This struck me odd at the time, because it was a dry year; the lagoons even were low; but I didn't stop to worry about it. I just crawled through till I found the hole, and stuck my head in and guzzled. Then I filled the canteen and a plastic bag I had, and got everything on me soppy wet, for that poor lad down below. I remember thinking this would be a nice spot to camp out for a couple days til we got our strength back, so I stood up to orient myself. The moon was still on the *laguna* right down below me and I sighted on an islet with a big strangler fig. The lagoon was high here, but that didn't bother me—you know how this weather varies; one place can get soaked while the rest of the coast dries up. Then I cut straight up over the dune and more or less fell down to the beach, and went back south on the last edge of moonlight to where I'd left him.

"I found him easy; he'd had the sense to crawl to a patch of light before he collapsed. Now he was lying face-up, asleep or unconscious. I was scared for a minute, but his head was thrown back and I could actually see the pulse going by his long, full throat. The jaw-line was delicate, like a child's or a girl's, and those great soft black lashes on his cheeks made him look more than ever like a beautiful woman. I knelt down by him, wondering if it could possibly be. I'd only seen the bottom of his ribs, you know. And those stuffed pants could be a fake—people do crazy things. And I'd felt that tiny waist. I was just getting my nerve to pull the shirt up, when the lashes lifted and the huge dark eyes met mine.

" '*Agua pura.*' I held the canteen by his mouth. 'Drink—*tome.*'

"The hands made a feeble movement, but they were too weak to hold the canteen. I could see the fight was gone too; the eyes looked like a bewildered child's.

" '*Perdon,*' I said, just in case, and slid one hand carefully through that glossy mass of hair to join canteen and mouth.

" 'Slowly. Drink slowly, *despacio.*'

"Obediently, my patient took long, slow sips, breathing deeply and stopping now and then to stare up at me. Presently an innocent, beautiful smile came on the lips. I smiled back, realizing that this stranger had in all probability decided that I had taken his gem and left him there to die. But just as my hand went to my pocket to give it back to him, his head fell back again across my arm. It was so heavy that I had to lie down alongside to support it, and the canteen was finished that way. I bathed the forehead and face with my wet bandanna, too.

"When I produced my plastic water-bag the smile changed to pure wonder, and the eyes grew wider still. Despite thirst, that transparent plastic had to be felt and poked at before my patient would drink . . . I can remember how oval and shiny the nails were. Not

JAMES TIPTREE, JR.

polished, you know, but buffed in some way. And very clean; I could even see their white half-moons.

"The real moon was going down fast behind us. In the last light on the shore, I noticed that the long-boat had washed close in. She was riding heeled over, dousing that broken mast in and out with every quiet swell. It would have been a torturing end for someone tied there. I guess I shuddered.

"The person in my arms raised up enough to follow my gaze, and for a second I saw again the furious aristocrat. Saw and *felt*—it was like a jolt of voltage through my arms and chest. I didn't like the idea of what so much rage could do in a person so weak. By luck I had just located an old piece of health-bar in my shirt. It was sodden but okay, so I broke it and touched it to the stranger's lips.

" *'Es bueno. Come.'*

"A tongue-tip came out to explore the lips, dainty as a cat.

" *'¡Chocolate!'* My patient stared at me open-mouthed, the boat forgotten.

" *'Sí*, it's good. Eat some.'

" *'¡Chocolate!'* And the next thing I knew the stranger had stuffed the whole thing in his or her mouth, like a kid, with me trying to say 'Take it easy' and both of us grinning like mad.

"I recall thinking that chocolate couldn't be all that rare in Peru or wherever. Was it possible the person I was holding in my arms was simply a refugee from some expensive nut-house?

"But there was one thing I was determined to find out, if I could just hold out until my companion went to sleep. It wouldn't be long now; another sip or two of water, and the furry lashes were sweeping low with fatigue. The only trouble was, I was almost asleep myself. And the darkness coming over us didn't help. Even the occasional muffled clanking from the boat was starting to sound like music. I wedged a sharp rock under my shoulder, and that helped a bit. The person in my arms was drifting off; I could feel the body softening and fitting against mine in a way that made me absolutely convinced it had to be a woman, or the damnedest gay earth ever created. But that rock was getting to feel soft. I was desperate enough to actually try pinching myself as hard as I could, with fingers that felt like Jello.

"The second time I did that, I hit the lump in my back pocket and remembered the ruby. That woke me a little; it seemed unbearable that this aristocrat might think the stone had bought that water. So I wriggled enough to unbutton and carefully pull it out. Or rather, I tried to. My fingers have never felt so clumsy. It was almost like the stone was hiding, it didn't want to come.

"But I finally managed to get hold of it and ease it across my body toward where one of her hands was lying on the sand beside her head. A star shone right through as I raised it. I guess a poet could find the right words, but the truth is that the only red flash I've ever seen like that was on a police squad-car.

"The hand was lying palm-up, with the fingers slightly curled, and I went to put the ruby in it. Again I had trouble. The hand moved but without moving, if I can describe it—maybe I was just too dead to focus right. And her body was half under mine now, and it moved in a way that—well, you wouldn't have thought mine could respond, in the state I was in, but I did. That made me more than ever eager to get rid of that damned stone. I made three grabs at that little hand and caught the wrist, and forced the thing in her palm and curled her fingers over it, so I could get my own hand back where it wanted to be.

"But by then her body had slackened and fallen away from me, and before I could stop myself my nose went down in her cool dark hair and I was dead to the world.

"I didn't remember until next day that just at the very end, as I was folding her warm fingers, they seemed to change too, and turn kind of cold and stiff. And there was a strange faint sound from away on the sea, I guess it might have been a kind of wail from the boat's scraping, or like a bird's voice . . . "

His own voice had grown cool and quiet.

"That's it, really."

He showed his teeth in a comfortless grin.

"I woke up in a blazing sunrise, all alone. There wasn't one mark on the beach, not even my own footprints. But lots of plastic trash now—there was a Clorox bottle by my head. It hadn't been there before. Maybe the tide sent up a little wavelet, enough to smooth everything out without waking me. It was far out again by then, farther than I've ever seen it. No sign of a boat, of course. I guess if this was a good ghost story, there'd have been *something*"—he gave that joyless grin—"but there wasn't a single trace. Not even one long black hair. I looked, you see. I looked. The only tiny thing was, my hip pocket was unbuttoned. Oh how I searched. And all the while hearing Lirios's damn radio yattering from over the bluff."

He made a sound somewhere between a cough and a sigh.

"After . . . after awhile I climbed up; the path was right behind me. When I looked back I noticed three or four dark knobs of wood sticking out of the water 'way far out, like in a line . . . I bought

JAMES TIPTREE, JR.

some tacos off Pedro, and filled up the canteen on his skunk-water, with the radio banging out mariachis and tire ads. The thing is, Pedro's *poso,* his well, was right where the old *cenote,* the water hole, had been. I checked—it was the same view, but the water was low, like everywhere else that year. So I went back on the beach and walked on north. It was like a dream—I mean, not the other; the dream was Lirios and Pedro's *chistas*—joking. Or no, it was more like two dreams at once . . . ever since."

He was eyeing me intently, Maya-style, out of the corners of his clear *gringo* eyes. I got very busy discouraging some sugar-ants that were after his pack-roll.

"When I came by next year, you weren't around."

"No. I was late."

"Yeah. And I was earlier . . . Nobody was around but some kids and that lad with the *machete.*"

He nodded his beard at Ek, who had resumed surveillance at extreme range.

"When I got by Lirios there were five *borrachos* from the *Gardia Nacional* roaring up and down the beach on their new Hondas and firing handguns at the moon. So I went on by. About sunrise I met an old *ranchero* walking down from Tuloom. We talked awhile. A fine old guy, I gave him my plastic water-bag. Turned out he knew all about me—you know how it goes around here."

"De vero. I've never yet gone anywhere I wasn't expected."

"Yeah." He wasn't listening. "Anyway, he wanted to make sure I'd passed by Lirios at full moon the year before. When I told him 'Yes,' he said, 'Good. In *la noche negra,* the moon-dark, the very bad ones come. Not often, you understand—but they *can.'* Then he asked me if anybody had given me anything there.

"I told him, 'No, at least, I didn't keep it.' He looked at me real hard and serious. *'Bueno,'* he said. 'If you had kept it, you would be *perdido*—lost. So long as you touch or hold anything. And are you free now? It is much the best that you go by day. Do you know the name of that place?'

" 'No.'

" *'El Paso del Muertes.* The pass or place of the dead, their *querencia.* Because all things come to the shore there. From Ascensión, Morales, Jamaica even. Sometimes quite big *lanchas,* shrimp-boats even from the Gulf. The rocks turn the current under water, you see, very far out. People used to make *mucho dinero* from what came there. But only by day, you understand. Only in the light of the sun. But that's all finished now. The *Gardia Aereo* finds them first from their planes.' He pointed out east. 'Where the sea turns by the *rifé de Cozumel.* Only wood and *basura,* worthless things come now.'

" 'I think I saw the ribs of one old wreck. The tide was very far out.'

" 'Ah?' He gave me that penetrating stare again. 'It must have been indeed very low water,' he said. 'Only once, in my youth, have I seen such a thing. I waded out to see it—in the day. It had been a sailing-boat. You know the metal *grimpas* used to hold the mast-ropes?' He did a little sketch in the sand, showing the stays. 'These were not fitted in, my friend, the way they do today. They were made of hot metal, poured right into the side of the ship. Which has not been done for two, three hundred years.' "

My visitor gave a deep sigh, or shudder, and tried the grin again.

"Anyway, we said goodbye and went our ways, and when I got to Tulum I heard that something had happened to one of the drunk *soldarero* kids the night before. I found out later that Pedro's brother dragged the Honda out of the drink and filed off all the numbers. He's trying to fix it up."

Abruptly, the light eyes locked on mine. I couldn't dodge.

"Look. *Is it* possible?" He nodded at the shelves behind the glass. "You're supposed to know things. Aren't you? Could I have, well, *dreamed* all that? I mean, it went on so long—it started right over there, you know. I must have walked after that thing for ten miles."

His voice got low and slow, the words almost forced out.

"Could I have—made it up? Believe me, I'm not a day-dreamer, I don't even dream much at night. And I don't drink, only a few beers. No grass for years now. And the other shit they have down here, I learnt not to mess with that the first week I was here. And fiction, movies, mystic stuff—forget it. Here, look—" He bent and fished a thick pamphlet out of his pack. It was titled *Hydraulic Properties of Natural Soil Aggregates.* He put it back and looked straight up at me.

"Am I—crazy? How could I have made up all that? Was I in a different time? *Am I crazy? . . .* What do you think?"

He was really asking.

I was thinking that I knew many people who would be delighted to take charge, to enlighten him on the ultimate nature and limits of reality, or the effects of dehydration and solitude on cerebral function. But some minutes earlier I had discovered I wasn't one of them. What in hell *did* I think, what had I been doing all during that long account, except believing him? . . . I knew what I *should* think, of course. All too well I knew. But, well—maybe one can dwell too long on the sands of the Quintana Roo.

I started a tentative mumble when he interrupted me, almost whispering: "How could I have made up that song?"

"Song?"

"I—I guess I didn't tell you about that." His face had turned back toward the sea, so that all I could catch from the fading gusts of the Stuffer was something about "at the end, see . . . and even this year."

He coughed again, and began to hum tunelessly, and finally sang a phrase or two, still watching the far reefs. His voice was clear and pleasing, but totally off any conceivable key.

"You see?" He glanced briefly at me. "I can't sing *at* all. So how could I . . . ? I can hear it, though."

The tune he had produced could have been any of a hundred Spanish wails—*amorado, corazon de oro, amor dorados lejos, lejos por la mar—Quisierra viajar;* that sort of thing: love, golden love far over the sea, who would not journey to the golden heart of the sea? . . . If there was anything extraordinary there, my Spanish could not detect it. Yet it seemed to have significance for him, as sometimes the most ordinary phrases do, in our dreams. Could I salvage my own sanity by hinting at this?

But whatever I might have said, I had delayed too long. His gaze was on the sea again, and he spoke in a whisper, not to be.

"No. I didn't make up that song."

Our moment had passed. Abruptly, he was on his feet, picking up his pack and canteen. The sea was almost calm now, a burnished splendor of green-gold and salmon, flushed with unearthly lavender and rose, reflections of the tropic sunset behind us. My dismayed protests blended with his farewell.

"Please wait. I'd assumed you'd spend the night here. I have a good spare *amaca.*"

He shook his flaming head, smiling politely.

"No. But thanks for the stuff and everything, I mean, really."

"Can't you wait a moment?—I meant to give you some—"

But he was already moving away, turning to stride down the beach. My last view of his expression was a mingled eagerness and sadness, a young face shadowed by a resolution I couldn't hope to break. The sunset behind us was now filling the air with golden haze, the palms were still.

After a moment I followed him down to the beach, irresolute. His easy stride was deceptive; by the time I reached the tide-line his thin figure was already filmed by the soft twilight air between us. Even to catch him now I would have to run. The mad notion of accompanying him on his walk through the night died before the reality of the old heart jittering in my ribs.

I could only stand and watch him dwindle, fade into the stick-figure I had seen at first. Tropic dusks come fast. By the time he was rounding the point I could barely make him out, had it not been for an occasional glint of red hair. Just as he turned the corner of the mangroves a new light came from sea-ward and lit up his head with rosy fire. Then he was gone.

I turned and saw that the full moon was rising through the cloud-castles on the sea, a great misshapen ball of cold, gaseous light. For a moment it shone clear, at the apex of its luminous sea-path; and the beach became a snow-scape in silver and black. Then the high clouds took it again, in racing patterns of lemon and smoky bronze; and I turned to make my way up to the dark *casa*. Automatically I registered the high cirrus from the east—tomorrow would be fine. As I neared the patio, Ek's hat scuttled behind a dune on the road. He too had been watching the stranger go.

And that's it, really, as the strange boy said.

The night turned greasy-hot, so that about midnight I went down to cool myself in the placid sea. Mayas do not do this; they say that the brown sharks come close in on calm nights, to bear their young in the shallows. I waded out hip-deep to my sand-bar, wondering where my visitor was now. Great Canopus had risen, and in the far south I could just see Alpha Centauri, magnificent even in the horizon veils. The sheer beauty of the scene was calming. No wonder my young friend wanted to make his way by night. Doubtless he was already near Tuloom, perhaps curled up in one of his wayside nets, savoring a grapefruit, fighting off the *chiquitistas*.

The thought of the grapefruits had reassured me some time back. Surely a man does not set out to meet God knows what, to follow delusions or invoke spirits or yield to succubi—armed with two mediocre grapefruits and a baggie of maple-syrup?

But as I stood there in the quicksilver Caribbean, a triangular shadow with something large and dark below it caught my attention. Only a sea-fan, no doubt. But I decided it would be prudent to return to land before it came into the channel I had to cross. And as I splashed ashore another memory came back; my young friend claimed to have fed chocolate to his particular apparition. Was my maple-syrup possibly destined for the same?

This troubling notion combined with the extraordinary heat and heavy calm—effects not often met on this shore—and with an over-active conscience to give me a very bad hour on the patio that night.

JAMES TIPTREE, JR.

What had I done, letting him go on? Hallucinated or sane, it was equally bad. Several times I came within a gull-feather of rousing out Don Pa'o's son to ride me to Lirios on his bike. But what then? Either we would find nothing, or ignominiously come upon my young man eating Pedro's tacos. And either way, my hard-won reputation of being fairly sensible, for a *gringo,* would be gone for good. . . . I fear that selfishness, rather than good sense, drove me finally to my hammock and uneasy sleep. And in the fresh morning breeze, what passes for sanity prevailed.

The tale has no real ending, but only one more detail which may have no bearing at all.

The next week of fine weather saw me plunged back into some long-overdue paperwork, during which no gossip came by. And then the advent of the *rancho's* first real live school-teacher threw everyone into a great bustle. She was a resolute and long-suffering Maya maiden, sent by the *Goberniente* to see that the *rancho's* grandchildren did not grow up as wild as their parents had. I found myself involved in making peace between her and the owner, who paid one of his rare visits expressly to get her out. My task was almost hopeless, until the generator conveniently—and expensively—broke down, and I was able to convince him that it might be useful if someone could read the manual. Thus, with one thing and another, I found no occasion to query Don Pa'o about the *gringo caminante* before it was time for me to go.

The next year I came early, and found myself keeping one eye on the beach. Nothing came by, until there was a little excitement at Lirios: a body did wash ashore. But I quickly discovered it was the corpse of a small dark man with the name OLGA tattooed on his arm.

That evening was another windless one, and I strolled over to where Don Pa'o and his lady were dining alone in their outdoor kitchen. The last of their resident sons was staying in Cozumel that year, learning to lay bricks.

After the ritual greetings, I remarked that one was reminded of the red-haired *gringo* walker, who did not seem to have come by this year. As I spoke, the old man's mouth drew down, until he looked exactly like the petty Maya chieftain his grandfather had been.

"Do you think he will come this year?"

Don Pa'o shrugged, and the globular brown matron who had borne his ten children gave the all-purpose Maya matron's cackle, intended to convey nothing except possibly a low opinion of her conversant.

"Perhaps he has gone back to Norte America?" I persisted.

Don Pa'o squinted at me hard for an instant, and then his slant eyes drooped, and his chin swung slowly from shoulder to shoulder.

"No," he said with finality.

At the same moment his wife made an extraordinary complex criss-cross of one hand across her abdomen. It puzzled me, until I recalled that some of the high-status older ladies here profess a brand of Catholicism whose rites and dogmas would doubtless astonish the Roman church. Then she got up to take the plates.

I did not need another look at the old man's archaic face to know that the subject was closed—and to sense too that I would not be seeing the strange red-haired boy again.

But why? I thought, as I made my farewells. What do they, what can they know? I have enough casual informants along this coast to ensure that nothing really disastrous or sensational could have occurred without my catching at least an echo of it, after this long. Mayas love morbidity; the actual fact was probably that my young friend was minting money in the swimming pool business, or had decided to explore someplace else.

Yet as I sat on my moonlit patio, listening to the quiet splash of the wavelets on the beach below, they seemed to be sighing out the odd little tuneless tune my visitor had tried to sing. *Amor dorado, lejos, lejos por la mar.* I realized I'd been half-hearing it now and again, particularly when I swam on quiet days, but I had put it down to the murmur in my bad ear. Now it was plainer. And the stranger's whole tale came back to me, as I had not let it do before. A year had passed and cooled; I could reflect.

I found I did not believe it—or rather, I did not believe in its outward detail and aspect. It could, I suppose, be some unquiet spirit who came to my young friend, some long-dead Spaniard or revenant Conquistador, some androgynous adventurer proffering ghostly gold; a life-hungry succubus from the shadows between the living and the dead. Or he could have been, very simply, out of his head. Yet I didn't quite believe that either.

What haunts me is the idea that something . . . did come to him there, something deeper than all these, which took on those manifestations to lure and seek him out. Something to which he was peculiarly vulnerable; and which, I fear, took him to itself on the night he left me. (For it has been five years now that he has not been seen here, and there is word that his partner in Des Moines has never seen him back.) What could it be?

I gazed out long at the impersonal beauty before me, scarcely daring to name it: the last great wonder of the world . . . "Anything you need," the boy had said. Whimsical as a tea-tray, seductive as

JAMES TIPTREE, JR.

a ruby, more terrible than all the petty armies of man. Who could say what was not in it, despite all our tiny encroachments and sorties? Perhaps we will kill it. And with it, ourselves. But it is far from dead yet—and its life is ours. As the boy had said too, our blood is its very substance, moving in our veins.

As I prepared to cease gazing and go to my human sleep, I recalled a trivial detail which carried an odd conviction. The Spanish word *mar* has one extraordinary aspect: *El mar, la mar*—the sea is the only word in Spanish, or any other tongue known to me, which is both female and male indifferently and alike. If it was indeed the sea itself which came for my friend, is it any wonder that it came in double guise?

> *Quintana Roo, maps call it,*
> *That blazing, blood-soaked shore;*
> *Which brown men called Zama, the Dawn,*
> *And other men called names long gone*
> *Four centuries years before.*
> *Still songs of Gold that dead men sought,*
> *And lures of Love whom Death forgot,*
> *And hungry Life by Death begot,*
> *Murmur from ocean's floor.*
> *For those who myth from fact would know*
> *Dwell not in the Quintana Roo.*

LIRIOS: A TALE OF THE QUINTANA ROO

art: Rick Sternbach

by Gregory Benford

EXPOSURES

The author is Professor of Physics
at the University of California,
Irvine. His astronomical
research centers on the dynamics
of pulsars, radio galaxies, and quasars.
His recent novel, Timescape,
won several major awards, including
the Nebula and John W. Campbell Award.

Puzzles assemble themselves one piece at a time. Yesterday I began laying out the new plates I had taken up on the mountain, at Palomar. They were exposures of varying depth. In each, NGC 1097—a barred spiral galaxy about twenty megaparsecs away—hung suspended in its slow swirl.

As I laid out the plates I thought of the way our family had always divided up the breakfast chores on Sunday. On that ritual day our mother stayed in bed. I laid out the forks and knives and egg cups and formal off-white china, and then stood back in the thin morning light to survey my precise placings. Lush napkin pyramids perched on lace table cloth, my mother's favorite. Through the kitchen door leaked the mutter and clang of a meal coming into being.

I put the exposures in order according to the spectral filters used, noting the calibrated photometry for each. The ceramic sounds of Bridge Hall rang in the tiled hallways and seeped through the door of my office: footsteps, distant talk, the scrape of chalk on slate, a banging door. Examining the plates through an eye piece, I felt the galaxy swell into being, huge.

The deep exposures brought out the dim jets I was after. There were four of them pointing out of NGC 1097, two red and two blue, the brightest three discovered by Wolsencroft and Zealey, the last red one found by Lorre over at JPL. Straight lines scratched across the mottling of foreground dust and stars. No one knew what colored a jet red or blue. I was trying to use the deep plates to measure the width of the jets. Using a slit over the lens, I had stopped down the image until I could employ calibrated photometry to measure the wedge of light. Still further narrowing might allow me to measure the spectrum, to see if the blues and reds came from stars, or from excited clouds of gas.

They lanced out, two blue jets cutting through the spiral arms and breaking free into the blackness beyond. One plate, taken in that spectral space where ionized hydrogen clouds emit, giving H II radiation, showed a string of beads buried in the curling spiral lanes. They were vast cooling clouds. Where the jets crossed the H II regions, the spiral arms were pushed outward, or else vanished altogether.

Opposite each blue jet, far across the galaxy, a red jet glowed. They, too, snuffed out the H II beads.

From these gaps in the spiral arms I estimated how far the barred spiral galaxy had turned, while the jets ate away at them: about fifteen degrees. From the velocity measurements in the disk, using the Doppler shifts of known spectral lines, I deduced the rotation rate of the NGC 1097 disk: approximately a hundred million years. Not surprising; our own sun takes about the same amount of time to circle around our galactic center. The photons which told me all these specifics had begun their steady voyage sixty million years ago, before there was a *New General Catalog of Nebulae and Clusters of Stars* to label them as they buried themselves in my welcoming emulsion. Thus do I know thee, NGC 1097.

These jets were unique. The brightest blue one dog-legs in a right angle turn and ends in silvery blobs of dry light. Its counter-jet, off-set a perverse eleven degrees from exact oppositeness, continues on a warmly rose-colored path over an immense distance, a span far larger than the parent galaxy itself. I frowned, puckered my lips in concentration, calibrated and calculated and refined. Plainly these ramrod, laconic patterns of light were trying to tell me something.

But answers come when they will, one piece at a time.

I tried to tell my son this when, that evening, I helped him with his reading. Using what his mother now knowingly termed "word attack skills," he had mastered most of these tactics. The larger strategic issues of the sentence eluded him still. *Take it in phrases,* I urged him, ruffing his light brown hair, distracted, because I liked the nutmeg smell. (I have often thought that I could find my children in the dark, in a crowd, by my nose alone. Our genetic code colors the air.) He thumbed his book, dirtying a corner. Read the words between the commas, I instructed, my classroom sense of order returning. Stop at the commas, and then pause before going on, and think about what all those words mean. I sniffed at his wheatlike hair again.

I am a traditional astronomer, accustomed to the bitter cold of the cage at Palomar, the Byzantine marriage of optics at Kitt Peak, the muggy air of Lick. Through that long morning yesterday I studied the NGC 1097 jets, attempting to see with the quick eye of the theorist, "dancing on the data" as Roger Blandford down the hall had once called it. I tried to erect some rickety hypothesis that my own uncertain mathematical abilities could brace up. An idea came. I caught at it. But holding it close, turning it over, pushing terms about in an overloaded equation, I saw it was merely an old idea tarted up, already disproved.

Perhaps computer enhancement of the images would clear away some of my enveloping fog, I mused. I took my notes to the neighboring building, listening to my footsteps echo in the long arcade.

The buildings at Caltech are mostly done in a pseudo-Spanish style, tan stucco with occasional flourishes of Moorish windows and tiles. The newer library rears up beside the crouching offices and classrooms, a modern extrusion. I entered the Alfred Sloan Laboratory of Physics and Mathematics, wondering for the nth time what a mathematical laboratory would be like, imagining Lewis Carroll in charge, and went into the new computer terminal rooms. The indices which called up my plates soon stuttered across the screen. I used a median numerical filter, to suppress variations in the background. There were standard routines to subtract particular parts of the spectrum. I called them up, averaging away noise from dust and gas and the image-saturating spikes that were foreground stars in our own galaxy. Still, nothing dramatic emerged. Illumination would not come.

I sipped at my coffee. I had brought a box of crackers from my office; and I broke one, eating each wafer with a heavy crunch. I swirled the cup and the coffee swayed like a dark disk at the bottom, a scum of cream at the vortex curling out into gray arms. I drank it. And thumbed another image into being.

This was not NGC 1097. I checked the number. Then the log. No, these were slots deliberately set aside for later filing. They were not to be filled; they represented my allotted computer space. They should be blank.

Yet I recognized this one. It was a view of Sagittarius A, the intense radio source that hides behind a thick lane of dust in the Milky Way. Behind that dark obscuring swath that is an arm of our Galaxy, lies the center. I squinted. Yes: this was a picture formed from observations sensitive to the 21-centimeter wavelength line, the emission of nonionized hydrogen. I had seen it before, on exposures that looked radially inward at the Galactic core. Here was the red band of hydrogen along our line of sight. Slightly below was the well-known arm of hot, expanding gas, nine thousand light years across. Above, tinted green, was a smaller arm, a ridge of gas moving outward at 135 kilometers per second. I had seen the seminars years ago. In the very center was the knot no more than a light year or two across, the source of the 10^{40} ergs per second of virulent energy that drove the cooker that caused all this. Still, the energy flux from our Galaxy was ten million times less than that of a quasar. Whatever the compact energy source there, it was comparatively quiet. NGC 1097 lies far to the south, entirely out of the Milky Way. Could the aim of the satellite camera have strayed so much?

Curious, I thumbed forward. The next index number gave another

GREGORY BENFORD

scan of the Sagittarius region, this time seen by the spectral emissions from outward-moving clouds of ammonia. Random blobs. I thumbed again. A formaldehyde-emission view. But now the huge arm of expanding hydrogen was sprinkled with knots, denoting clouds which moved faster, Dopplered into blue.

I frowned. No, the Sagittarius A exposures were no aiming error. These slots were to be left open for my incoming data. Someone had co-opted the space. Who? I called up the identifying codes, but there were none. As far as the master log was concerned, these spaces were still empty.

I moved to erase them. My finger paused, hovered, went limp. This was obviously high-quality information, already processed. Someone would want it. They had carelessly dumped it into my territory, but. . . .

My pause was in part that of sheer appreciation. Peering at the color-coded encrustations of light, I recalled what all this had once been like: impossibly complicated, ornate in its terms, caked with the eccentric jargon of long-dead professors, choked with thickets of atomic physics and thermodynamics, a web of complexity that finally gave forth mental pictures of a whirling, furious past, of stars burned now into cinders, of whispering, turbulent hydrogen that filled the void between the suns. From such numbers came the starscape that we knew. From a sharp scratch on a strip of film we could catch the signature of an element, deduce velocity from the Doppler shift, and then measure the width of that scratch to give the random component of the velocity, the random jigglings due to thermal motion, and thus the temperature. All from a scratch. No, I could not erase it.

When I was a boy of nine I was brow-beaten into serving at the altar, during the unendurably long Episcopal services that my mother felt we should attend. I wore the simple robe and was the first to appear in the service, lighting the candles with an awkward long device and its sliding wick. The organ music was soft and did not call attention to itself, so the congregation could watch undistracted as I fumbled with the wick and tried to keep the precarious balance between feeding it too much (so that, engorged, it bristled into a ball of orange) and the even worse embarrassment of snuffing it into a final accusing puff of black. Through the service I would alternately kneel and stand, murmuring the worn phrases as I thought of the softball I would play in the afternoon, feeling the prickly gathering heat underneath my robes. On a bad day the sweat would accumulate and a drop would cling to my nose. I'd let it hang there in mute testimony. The minister never seemed to notice. I would often slip off into decidedly untheological daydreams, intoxicated by the pressing moist heat, and miss the telltale words of the litany which signalled the beginning of communion. A whisper would come skating across the layered air and I would surface, to see the minister turned with clotted face toward me, holding the implements of his forgiving trade, waiting for me to bring the wine and wafers, swearing that once the polished walnut altar rail was emptied of its upturned and strangely blank faces, once the simpering organ had ebbed into silence and I had shrugged off these robes swarming with the stench of mothballs, I would have no more of it, I would erase it.

I asked Redman who the hell was logging their stuff into my inventory spaces. He checked. The answer was: nobody. There were no recorded intrusions into those sections of the memory system. *Then look further,* I said, and went back to work at the terminal.

They were still there. What's more, some index numbers that had been free before were now filled.

NGC 1097 still vexed me, but I delayed working on the problem. I studied these new pictures. They were processed, Doppler-coded, and filtered for noise. I switched back to the earlier plates, to be sure. Yes, it was clear: these were different.

Current theory held that the arm of expanding gas was on the outward phase of an oscillation. Several hundred million years ago, so the story went, a massive explosion at the galactic center had started the expansion: a billowing, spinning doughnut of gas swelled outward. Eventually its energy was matched by the gravitational attraction of the massive center. Then, as it slowed and finally fell back toward the center, it spun faster, storing energy in rotational motion, until centrifugal forces stopped its inward rush. Thus the hot cloud could oscillate in the potential well of gravity, cooling slowly.

These computer-transformed plates said otherwise. The Doppler shifts formed a cone. At the center of the plate, maximum values, far higher than any observed before, over a thousand kilometers per second. That exceeded escape velocity from the Galaxy itself. The values tapered off to the sides, coming smoothly down to the shifts that were on the earlier plates.

I called the programming director. He looked over the displays, understanding nothing of what it meant but everything about how it could have gotten there; and his verdict was clean, certain: human error. But further checks turned up no such mistake. "Must be comin' in on the transmission from orbit," he mused. He seemed half-asleep as he punched in commands, traced the intruders. These data had come in from the new combination optical, IR, and UV 'scope in orbit, and the JPL programs had obligingly performed the routine miracles of enhancement and analysis. But the orbital staff were sure no such data had been transmitted. In fact, the 'scope had been down for inspection, plus an alignment check, for over two days. The programming director shrugged and promised to look into it, fingering the innumerable pens clipped in his shirt pocket.

I stared at the Doppler cone, and thumbed to the next index number. The cone had grown, the shifts were larger. Another: still larger. And then I noticed something more; and a cold sensation seeped into me, banishing the casual talk and mechanical-printout stutter of the terminal room.

The point of view had shifted. All the earlier plates had shown a particular gas cloud at a certain angle of inclination. This latest plate was slightly cocked to the side, illuminating a clotted bunch of minor H II regions and obscuring a fraction of the hot, expanding arm. Some new features were revealed. If the JPL program had done such a rotation and shift, it would have left the new spaces blank, for there was no way of filling them in. These were not empty. They brimmed with specific shifts, detailed spectral indices. The JPL program would not have produced the field of numbers unless the raw data contained them. I stared at the screen for a long time.

That evening I drove home the long way, through the wide boulevards of Pasadena, in the gathering dusk. I remembered giving blood the month before, in the eggshell light of the Caltech dispensary. They took the blood away in a curious plastic sack, leaving me with a small bandage in the crook of my elbow. The skin was translucent, showing the riverwork of tributary blue veins, which—recently tapped—were nearly as pale as the skin. I had never looked at that part of me before and found it tender, vulnerable, an unexpected opening. I remembered my wife had liked being stroked there when we were dating, and that I had not touched her there for a long time. Now I had myself been pricked there, to pipe brimming life into a sack, and then to some other who could make use of it.

That evening I drove again, taking my son to Open House. The school bristled with light and seemed to command the neighborhood with its luminosity, drawing families out of their homes. My wife was taking my daughter to another school, and so I was unshielded by her ability to recognize people we knew. I could never sort out their names in time to answer the casual hellos. In our neighborhood the PTA nights draw a disproportionate fraction of technical types, like me. Tonight I saw them without the quicksilver verbal fluency of my wife. They had compact cars that seemed too small for their large families, wore shoes whose casualness offset the formal, just-come-from-work jackets and slacks, and carried creamy folders of their children's accumulated work, to use in conferring with the teachers. The wives were sun-darkened, wearing crisp, print dresses that looked recently put on, and spoke with ironic turns about PTA politics, bond issues, and class sizes. In his classroom my son tugged me from board to board, where he had contributed paragraphs on wildlife. The crowning exhibit was a model of Io, Jupiter's pizza-mocking moon, which he had made from a tennis ball and thick, sulphurous paint. It hung in a box painted black and looked remarkably, ethereally real. My son had won first prize in his class for the mockup moon, and his teacher stressed this as she went over the less welcome news that he was not doing well at his reading. Apparently he arranged the plausible phrases—A, then B, then C—into illogical combinations, C coming before A, despite the instructing commas and semicolons which should have guided him. It was a minor problem, his teacher assured me, but should be looked after. Perhaps a little more reading at home, under my eye? I nodded, sure that the children of the other scientists and computer programmers and engineers did not have this difficulty, and already knew what the instructing phrase of the next century would be, before the end of this one. My son took the news matter-of-factly, unafraid, and went off to help with the cake and Koolaid. I watched him mingle with girls whose awkwardness was lovely, like giraffes'. I remembered that his teacher (I had learned from gossip) had a mother dying of cancer, which might explain the furrow between her eyebrows that would not go away. My son came bearing cake. I ate it with him, sitting with knees slanting upward in the small chair; and quite calmly and suddenly an idea came to me and would not go away. I turned it over and felt its shape, testing it in a preliminary fashion. Underneath I was both excited and fearful and yet sure that it would survive: it was right. Scraping up the last crumbs and icing, I looked down, and saw my son had drawn a crayon design, an enormous father playing ball with a son, running and catching, the

GREGORY BENFORD

scene carefully fitted into the small compass of the plastic, throw-away plate.

The next morning I finished the data reduction on the slit-image exposures. By carefully covering over the galaxy and background, I had managed to take successive plates which blocked out segments of the space parallel to the brightest blue jet. Photometry of the resulting weak signal could give a cross section of the jet's intensity. Pinpoint calibration then yielded the thickness of the central jet zone.

The data was somewhat scattered, the error bars were larger than I liked, but still—I was sure I had it. The jet had a fuzzy halo and a bright core. The core was less than a hundred light years across, a thin filament of highly ionized hydrogen, cut like a swath through the gauzy dust beyond the galaxy. The resolute, ruler-sharp path, its thinness, its profile of luminosity: all pointed toward a tempting picture. Some energetic object had carved each line, moving at high speeds. It swallowed some of the matter in its path; and in the act of engorgement the mass was heated to incandescent brilliance, spitting UV and x-rays into an immense surrounding volume. This radiation in turn ionized the galactic gas, leaving a scratch of light behind the object, like picnickers dumping luminous trash as they pass by.

The obvious candidates for the fast-moving sources of the jets were black holes. And as I traced the slim profiles of the NGC 1097 jets back into the galaxy, they all intersected at the precise geometrical center of the barred spiral pattern.

Last night, after returning from the Open House with a sleepy boy in tow, I talked with my wife as we undressed. I described my son's home room, his artistic achievements, his teacher. My wife let slip offhandedly some jarring news. I had, apparently, misheard the earlier gossip; perhaps I had mused over some problem while she related the story to me over breakfast. It was not the teacher's mother who had cancer, but the teacher herself. I felt an instant, settling guilt. I could scarcely remember the woman's face, though it was a mere hour later. I asked why she was still working. Because, my wife explained with straightforward New England sense, it was better than staring at a wall. The chemotherapy took only a small slice of her hours. And anyway, she probably needed the money. The night beyond our windows seemed solid, flinty, harder than the soft things inside. In the glass I watched my wife take off a print dress and stretch backward, breasts thinning into crescents, her nobbed spine describing a serene curve that anticipated bed. I went over to my chest of drawers and looked down at the polished walnut surface, scrupulously rectangular and arranged, across which I had tossed the residue of an hour's dutiful parenting: a scrawled essay on marmosets, my son's anthology of drawings, his reading list, and on top, the teacher's bland paragraph of assessment. It felt odd to have called these things into being, these signs of a forward tilt in a small life, by an act of love or at least lust, now years past. The angles appropriate to cradling my children still lived in my hands. I could feel clearly the tentative clutch of my son as he attempted some upright steps. Now my eye strayed to his essay. I could see him struggling with the notion of clauses, with ideas piled upon each other to build a point, and with the caged linearity of the sentence. On the page above, in the loops of the teacher's generous flow pen, I saw a hollow rotundity, a denial of any constriction in her life. She had to go on, this schoolgirlish penmanship said, to forcefully forget a gnawing illness among a roomful of bustling children. Despite all the rest, she had to keep on doing.

What could be energetic enough to push black holes out of the galactic center, up the slopes of the deep gravitational potential well? Only another black hole. The dynamics had been worked out years before—as so often happens, in another context—by William Saslaw. Let a bee-swarm of black holes orbit about each other, all caught in a gravitational depression. Occasionally, they veer close together, deforming the space-time nearby, caroming off each other like billiard balls. If several undergo these near-miss collisions at once, a black hole can be ejected from the gravitational trap altogether. More complex collisions can throw pairs of black holes in opposite directions, conserving angular momentum: jets and counterjets. But why did NGC 1097 display two blue jets and two red? Perhaps the blue ones glowed with the phosphorescent waste left by the largest, most energetic black holes; their counter-jets must be, by some detail of the dynamics, always smaller, weaker, redder.

I went to the jutting, air-conditioned library, and read Saslaw's papers. Given a buzzing hive of black holes in a gravitational well—partly of their own making—many things could happen. There were compact configurations, tightly orbiting and self-obsessed, which could be ejected as a body. These close-wound families could in turn be unstable, once they were isolated beyond the galaxy's tug, just as the group at the center had been. Caroming off

GREGORY BENFORD

each other, they could eject unwanted siblings. I frowned. This could explain the astonishing right-angle turn the long blue jet made. One black hole thrust sidewise and several smaller, less energetic black holes pushed the opposite way.

As the galactic center lost its warped children, the ejections would become less probable. Things would die down. But how long did that take? NGC 1097 was no younger than our own Galaxy; on the cosmic scale, a sixty-million-year difference was nothing.

In the waning of afternoon—it was only a bit more than twenty-four hours since I first laid out the plates of NGC 1097—the Operations report came in. There was no explanation for the Sagittarius A data. It had been received from the station in orbit and duly processed. But no command had made the scope swivel to that axis. Odd, Operations said, that it pointed in an interesting direction, but no more.

There were two added plates, fresh from processing. I did not mention to Redman in Operations that the resolutions of these plates was astonishing, that details in the bloated, spilling clouds were unprecedented. Nor did I point out that the angle of view had tilted further, giving a better perspective on the outward-jutting inferno. With their polynomial percussion, the computers had given what was in the stream of downward-flowing data, numbers that spoke of something being banished from the pivot of our Galaxy.

Caltech is a compact campus. I went to the Athenaeum for coffee, ambling slowly beneath the palms and scented eucalyptus, and circumnavigated the campus on my return. In the varnished perspectives of these tiled hallways, the hammer of time was a set of Dopplered numbers, blue-shifted because the thing rushed toward us, a bulge in the sky. Silent numbers.

There were details to think about, calculations to do, long strings of hypothesis to unfurl like thin flags. I did not know the effect of a penetrating, ionizing flux on Earth. Perhaps it could affect the upper atmosphere and alter the ozone cap that drifts above our heedless heads. A long trail of disturbed, high-energy plasma could fan out through our benign spiral arm—odd, to think of bands of dust and rivers of stars as a neighborhood where you have grown up—churning, working, heating. After all, the jets of NGC 1097 had snuffed out the beaded H II regions as cleanly as an eraser passing across a blackboard, ending all the problems that life knows.

The NGC 1097 data was clean and firm. It would make a good

paper, perhaps a letter to *Astrophysical Journal Letters*. But the rest—there was no crisp professional path. These plates had come from much nearer the Galactic center. The information had come outward at light speed, far faster than the pressing bulge, and tilted at a slight angle away from the radial vector that led to Earth.

I had checked the newest Palomar plates from Sagittarius A this afternoon. There were no signs of anything unusual. No Doppler bulge, no exiled mass. They flatly contradicted the satellite plates.

That was the key: old reliable Palomar, our biggest ground-based 'scope, showed nothing. Which meant that someone in high orbit had fed data into our satellite 'scope—exposures which had to be made nearer the Galactic center and then brought here and deftly slipped into our ordinary astronomical research. Exposures which spoke of something stirring where we could not yet see it, beyond the obscuring lanes of dust. The plumes of fiery gas would take a while longer to work through that dark cloak.

These plain facts had appeared on a screen, mute and undeniable, keyed to the data on NGC 1097. Keyed to a connection that another eye than mine could miss. Some astronomer laboring over plates of eclipsing binaries or globular clusters might well have impatiently erased the offending, multicolored spattering, not bothered to uncode the Dopplers, to note the persistent mottled red of the Galactic dust arm at the lower right, and so not known what the place must be. Only I could have made the connection to NGC 1097, and guessed what an onrushing black hole could do to a fragile planet: burn away the ozone layer, hammer the land with high-energy particles, mask the sun in gas and dust.

But to convey this information in this way was so strange, so—yes, that was the word—so alien. Perhaps this was the way they had to do it: quiet, subtle, indirect. Using an oblique analogy which only suggested, yet somehow disturbed more than a direct statement. And of course, this might be only a phrase in a longer message. Moving out from the Galactic center, they would not know we were here until they grazed the expanding bubble of radio noise that gave us away, and so their data would use what they had, views at a different slant. The data itself, raw and silent, would not necessarily call attention to itself. It had to be placed in context, beside NGC 1097. How had they managed to do that? Had they tried before? What odd logic dictated this approach? How. . . .

Take it in pieces. Some of the data I could use, some not. Perhaps a further check, a fresh look through the dusty Sagittarius arm, would show the beginnings of a ruddy swelling, could give a veri-

GREGORY BENFORD

fication. I would have to look, try to find a bridge that would make plausible what I knew but could scarcely prove. The standards of science are austere, unforgiving—and who would have it differently? I would have to hedge, to take one step back for each two forward, to compare and suggest and contrast, always sticking close to the data. And despite what I thought I knew now, the data would have to lead, they would have to show the way.

There is a small Episcopal church, not far up Hill Street, which offers a Friday communion in early evening. Driving home through the surrounding neon consumer gumbo, musing, I saw the sign, and stopped. I had the NGC 1097 plates with me in a carrying case, ripe beneath my arm with their fractional visions, like thin sections of an exotic cell. I went in. The big oak door thumped solemnly shut behind me. In the nave two elderly men were passing woven baskets, taking up the offertory. I took a seat near the back. Idly I surveyed the people, distributed randomly like a field of unthinking stars, in the pews before me. A man came nearby and a pool of brassy light passed before me and I put something in, the debris at the bottom clinking and rustling as I stirred it. I watched the backs of heads as the familiar litany droned on, as devoid of meaning as before. I do not believe, but there is communion. Something tugged at my attention; one head turned a fraction. By a kind of triangulation I deduced the features of the other, closer to the ruddy light of the altar, and saw it was my son's teacher. She was listening raptly. I listened, too, watching her, but could only think of the gnawing at the center of a bustling, swirling galaxy. The lights seemed to dim. The organ had gone silent. *Take, eat. This is the body and blood of* and so it had begun. I waited my turn. I do not believe, but there is communion. The people went forward in their turns. The woman rose; yes, it was she, the kind of woman whose hand would give forth loops and spirals and who would dot her i's with a small circle. The faint timbre of the organ seeped into the layered air. When it was time I was still thinking of NGC 1097, of how I would write the paper—fragments skittered across my mind, the pyramid of the argument was taking shape—and I very nearly missed the gesture of the elderly man at the end of my pew. Halfway to the altar rail I realized that I still carried the case of NGC 1097 exposures, crooked into my elbow, where the pressure caused a slight ache to spread: the spot where they had made the transfusion in the clinic, transferring a fraction of life, blood given. I put it beside me as I knelt. The robes of the approaching figure were cobalt blue and red, a change from the decades since I had been an acolyte. There were no acolytes at such a small service, of course. The blood would follow; first came the offered plate of wafers. Take, eat. Life calling out to life. I could feel the pressing weight of what lay ahead for me, the long roll of years carrying forward one hypothesis, and then, swallowing, knowing that I would never believe this and yet I would want it, I remembered my son, remembered that these events were only pieces, that the puzzle was not yet over, that I would never truly see it done, that as an astronomer I had to live with knowledge forever partial and provisional, that science was not final results but instead a continuing meditation carried on in the face of enormous facts—*take it in phrases*—let the sentences of our lives pile up.

GREGORY BENFORD

FOR THE BIRDS
by Isaac Asimov
art: Vincent Di Fate

Dr. Asimov's Foundation's Edge,
the long-awaited sequel to the
"Fountain Trilogy," will
be out shortly from Doubleday, Inc.

Charles Modine, despite the fact that he was in his late thirties and in perfect health, had never been in space. He had seen space settlements on television and had occasionally read about them in the public prints, but it went no farther than that.

To tell the truth, he was not interested in space. He had been born on Earth, and Earth was enough for him. When he wanted a change of environment, he turned to the sea. He was an avid and skilled sailor.

He was therefore repelled when the representative of Space Structures, Limited, finally told him that in order for him to do the job they were asking him to do, he would have to leave Earth.

Modine said, "Listen. I'm not a space person. I design clothes. What do I know about rockets and acceleration and trajectories and all the rest of it?"

"We know about that. You don't have to," said the other, urgently. Her name was Naomi Baranova and she had the queer, tentative walk of someone who had been in space so long she wasn't sure what the gravitational situation was at the moment.

Her clothes, Modine noted with some irritation, functioned as coverings and as little else. A tarpaulin would have done as well.

"But why need I come out to a space station?"

"For what *you* know. We want you to design something for us."

"Clothes?"

"Wings."

Modine thought about it. He had a high, pale forehead and the process of thought always seemed to flush it somewhat. He had been told that at any rate. This time, if it flushed, it was partly in annoyance. "I can do that here, can't I?"

Baranova shook her head firmly. She had hair with a dark reddish tinge that was slowly being invaded by gray. She didn't seem to mind. She said, "We want you to understand the situation, Mr. Modine. We've consulted the technicians and the computer experts, and they've built the most efficient possible wings, they tell us. They've taken into account stresses and surfaces and flexibilities and maneuverabilities and everything else you can imagine—but it doesn't help. We think perhaps a few frills—"

"Frills, Ms. Baranova?"

ISAAC ASIMOV

"Something other than scientific perfection. Something to rouse interest. Otherwise, the space settlements won't survive. That's why I want you there; to appreciate the situation for yourself. We're prepared to pay you very well.

It was the promised pay, including a healthy retainer, win or lose, that brought Modine into space. He was no more money-mad than the average human being, but he was not money-insensitive either, and he liked to see his reputation appreciated.

Nor was it actually as bad as he had expected. In the early days of space travel, there had been short periods of high acceleration and long cramped periods in small modules. Somehow that was what Earth-bound people still thought of in connection with space travel. But a century had passed, and the shuttles were commodious, while the hydraulic seats seemed to sop up the acceleration as though it were nothing more than a coffee-spill.

Modine spent the time studying photographs of the wings in action and in watching holographic videotapes of the flyers.

He said, "There's a certain grace to the performance."

Naomi Baranova smiled rather sadly, "You're watching experts—athletes. If you could see me trying to handle those wings and manage to tumble and side-slip, I'm afraid you would laugh. And yet I'm better than most."

They were approaching Space Settlement Five. Its name was Chrysalis, officially; but everyone called it Five.

"You might suppose," said Baranova, "that it would be the other way around, but there's no feeling of poetry about the place. That's the trouble. It's not a home; it's just a job, and it is hard to make people establish families and settle down. Until it's a home—"

Five showed up as a small cylinder, far away, looking much as Modine had seen it on television on Earth. He knew it was larger than it looked, but that was only an intellectual knowledge. His eyes and his emotions were not prepared for the steady increase in size as they approached. The spaceship and he dwarfed steadily, and—eventually—they were circling an enormous object of glass and aluminum.

He watched for a long time before he became aware that they were still circling. He said, "Aren't we going to land on it?"

"Not that easy," said Baranova. "Five rotates on an axis about once in two minutes. It has to in order to set up a centrifugal effect that will keep everything inside pressed against the inner wall and create an artificial gravity. We have to match that speed before we can land. It takes time."

"Must it spin that quickly?"

"To have the centrifugal effect mimic Earth-strength gravity, yes. That's the basic problem. It would be much better if we could use a slow spin to produce a tenth-normal gravity or even less, but that interferes with human physiology. People can't take low gravity for too long."

The ship's speed had nearly matched the rotation period of Five. Modine could clearly see the curve of the outer mirror that caught the sunlight and with it illuminated Five's interior. He could make out the Solar power station that supplied the energy for the station, with enough left over for export to Earth.

And they finally entered at the pole of the cylinder's hemispherical end-cap and were inside Five.

Modine had spent a full day on Five, and he was tired—but he had, rather unexpectedly, enjoyed it. They were sitting now on lawn furniture—on a wide stretch of grass—against a vista of suburbia.

There were clouds overhead—sunshine, without a clear view of the Sun itself—a wind—and, in the distance, a small stream.

It was hard to believe he was on a cylinder floating in space in the Moon's orbit, circling Earth once a month. He said, "It's like a world."

Baranova said, "So it seems when you're new here. When you've been here a time, you discover you know every corner of it. Everything repeats."

Modine said, "If you live in a particular town on Earth, everything repeats too."

"I know. But on Earth you can travel widely if you wish. Even if you don't travel, you know you can. Here you can't. That's not so good; but it's not the worst."

"You don't have the Earth's worst," said Modine. "I'm sure you don't have weather extremes."

"The weather, Mr. Modine, is indeed Garden of Edenish, but you get used to that. —Let me show you something. I have a ball here. Could you throw it high up, straight up, and catch it.'

Modeen smiled. "Are you serious?"

"Quite. Please do."

Modeen said, "I'm not a ball-player, but I think I can throw a ball. I might even catch it when it comes down."

He threw the ball upward. It curved parabolically, and Modeen found himself drifting forward in order to catch it, then running. It fell out of reach.

Baranova said, "You didn't throw it straight up, Mr. Modine."

"Yes I did," gasped Modine.

"Only by Earth-standards," said Baranova. "The difficulty is that what we call the Coriolis force is involved. Here at the inner surface of Five, we're moving quite rapidly in a great circle about the axis. If you throw the ball upward it moves nearer the axis where things make a smaller circle and move more slowly. However, the ball retains the speed it had down here, so it moves ahead and you couldn't catch it. If you had wanted to catch it, you would have had to throw it up and back so that it would loop and return to you like a boomerang. The details of motion are different here on Five than on Earth."

Modine said, thoughtfully, "You get used to it, I suppose."

"Not entirely. We live on the equatorial regions of our small cylinder. That's where the motion is fastest and where we get the effect of normal gravity. If we move upward toward the axis, along the end-caps toward the poles, the gravitational effect decreases rapidly. We frequently have to go up or axis-ward, and—whenever we do—the Coriolis effect must be taken into account. We have small monorails that must move spirally toward either pole; one track poleward, another returning. In the trip we feel ourselves perpetually canted to one side. It takes a long time to get used to it and some people never learn the trick of it. No one really likes to live here for that reason."

"Can you do something about that twisting effect?"

"If we could make our rotation slower, we would lessen the Coriolis, but we would also lessen the feel of gravitation, and we can't do that."

"Damned if you do; damned if you don't."

"Not entirely. We could get along with less gravitation, if we exercise; but it would mean exercise every day for considerable periods. That would have to be fun. People won't indulge in daily calisthenics that are troublesome or a bore. We used to think that flying would be the answer. When we go to the low-gravity regions near the poles, people are almost weightless. They can almost rise into the air by flapping their arms. If we attach light plastic wings to each arm, stiffened by flexible rods, and if those wings are folded and extended in just the right rhythm, people can fly like birds."

"Will that work as exercise?"

"Oh, yes. Flying is hard work, I assure you. The arm and shoulder muscles may not have to do much to keep you aloft but they must be in continuous use to maneuver you properly. It keeps up the muscle tone and bone calcium, *if* it's done on a regular basis. —But people won't do it."

"I should think they'd love to fly."

Baranova sniffed. "They would, if it were easy enough. The trouble is that it requires skillful coordination of muscles to keep steady. The slightest errors result in tumbling and spinning and almost inevitable nausea. Some can learn how to fly gracefully as you saw on the holo-casettes, but very few."

"Birds don't get sea-sick."

"Birds fly in normal gravity fields. People on Five don't."

Modine frowned and grew thoughtful.

Baranova said, "I can't promise that you'll sleep. People don't usually their first few nights on a space settlement. Still, please try to do so and tomorrow we'll go to the flying areas."

Modine could see what Baranova had meant by saying the Coriolis force was unpleasant. The small monorail coach that took them poleward seemed constantly to be sliding leftward, and his entrails seemed to be doing the same. He held on to the hand-grips, white-knuckled.

"I'm sorry," said Baranova, sympathetically. "If we went more slowly, it wouldn't be so bad, but we're holding up traffic as it is."

"Do you get used to this?" groaned Modine.

"Somewhat. Not enough."

He was glad to stop finally, but only limitedly so. It took a while to get used to the fact that he seemed to be floating. Each time he tried to move, he tumbled; and each time he tumbled he didn't fall but drifted slowly forward or upward and returned only gradually. His automatic kicking made things worse.

Baranova left him to himself for a while, then caught at him and drew him slowly back. "Some people enjoy this," she said.

"I don't," gasped Modine, miserably.

"Many don't. Please put your feet into these stirrups on the ground and don't make any sudden movements."

There were five of them—people wearing wings—flying in the sky. Baranova said, "Those five 'birds' are here just about every day. There are a few hundred more who are there now and then; and we could accommodate, here and at the other pole, as well as along the axis, something like five thousand flyers at a time. That is enough to keep Five's thirty thousand in condition. What do we do?"

Modine gestured and his body swayed backward in response.

ISAAC ASIMOV

"They must have learned how, those—birds—up there. They weren't born birds. Can't the others learn it, too?"

"Those up there have natural coördination."

"What can I do then? I'm a fashion designer. I don't create natural coordination."

"Not having natural coordination doesn't stop you altogether. It just means working hard, practicing longer. Is there any way you could make the process more—fashionable? Could you design a flying-costume; suggest a psychological campaign to get the people out? If we could arrange proper programs of exercise and physical fitness, we could slow Five's rotation, weaken the Coriolis effect, make this place a home."

"You may be asking for a miracle. —Could you have them come closer?"

Baranova waved, and one of the birds saw her and swooped toward them in a long, graceful curve. It was a young woman. She hovered ten feet away, smiling, her wings flicking slightly at the tips.

"Hi," she called out. "What's up?"

"Nothing," said Baranova. "My friend wants to watch you handle the wings. Show him how they work."

The young woman smiled and, twisting first one wing, then the other, performed a slow somersault. She straightened to a halt with a back-handed twist, of both wings, then rose slowly, her feet dangling and her wings moving slowly. The wing-motion grew more rapid, and she was off in wild acceleration.

Modine said, after a while, "Rather like ballet-dancing, but the wings are ugly."

"Are they? Are they?"

"Certainly," said Modine. "They look like bat-wings. The associations are all wrong."

"Tell us what to do then? Should we put a feather-design on them? Would that bring out the flyers and make them try harder to learn?"

"No." Modine thought for a while. "Maybe we can make the whole process easier."

He took his feet out of the stirrups, gave himself a little push and floated into the air. He moved his arms and legs experimentally and rocked erratically. He tried to scramble back for the stirrups, and Baranova reached up to pull him down.

Modine said, "I'll tell you what: I'll design something; and if someone here can help me construct it according to the design, *I'll* try to fly. I've never done any such thing; you've just seen me try to wriggle in the air and I can't even do that. Well, if I use my design and *I* can fly, then anyone can."

"I should think so, Mr. Modine," said Baranova, in a tone that seemed suspended between skepticism and hope.

By the end of the week, Modine was beginning to feel that Space Settlement Five was home. As long as he stayed at ground level in the equatorial regions, where the gravitational effect was normal, there was no Coriolis effect to bother him and he felt his surroundings to be very Earth-like.

"The first time out," he said, "I don't want to be watched by the population generally, because it may be harder than I think and I don't want to get this thing to a bad start. —But I would like to be watched by some of the officials of the Settlement, just in case I make it."

Baranova said, "I should think we would try in private first. A failure the first time, whatever the excuse—"

"But a success would be *so* impressive."

"What are the chances of success? Be reasonable."

"The chances are good, Ms. Baranova. Believe me. What you have been doing here is all wrong. You're flying in air—like birds—and it's hard. You said it yourself. Birds on Earth operate under gravity. The birds up here operate without gravity—so everything has to be designed differently."

The temperature, as always, was perfectly adjusted. So was the humidity. So was the wind speed. The atmosphere was so perfect it was as though it weren't there. —And yet Modine was perspiring with a bad case of stage fright. He was also gasping. The air was thinner in these gravity-free regions then at the equator—not by much, but enough thinner for him to have trouble gathering enough with his heart pounding so.

The air was empty of the human birds; the audience was a handful—the Coordinator, the Secretary of Health, the Commissioner of Safety, and so on. There were a dozen men and women present. Only Baranova was familiar.

He had been outfitted with a small mike, and he tried to keep his voice from shaking.

He said, "We are flying without gravity, and neither birds nor bats are a good model for us. They fly *with* gravity. —It's different in the sea. There's little effective gravity in water, since buoyancy lifts you. When we fly through no-gravity water, we call it swimming. In Space Station Five, where there's no gravity in this region, the air is for swimming, not for flying. We must imitate the dolphin and not the eagle."

He sprang into the air as he spoke, wearing a graceful one-piece suit that neither clung skin-tight, nor billowed. He began to tumble at once, but stretching one arm was sufficient to activate a small gas cartridge. A smoothly curved fin emerged along his spinal column, while a shallow keel marked the line of his abdomen.

The tumbling ceased. "Without gravity," he said, "this is enough to stabilize your flight. You can still tip and turn, but always under control. I may not do it well at first, but it won't take much practice."

He stretched his other arm and each foot was suddenly equipped with a flipper—each elbow with another.

"These," he said, "offer the propulsive force. You needn't flap the arms. Gentle motions will suffice for everything but you have to bend your body and arch your neck in order to make turns and veers. You have to twist and alter the angle of your arms and legs. The whole body is engaged, but smoothly and non-violently. —Which is all the better, for every muscle in your body is involved and you can keep it up for hours without tiring."

He could feel himself moving more surely and gracefully—and faster. Up, up, he was suddenly going, with the air rushing up past him until he was almost in a panic for fear he would not be able to slow up. But he turned his heels and elbows almost instinctively and felt himself curve and slow.

Dimly, through the pounding of his heart, he could hear the applause.

Baranova said, admiringly, "How did you see this when our technicians couldn't?"

"The technicians started with the inevitable assumption of wings, thanks to birds and airplanes, and designed the most efficient ones possible. That's a technician's job. The job of a fashion designer is to see things as an artistic whole. I could see that the wings didn't fit the conditions of the space settlement. Just my job."

Baranova said, "We'll make these dolphin suits and get the population out into the air. I'm sure we can now. And then we can lay our plans to begin to slow Five's rotation."

"Or stop it altogether," said Modine. "I suspect that everyone will want to swim all the time instead of walking." He laughed. "They may not ever want to walk again. *I* may not."

They made out the large check they had promised and Modine, smiling at the figure, said, "Wings are for the birds."

©Borth '80

THE WOMAN THE UNICORN LOVED
by Gene Wolfe
art: Frank Borth

Gene Wolf's novel The Shadow of the Torturer, *the first volume of the tetralogy* The Book of the New Sun, *received the 1981 World Fantasy Award. The second volume,* The Claw of the Conciliator *received the Nebula for best novel in 1982.*

At the western edge of the campus the parkway sent a river of steel and rubber roaring out of the heart of the city. Fragrant pines fringed the farther side. The unicorn trotted among them, sometimes concealed, sometimes treading the strip of coarse grass that touched the strip of soiled gravel that touched the concrete. That was where Anderson, looking from his office window, first saw him.

Drivers and passengers saw him too. Some waved; no doubt some shouted, though their shouts could not be heard. Faces pale and faces brown pressed against glass, but no one stopped. Possibly some trucker with a CB informed the police.

The unicorn was so white he gleamed. His head looked Arabian, but his hooves were darkly red, like pigeon's-blood rubies, and his tail was not like a horse's tail at all, but the kind of tail—like the tail of a bull, but with an additional guidon of hair halfway to the tip—that is seen only in heraldic beasts. His horn shone like polished ivory, straight as the blade of a rapier and as long as a man's forearm. Anderson guessed his height at fourteen hands.

He turned away to lift his camera bag down from the top of the filing cabinet, and when he got back to the window the unicorn was in the traffic. Across two hundred yards of campus lawn he could hear the squealing of brakes.

"Pluto, the grisly god, who never spares,
Who feels no mercy, who hears no prayers."

Anderson recited the couplet to himself, and only as he pronounced the word *prayers* was he aware that he had spoken aloud.

Then the unicorn was safe on the other side, cantering across the shaven grass. (Pluto, it appeared, might hear prayers after all.) As the armed head lifted to test the wind, Anderson's telephone rang. He picked it up.

"Hello, Andy? Dumont. Look out your window."

"I am looking," Anderson said.

"Dropped right into our laps. Can you imagine anybody letting something like that go?"

"Yes, pretty easily. I can also imagine it jumping just about any fence on earth. But if we're going to protect it, we'd better get on the job before the kids run it off." Anderson had found his telephoto zoom and coupled it to the camera body. With the phone clamped between his shoulder and his ear, he took a quick picture.

"I'm going after it. I want a tissue specimen and a blood sample."

"You can get them when the Army shoots it."

"Listen, Andy, I don't want to see it shot any more than you do. A piece of work like that? I'm going out there now, and I'll appreciate any help I can get. I've already told my secretary to phone some members. If the military comes in—well, at least you'll be able to get some stills to send the TV people. You coming?"

Anderson came, a big, tawny man of almost forty, with a camera hanging from his neck. By the time he was out of the Liberal Arts Building, there were a hundred or so students around the unicorn. He must have menaced them; their line bent backward, then closed again. His gleaming horn was lifted above their heads for a moment, half playful, half triumphant. Anderson used his size and faculty status to elbow his way to the front of the crowd.

The unicorn stood—no, trotted, almost danced—in the center of a circle fifty feet wide, while the students shouted jokes and cheered. A little group who must have known something of his lore grabbed a blonde in a cheerleader's sweater and pushed her forward. He put his head down, a lancer at the charge; and she scampered back into the jeering crowd, breasts bobbing.

Anderson lowered his camera.

"Get it?" a student beside him asked.

"I think so."

A Frisbee sailed by the unicorn's ears, and he shied like a skittish horse. Someone threw it back.

Anderson yelled, "If that animal gets frightened, he's going to hurt somebody."

Dumont heard him, whether the students did or not. He waved from the farther side of the circle, his bald head gleaming. As the unicorn trotted past him, he thrust out a loaf of bread and was ignored.

Anderson sprinted across the circle. The students cheered, and several began running back and forth.

"Hi," Dumont said. "That took guts."

"Not really." Anderson found he was puffing. "I didn't come close. If he was angry, none of us would be here."

"I wish none of them were—nobody but you and me. It would make everything a hell of a lot simpler."

"Don't you have that tranquilizer gun?"

"At home. Our friend there would be long gone by the time I got back with it. Maybe I should keep one in the lab, but you know how it is—before this, we've always had to go after them."

Anderson nodded, only half listening as he watched the unicorn.

"We had this bread to feed to mice in a nutrition project. I put some stuff in it to quiet him down. On the spur of the moment, it was the best I could do."

Anderson was wondering who would arrive first—their Mythic Conservationists with protest signs or the soldiers and their guns. "I doubt that it's going to be good enough," he told Dumont.

A young woman slipped between them. "Here," she asked, "can I try?" Before Dumont could object, she took the bread and jogged to the center of the circle, the wind stirring her short, brown hair and the sunlight flashing from her glasses.

The unicorn came toward her slowly, head down.

Dumont said, "He'll kill her."

The students were almost quiet now, whispering. Anderson had to fight the impulse to dash out, to try to hold back the white beast, to knock him off his feet and wrestle him to the ground if he could. Except that he could not; that a dozen like him could not, no more than they could have overthrown an elephant. If he, or anyone here, were to attempt such a thing now, people would surely die.

The young woman thrust out Dumont's loaf—common white bread from some grocery store. After a moment she crouched to bring her eyes on a level with the unicorn's.

Anderson heard himself murmur,

"Behold a pale horse:
And his name that sat on him was Death."

Then, when tension had been drawn so fine that it seemed to him that he must break, *it* broke instead. The ivory lance came up; and the shining, impossible lancer trotted forward, nibbled at the bread, nuzzled the young woman's neck. Still quiet, indeed almost hushed, the students surged forward. A boy with a feathery red beard patted the unicorn's withers, and a girl Anderson recognized from one of his classes buried her face in the flowing mane. The young woman herself, the girl with the bread, stroked the fierce horn. Anderson found that he was there too, his hand on a gleaming flank.

Then the magic blew away beneath the threshing of a helicopter, dissolved like a dream at cockcrow. It came in low across the park, a dark blue gunship. (Police, Anderson thought crazily, police and not the Army this time.) A dozen people yelled, and the students began to scatter.

It banked in a tight turn and came back trailing a white plume of tear gas. Anderson ran with the rest then, hearing the thunder of the unicorn's hooves over—no, under—the whicker of the four-bladed prop. There was a sputter of fire from some automatic weapon.

Back in the Liberal Arts Building several hours later, he went to the restroom to wash the traces of the gas from his face and hands and put drops in his faintly burning eyes. The smell of the gas was in his trousers and jacket; they would have to be cleaned. He wished vaguely that he had been prescient enough to keep a change of clothes on campus.

When he opened the door to his office, the young woman was there. Absurdly, she rose when he entered, as though sex roles had not just been eliminated but reversed.

He nodded to her, and she extended her hand. "I'm Julie Coronell, Dr. Anderson."

"It's a pleasure," he said. She might have been quite pretty, he decided, if she were not so thin. And so nervous.

"I—I noticed you out there. With the unicorn. I was the one who fed him bread."

"I know you were," Anderson said. "I noticed you, too. Everyone did."

She actually blushed, something he had not seen in years. "I've some more." She lifted a brown paper sack. "The other wasn't mine, really—I got it from some man there. He's in the Biology Department, I think."

Anderson nodded. "Yes, he is."

"That was white. That bread. This is pumpernickel. I thought he—the unicorn. I thought he might like it better."

Anderson could not keep from grinning at that, and she smiled too.

"Well, anyway, *I* like it better. Do you know the story about the general's horse? Or am I being a pest?"

"Not at all. I'd love to hear the story of the general's horse, especially if it has anything to do with unicorns."

"It doesn't, really. Only with horses, you know, and pumpernickel. The general was one of Napoleon's, I think Bernadotte, and he had a favorite charger named Nicole—we would say Nicholas or Nick. When the Grand Army occupied Germany and the officers ate at the German country inns, they were served the coarse, brown German bread with their meals. All Frenchmen hate it, and none of them would eat it. But the others saw that Bernadotte slipped it into his pockets, and when they asked him about it, he said it was for his horse—*Pain pour Nicole*, bread for Nick. After that the others joked about the German 'horse bread,' *pain pour Nicole*, and the Germans thought that was the French name for it, and since anything French has always been very posh on menus, they used it."

Anderson chuckled and shook his head. "Is that what you're going to call him when you find him? Nicholas? Or will it be Nicole?"

"Nick, actually. The story is just folk-etymology, really. But I thought of it, and it seemed to fit. Nick, because we're both Americans now. I was born in New Zealand, and that brings me to one of the things I came to ask you—what nationality are unicorns? I mean originally. Greek?"

"Indian," Anderson told her.

"You're making fun of me."

He shook his head. "Not American Indian, of course. Indian like the tiger. A Roman naturalist called Pliny seems to have begun the story. He said that people in India hunted an animal he called the monoceros. Our word *unicorn* is a translation of that. Both words mean 'one-horned.' "

Julie nodded.

"Pliny said this unicorn had a head like a stag, feet like an elephant, a boar's tail, and the body of a horse. It bellowed, it had one black horn growing from its forehead, and it could not be captured alive."

She stared at him. He stared expressionlessly back, and at last she said, "That's not a unicorn! That's not a unicorn at all. That's a rhinoceros."

"Uh huh. Specifically, it's an Indian rhinoceros. The African ones actually have two horns, one in front of the other. Pliny's description fell into the hands of the scholars of the Dark Ages, who knew nothing about rhinoceroses or even elephants; and the unicorn became a one-horned creature that was otherwise much like a horse. Unicorn horn was supposed to neutralize poisons, but the Indians didn't ship their rhinoceros horns west—China was much closer and much richer, and the Chinese thought rhinoceros horn was an aphrodisiac. Narwhale horns were brought in to satisfy the demand, and narwhale horns succeeded wonderfully, because narwhale horns are so utterly fantastic that no one who hasn't seen one can believe in them. They're ivory, and spiraled, and perfectly straight. You know, of course. You had your hand on one today, only it was growing out of a unicorn's head. Dumont would say out of the head of a genetically re-engineered horse, but I think we both know better."

Julie smiled. "It's wonderful, isn't it? Unicorns are real now."

"In a way, they were real before. As Chesterton says somewhere, to think of a cow with wings is essentially to have met one. The unicorn symbolized masculine purity—which isn't such a bad thing to symbolize, after all. Unicorns were painted on shields and sewn into flags. A unicorn rampant is the badge of Scotland, just as the bald eagle is the badge of this country, and eventually that unicorn became one of the supporters of the British arms. The image, the idea, has been real for a long time. Now it's tangible."

"And I'm glad. I like it like that. Dr. Anderson, the real reason I came to see you was that a friend told me you were the president of an organization that tries to save these animals."

"Most of them are people. All right if I smoke?" She nodded, and Anderson took a pipe from his desk and began to pack it with tobacco. "Many of the creatures of myth were partly human and had human intelligence—lamias, centaurs, fauns, satyrs, and so forth. Often that seems to appeal to the individuals who do this sort of thing. Then too, human cellular material is the easiest of all for them to get—they can use their own."

"Do you mean that I could make one of these mythical animals if I wanted to? Just go off and do it?"

The telephone rang and Anderson picked it up.

"Hello, Andy?" It was Dumont again.

"Yep," Anderson said.

"It seems to have gotten away."

"Uh huh. Our bunch certainly couldn't find it, and our operator said there was nothing on the police radio."

"Well, it gave them the slip. A student—an undergraduate, but I know him, and he's pretty reliable—just came and told me. He saw it over on the far side of the practice field. He tried to get up close, but it ran behind the field house, and he lost it."

Anderson covered the mouthpiece with his hand and said, "Nick's all right. Someone just saw him." He asked Dumont, "You send a bunch to look for him?"

"Not yet. I wanted to talk to you first. I gave the boy the key to my place and asked him to fetch my tranquilizer gun. He's got my van."

"Fine. Come up here and we'll talk. Leave this student a note so he'll know where you are."

"You don't think we ought to send some people out after the unicorn?"

"We've had searchers out after him for a couple of hours, and so have the police. I don't know about you; but while I was beating the bushes, I was wondering just what in the name of Capitoline Jove I was going to do with him if I found him. Try to ride him? Put salt on his tail? We can't do a damn thing until we've got your tranquilizer gun or some other way to control him, and by the time the boy gets back from your house in Brookwood it will be nearly dark."

When he had cradled the telephone, Anderson said, "That should give you an idea of how well organized we are."

Julie shrugged sympathetically.

"In the past, you see, it was always a question of letting the creature get away. The soldiers or the police wanted to kill it, we wanted to see it spared. Usually they head for the most lightly populated area they can find. We should have anticipated that sooner or later we'd be faced with one right here in the city, but I suppose we assumed that in a case like that we'd have no chance at all. Now it turns out that we've got a chance—your friend Nick is surprisingly elusive for such a big beast—and we haven't the least idea of what to do."

"Maybe he was born—do you say born?"

"We usually say created, but it doesn't matter."

"Well, maybe he was created here in the city, and he's trying to find his way out of it."

"A creature that size?" Anderson shook his head. "He's come in from outside, from some sparsely settled rural area, or he'd have been turned in by a nosy neighbor long ago. People can—people do—perform DNA engineering in the city. Sometimes in basements or garages or kitchens, more often on the sly in college labs or some big corporation's research and development facility. They keep the creatures they've made, too; sometimes for years. I've got a seahorse at home in an aquarium, not one of those fish you buy cast in plastic paperweights in the Florida souvenir shops, but a little fellow about ten inches long, with the head and forelegs of a pony and the hindquarters of a trout. I've had him for a year now, and I'll probably have him for another ten. But suppose he were Nick's size—where would I keep him?"

"In a swimming pool, I imagine," Julie said. "In fact, it seems rather a nice idea. Maybe at night you could take him to Lake Michigan and ride him there, in the lake. You could wear scuba gear. I'm not a terribly good swimmer, but I think I'd do it." She smiled at him.

He smiled back. "It does sound like fun, when you describe it."

"Just the same, you think Nick's escaped from some farm—or perhaps an estate. I should think that would be more likely. The

GENE WOLFE

rich must have these poor, wonderful animals made for them sometimes."

"Sometimes, yes."

"Unicorns. A sea-horse—that's from mythology too, isn't it?"

Anderson was lighting his pipe; the mingled fumes of sulfur and tobacco filled the office. "Balios and Xanthos drew the chariot of Poseidon," he said. "In fact, Poseidon was the god of horses as well as of the sea. His herds were the waves, in a mystic sense few people understand today. The whitecaps were the white manes of his innumerable steeds."

"And you mentioned lamias—those were snake women, weren't they?"

"Yes."

"And centaurs. And fauns and satyrs. Are all the animals like that, that the biologists make, from mythology?"

Anderson shook his head. "Not all of them, no. But let me ask you a question, Ms. Coronell—"

"Call me Julie, please."

"All right, Julie. Now suppose that you were a biologist. In genetic engineering they've reached the stage at which any competent worker with a Master's or a Ph.D.—and a lot of bright undergraduates—can do this sort of thing. What would you make for yourself?"

"I have room for it, and privacy, and lots of money?"

"If you like, yes."

"Then I'd make a unicorn, I think."

"You're impressed with them because you saw a beautiful one today. After that. Suppose you were going to create something else?"

Julie paused, looking pensive. "We talked about riding a sea-horse in the lake. Something with wings, I suppose, that I could ride."

"A bird? A mammal?"

"I don't know. I'd have to think about it."

"If you chose a bird, it would have to be much larger, of course, than a natural bird. You'd also find that it could not maintain the proportions of any of the species whose genetic matter you were using. Its wings would have to be much larger in proportion to its body. Its head would not have to be much bigger than an eagle's—and so on. When you were through and you were spotted sailing among the clouds, the newspapers would probably call your bird a roc, after the one that carried Sinbad."

"I see."

"If you decided on a winged horse instead, it would be Pegasus. I've never yet seen one of those that could actually fly, by the way.

THE WOMAN THE UNICORN LOVED

A winged human being would be an angel, or if it were more bird-like, with claws and tail feathers and so on, perhaps a harpy. You see, it's quite hard to escape from mythological nomenclature, because it covers so much. People have already imagined all these things. It's just that now we—some of us—can make them come true."

Julie smiled nervously. "An alligator! I think I'll choose an alligator with wings. I could make him smarter at the same time."

Anderson puffed out a cloud of smoke. "That's a dragon."

"Wait, I'll—"

The door flew open and Dumont came in. Anderson said, "Here's the man who can tell you about recombinant DNA and that sort of thing. I'd only make a hash of it." He stood. "Julie, may I present Henry A. Dumont of Biology, my good friend and occasionally my rival."

"Friendly rival," Dumont put in.

"Also the treasurer and technical director of our little society. Dumont, this is Julia Coronell, the lady who's hiding the unicorn."

For a moment no one spoke. Julie's face was guarded, expressionless save for tension. Then she said, "How did you know?"

Anderson sat down again, and Dumont took the office's last chair. Anderson said, "You came here because you were concerned about Nick." He paused, and Julie nodded. "But you didn't seem to want to *do* anything. If Nick was running around while the police looked for him, the situation was urgent; but you told me that story about pumpernickel and let me blather on about fauns and centaurs. You were worried, you were under a considerable strain, but you weren't urging me to get busy and reactivate the group we had looking for Nick this afternoon. When Dumont here called, I was very casual about the whole thing and just asked him to come over and talk. You didn't protest, and I decided that you knew where Nick was already. And that he was safe, at least for the time being."

"I see," Julie whispered.

"I don't," Dumont said. "That boy told me he saw the unicorn."

Anderson nodded. "A friend of yours, Julie?"

"Yes . . ."

Dumont said, "Honey, it's nothing to be ashamed of. We're on your side."

"You hid Nick," Anderson continued, "after the police dropped their tear gas. He was tame with you, as we saw earlier. He may even have eaten enough of Dumont's bread to calm him down a bit—there was a sedative in it. For a while after that, you were

GENE WOLFE

probably too frightened to do anything more; you just lay low. Then the police went away and our search parties gave up, and you went off campus to buy that bread you're holding. On the way back to give it to Nick, you met someone who told you about me."

Dumont asked, "Was it Ed? The boy who told me he saw the unicorn?"

Julie's voice was nearly inaudible. "Yes, it was."

"And between the two of you, you decided it would be smart to start some rumors indicating that Nick was still free and moving in a direction away from the place where you had him hidden." Anderson paused to relight his pipe. "So the first report had him disappearing behind the field house. The next one would have put him even farther away, I suppose. But more or less on impulse, you decided that we might help you, so you came up here to wait for me. Anyway, it would be safer for you to take that bread to Nick after dark. All right, we will help you. At least, we'll try. Where is Nick?"

Ed was no more a boy, actually, than Julie Coronell was a girl—a studious looking young man of nineteen or twenty. He had brought Dumont's tranquilizer gun, and Dumont had it now, though all of them hoped it would not be needed. Julie led the way, with Anderson beside her and Dumont and Ed behind them. A softness as of rose petals was in the evening air.

Anderson said, "I've seen you around the campus, haven't I? Graduate school?"

Julie nodded. "I'm working on my doctorate, and I teach some freshman and sophomore classes. Ed's one of my students. Most of the people I meet seem to think I'm a sophomore or a junior myself. How did you know I wasn't?"

"The way you're dressed. I guessed, actually. You look young, but you also look like a woman who looks younger than she is."

"You ought to have been a detective," she told him.

"Yes, anything but this."

The sun had set behind the trees of the park, trees whose long shadows had all run together now, flooding the lawns and walks with formless night. Most of the windows in the buildings the four passed were dark.

"What department?" Anderson asked when Julie said nothing more.

"English. My dissertation will be on twentieth century American novelists."

"I should have recognized you, but I'm more than two thousand years behind you."

"I'm easy to overlook."

"Let's hope Nick is too." For a moment, Anderson studied the building looming before them. "Why the library?"

"I've been doing research; they let me have a key. I knew it had just closed, and I couldn't think of anything else." She held up the key.

A minute or two later, it slid into the lock. The interior was dim but not dark—a scattering of lights, lonely and almost spectral, burned in the recesses of the building, as though the spirits of a few geniuses lingered, still awake.

Dumont said, "You'd better let me go in front," and hurried past them with the tranquilizer gun. The doors closed with a hollow boom; suddenly the air seemed stale.

"Isn't there a watchman?" Anderson asked.

Julie nodded. She was near enough for Anderson to smell her faint perfume. "You said Ed was a friend of mine. I don't have a lot, but I suppose Bailey—he's the watchman—is a friend too. I'm the only one who never calls him Beetle. I told you Nick was in the Sloan Fantasy Collection. Have you heard of it?"

"Vaguely. My field is classical literature."

Behind them, Ed said, "That's what fantasy is—classical lit that's still alive. When the people who wrote those stories did it, their books were called fantasy."

"Ed!" Julie protested.

"No," Anderson said. "He's right."

"Anyway," Julie continued, "the Sloan Collection isn't the best in the country, or even a famous collection. But it's a jolly good one. It's got James Branch Cabell in first editions, for example, and a lot of his letters. And there's some wonderful John Gardner material. So that's where I put Nick."

Stamping among the books, Anderson thought to himself. Couchant at the frontiers of Overworld and Oz.

Pity the Unicorn,
Pity the Hippogriff,
Souls that were never born
Out of the land of If!

Somewhere ahead, Dumont called, "*He's dead!*" and suddenly all three of them were running, staggering, stumbling down a dark and narrow corridor, guided by the flame of Dumont's lighter.

Anderson heard Julie whisper, "Nick! Oh, God, Nick!" Then she was quiet. The thing on the floor was no white unicorn.

Dumont rasped, "Hasn't anybody got a light?"

"Just matches," Anderson said. He lit one.

Ed told them, "I've got one," and from the pocket of his denim shirt produced a little, disposable pen light.

Julie was bending over the dead man, trying not to step in his blood. There was a great deal of it, and Dumont had stepped in it already, leaving a footprint. Ed played his light upon the dead man's face—cleanshaven; about sixty, Anderson guessed. He had worn a leather windbreaker. There was a hole in it now, a big hole that welled blood.

"It's Bailey," Julie said. And Dumont, thinking that she spoke to him (as perhaps she did), answered, "Is that his name? Everybody called him Beetle."

Bailey had been gored in the middle of the chest, very near the heart, Anderson decided. No doubt he had died instantly, or almost instantly. His face was not peaceful or frightened or anything else; only twisted in the terrible rictus of death. The match burned Anderson's fingers; he shook it and dropped it.

"Nick . . ." Julie whispered. "Nick did this?"

"I'm afraid so," Dumont told her.

She looked around, first at Dumont, then at Anderson. "He's dangerous. . . . I suppose I always knew it, but I didn't like to think about it. We'll have to let the police . . ."

Dumont nodded solemnly.

"Like hell," Anderson said, and Julie stared at him. "You put him here, in this room"—Anderson glanced at the half open door—"and went away and left him. Is that right?"

"Mr. Bailey was with us. He heard us as soon as I brought Nick inside. Nick's hooves made a lot of noise on the terrazzo floor. We took him to this room, and Mr. Bailey locked it for me."

Ed asked, "Hold this, will you, Dr. Dumont?" and handed Dumont the pen light, then took three steps, stooped, and straightened up with a much larger flashlight. After the near darkness, its illumination seemed almost a glare. Dumont let his lighter go out and dropped it into his pocket.

Ed was grinning weakly. "This must be the old man's flash," he said. "I thought I saw something shine over here."

"Yes." Anderson nodded. "He would have had it in his hand. After Julie left he came here to take another look at the unicorn. He opened the door and turned on his flashlight."

Julie shivered. "It could have been me."

"I doubt it. Even if Nick doesn't have human or almost human intelligence—and I suspect he does—he would have winded the watchman and known it wasn't your smell. No matter what kind of brain his creator gave him, his sensory setup must be basically the one that came with his equine DNA. Am I right, Dumont?"

"Right." The biologist glanced at his wrist. "I wish we had more information about the time Beetle died."

Ed asked, "Can't you tell from the clotting of the blood?"

"Not close enough," Dumont said. "Maybe a forensic technician could, but that's not my field. If this were one of those mysteries on TV, we could tell from the time his watch broke. It didn't, and it's still running. Anybody want to guess how far that unicorn's gone since he did this?"

"I will," Anderson told him. "Not more than about two hundred and fifty feet."

They stared at him.

"The front doors were locked when we came in—Julie had to open them for us. I'd bet the side door is locked too, and this building has practically no windows."

"You mean he's still in here?"

"If he's not, how did he get out?"

Julie said, "We'd hear him, wouldn't we? I told you—his hooves made a racket when I let him in."

"He heard them too," Anderson told her. "He wouldn't have to be a tenth as intelligent as he probably is to keep quiet. Almost any animal will do that by instinct. If it can't run—or doesn't think running's a good idea—it freezes."

Ed cleared his throat. "Dr. Anderson, you said he could tell by the smell that Beetle wasn't Julie. He'll know we aren't Julie too."

"Conversely, he'll know that she is. But if we separate to look for him and the wrong party finds him, there could be trouble."

Dumont nodded. "What do you think we ought to do?"

"To start with, give Ed here the keys to your van so he can bring it around front. If we find Nick, we're going to have to have some way to get him out of town. We'll leave the front doors open—"

"And let him get away?"

"No. But we need unicorn bait, and freedom's about as good a bait as anybody's ever found. Nick's probably hungry by now, and he's almost certainly thirsty. My mind runs to quotations anyway, so how about:

One by one in the moonlight there,
Neighing far off on the haunted air,

GENE WOLFE

The unicorns come down to the sea'.
Do you know that one?"

All three looked blank.

"It's Conrad Aiken, and of course he never saw a unicorn. But there may be some truth in it—in the feeling of it—just the same. We'll prop the doors wide. Dumont, you hide in the darkest shadow you can find there; the open doors should let in enough light for you to shoot by, particularly since you'll be shooting at a white animal. Julie and I will go through the building, turning on lights and looking for Nick. If we find him and he's docile with her, we can just lead him out and put him in the van. If he runs, you should get him on the way out."

Dumont nodded.

When the two of them were alone, Julie asked, "That gun of Dr. Dumon's won't really hurt Nick, will it?"

"No more than a shot in the arm would hurt you. Less."

The beam of the dead watchman's flashlight probed the corridor, seeming to leave a deeper twilight where it had passed. A few moments before, Anderson had talked of turning on more lights, but thus far they had failed to find the switches. He asked Julie if it were always this dim when she came to do research after the library had closed.

"Bailey used to take care of the lights for me," she said. "But I don't know where. I'd begin setting up my things on one of the tables, my notebooks and so forth; and the lights would come on." Her voice caught on *lights*.

She sniffled, and Anderson realized she was crying. He put his arm about her shoulders.

"Oh, rot! Why is it that one can—can try to do something fine, and have—have it end . . ."

He chanted softly:

"Twist ye, twine ye! Even so,
Mingled shades of joy and woe,
Hope and fear, and peace, and strife,
In the thread of human life."

"That's b—beautiful, but what does it mean? That the good and bad are mixed together so we can't pull them apart?"

"And that this isn't the end. Not for men or women or unicorns. Probably not even for poor old Bailey. Threads are long."

She put her arms about his neck and kissed him, and he was so busy pressing those soft, fragrant lips in return that he hardly heard the sudden thunder of the unshod hooves.

He pushed her away just in time. The spiraled horn raked his belly like a talon; the beast's shoulder hit him like a football player's, sending him crashing into a high bookcase.

Julie screamed, "No, Nick! Don't!" and he tried to stand.

The unicorn was rearing to turn in the narrow aisle, tall as a giant on his hind legs. Anderson clawed at the shelves, bringing down an avalanche of books. He found himself somehow grasping the horn, holding on desperately. A hoof struck his thigh like a hammer and he was careening down some dark passage, half carried, half dragged.

Abruptly, there was light ahead. He tried to shout for Dumont to shoot; but he had no breath, grasping the horn, grappling the tossing white head like a bulldogger. If the soft pluff of the gun ever came, it was lost in the clattering hoof-beats, in the roar of the blood in his ears. And if it came, the dart surely missed.

They nearly fell on the steps. Reeling they reached the bottom like kittens tossed from a sack. Anderson managed then to get his right leg under him; and with the unicorn nearly sprawling, he tried to get his left across the broad, white back and found that leg was broken.

He must have shrieked when the ends of splintered bone grated together, and he must have lost his hold. He lay upon his back, on grass, and heard the gallop of approaching death. Saw Death, white as bone.

Stallions fight, he thought. Fight for mares, kicking and biting. Only men kill other men for a woman.

He lay without moving, his left leg twisted like a broken doll's. Stallions don't kill—not if the other lies down, surrenders.

The white head was silhouetted against the twinkling constellations now, the colors seemingly reversed as in a negative, the longsword horn both new and ancient to the sky of Earth.

Later, when he told Julie and Dumont about it, Dumont said, "So he was only a horse after all. He spared you."

"A super horse. A horse armed, with size, strength, grace, and intelligence all augmented." They had wanted to carry him somewhere (he doubted if they themselves knew where), but he had stopped them. Now, after Dumont had phoned for an ambulance, they sat beside him on the grass. His leg hurt terribly.

"Which way did he go? The park again?"

"No, the lake shore. '*The unicorns come down to the sea*,' remem-

GENE WOLFE

ber? You'll have to drum up a group and go after him in the morning."

Julie said, "I'll come, and I'm sure Ed will too."

Anderson managed to nod. "We've got a couple of dozen others. Some here, some in town. Dumont has the phone numbers."

She forced a smile. "Andy—can I call you Andy? You like poems. Do you recall this one?

The lion and the unicorn
Were fighting for the crown;
The lion beat the unicorn
And sent him out of town.
Some gave them white bread,
And some gave them brown.
Some gave them plum-cake,
And drummed them out of town."

We've just had it come true, all except for that bit about the plum-cake."

"And the lion," Anderson said.

DEATH IN VESUNNA
by Eric G. Iverson & Elaine O'Byrne
art: Karl B. Kofoed

Mr. Iverson tells us that it's all the fault of L. Sprague de Camp and his book, Lest Darkness Fall, *that he wound up with a doctorate in Byzantine history from UCLA, and—eventually—wrote this story (which, however, is set in the western end of the Roman Empire, in Gaul, during the reign of Antoninus Pius, around A.D. 150). The story's co-author, Ms. O'Byrne, is a Senior Executive Secretary with a large aerospace firm, working for the man who invented the laser. She is also a violinist with the local symphony orchestra, occasionally belly-dances, and once had a brief fling with cabinetmaking.*

"More wine, gentlemen?" Clodius Eprius asked, eyeing his two guests with faint distaste. He had wanted to leave for his country estate to supervise the harvest, but this dinner meeting was keeping him stranded in Vesunna like some vulgar lampseller. When both men nodded, he sighed and rose from his couch. Picking up the red earthenware jug, he filled their cups and poured himself a hefty dollop as well.

All drank; the two strangers murmured appreciatively. That warmed Eprius a little. He said, "It's not Falernian, but this is a fine vintage. It was laid down the year Hadrian died, eight—no, nine years ago now. A fine vintage," he repeated. "Do you know, they're even shipping our Aquitanian wine to Britain these days."

"Really?" One of his visitors, a short blondish fellow who called himself Lucius, looked interested. His comrade kept his nose in his cup. A tall, solidly built man with hard, dark eyes, he had not said three words all through dinner. Lucius had introduced him as Marcus.

For no reason he could name, Eprius's guests disturbed him. It was not their accent, though Lucius, who did most of the talking, flavored his Latin in a curious fashion. No, the way they looked at their surroundings nettled their host more. Itinerant booksellers like these men would have seen many splendid villas in their travels, to be sure. Eprius knew his house would not have seemed imposing to anyone newly come from Rome or Antioch. But a fountain laughed in the courtyard, and the statues around it were good work. So was the hunting scene picked out in mosaic on the dining room floor; craftsmen from Rome had created it. His home was no hovel. It did not deserve Lucius's patronizing stare or the contempt Marcus scarcely bothered to conceal.

He drained his wine. "Well, good sirs," he said, "you told me you had a proposition I might find interesting, could it be kept in sufficient privacy. I have met your request. My servants are already at my other home, and I've given my valet the evening off. I am at your disposal, gentlemen. How do you wish to entice me?"

"We thank you, my friend," Lucius replied, "for a fine meal, and for the kindness you have shown two men you do not know. We will think your courtesy limitless indeed if you answer one question for us."

"Ask, sir, ask."

"I am sure you know Vesunna is not a town to which we usually travel, fine though it may be. But while we were in Massilia we heard a rumor so astounding, if true, that we hurried north to investigate."

"You have not asked your question," Eprius pointed out. There was a tinge of smugness in his voice, and Lucius did not miss it.

"It's true, then. You do have a copy of Sophokles's *Aleadai*?"

"And if I should?"

"May we see it?" For the first time, Lucius displayed real eagerness. Even Marcus's dour features almost smiled.

"I keep it in my private suite. Wait here a moment, if you will." Taking a lamp to light his way, Eprius bustled out of the dining room, down the hall, and into his sanctum. The first thing he spied there was a stout walking-stick. He seized it gratefully, for he had been a trifle lame since falling from a horse a couple of years before.

He shuffled rolls of papyrus, finding book three of the *Aeneid,* book one of the *Iliad,* a bill from the sheep-doctor Valerius Bassus ("Damn it, I thought I paid that two weeks ago!" he grumbled), book seven of the *Aeneid,* and, at last, the work he sought. A copy of the *Aleadai* had been in his family for almost three hundred years. One of his ancestors had been a centurion in Lucius Mummius's army when that general sacked Corinth, and had taken the original document as part of his loot. Finding that the ravages of time had made it almost illegible, Eprius's grandfather had had it recopied. It had been rare then; Eprius still recalled the old man chuckling as he described the surprise of the copyist who redid it. He could well understand booksellers coming a long way in search of such a work.

Lucius took the roll like a lover carressing his beloved. Yet he handled its spindles clumsily, almost, thought Eprius, as if he were not used to unrolling a book to read it. Don't be a fool, he told himself: a book-dealer sees more books in a month than you will in ten years. The wine has simply made his fingers awkward. He certainly reads well enough—he isn't even moving his lips, which is more than you can claim for your reading.

A passage seemed to please the stranger, who began to read aloud. His accent was, if anything, stronger in Greek than in Latin, but he paid scrupulous heed to the complex meter of the tragedian's verse. Despite himself, Eprius was impressed.

Lucius read silently once more, faster and still faster, whipping through the scroll now with a speed that left Eprius blinking. A lamp went out, but Lucius never noticed. He read aloud again:

> " 'Stop! It is enough to have been called father,
> If indeed I begot you. But if not, the harm is less,
> For what one believes carries more weight than the truth.' "

He turned in triumph to Marcus. "That clinches it!" he said. "This is one of the sections Stobaeus quotes, and this is the genuine *Aleadai!*"

"Of course it's genuine," Eprius said in aggrieved tones. These fellows had approached him. Did they now think he was trying to cheat them? And who was Stobaeus? The name was not familiar.

Neither of his guests was listening to him. They sprang from their couches (Lucius carefully put the *Aleadai* down first) and capered about in ridiculous fashion. They slapped each other's backs, swatted each other's palms, and clasped each other's wrists, the while making interlocking rings of thumbs and forefingers. Barbarians after all, Eprius thought.

Little by little they calmed down. Marcus's glee subsided into wariness, but Lucius's face was lit by that special joy felt when something long sought is at last found. "This is indeed a treasure," he said. "What price would you put on it?"

Eprius smiled. "A curious sort of merchant you are, to let a prospective seller know how much you esteem his goods."

Marcus looked alarmed, but Lucius said smoothly, "Under any other circumstances you would be right, but not today. You see, I have a standing offer for this work from a gentleman at Rome whose name I am sure you would recognize were I at liberty to disclose it. Quite a sizeable offer, in fact."

That made sense. Many senators and other officials were zealots in the pursuit of culture. Eprius nodded, and as he did Marcus's watchful mask settled back over his face. "How sizeable an offer?" Eprius asked.

"Large enough so that I can afford to offer you—hmm—seventy-five aurei and still turn a handsome profit."

"Seventy-five aurei?" Eprius tried hard not to show how startled he was. That was many, many times the going rate, even for a rare book. "A princely sum! Why is your unnamed patron so anxious to acquire the *Aleadai*?"

"It is the only play of Sophokles he lacks."

"Come now, do you take me for an utter idiot? I doubt if even the library of Alexandria could make that claim. My friend, I do not know what your game is, but find someone else to play the dupe."

"Do you think we are trying to defraud you? This will persuade you otherwise." Lucius drew out a leather purse and tossed it to Eprius. He opened it. Ruddy in the lamplight, goldpieces spilled into his palms. They clinked sweetly.

"Well, well," he said at last. "I owe you an apology, good sirs, both for what I said and what I thought. Let me take the roll to our local copyist, and you may have either the original or the copy within a week, just as you please. Aemilius Ruso is a friend of mine; I assure you he has a fine hand, and he is careful too."

"I am afraid that won't quite do, friend Eprius. A condition of the sale is absolute privacy, and it is a condition on which I have no discretion whatever. We must have this work now. Is the price inadequate? I can sweeten it a bit, I think."

" 'Money buys men friends, and honors too.' So says the poet in this very play. But money will not buy the only copy of the *Aleadai*, for it has been an heirloom in my family for eleven generations. I see no reason not to share it, but I will not give it up."

"A hundred aurei?"

Eprius' face froze. He refilled the purse and threw it at Lucius's feet. "You insult me, sir. I must bid you a good evening." He held out his hand for the play.

Reluctantly, Lucius began to give it back to him, but Marcus reached out and held him back. His smile and his heavily-accented voice were deliberately offensive. "I think we keep this," he said.

"What? Get out, you rogues, you lashworthy rascals!" Despite graying hair and growing paunch, Eprius was still fairly quick on his feet. His walking-stick thudded down on Marcus's shoulder. The *Aleadai* fell to the floor. "Get out, robbers, get out!" Eprius shouted.

"Bastard!" Marcus snarled. He ducked the next swing of the stick. Stars exploded inside Eprius's head as a solid right sent him spinning back over his couch to the floor. Somehow he held onto his stick. Too angry to fear facing two younger men, he surged forward, crying, "Thieves! Thieves!" at the top of his lungs.

Marcus's hand snaked under his tunic. Eprius saw it emerge with a curiously-shaped metal object. One of Marcus's fingers twitched on it, and Eprius heard the beginning of a barking roar. Something sledged him in the forehead, and he never saw or heard anything again.

Lou Muller, who in Vesunna called himself Lucius the book-dealer, stared in horror at the crumpled corpse that had been Clodius Eprius. The gunshot still seemed to echo in the room. "Jesus H. Christ, Mark!" he said, and he was not speaking Latin at all. "The Patrol—"

"Lou, you can take the Patrol and stuff it right on up—" Mark Alvarez tucked away the pistol and rubbed his shoulder. "The old son of a bitch damn near broke my collarbone. What was I supposed to do, let him yell until all the neighbors came? Speaking of which—" He scooped up the *Aleadai* and trotted into the street. His partner followed, still expostulating.

"Oh, shut up and listen to me, will you please?" Alvarez growled. "Why do we make a good team, anyway? It's not just because you're the fellow who knows his way around the second-century Empire and I'm the one with the pull to get a timer. I've got the brains to get you out of trouble when you screw up, which you did. For one thing, even I know—you've told me often enough—Stobaeus isn't going to be born for a couple of hundred years yet. For another, and worse, that geezer was never going to sell us the play after you got his back up."

"But I offered him seventy-five aurei!"

"That didn't impress him, now did it? And it doesn't impress me either. What're seventy-five aurei to us? Thirty credits for the gold (always thanking God for fusion-powered transmutation), the same for some authentic molds, and voilà! Aurei! Whereas we can—and we will—get an easy fifty thousand credits for a lost play of Euripides."

"Sophokles," Muller corrected absently.

"Whatever. And as for the Time Patrol, why are we here in the boondocks instead of at the library of Alexandria? Why do we insist on so much privacy when we make our deals? Just so they won't run across us. And they won't. Erasing this fellow won't leave any clues downtime. We don't change anyone's ancestry, because his wife's been dead for years. We *did* check him out, you know." He glanced over his shoulder. "Did anyone see us leave?"

"I don't think so. But my God, Mark, a bullet—"

"What about it? Nobody here will ever figure out how he died. The local yokels'll call it the wrath of the gods or something and then they'll forget it. All we have to do is sit tight for three weeks until the timer recharges and then it's back to 2059 and lots of lovely money."

"I suppose so," Muller agreed slowly. "I kind of liked old Eprius, though."

"Liked him? Lou, he was just a stupid savage, like all the other stupid savages here and now. Look around. Is there anything here but filth and disease and superstition? You couldn't pay me to time if it weren't for xanthomycin. Come on, let's get back to the inn. Like the fellow said, my man, the play's the thing, and we've got it."

"What about the gold?"

"You want to go back and get it? Relax, it'll confuse the issue anyway." They walked on in silence until they came to the inn. "What a dump," Alvarez sighed. "Oh well, at least it has a bed, and I need sleep right now. We've had a busy night."

The sound of a fist crashing against his door hauled Gaius Tero from the depths of slumber. Stifling a curse, he climbed out of bed and threw on a mantle. His wife stirred and muttered drowsily. "It sounds like business, Calvina," he said. "Go back to sleep." A forlorn hope indeed, with his door being battered down. "I'm coming, I'm coming!" he shouted, and the pounding stopped. As tesserarius of Vesunna's seven-man detachment of vigiles, he wondered what had gone wrong now. Had someone knocked over Porcius's wineshop (again!), or had Herennius Fundanus's firetrap of a stable finally decided to go up in smoke? Either way, the responsibility fell on him, for the vigiles were constabulary and fire brigade both.

He threw open the door. Just as he expected, there stood the panting figure of Larcius Afer, who had the watch tonight. "Well, what is it?" Tero demanded, adding hopefully, "I don't smell smoke." The siphon, which was the city's chief fire-fighting implement, was a pain in the fundament to deploy and use.

"No, sir," Afer agreed. He paused to wipe sweat from his face. The night was warm, and he had plainly run some distance. Tero, who was not the most patient of men, glared at him until he continued, "Clodius Eprius has been killed."

"What do you mean, killed? Has he been murdered?"

"Killed, sir," Afer repeated stolidly. "Kleandros is with the body now. He'll be able to tell you more than I can, I'm sure."

"Obviously," Tero snapped. Still, he was glad the Greek doctor would be there. They were old friends, though they argued constantly.

The tesserarius ducked back into his house for sandals, then accompanied his fellow vigil to the dead man's home. It was a couple of hours before dawn, and a waning crescent moon shed a wan light over the town. Nevertheless, it was dark enough to make Tero glad his companion carried a torch.

Eprius lived (or rather, had lived) at the opposite end of town from Tero's home. He and Afer tramped through Vesunna's central forum, silent save for the sound of their footsteps. At its very heart was the temple dedicated to the city's tutelary gods. Its huge circular cella made it currently the biggest structure in Vesunna, but the amphitheater being built not far away promised to dwarf it and everything else in the town.

Tero wondered idly what the old Petrocorii, the Celtic tribe who had founded Vesunna, would have thought of such an incredibly huge edifice. Magic, without a doubt: anything was magical to someone who did not know how to do it.

His thoughts turned back to Eprius. Why would anyone want to kill the old fool? Tero knew him fairly well, and also knew he had not a single enemy in town. Had some footpad done away with him? Tero tried to pump Larcius Afer; but Afer shook his head, saying, "You'll have to see for yourself, sir." With a small shock, the tesserarius realized his subordinate was frightened. That was very strange. Before settling in Vesunna, the two of them had served together on the Rhine, and Tero knew full well that the skirmishes there had thoroughly inured Afer to the sight of gore.

It seemed as if most of Eprius's neighbors were gathered outside his front door. Well, Tero thought, that's scarcely surprising. Everyone started talking at once when they saw him, raining questions down on his unprepared head. "I don't know a damned thing yet," he said, pushing his way through the crowd. "If you'll let me by, maybe I'll find out something."

Kleandros met him at the entrance. Tero liked the sharp-tongued physician. They had worked together before; and once or twice a month they would meet for wine, a friendly game of draughts, and much good talk. Still, the doctor's elegant slimness always made the squarely-built Tero feel like a poorly-trained dancing bear. Just by standing before him, Kleandros made him suddenly and acutely aware of his own uncombed hair, the patches and stains on his cloak, and the ragged bit of leather hanging from one sandal. As usual, he disguised his feelings with raillery. "Hello, quack," he said. "What do you have for me today?"

An opening like that would normally make Kleandros sputter and fume, but today he did not rise to the bait. Under the curling black ringlets he combed low on his forehead, his face was grim as he answered, "Hello, Tero. I'm glad to see you. You'd best come look for yourself." He was speaking Greek instead of Latin, something he did only when very upset. Tero began to worry in earnest.

The physician led him down the dark entry-hall to the dining room. Someone had refilled and lit all the lamps there; the flames cast multiple dancing shadows. Three couches had been grouped together in one corner of the room. One was overturned, and the wall behind it bore a sinister stain. The vigil looked a question at Kleandros, who nodded. "Poor Eprius is behind the courch," Kleandros said. "Tell me what you make of him."

"Why me? You're the doctor," Tero said, but he walked around the couch.

Both on the Rhine and as a vigil in Vesunna, Gaius Tero had seen the results of more violent deaths than he liked to remember. Yet the corpse in this quiet room shook him in a way none of the others, however grisly, ever had. He was in the presence of the unknown, and little fingers of ice crawled up his back as he viewed its handiwork.

Eprius's body lay on its right side; its right hand still clutched a stick. Tero barely noticed, for his gaze was fixed in horrified fascination at the ruin that had been its head. There was a neat hole about the width of Tero's little finger over the left eye. A small stream of blood ran down over Eprius's face to join the pool beneath his head. Already flies were beginning to buzz about it.

Bad as that was, it was far from the worst. Whatever had drilled through Eprius's forehead had smashed out through the back of his head, tearing his skull open from the inside out. Much of the left rear quadrant of his head was a sickening soup of brain, pulverized bone, scalp, and hair. It was that which had stained the wall; blood cemented the gory fragments to the plaster.

The hobnails of Larcius Afer's sandals clicked on mosaic tiles as he came up. Dread was on his face; his fingers writhed in a sign to

ERIC G. IVERSON & ELAINE O'BYRNE

avert evil. "It was Jupiter's thunderbolt slew him," Afer said. "Two or three of the neighbors heard him cry out, and then the terrible roar of the thunderbolt itself—and not a cloud in the sky. His man Titus had the evening free, and when he got home he found this."

Tero had never been one to fear the gods unduly, but he felt the little hairs on the back of his neck trying to rise as he listened to Afer. Surely nothing in his experience could have produced the ghastly wound he saw. To have Kleandros throw back his head and laugh was unbelievable. Tero wondered if the doctor had taken leave of his senses, and Afer stared at him indignantly.

"How many men have either of you known to be killed by the gods?" Kleandros demanded. "I've been a doctor for twenty years now, and I've never seen one yet."

"There's always a first time," Afer said.

"I suppose so," Kleandros conceded. "But Clodius Eprius? Good heavens, man, use your head for something more than a place to hang your hair. The worst thing Clodius Eprius ever did in his whole life was to drink so much wine a couple of his friends had to carry him home. If the gods started killing everybody who did that, why, there wouldn't be five men left alive in the Empire by this time tomorrow. No, I'm afraid that if the gods left it to Nero to kill himself and soldiers to do away with Caligula, they wouldn't have much interest in Clodius Eprius."

Afer was still far from convinced. "What did kill him, then?" he demanded.

"I haven't the slightest idea right now, but I intend to try to find out instead of moaning about Jupiter."

The physician's healthy skepticism gave Tero the heartening he needed to shake off his superstitious fear and begin thinking like a vigil once more. He quizzed Eprius's neighbors, but learned nothing Afer had not already told him. There had been shouts and then a crash, but nobody had seen anyone fleeing Eprius's home. Titus proved even less informative than the neighbors. He was grief-stricken and more than a little hung over. When Eprius gave him the night off he had not questioned his master, but headed straight for the wine and girls of Aspasia's lupanar, where he had roistered the night away. When he came back and found Eprius's body he rushed out to get Kleandros, and that was all he knew. Tero left him sitting with his head in his hands and went back to the dining room.

"Learn anything?" Kleandros asked.

"Nothing. Maybe Jupiter did kill him."

Kleandros's one-word reply was rude in the extreme. Tero managed an aswering grin, but it was strained. His eyes kept going back to the redly-spattered wall. In the midst of the spatters was a ragged hole. "What's this?" he said.

"How should I know?" Kleandros said. "Maybe Eprius used to keep a tapestry nailed there, and was clumsy taking it down."

"I don't think so. I've been here more than once, and I don't remember any wall hangings." Tero took a knife from his belt and chipped away at the plaster, enlarging the hole. At its bottom was a little button of metal. No, not a button, a flower, for as Tero dug it out he saw that little petals of lead had peeled back from a brass base. Never in all his years had he seen anything like it. He tossed it up and down, up and down, whistling tunelessly.

"Give me that!" Kleandros said, grabbing it out of the air. He examined it curiously. "What is it, anyway?"

"I was hoping you could tell me."

"I couldn't begin to, any more than I could begin to tell you what killed Eprius."

Something almost clicked in Tero's mind, but the thought would not come clear. "Say that again!" he demanded.

Kleandros repeated.

He had it. "Look," he said, "where did we find this strange thing?"

"Is this your day to do Sokrates? Very well, best one, I'll play along. We found this strange thing in a hole in the wall."

"And what was all around the hole in the wall?"

"Clodius Eprius's brains."

"Very good. Bear with me one more time. How did Clodius Eprius's brains get there?"

"If I knew that I wouldn't be standing here pretending to be Euthyphron," Kleandros snapped. "I've seen a fair number of dead men, but never one like this." He looked at the piece of metal in his hand and his voice grew musing. "And I've never seen anything like this, either—you think the one had something to do with the other, don't you?"

Tero nodded. "If you could somehow make that thing go fast enough, it would make a respectable hole—it didn't make a bad hole in the wall, you know."

"So it didn't. It probably used to have a tip shaped more like an arrowhead, too; that lead is soft, and it would get smashed down when it hit. See what a brilliant pair we are? We only have one problem left: how in Zeus's holy name does the little hunk of metal get moving so fast?"

90   ERIC G. IVERSON & ELAINE O'BYRNE

"Two problems," Tero corrected. "Once you get the little piece of metal moving, why do you use it to blow out Clodius Eprius's brains?"

"Robbery, perhaps?"

"Maybe. Titus should know if anything is missing. Until he can figure that out, I think I'm going home and back to bed. Wait a moment, what's this?" Almost out of sight under one of the couches was a small leather bag. Tero stooped to pick it up and exclaimed in surprise. It was far heavier than he'd expected. He knew of only two things combining so much weight with so little bulk, lead and—he opened the bag and aurei flooded into his hand.

"So much for robbery," Kleandros said, looking over his shoulder. The images of Trajan, Hadrian, and Antoninus Pius looked mutely back, answering none of the questions the two men would have put to them. The only time Tero had ever held so much gold at once was when he'd got his mustering-out bonus on leaving his legion.

He looked up to find Kleandros still studying the coins, a puzzled expression on his face. "What now?" Tero asked.

It was the doctor's turn to have trouble putting what he saw into words. "Does anything strike you as odd about this money?" he said at last.

"Only that no robber in his right mind would leave it lying under a couch."

"Apart from that, I mean. Is there anything wrong about the money itself?"

"An aureus is an aureus," Tero shrugged. "The only thing wrong with them is that I see them too seldom."

Kleandros grunted in exasperation. He plucked an aureus of Trajan from the pile in Tero's hand and held it under the vigil's nose, so close that his eyes started to cross as he looked at it. Tero shrugged again; to him it seemed like any fresh-minted goldpiece. He said so.

"To me too," Kleandros said. "And that is more than a little out of the ordinary, since Trajan has been dead—what is it? Thirty years now, I think. I was somewhere in my teens when he died, and I'm far from a youth now, worse luck. Yet here is one of his coins, bright and unworn. More than one, in fact," he said, picking out three or four more. They lay in his hand, like as peas in a pod.

And that was wrong, too. No coin had the right to be identical to its fellows; they were stamped out by hand, one at a time. There were always differences, sometimes not small ones, in shape and thickness. Not here, though. Both men noticed it at the same time, but neither was as disturbed as he would have been a few hours before. "Everything we've found here is impossible," Tero said, "and this is just one little impossibility among the big ones."

It was growing light outside. Tero swore disgustedly. "I might as well stay up now. Care to join me for an early cup of wine?"

"Thank you, no. But if you don't mind, I'll cadge a meal from you and Calvina this evening. We can talk more then, and maybe squeeze some sense from all this."

"I doubt it, truth to tell. But I'll expect you a little past sunset."

"Fine."

Tero swallowed his last morsel of ham, wiped his fingers, and sighed loudly. "Why did I ever quit the legions?" he said. "I'd twenty times rather fight the German lurking in his gloomy forest than face another day like this one."

"That bad?" Kleandros asked between bites of apple.

"You should know—you started me on it." The vigil did not feel right about dropping all his troubles on his friend, but he had had a bellyful. The story of Clodius Eprius's death had raced through Vesunna, gaining fresh embellishments with each teller. It did not take long for people to be saying all the twelve immortals had visited the town, destroying not only Eprius but his house and those of his neighbors, too. More than one panicky citizen hastily packed up his belongings and headed for the country.

None of that sat well with Vesunna's two duumvirs, and both of those worthies came down heavily on Tero, demanding he find the murderer at once. "What will this do to the name of our city?" said one, though Tero knew what he meant was, I do not want my year in office recalled only for a gruesome killing. He promised to do his best, though he had few illusions on how good that was going to be.

Late in the afternoon, Eprius's servant Titus came in with two more bits of depressing news: first, the gold the vigil had found was definitely not Eprius's; and, second, as far as he could tell after a quick search, nothing was missing from his late master's home. Larcius Afer was there to hear that, and his superior smile made Tero want to kick him in the teeth.

That he did tell Kleandros; it galled him too much for silence. The doctor pursed his lips and said judiciously, "If a fool laughed at me, I'd take it for a compliment."

"So would I, were I sure he was wrong. But what do we have here? A murder committed for no reason with an impossible weapon that produces an incredible wound. I think I'd rather believe in an angry god."

ERIC G. IVERSON & ELAINE O'BYRNE

"Who leaves behind a purse full of counterfeit aurei? No god would do that."

"No person would, either," Tero pointed out. "And they aren't counterfeits, either; they're pure gold. Rusticius the jeweler checked them for me this afternoon."

"Did he? How interesting. Yes." Kleandros said nothing more, but a look of satisfaction spread across his face.

"You know something!" Tero accused.

"I have some ideas, at any rate. Did I ever tell you that I studied medicine under Diodoros of Alexandria?"

There were times when Tero found his friend's evasiveness maddening. This, it seemed, was going to be one of them. "No," he said, "you never did. Why do you see fit to impart this bit of information to me now?"

"I am coming to that, never fear. You see, Diodoros himself was learning his skill in Alexandria when Heron son of Ktesibios was at the height of his fame."

Tero had to admit he did not know the name.

"Do you not? A pity; he was a remarkable man, probably one of the finest machine-makers the world has ever seen. Diodoros was fascinated by his contraptions, and he never tired of talking about them. Really amazing things: a device for dispensing sacramental water that only worked when a copper was inserted, a trumpet made to sound by opening a nearby door, bronze animals that moved like live ones, and many other things."

"He sounds like a sorcerer."

"No, he was an artificer and nothing more. One of the things he made, not really more than a toy, was what he called an aeolipile."

"All of this must lead somewhere, I suppose. What might an aeolipile be?"

Kleandros explained: a water-filled cauldron was fitted atop with a hollow ball mounted on a hollow tube. Directly opposite the tube's entrance into the ball was a pivot, which was attached to the cauldron's lid. The ball itself was fitted with bent nozzles; when a fire was lit beneath the cauldron, steam traveled up the hollow tube and out through the nozzles, making the ball spin merrily. "Do you see what I'm getting at?" the doctor asked. "In this device the force of the steam escaped continuously; but if some way were found to block it up for a time and then release it all at once, it could give a little metal pellet a very strong push indeed."

Tero took another pull at his wine while he thought. The idea had more than a little appeal, for it gave a rational picture of how the killing might have taken place. Still . . . "A cauldron, you say? How big a cauldron?"

"I have no idea. I've never seen the machine in action myself, only heard Diodoros talk about it."

"Somehow I find it hard to imagine Clodius Eprius letting anyone set up a cauldron in the middle of the room and then aim a little ball at him. And whoever would be using it would have to wait for his water to boil before it could go off, wouldn't he?"

"I suppose so," Kleandros said sulkily.

"Not only that, anyone hauling a cauldron through the middle of Vesunna will get himself noticed. Even if I don't know what killed Eprius, I can tell you a couple of things about it: you can use it right away, and you can carry it around without having it seen. I'm afraid your whatever-you-call-it misses the mark both ways." Seeing his friend's hurt expression, Tero went on, "If you could make one big enough, it might make a good ballista, though." I wonder why our generals never thought of anything like that, he thought, a little surprised at himself.

"Your logic is convincing," Kleandros said, adding, "Damn it!" a moment later.

"Let's give up on the weapon for now," Tero suggested. "It matters less than the person who used it. If we had some way of knowing who he was, we might catch him, thunderbolt thrower or no."

"A good point," Kleandros said. "Whoever he was, we can be fairly sure he was from outside the Empire."

"Why do you say that?"

"We know of no weapons to fit the bill within our land, do we? Also, why would a citizen need to carry coins that weren't genuine but would pass one by one? If they are true gold, that only makes the argument stronger."

"A spy!"

"You may have something there. But who would want to spy on Vesunna, and why?"

Tero opened his mouth for a reply, then realized he did not have a good one. No one had ever seen a German in the town, and Parthia was at the other end of the world. Besides, he was sure neither the Germans nor the Parthians had weapons that could blow large holes in men's head. If they did, they would have used them on Roman soldiers long ago. In fact, anyone who had such a weapon could master the world and surely would have done so by now. It made no sense at all.

What other foreigners were there? There were nomads south of

94   ERIC G. IVERSON & ELAINE O'BYRNE

Roman Africa, and others east of the Germans. There was an island off the coast of Britain, but it was full of savages, too. There was—

"Men from Atlantis, perhaps?"

"My dear Tero, I would be the last to deny Platon was a man of godlike intellect, and the *Timaios* has always been one of my favorite dialogues. Still, as far as I can see, in it he invents Atlantis in order to portray an idealized way of life. And, as Aristoteles said, 'He who invented it destroyed it,' for, if you'll remember, Platon says it sank beneath the waves thousands of years ago."

"That's a pity, because I don't see how a spy could come from any country we know well." He explained his reasoning to the doctor, who nodded.

"Where does that leave us?" Kleandros asked.

"Right where we started—ramming our heads into a stone wall. A plague on it, for now. Did you bring your *Iliad* with you? I'd sooner bend my brain around that for a while." Slowly but surely, over the course of years, Kleandros was teaching the vigil to read Greek; most cultured citizens of the Empire were bilingual. Tero spoke Greek fairly well: though more elastic, its basic structure was much like that of Latin; and there were more than a few similarities of vocabulary as well. But Homer was something else. His hexameters were splendid, his picture of the heroes of the Trojan war supremely human, but his antique vocabulary and archaic grammatical forms often made Tero want to tear his hair.

Line by line they fought their way through the opening of book sixteen, where Patroklos begs Akhilleus to let him borrow his armor and drive the Trojans from the ships of the Akhaians, which they had begun to burn. Akhilleus, hesitant at first, assented when he saw the fire going up, and

"Patroklos armed himself with shining bronze."

("I hate these funny-looking datives," Tero said, but went on:)

"First he put well-made greaves on his calves;
They had guards of silver on them.
Then on his breast he put the cleverly-made shining
Corselet of Aikos' swift-footed scion.
He slung his silver-nailed bronze sword from his shoulder,
And after it a great stout shield as well."

"Bronze, bronze, bronze!" Tero said. "Bronze this, bronze that. One cohort of my legion could have gone through all the heroes of the Trojan War, Akhaians and Trojans both, in about an hour and a half. Ten years? No wonder it took them ten years, with tactics like theirs. They run at each other, throw their spears, and then start looking for rocks to fling. And nobody cares about the fellow next to him until the poor sod gets a spear in the groin. Then they fight over his armor, not him."

"You have the soul of a turnip," said Kleandros, who had heard Tero's complaints many times. "That we are better at killing people than they were in Akhilleus's day is no cause for celebrating."

"Nevertheless, I wonder what shining-helmed Hektor would have thought if one morning he woke up and found my old legion round his walls instead of those Akhaian cattle-thieves. Can you imagine it? Earthworks, siege-towers, catapults, rams. He couldn't have held that town three days against us. I think I'd have paid money to see his face."

"He probably would have been like Afer, convinced all the gods were angry at him."

"And yet we would just have been men with skills he didn't have, not demigods or heroes. It's very strange." Tero returned to his Homer and plowed on doggedly even after his attention began to wander. The truth was that he did not want to think about Eprius's corpse, though he suspected he would see it in his dreams for years to come. Crimes were hard enough to solve at any time; but this one had an impossible wound, an unknown but highly potent weapon, a good many cleverly-counterfeited aurei (why, in the name of the gods?), and, to make matters worse, no visible motive. . . . "What verb does *lelalesthô* come from?" he asked Kleandros.

The knock on Tero's door a few days later was so tentative he was only half-sure he'd heart it. Nonetheless he went to the door and opened it, to find Eprius's valet Titus waiting for him.

"Come in, come in," the vigil said. "What can I do for you?"

"Thank you very much," replied the servant. His Latin, though grammatically perfect, still carried a faint guttural touch of his native Syriac. When comfortably seated, he went on, "I've had the time now to go through my late master's effects more thoroughly, and I've found something I think you ought to know."

"Ah?" Tero leaned forward. "Tell me more. . . ."

The two time-travelers walked through the center of Vesunna. The tune Alvarez was whistling would not be written for another

ERIC G. IVERSON & ELAINE O'BYRNE

nineteen centuries, but he couldn't have cared less. In less than a day, the timer would recharge itself and he'd return to the era where he belonged, a richer man. He looked about. Enough of painted marble statues littering the city square, enough of the stink of ordure and the slimy feel of it under his feet, enough of drafty clothes, bad syrupy wine, and a language he barely understood! And enough of bedbugs too; he scratched under his mantle. His fingers brushed the leather of his shoulder holster, and he smiled a little. The weight of the revolver was a comfort, like a paid-up insurance policy.

Lou was silent beside him, watching tides of humanity ebb and flow. Today was market day, and the square was packed. To Alvarez the merchants and their customers were so many gabbling barbarians, but for some incomprehensible reason Lou chose to regard them as people. Most of the time this inspired nothing but disdain in Alvarez, but now his all-encompassing good humor even included his partner. Lou might be a weakling, but he knew his stuff. He had tracked that play of Sophokles from nothing but the vaguest rumor, and now it looked like there would be an unexpected bonus in this squalid town. Who would have thought a copy of Hieronymos of Kardia's lost history would have ended up here? It would be worth plenty: not as much as the Sophokles, perhaps, but still a nice piece of change.

Whoever this fellow was, this Kleandros Harmodios's son who owned the Hieronymos, he wanted enough for it. Aemilius Ruso, the local scribe, had offered what was a good price by here-and-now standards and Kleandros turned him down flat. Alvarez chuckled. He and Lou would have no trouble on that score.

Despite directions, they got lost more than once searching out Kleandros's house. The streets of Vesunna were winding alleyways, and one blank housefront looked very much like another; to the locals, display belonged to the interior of a house, not the outside. Alvarez was beginning to mutter to himself with Lou stopped at a door no different from half a from half a dozen others nearby and said, "This is it, I think."

"How can you tell?" Alvarez asked, but Lou was already knocking. The door swung open, revealing a spare but handsome man wearing a white chlamys and sandals whose leather lacings reached almost to his knees. Greek dress, Alvarez realized: this must be Kleandros himself. Good. If Kleandros was answering the door himself, that must mean he was taking seriously the privacy instructions he'd got. Alvarez looked him over. In his own time he would have guessed Kleandros to be in his mid-fifties, but the wear and tear was harder here, so he was probably younger. Still, if he was a doctor he might take better care of himself than most of the locals. Maybe not, though—some of the things the second century judged medicinal were amazing.

"Come in, come in," Kleandros was saying. "You must be the gentlemen who inquired about my history." Lou admitted it. "Very good. Will you join me in the courtyard? The day is far too fine to be cooped up inside without need."

Kleandros was not as rich a man as Clodius Eprius, who had used the income of his country estate to beautify his home in Vesunna. Fewer rooms opened onto this courtyard, and it was bare of the elegant statuary that had been Eprius's delight. There was a fountain at the center of the courtyard, though, and flowers of many kinds and colors grew in neatly-trimmed rows, bright against drab plaster and pale stone.

The doctor seated his guests on a limestone bench and offered them wine. When they accepted, he served it to them in cups of the same red-glazed ware Eprius had used. It was decorated with embossed reliefs, and called terra sigillata, or sealing-wax ware, after the color of the glaze. The stuff was everywhere in Gaul; it was made locally and had nearly driven the more costly Italian pottery from the market.

Putting down his cup, Kleandros said, "Now to business. I am not eager to sell the history of Hieronymos, but I have a need for ready cash. What will you give me for it?"

A long haggle ensued. Lou had learned from his mistake with Eprius not to show too much eagerness, and as for Kleandros, he might have been arguing with some farmer over the price of a sack of beans. Alvarez was stifling yawns when they finally agreed that twenty-eight aurei did not seem too unreasonable. Lou was not yawning; he was sweating.

"Whew!" Kleandros said. "You drive a hard bargain, my friend. I suppose you would like to inspect the work now?"

"I would," Lou agreed.

"Wait a moment, then, and I will fetch it." Kleandros disappeared into the house. While he was gone, Lou counted out the requisite number of gold coins and made a little pile of them.

Kleandros's face lit up when he returned with the scrolls and saw the money. "Splendid!" he said, scooping up the aurei. "I'm glad you brought what money you needed with you; waiting is hard on the nerves." He studied the coins intently, so much so that Alvarez began to worry. Perhaps noticing the time-traveler watching him, the doctor grinned and said, "It's amazing how much more handsome an Emperor's face is when you see it on gold."

"True," Mark said, and he grinned back. For the first time he got a hint of his partner's point of view; Kleandros didn't seem like a bad fellow, for a savage. The doctor idly flipped a gold piece in the air, once, twice, three times.

Lou had been reading the work Kleandros gave him. At first his grin had been as wide as the Greek's; but little by little it fell from his face, replaced first by puzzlement and then anger. "What are you trying to palm off on us?" he demanded of Kleandros. "This is not Hieronymos of Kardia's history; it's the work of Diodoros of Sicily, who borrowed from him."

Alvarez's new-found liking for Kleandros flickered and blew out. Muscles bunched in his arms as he rose. If this downtime dimbulb was trying to cheat them, he was going to remember it for the rest of his life.

A crash behind him made him whirl, hand darting for his gun. Half a dozen fully armored Romans had burst from their concealment within Kleandros's house and were rushing him, swords drawn, faces grim over their shields. Lou screamed in terror and started to run. Barking an oath, Alvarez snapped off a quick shot. It went wild. Before he could fire again, Kleandros seized his arm and dragged it down. Desperate now, Alvarez smashed at the doctor with his left fist. Kleandros fell with a groan, but by then the soldiers were on the time-traveler. A sword knocked the gun from his hand. It flew spinning into the flowers. Punching and kicking to the last, he was borne to the ground and trussed like a hog on the way to the slaughterhouse. Lou Muller got the same treatment; a magnificent flying tackle had brought him down just inside Kleandros's front door.

One of Alvarez's captors, a broad-shouldered, grizzled fellow of about fifty, knelt over him, saying, "I arrest you for the murder of Clodius Eprius." Alvarez spat at him; in return he got a buffet that loosened his teeth. "Eprius was a friend of mine," the Roman said.

"You were right, Tero," said another trooper. "They are human, after all."

"I told you so, Afer. You owe me two aurei." Tero turned to Kleandros and helped him to his feet. A dark bruise was forming under the doctor's left eye, but he did not seem badly hurt.

The byplay went on without much attention from Alvarez. He was in pain and sunk deep in despair; the timer would automatically return to 2059 twenty-four hours after it recharged unless someone

DEATH IN VESUNNA

reset it, and it did not look as if he or Lou would have the chance. He was stuck here-and-now forever. No, revise that—his future here looked limited, too.

He realized Tero was saying something to him, but did not take the trouble to understand. Tero kicked him in the ribs, not unkindly, and repeated: "Tell me, barbarian, how many years lie between our time and yours?"

Alvarez felt his world coming apart. Somehow these savages had managed to seize him, and now they knew his secret as well. He strained wildly at his bonds, trying to break free, but one thing the Romans plainly knew was how to tie firm knots. "You are the barbarians!" he shouted.

Tero and Kleandros bent over him, faces intent. "It's true, then?" the Greek whispered. "You do come from the future?"

Utterly beaten, Alvarez said, "Yes."

"I thought so," Tero breathed. "Quite by accident, it occurred to me how much more we know, now, than the heroes of the Trojan Wars. That set me thinking—how much more still would the men who came after us learn? Surely they would have powers we do not: terrible weapons, who knows what? Simpler things, too: the ability to make one coin just like another, for instance. How do you do that, anyway?"

"Molds," Alvarez said dully.

"Ah? Interesting. It's neither here nor there, though. Even after I got my notion, I still had to figure out why the men of the future would want anything from *us* in the first place. That stymied me for a long, long time. By my own logic, you had to have everything we do, and more besides. And then Eprius's body-servant found that one of his master's books was missing, a rare one."

"Rare?" Kleandros interjected. "If I had known Eprius had a copy of the *Aleadai,* I might have killed him myself."

"You see?" Tero said. "It's so easy for a book to be lost forever, if few copies are made of it. Works like the *Aleadai* are valuable now—how much more would they be worth in some future time if between now and then they'd been lost altogether? A great deal, I have no doubt. Enough to steal for, enough to kill for? Once we knew the sort of thing you were after, it was easy enough to set a trap, and you walked right into it."

Kleandros added, "My apologies for not using an authentic copy of Hieronymos of Kardia, but, you see, no one in town owns one."

This was all a bad dream, Alvarez thought. It could not be happening. To be caught was bad enough, but then to be lectured by

ERIC G. IVERSON & ELAINE O'BYRNE

these stupid barbarians . . .

He must have said that aloud, for Tero's lips tightened. He realized the English phrase was close enough to the Latin from which it had come to let the Romans understand him.

"Us, barbarians?" Tero said. "On the contrary. What are the marks of the barbarian? Surely one is acting without thinking ahead to see what results might come of what you do. Did you do that, when you used your thunder-weapon? Hardly. And because we were ignorant of your device, did you think us dolts? You were stupid to reveal it to us at all. No, man from another time, if either of us deserves to be called a barbarian, it is you."

He stood and turned to his men. "Take them away," he said.

I DREAM OF A FISH, I DREAM OF A BIRD

by Elizabeth A. Lynn

Elizabeth A. Lynn has written five novels,
the most recent of which is The Sardonyx Net
(Berkley 1982). Her second novel, Watchtower,
won a World Fantasy Award in 1980.
She has a first degree black belt in aikido,
has taught science fiction at San Francisco State
University, the University of California at Berkeley,
the Haystack Writer's Workshop,
and at Clarion, and currently lives in San Francisco.

Forty miles off the coast, anchored in the sea floor, Vancouver stood.

It had been designed and built before the Change, for bored, rich land-dwellers to play in. Sixty years after the Change, it was a tower filled with refugees. Pictures in the library showed the abandoned land: brown, bleak, and ruined, with skeletal steel buildings twisted and broken across it, like the torn masts of wrecked ships. War, disease, famine, and madness had created that.

The names of the lost cities—New York, Boston, Ellay, Tokyo, Cairo, Capetown—and of the burnt lands, were a litany of lament in their history lessons.

Where the radiation levels let them get to it, the shards of steel engraving the gullied lands were City salvage—a needed, dangerous harvest.

Illis swung on the handle of the door, and pushed. It opened grudgingly, silently, as he thrust his weight against it. Smooth metal felt cold on his palms. He slipped through the narrow space into the dark hallway. This made the fifth time he had sneaked out into the sleeping skyscraper, to climb the webway. He was not supposed to go out of the Children's Floor at night.

But it was hard to stay still in bed, when dreams left him with a dry mouth, twitching muscles, and visions winging through his brain.

He ran to the window at the end of the corridor, and looked

out—and down. Waves beneath him humped and bumped in dark, endless circles.

Nose against the cold glass, he looked east, towards land. On clear bright days he saw it, or thought he saw it. He dreamed about it: only in his dreams it was green, and there were birds. He had never seen a bird; there were none, but in his dreams they soared against the clouds in graceful spirals, making odd mewing sounds. *I want to be a bird.*

He had told his mother Janna about the birds in his dreams. "Maybe there is memory in your blood," she'd said. "I dream of birds, too."

"Have you seen one?"

But no, she had shaken her head.

He walked back down the hall. Set in the wall, like a mosaic or a painting, was the round, rainbow-colored webway door. Illis wiped his palms on his jumpsuit. "A climbing fool," Janna called him. She was one, too; she had taught him to climb. He liked sailing. He was good at handling the boats, careful and attentive, though he was only ten, and uncomfortably small for his age. But he was a City child, and his delight was in climbing.

Even on tiptoe, he couldn't hold down the release set at the top of the door. It was there on purpose, he well knew, so that small children could not finger it curiously and by mistake open the door. There was no one in the shadowy hall to stop him. He took a breath, and jumped for the release, holding with both hands, hanging from the handle, pulling it sideways with his weight. The door slid back. He looked down.

Imagine a spider, trapped in a long vertical pipe, spinning web after web at regular intervals from the bottom to the top of the pipe. Look down the pipe. You will see layer upon layer of web, until the layers blend to your eyes. Look up. It looks the same. Illis checked to see that there was no one on the net beneath him. Then he hooked his fingers over the rope that dangled from just inside the entrance.

He swung out, twisting around to touch the red button that opened and closed the door from the inside. Then he set his feet against the lip of the doorway and kicked off into the center of the web.

Falling—falling—sproong! He landed bouncing, curling his body like a ball to take the shock. The net bucked and quivered. He balanced on it and looked around for a "hole." There was one, a meter away. He slid easily through it, hung one-handed from the rope next to it, and dropped. SPROONG.

The webway was playground, gymnasium, and stairway to the

skyscraper city. Illis couldn't see why anyone bothered to use the lifts, except for going up. Climbing up on the webway, going up the knotted ropes, hauling himself back up through the holes, made his arms ache. But going down was like flying! He dropped again. That was three. The farther he got from his floor, the harder it was for him to get back there. The danger of being caught excited him almost as much as the webway itself.

Above him the door slid back.

Illis looked up, counting. Go in! he thought at the net-obscured form. Be lazy. Take the lift! But the person was not being lazy. Illis's jumpsuit felt suddenly tight and hot. He scuttled for the webway door and punched the inside button. The door opened and he swung through it. He pressed against the wall by the hole in the wall, listening to the steady descent. I'll wait till there's no one there, he thought. Then I'll get back on the web and I'll climb home, to the Children's Floor.

"What are *you* up to?" asked an amused voice above his intent head.

Illis looked up. Leaning over him was a very tall woman, with black hair and brown skin and amber eyes. She looked exactly like his mother. "Nothing," he said, and ducked under her arm. He ran down the hall. A door came slapping in front of him. He hauled on the handle with all his strength, and scooted inside. It smelled of soap, and fish. It was cold. He heard water running. Around him the tall bulk of machinery gleamed metal. He searched for a corner to hide in, careful as he went scrambling to keep his elbows in.

"Hey!" He shrank against a door. "Did you see a kid?"

A man's voice answered, through the sound of rushing water: "What would a kid be doing in here?"

"I chased one down the hall," said the woman. "Take a look around, will you? I'll check the refectory."

"Sure." Illis, crouching very still, heard her open the door. He looked cautiously for the source of the other voice. There he was—hosing down the floor. He doesn't look in a hurry to find me, Illis thought. Where am I? Around him, above him, hanging from pegs on the wall, were pots, pans, knives, cleavers, spoons, and forks as big as brooms, or almost. I'm in a kitchen, he realized. That's why it smells of fish. He listened again. The man was looking for him, not very hard, grumbling disbelief, rolling up the hose. The man wanted to get home. I wonder where the freezers are, Illis thought, one ear towards the grumbles. And the stoves. His legs felt cramped.

ELIZABETH A. LYNN

He stood up to ease them. He heard the door open, and close. Wait'll I tell mother I got inside a kitchen!

He found the freezers. They had dials and signs all over them, and even if he'd wanted to look inside, the handle was too far away for him to swing on it. He pictured fish from the farms in there, all frozen and silvery, like pieces of ice with eyes. He found a huge bin of dried kelp. He found the giant broilers; four of them, protected by steel-mesh gates.

I could climb over *these*.

He measured the gates with his eyes. The broilers sat silent, empty, mouths shut, DANGER! WHEN LIGHT FLASHES RED, BROILER IS ON! There were no flashing red lights. The broilers were off. I could even open the door, he thought. Easily, quietly, he climbed the fence. The broilers looked even bigger from close up. The button marked "Open Door" was sitting only centimeters above his head.

It was a freak of time, incalculable and unforeseen, that his finger on the button opened the broiler door just as that broiler — preset — began a self-cleaning cycle.

A red light flashed.

As the door gaped wider, the broiler shut itself off, and the door stopped moving—but not in time.

Illis's clothes flamed.

They packed him round with ice before moving him to Medica.

"You're a mess," Lazlo, Senior Medic, told him. "Does it hurt?"

"No." Two amber eyes looked up at him. Christ! What am I going to do for him? Lazlo thought.

"Well, you have to stop climbing for a while," he said. "You got to stay in here and grow new skin." *Damned if I know where it's going to come from.* The boy had flung his left arm across his eyes. The skin round his eyes, his eyelids, his mouth and nose, a strip on his left cheek, and another strip on his left arm, remained untouched. Methodically he checked the IV tubing and the catheter. "Are you warm enough?" Already, under his light sterile gown, he was sweating.

"Yes." Something—laughter?—touched the boy's eyes. "That's funny," he murmured. Lazlo grinned at him with his eyes, over the top of his mask.

"Is it?" he said. "Good. You know how to call people if you want anything? Good. There'll be people in and out of here all the time, and anyone you want to see, you tell us. You get to float in here, we call it the G-room, for a bit. Tomorrow we'll take you to surgery and remove all the old burned skin that's still sticking to you. You'll be all peeled. After that we'll take skin from your arm and your cheek and start growing it all over you."

"Grafts," Illis said, knowledgeably. He must know that word from Janna, Lazlo thought, with all her years of working here.

"Exactly. What you have to do now is, you have to move, and you have to eat."

"It's real easy to move in here," Illis said, looking at the gold-painted walls, the white net bed holding him, and the piles of machines humming in the corners of the small room.

"That's why you're in here, and not in a regular bed, in a room with regular gravity. We can increase the gravity in here, slowly, so that your muscles don't get weak. And you have to eat. Lots. Whatever you like, you tell us. You can have anything, anytime. You *must* eat."

"I understand," whispered the boy, staring at his raw, scorched flesh, from which fluid was leaking.

"I'll be in to see you every day."

A set of sealed doors with a tiny supply room between them kept Illis in strict reverse isolation. It was called the Lock. Lazlo inventoried the supplies as he went through it: sterile cloths, gowns, masks, gloves, bottles of fluids. The blood was in its freezer. For the thousandth time he praised the foresight of the first City generation, who had guessed how badly the city would need medical supplies. The hum of the air purifier filled the tiny room. He couldn't put it off. He opened the outer door and stepped into the corridor. Janna was waiting for him there.

Bright polished tools swung from loops on her hips. Every City adult worked part of the year on Maintenance. The glare of the sun through the window gave her the cut-away carved look of a mahogany figurehead. She saw his face—"It's bad," she said, before he could say it. And glared at him as if he were an enemy. "I want to stay with him."

"No," he said. "You can visit him—"

"You're an arbitrary absolutist son-of-a-bitch!" she said furiously. "Why?"

"It will upset him," he said reasonably. "And it will break you. If he asks to see more of you, we'll get Maintenance to set up a direct com-screen link, your room to G-room."

"I want to be with him," she repeated.

"What does he like to eat? Get me a list. Your pain will only distract him from healing. He *has* to eat, or he won't live long enough to grow new skin."

"I want to take care of him—"

"The City will take care of Illis. You want to help him—make me a list."

"Damn you!" she cried at him. "No, don't touch me! I'll make you a list."

Janna was shaking by the time she reached her rooms. It was not *fair* to keep her from her son. Obsessively, she had pictured Illis dead a hundred times since his birth, from any one of a hundred birth defects—but never hurting, wasting and hurting! She paced and raged. *I taught Illis to climb.* She twisted in anger and guilt.

It was not *fair* . . .

His father had died of radiation poisoning. Had that been fair?

She had done it before. She knew the routine. She could sit with him, coax him to eat, change his dressings, regulate his fluids, . . . Maintenance would let her go. The beeper on her belt screeched at her. She fumed at it. Hadn't they heard Illis was hurt? She was supposed to be in the soil lab, working on some defective wiring—but every adult in the City could use pliers! They could find someone to take her place.

You taught him to climb.

She had had six miscarriages before Illis. She was thirty-five, and likely not to have another child. If Illis died—the light on the com-screen was flashing. A neighbor, maybe, calling to console, to patter platitudes into her ears. I will have a seventh ghost face, she thought, to add to the six that anguish my dreams . . .

Don't give up hope—we will survive, Vancouver will survive—*I don't give a damn,* Janna thought. I don't care about the City—but my son is hurting—why? For what?

Floating in the isolation of his room, Illis slept and ate, slept and ate more, replenishing the nourishment leaking from his flesh. He developed pneumonia, and recovered from it. He exercised, painfully. But at the end of two months he weighed twenty-nine kilos.

"His body's rejecting the secondary grafts," Lazlo said, in staff conference. "We expected it. Skin from the freezer or from donors doesn't last very long. It's a temporary protection. But he seems to be rejecting it with uncommon swiftness—and there's too little of his own skin. It just isn't growing fast enough." Dressed in her

Maintenance jumpsuit, jangling with tools, Janna sat at the table, making notes. Lazlo did not look at her as he talked.

"How about plastics?" someone asked.

Mitra, from Research, answered. "We've been using a laminated nylon dressing," she said. "And we are working now on an adaptive protein paint, to be used in all kinds of wound cases. But it's still experimental. Our supply of plastic is very limited, and anyway, the dressing lasts no longer than the secondary grafts. There's no substitute for skin."

Someone else asked: "What happens now?"

"We keep on," Lazlo said. "The boy's very tough. He may yet make it. We keep on."

After the others cleared out, Lazlo walked around to where Janna was sitting. "How are you?" he asked.

"I'm fine." She would not give an inch. Illis's condition has become a battleground on which we maneuver, he thought. "I am coming to work in the labs tomorrow," she said. "Perhaps they will find me something on which I can work off my obsession."

"Are you eating?" he persisted. "You look thinner."

"I!" She glared at him. Then she relented. Lazlo spent an hour every day in the G-room, talking with Illis, playing games to make him move, checking the too-few patches of new skin, changing the bio-adherent dressings. *Doing the things he will not let me do.* "I'm all right, Lazlo. Thank you." She touched his hand. Then her spine straightened. She picked up her notes. "Maybe I will see you tomorrow," she said to him. "Tell me when I may be permitted to spend more time with my son."

In the morning, Mitra took Janna to a table with a shelf and a bank of machines. The shelf had her name on it; as if, Janna thought, I had never been away. "You work here," Mitra said. She pointed at a stack of papers. "The problem's there. Read."

Janna ate dinner in the refectory in Medica that evening. Lazlo came to sit with her. "How're you doing?" he asked.

She grinned at him. "I'm eating."

It made him smile, and emboldened him. "I see you're dressed in whites," he said. "What are you working on? Something good?"

Her eyes gleamed out of her dark face, a look fierce as a predator's. "Skin," she said. "I'm working on skin."

Somewhere amid the piles of print-outs on her shelf was a fact or formula that would help Illis.

Working with epithelial cells grown in culture media, she sorted through a dozen experiments designed to stimulate or regenerate damaged tissue. She haunted her desk late at night; she dreamed about the helical collagen molecule. She plunged into the library to scour the pre-Change records on immuno-suppressive nutrient solutions, a way to counteract the rejector mechanisms that kept Illis from using her skin, Lazlo's skin, anybody's skin. Mitra, at her desk nearby, was working on her own project, the all-purpose protein paint. She wanted a substance—like synthetic insulin—which the City's bioengineers could make. Janna listened to her grumbles, in between her own. *Skin. I'm working on skin.*

Lazlo came from a late visit to the wards, one night, and saw her in silhouette against a western window. Summer sunset had left streaks of red and lavender across the sky. He went to her. "It's getting late."

Her voice was heavy with fatigue. "Yes."

"Illis gained weight this week," he said.

She turned around. "How much?"

"Almost two kilos."

"That's good."

"Two grafts on his left arm seem to be taking."

"That's good."

"Have you stopped at all today?" he demanded. "You're punchy! Come on, you're getting out of here. I'll help you close up." He went around the lab for her, turning off the lights. She leaned on him as they left. "Fool woman!" he said. Her shoulder blades winged sharply under his fingers, and there were dark hollows under her eyes. "Don't you *dare* get sick! How would I tell Illis?"

He took her to the refectory. She ate in absent-minded gulps, not looking at the food, fork and fingers moving like the claw of an automaton.

"What keeps you up so late?" Lazlo asked.

"New skin for Illis."

"You're not going to get anywhere if you don't sleep at night."

She looked directly at him. "I used to have nightmares when I slept," she said. "I dreamed about Illis, a dark little ghost face crying, going away from me, going to join the others. I hated to sleep alone."

"You don't have to sleep alone," Lazlo said.

"I don't dream that anymore. I don't dream at all anymore. I am a dream, Laz, a dream that the City is dreaming."

"I think you need to go to bed," Lazlo said.

She let him take her there.

Janna woke in the night.

Her pillow smelled of Lazlo. The room smelled of sex and of growing things; some of her plants were blossoming. She had just dreamed, and the memory of pain had awakened her. She had dreamed that Illis had turned into a bright silver fish, and she had swallowed him. He swam into her womb, and all over again, she gave birth to him. She passed her hands across her belly. It was flat and muscular, smooth—of course.

What was the dream telling her?

Silver—her memory jumped to the lab, and Mitra holding up a test tube filled with silver liquid. "Promising," she had commented tersely. "Needs more tests." Janna stalked naked to the com-screen and punched out a number.

"Mitra? What were you playing around with this morning? A test substance for the paint? It was silver."

The screen said two short sibilant words, and then said something rude, and was silent.

Janna reached for clothes. The lab will be empty, she thought, seeing deserted City corridors, passengerless lifts, herself alone, private, unobserved in the vacant lab—doing what? I will know, when I get there, what needs doing. Detachedly she saw herself open the door, leave her room, walk quickly down the hall—I am a dream of the City, she thought. The City is dreaming me.

Illis woke when the light went bright.

His mother was bending over him.

His mouth filled with questions. She had not come to visit him for ten days. "Hello," she said. Her voice was muffled in the fabric of the mask. He saw it stretch over her smile. "Hello, baby. You don't have to talk to me. Just lie back and watch."

He lay curious, feasting his eyes on her graceful movements, as she carried in a box through the door, and then knelt down by the inner door of the Lock, hands busy, head bent secretively. She had made the room heavy again. Painfully he pulled himself up in the bed to watch her. She saw him, and came to sit on the chair beside the bed.

"Look!" she commanded, and she pushed up the sleeve on her left arm with her right hand. "Look at my arm."

The skin along her left forearm was thickened and scaly, and it *glittered*.

"What—" Where it touched the dark of her own skin, it thinned away. He reached with his left arm, the good one, and touched the silver. It was warm and dry. "It's skin," she said.

"Is it real?"

"It's growing there."

"What's it made of?" He stroked it.

She chuckled, and watched his yearning face. "Fish scales. Mitra made it, in Research. It looks like paint, and it's made of protein, protein very like the components of your skin." She touched his left cheek with her gloved hand. "It's for you."

There was a loud click, and Lazlo's voice came into the room. "What's going on in there?"

Janna called out cheerfully, "I'm visiting my son!"

"At four in the morning?"

"Yes. And yes, I did jam the door. You aren't going to be able to get in here without screwing Illis's protective isolation all to hell." She walked over to the com-screen unit and did something to it. Then she came back to the bed. "That'll keep 'em busy," she said. "Hold still now. I want to look at you." She turned the light up, and pulled the netting away. The grafts looked better than they had ten days back—but there were still too few of them. Illis's bones poked up through the devastated body as if they were trying to climb out.

"I'm pretty ugly," Illis said.

"You're going to be pretty flashy soon," Janna answered. "I'm going to color you silver."

"Now?" Illis whispered.

"Now." She stepped to the box, and took from it an ordinary glass jar, filled with a thick silver liquid, and a prosaic brush. "I'm going to do one whole side of you," she said. "It'll be cold, at first, and then it will sink in. Which side shall I do?"

"My right one," Illis said.

Janna set her teeth, and began to slowly paint the iridescent fibrous material over the raw wounds on her son's body. He whimpered, but held still, as she dabbed his throat, chest, abdomen, and right side. She put down the brush and wiped her sweating forehead, and then continued, working down his groin and his right leg. "That's all," she said, as she brushed the paint over his heel, and she capped the jar with shaking hands.

"It is cold," he reported.

"It will pass."

"The cold is going away."

"Good." At last she was able to look at him. He looked like a starved harlequin. "It will itch," she warned him. "You'd better not scratch. Not even in your sleep!"

It took her a long time to unjam the door.

Lazlo was waiting on the other side. He grabbed her. "What did you do?"

"Go and look."

Careless of isolation procedure, he strode inside the room. Illis waved at him from the net bed. "What—what is it?"

She laughed, sagging against the wall, and held up her glittering arm. "It's the protein paint," she said. "I had a dream—and the dream told me something, Laz. I stole some. And then I burned myself a third degree burn. I poured the paint on. It healed—like this, Lazlo. With no grafting, just like this!" She was crying. He grabbed her by the shoulders and shook her. One or two tears splashed his face.

From the bed, Illis watched with undiminished curiosity.

"You did this because of a *dream!* Blast you, Janna. How could you take such a risk!"

"For Illis," she said. And grinned. "Now I can stay with him."

"Ah, Christ!"

The whole City heard the news, and waited. Lazlo became an unwilling daily reporter. The paint remained unchanged on the emaciated boy for two weeks. Three weeks. After twenty-two days, it began to grow along the right arm, up the collarbone, to meet the healthy skin growing down the neck. They installed a mirror at the foot of Illis's bed, so that he could watch. "It's growing," he said with wonder, flexing the elbow of his right arm, touching his shoulder with his finger.

"Yes," said Lazlo. *"Don't scratch."*

With novel luxury, Illis wriggled in bed.

They patch-painted him all over. The new skin grew in faster each day. "Hey—will I be able to go home soon?" he asked his mother.

"Soon."

And Illis ate for three, watched the mirror, and wept when his new skin itched.

When she came to get him, to take him home, Illis was standing at the window, looking up at the sky. She went to stand beside him. So close, one could see their kinship in the shape of noses and ears, the way their mouths were set, their amber eyes—only Janna's skin was a warm, dark brown, and Illis's shone bright, scaly, hairless, and delicately mottled, like the integument of an eel.

ELIZABETH A. LYNN

"What are you doing?" she asked him.

"Dreaming." He turned to her, intrigue in his eyes, looking like a quicksilver monkey. "I'm going to go there someday," he said.

It was the City's dream—the return. "Sure you are," she said gently.

He danced a little, phoenix-brilliant in the summer sunlight. Her heart clenched.

"Have you been there?"

"No."

"Why not?" he demanded.

"The radiation level's too high. The only people who can go are those who've had their children, or who are sterile."

"Is it green yet?"

"No." It was still too early for renaissance. Throughout the City, desire fleshed a vision of plowable soil, drinkable water, rivers brimming with fish instead of chemical death. But the City scavengers would find rocks and steel, lichens, moss, and insects. The insects had re-inherited the earth.

"I *will* go." Illis said. "I will swim there." He grinned. "I'm a fish, now."

"You are an imp."

He looked up again. "I dream about them," he said. "In the sky, with the sun shining on their wings. Next time, Mama—make me feathers. I want to be a bird."

FIRE WATCH
by Connie Willis
art: James Odbert

*Ms. Willis wrote "Firewatch" while
working under a generous National
Endowment for the Arts government
grant which enabled her to quit
substitute teaching and start
writing full-time. The extra time is
helpful because she is also
the hassled mother of a
thirteen-year-old with braces
and the wife of an even
more hassled physics teacher.*

"History hath triumphed over time, which besides it nothing but
eternity hath triumphed over."

—Sir Walter Raleigh

September 20—Of course the first thing I looked for was the firewatch stone. And of course it wasn't there yet. It wasn't dedicated
until 1951, accompanying speech by the Very Reverend Dean Walter
Matthews, and this is only 1940. I knew that. I went to see the firewatch stone only yesterday, with some kind of misplaced notion that
seeing the scene of the crime would somehow help. It didn't.

The only things that would have helped were a crash course in
London during the Blitz and a little more time. I had not gotten
either.

"Travelling in time is not like taking the tube, Mr. Bartholomew,"
the esteemed Dunworthy had said, blinking at me through those
antique spectacles of his. "Either you report on the twentieth or you
don't go at all."

"But I'm not ready," I'd said. "Look, it took me four years to get
ready to travel with St. Paul. *St. Paul.* Not St. Paul's. You can't
expect me to get ready for London in the Blitz in two days."

"Yes," Dunworthy had said. "We can." End of conversation.

"Two days!" I had shouted at my roommate Kivrin. "All because
some computer adds an apostrophe **s**. And the esteemed Dunworthy
doesn't even bat an eye when I tell him. 'Time travel is not like
taking the tube, young man,' he says. 'I'd suggest you get ready.
You're leaving day after tomorrow.' The man's a total incompetent."

"No," she said. "He isn't. He's the best there is. He wrote the book

CONNIE WILLIS

on St. Paul's. Maybe you should listen to what he says."

I had expected Kivrin to be at least a little sympathetic. She had been practically hysterical when she got her practicum changed from fifteenth to fourteenth century England, and how did either century qualify as a practicum? Even counting infectious diseases they couldn't have been more than a five. The Blitz is an eight, and St. Paul's itself is, with my luck, a ten.

"You think I should go see Dunworthy again?" I said.

"Yes."

"And then what? I've got two days. I don't know the money, the language, the history. Nothing."

"He's a good man," Kivrin said. "I think you'd better listen to him while you can." Good old Kivrin. Always the sympathetic ear.

The good man was responsible for my standing just inside the propped-open west doors, gawking like the country boy I was supposed to be, looking for a stone that wasn't there. Thanks to the good man, I was about as unprepared for my practicum as it was possible for him to make me.

I couldn't see more than a few feet into the church. I could see a candle gleaming feebly a long way off and a closer blur of white moving toward me. A verger, or possibly the Very Reverend Dean himself. I pulled out the letter from my clergyman uncle in Wales that was supposed to gain me access to the Dean, and patted my back pocket to make sure I hadn't lost the microfiche *Oxford English Dictionary, Revised, with Historical Supplements,* I'd smuggled out of the Bodleian. I couldn't pull it out in the middle of the conversation, but with luck I could muddle through the first encounter by context and look up the words I didn't know later.

"Are you from the ayarpee?" he said. He was no older than I am, a head shorter and much thinner. Almost ascetic looking. He reminded me of Kivrin. He was not wearing white, but clutching it to his chest. In other circumstances I would have thought it was a pillow. In other circumstances I would know what was being said to me, but there had been no time to unlearn sub-Mediterranean Latin and Jewish law and learn Cockney and air-raid procedures. Two days, and the esteemed Dunworthy, who wanted to talk about the sacred burdens of the historian instead of telling me what the ayarpee was.

"Are you?" he demanded again.

I considered shipping out the *OED* after all on the grounds that Wales was a foreign country, but I didn't think they had microfilm in 1940. Ayarpee. It could be anything, including a nickname for the fire watch, in which case the impulse to say no was not safe at all. "No," I said.

He lunged suddenly toward and past me and peered out the open doors. "Damn," he said, coming back to me. "Where are they then? Bunch of lazy bourgeois tarts!" And so much for getting by on context.

He looked at me closely, suspiciously, as if he thought I was only pretending not to be with the ayarpee. "The church is closed," he said finally.

I held up the envelope and said, "My name's Bartholomew. Is Dean Matthews in?"

He looked out the door a moment longer, as if he expected the lazy bourgeois tarts at any moment and intended to attack them with the white bundle, then he turned and said, as if he were guiding a tour, "This way, please," and took off into the gloom.

He led me to the right and down the south aisle of the nave. Thank God I had memorized the floor plan or at that moment, heading into total darkness, led by a raving verger, the whole bizarre metaphor of my situation would have been enough to send me out the west doors and back to St. John's Wood. It helped a little to know where I was. We should have been passing number twenty-six: Hunt's painting of "The Light of the World"—Jesus with his lantern—but it was too dark to see it. We could have used the lantern ourselves.

He stopped abruptly ahead of me, still raving. "We weren't asking for the bloody Savoy, just a few cots. Nelson's better off than we are—at least he's got a pillow provided." He brandished the white bundle like a torch in the darkness. It was a pillow after all. "We asked for them over a fortnight ago, and here we still are, sleeping on the bleeding generals from Trafalgar because those bitches want to play tea and crumpets with the tommies at Victoria and the Hell with us!"

He didn't seem to expect me to answer his outburst, which was good, because I had understood perhaps one key word in three. He stomped on ahead, moving out of sight of the one pathetic altar candle and stopping again at a black hole. Number twenty-five: stairs to the Whispering Gallery, the Dome, the library (not open to the public). Up the stairs, down a hall, stop again at a medieval door and knock. "I've got to go wait for them," he said. "If I'm not there they'll likely take them over to the Abbey. Tell the Dean to ring them up again, will you?" and he took off down the stone steps, still holding his pillow like a shield against him.

He had knocked, but the door was at least a foot of solid oak, and

CONNIE WILLIS

it was obvious the Very Reverend Dean had not heard. I was going to have to knock again. Yes, well, and the man holding the pinpoint had to let go of it, too, but even knowing it will all be over in a moment and you won't feel a thing doesn't make it any easier to say, "Now!" So I stood in front of the door, cursing the history department and the esteemed Dunworthy and the computer that had made the mistake and brought me here to this dark door with only a letter from a fictitious uncle that I trusted no more than I trusted the rest of them.

Even the old reliable Bodleian had let me down. The batch of research stuff I cross-ordered through Balliol and the main terminal is probably sitting in my room right now, a century out of reach. And Kivrin, who had already done her practicum and should have been bursting with advice, walked around as silent as a saint until I begged her to help me.

"Did you go to see Dunworthy?" she said.

"Yes. You want to know what priceless bit of information he had for me? 'Silence and humility are the sacred burdens of the historian.' He also told me I would love St. Paul's. Golden gems from the master. Unfortunately, what I need to know are the times and places of the bombs so one doesn't fall on me." I flopped down on the bed. "Any suggestions?"

"How good are you at memory retrieval?" she said.

I sat up. "I'm pretty good. You think I should assimilate?"

"There isn't time for that," she said. "I think you should put everything you can directly into long-term."

"You mean endorphins?" I said.

The biggest problem with using memory-assistance drugs to put information into your long-term memory is that it never sits, even for a micro-second, in your short-term memory, and that makes retrieval complicated, not to mention unnerving. It gives you the most unsettling sense of *déjà vu* to suddenly know something you're positive you've never seen or heard before.

The main problem, though, is not eerie sensations but retrieval. Nobody knows exactly how the brain gets what it wants out of storage, but short-term is definitely involved. That brief, sometimes microscopic, time information spends in short-term is apparently used for something besides tip-of-the-tongue availability. The whole complex sort-and-file process of retrieval is apparently centered in short-term; and without it, and without the help of the drugs that put it there or artificial substitutes, information can be impossible to retrieve. I'd used endorphins for examinations and never had any difficulty with retrieval, and it looked like it was the only way to store all the information I needed in anything approaching the time I had left, but it also meant that I would *never* have known any of the things I needed to know, even for long enough to have forgotten them. If and when I could retrieve the information, I would know it. Till then I was as ignorant of it as if it were not stored in some cobwebbed corner of my mind at all.

"You can retrieve without artificials, can't you?" Kivrin said, looking skeptical.

"I guess I'll have to."

"Under stress? Without sleep? Low body endorphin levels?" What exactly had her practicum been? She had never said a word about it, and undergraduates are not supposed to ask. Stress factors in the Middle Ages? I thought everybody slept through them.

"I hope so," I said. "Anyway, I'm willing to try this idea if you think it will help."

She looked at me with that martyred expression and said, "Nothing will help." Thank you, St. Kivrin of Balliol.

But I tried it anyway. It was better than sitting in Dunworthy's rooms having him blink at me through his historically accurate eyeglasses and tell me I was going to love St. Paul's. When my Bodleian requests didn't come, I overloaded my credit and bought out Blackwell's. Tapes on World War II, Celtic literature, history of mass transit, tourist guidebooks, everything I could think of. Then I rented a high-speed recorder and shot up. When I came out of it, I was so panicked by the feeling of not knowing any more than I had when I started that I took the tube to London and raced up Ludgate Hill to see if the firewatch stone would trigger any memories. It didn't.

"Your endorphin levels aren't back to normal yet," I told myself and tried to relax, but that was impossible with the prospect of the practicum looming up before me. And those are real bullets, kid. Just because you're a history major doing his practicum doesn't mean you can't get killed. I read history books all the way home on the tube and right up until Dunworthy's flunkies came to take me to St. John's Wood this morning.

Then I jammed the microfiche *OED* in my back pocket and went off feeling as if I would have to survive by my native wit and hoping I could get hold of artificials in 1940. Surely I could get through the first day without mishap, I thought; and now here I was, stopped cold by almost the first word that was spoken to me.

Well, not quite. In spite of Kivrin's advice that I not put anything

CONNIE WILLIS

in short-term, I'd memorized the British money, a map of the tube system, a map of my own Oxford. It had gotten me this far. Surely I would be able to deal with the Dean.

Just as I had almost gotten up the courage to knock, he opened the door, and as with the pinpoint, it really was over quickly and without pain. I handed him my letter, and he shook my hand and said something understandable like, "Glad to have another man, Bartholomew." He looked strained and tired and as if he might collapse if I told him the Blitz had just started. I know, I know: Keep your mouth shut. The sacred silence, etc.

He said, "We'll get Langby to show you round, shall we?" I assumed that was my Verger of the Pillow, and I was right. He met us at the foot of the stairs, puffing a little but jubilant.

"The cots came," he said to Dean Matthews. "You'd have thought they were doing us a favor. All high heels and hoity-toity. 'You made us miss our tea, luv,' one of them said to me. 'Yes, well, and a good thing, too,' I said. 'You look as if you could stand to lose a stone or two.' "

Even Dean Matthews looked as though he did not completely understand him. He said, "Did you set them up in the crypt?" and then introduced us. "Mr. Bartholomew's just got in from Wales," he said. "He's come to join our volunteers." Volunteers, not fire watch.

Langby showed me around, pointing out various dimnesses in the general gloom and then dragged me down to see the ten folding canvas cots set up among the tombs in the crypt, also in passing Lord Nelson's black marble sarcophagus. He told me I didn't have to stand a watch the first night and suggested I go to bed, since sleep is the most precious commodity in the raids. I could well believe it. He was clutching that silly pillow to his breast like his beloved.

"Do you hear the sirens down here?" I asked, wondering if he buried his head in it.

He looked round at the low stone ceilings. "Some do, some don't. Brinton has to have his Horlich's. Bence-Jones would sleep if the roof fell in on him. I have to have a pillow. The important thing is to get your eight in no matter what. If you don't, you turn into one of the walking dead. And then you get killed."

On that cheering note he went off to post the watches for tonight, leaving his pillow on one of the cots with orders for me to let nobody touch it. So here I sit, waiting for my first air-raid siren and trying to get all this down before I turn into one of the walking or non-walking dead.

I've used the stolen *OED* to decipher a little Langby. Middling success. A tart is either a pastry or a prostitute (I assume the latter, although I was wrong about the pillow). Bourgeois is a catchall term for all the faults of the middle class. A Tommy's a soldier. Ayarpee I could not find under any spelling and I had nearly given up when something in long-term about the use of acronyms and abbreviations in wartime popped forward (bless you, St. Kivrin) and I realized it must be an abbreviation. ARP. Air Raid Precautions. Of course. Where else would you get the bleeding cots from?

September 21—Now that I'm past the first shock of being here, I realize that the history department neglected to tell me what I'm supposed to do in the three-odd months of this practicum. They handed me this journal, the letter from my uncle, and a ten-pound note, and sent me packing into the past. The ten pounds (already depleted by train and tube fares) is supposed to last me until the end of December and get me back to St. John's Wood for pickup when the second letter calling me back to Wales to sick uncle's bedside comes. Till then I live here in the crypt with Nelson, who, Langby tells me, is pickled in alcohol inside his coffin. If we take a direct hit, will he burn like a torch or simply trickle out in a decaying stream onto the crypt floor, I wonder. Board is provided by a gas ring, over which are cooked wretched tea and indescribable kippers. To pay for all this luxury I am to stand on the roofs of St. Paul's and put out incendiaries.

I must also accomplish the purpose of this practicum, whatever it may be. Right now the only purpose I care about is staying alive until the second letter from uncle arrives and I can go home.

I am doing makework until Langby has time to "show me the ropes." I've cleaned the skillet they cook the foul little fishes in, stacked wooden folding chairs at the altar end of the crypt (flat instead of standing because they tend to collapse like bombs in the middle of the night), and tried to sleep.

I am apparently not one of the lucky ones who can sleep through the raids. I spent most of the night wondering what St. Paul's risk rating is. Practica have to be at least a six. Last night I was convinced this was a ten, with the crypt as ground zero, and that I might as well have applied for Denver.

The most interesting thing that's happened so far is that I've seen a cat. I am fascinated, but trying not to appear so since they seem commonplace here.

September 22—Still in the crypt. Langby comes dashing through periodically cursing various government agencies (all abbreviated) and promising to take me up on the roofs. In the meantime, I've run out of makework and taught myself to work a stirrup pump. Kivrin was overly concerned about my memory retrieval abilities. I have not had any trouble so far. Quite the opposite. I called up fire-fighting information and got the whole manual with pictures, including instructions on the use of the stirrup pump. If the kippers set Lord Nelson on fire, I shall be a hero.

Excitement last night. The sirens went early and some of the chars who clean offices in the City sheltered in the crypt with us. One of them woke me out of a sound sleep, going like an air raid siren. Seems she'd seen a mouse. We had to go whacking at tombs and under the cots with a rubber boot to persuade her it was gone. Obviously what the history department had in mind: murdering mice.

September 24—Langby took me on rounds. Into the choir, where I had to learn the stirrup pump all over again, assigned rubber boots and a tin helmet. Langby says Commander Allen is getting us asbestos firemen's coats, but hasn't yet, so it's my own wool coat and muffler and very cold on the roofs even in September. It feels like November and looks it, too, bleak and cheerless with no sun. Up to the dome and onto the roofs which should be flat, but in fact are littered with towers, pinnacles, gutters, and statues, all designed expressly to catch and hold incendiaries out of reach. Shown how to smother an incendiary with sand before it burns through the roof and sets the church on fire. Shown the ropes (literally) lying in a heap at the base of the dome in case somebody has to go up one of the west towers or over the top of the dome. Back inside and down to the Whispering Gallery.

Langby kept up a running commentary through the whole tour, part practical instruction, part church history. Before we went up into the Gallery he dragged me over to the south door to tell me how Christopher Wren stood in the smoking rubble of Old St. Paul's and asked a workman to bring him a stone from the graveyard to mark the cornerstone. On the stone was written in Latin, "I shall rise again," and Wren was so impressed by the irony that he had the words inscribed above the door. Langby looked as smug as if he had not told me a story every first-year history student knows, but I suppose without the impact of the firewatch stone, the other is just a nice story.

Langby raced me up the steps and onto the narrow balcony circling the Whispering Gallery. He was already halfway round to the other side, shouting dimensions and acoustics at me. He stopped facing the wall opposite and said softly, "You can hear me whispering because of the shape of the dome. The sound waves are reinforced around the perimeter of the dome. It sounds like the very crack of doom up here during a raid. The dome is one hundred and seven feet across. It is eighty feet above the nave."

I looked down. The railing went out from under me and the black-and-white marble floor came up with dizzying speed. I hung onto something in front of me and dropped to my knees, staggered and sick at heart. The sun had come out, and all of St. Paul's seemed drenched in gold. Even the carved wood of the choir, the white stone pillars, the leaden pipes of the organ, all of it golden, golden.

Langby was beside me, trying to pull me free. "Bartholomew," he shouted, "What's wrong? For God's sake, man."

I knew I must tell him that if I let go, St. Paul's and all the past would fall in on me, and that I must not let that happen because I was an historian. I said something, but it was not what I intended because Langby merely tightened his grip. He hauled me violently free of the railing and back onto the stairway, then let me collapse limply on the steps and stood back from me, not speaking.

"I don't know what happened in there," I said. "I've never been afraid of heights before."

"You're shaking," he said sharply. "You'd better lie down." He led me back to the crypt.

September 25—Memory retrieval: ARP manual. Symptoms of bombing victims. Stage one—shock; stupefaction; unawareness of injuries; words may not make sense except to victim. Stage two—shivering; nausea; injuries, losses felt; return to reality. Stage three—talkativeness that cannot be controlled; desire to explain shock behavior to rescuers.

Langby must surely recognize the symptoms, but how does he account for the fact there was no bomb? I can hardly explain my shock behavior to him, and it isn't just the sacred silence of the historian that stops me.

He has not said anything, in fact assigned me my first watches for tomorrow night as if nothing had happened, and he seems no more preoccupied than anyone else. Everyone I've met so far is jittery (one thing I had in short-term was how calm everyone was during the raids) and the raids have not come near us since I got here. They've been mostly over the East End and the docks.

There was a reference tonight to a UXB, and I have been thinking about the Dean's manner and the church being closed when I'm almost sure I remember reading it was open through the entire Blitz. As soon as I get a chance, I'll try to retrieve the events of September. As to retrieving anything else, I don't see how I can hope to remember the right information until I know what it is I am supposed to do here, if anything.

There are no guidelines for historians, and no restrictions either. I could tell everyone I'm from the future if I thought they would believe me. I could murder Hitler if I could get to Germany. Or could I? Time paradox talk abounds in the history department, and the graduate students back from their practica don't say a word one way or the other. Is there a tough, immutable past? Or is there a new past every day and do we, the historians, make it? And what are the consequences of what we do, if there are consequences? And how do we dare do anything without knowing them? Must we interfere boldly, hoping we do not bring about all our downfalls? Or must we do nothing at all, not interfere, stand by and watch St. Paul's burn to the groun. if need be so that we don't change the future?

All those are fine questions for a late-night study session. They do not matter here. I could no more let St. Paul's burn down than I could kill Hitler. No, that is not true. I found that out yesterday in the Whispering Gallery. I could kill Hitler if I caught him setting fire to St. Paul's.

September 26—I met a young woman today. Dean Matthews has opened the church, so the watch have been doing duties as chars and people have started coming in again. The young woman reminded me of Kivrin, though Kivrin is a good deal taller and would never frizz her hair like that. She looked as if she had been crying. Kivrin has looked like that since she got back from her practicum. The Middle Ages were too much for her. I wonder how she would have coped with this. By pouring out her fears to the local priest, no doubt, as I sincerely hoped her lookalike was not going to do.

"May I help you?" I said, not wanting in the least to help. "I'm a volunteer."

She looked distressed. "You're not paid?" she said, and wiped at her reddened nose with a handkerchief. "I read about St. Paul's and the fire watch and all and I thought, perhaps there's a position there for me. In the canteen, like, or something. A paying position." There were tears in her red-rimmed eyes.

"I'm afraid we don't have a canteen," I said as kindly as I could, considering how impatient Kivrin always makes me, "and it's not actually a real shelter. Some of the watch sleep in the crypt. I'm afraid we're all volunteers, though."

"That won't do, then," she said. She dabbed at her eyes with the handkerchief. "I love St. Paul's, but I can't take on volunteer work, not with my little brother Tom back from the country." I was not reading this situation properly. For all the outward signs of distress, she sounded quite cheerful and no closer to tears than when she had come in. "I've got to get us a proper place to stay. With Tom back, we can't go on sleeping in the tubes."

A sudden feeling of dread, the kind of sharp pain you get sometimes from involuntary retrieval, went over me. "The tubes?" I said, trying to get at the memory.

126   CONNIE WILLIS

"Marble Arch, usually," she went on. "My brother Tom saves us a place early and I go—" She stopped, held the handkerchief close to her nose, and exploded into it. "I'm sorry," she said, "this awful cold!"

Red nose, watering eyes, sneezing. Respiratory infection. It was a wonder I hadn't told her not to cry. It's only by luck that I haven't made some unforgivable mistake so far, and this is not because I can't get at the long-term memory. I don't have half the information I need even stored: cats and colds and the way St. Paul's looks in full sun. It's only a matter of time before I am stopped cold by something I do not know. Nevertheless, I am going to try for retrieval tonight after I come off watch. At least I can find out whether and when something is going to fall on me.

I have seen the cat once or twice. He is coal-black with a white patch on his throat that looks as if it were painted on for the blackout.

September 27—I have just come down from the roofs. I am still shaking.

Early in the raid the bombing was mostly over the East End. The view was incredible. Searchlights everywhere, the sky pink from the fires and reflecting in the Thames, the exploding shells sparkling like fireworks. There was a constant, deafening thunder broken by the occasional droning of the planes high overhead, then the repeating stutter of the ack-ack guns.

About midnight the bombs began falling quite near with a horrible sound like a train running over me. It took every bit of will I had to keep from flinging myself flat on the roof, but Langby was watching. I didn't want to give him the satisfaction of watching a repeat performance of my behavior in the dome. I kept my head up and my sandbucket firmly in hand and felt quite proud of myself.

The bombs stopped roaring past about three, and there was a lull of about half an hour, and then a clatter like hail on the roofs. Everybody except Langby dived for shovels and stirrup pumps. He was watching me. And I was watching the incendiary.

It had fallen only a few meters from me, behind the clock tower. It was much smaller than I had imagined, only about thirty centimeters long. It was sputtering violently, throwing greenish-white fire almost to where I was standing. In a minute it would simmer down into a molten mass and begin to burn through the roof. Flames and the frantic shouts of firemen, and then the white rubble stretching for miles, and nothing, nothing left, not even the firewatch stone.

It was the Whispering Gallery all over again. I felt that I had said something, and when I looked at Langby's face he was smiling crookedly.

"St. Paul's will burn down," I said. "There won't be anything left."

"Yes," Langby said. "That's the idea, isn't it? Burn St. Paul's to the ground? Isn't that the plan?"

"Whose plan?" I said stupidly.

"Hitler's, of course," Langby said. "Who did you think I meant?" and, almost casually, picked up his stirrup pump.

The page of the ARP manual flashed suddenly before me. I poured the bucket of sand around the still sputtering bomb, snatched up another bucket and dumped that on top of it. Black smoke billowed up in such a cloud that I could hardly find my shovel. I felt for the smothered bomb with the tip of it and scooped it into the empty bucket, then shovelled the sand in on top of it. Tears were streaming down my face from the acrid smoke. I turned to wipe them on my sleeve and saw Langby.

He had not made a move to help me. He smiled. "It's not a bad plan, actually. But of course we won't let it happen. That's what the fire watch is here for. To see that it doesn't happen. Right, Bartholomew?"

I know now what the purpose of my practicum is. I must stop Langby from burning down St. Paul's.

September 28—I try to tell myself I was mistaken about Langby last night, that I misunderstood what he said. Why would he want to burn down St. Paul's unless he is a Nazi spy? How can a Nazi spy have gotten on the fire watch? I think about my faked letter of introduction and shudder.

How can I find out? If I set him some test, some fatal thing that only a loyal Englishman in 1940 would know, I fear I am the one who would be caught out. I *must* get my retrieval working properly.

Until then, I shall watch Langby. For the time being at least that should be easy. Langby has just posted the watches for the next two weeks. We stand every one together.

September 30—I know what happened in September. Langby told me.

Last night in the choir, putting on our coats and boots, he said, "They've already tried once, you know."

I had no idea what he meant. I felt as helpless as that first day when he asked me if I was from the ayarpee.

"The plan to destroy St. Paul's. They've already tried once. The

CONNIE WILLIS

tenth of September. A high explosive bomb. But of course you didn't know about that. You were in Wales."

I was not even listening. The minute he had said, "high explosive bomb," I had remembered it all. It had burrowed in under the road and lodged on the foundations. The bomb squad had tried to defuse it, but there was a leaking gas main. They decided to evacuate St. Paul's, but Dean Matthews refused to leave, and they got it out after all and exploded it in Barking Marshes. Instant and complete retrieval.

"The bomb squad saved her that time," Langby was saying. "It seems there's always somebody about."

"Yes," I said. "There is," and walked away from him.

October 1—I thought last night's retrieval of the events of September tenth meant some sort of breakthrough, but I have been lying here on my cot most of the night trying for Nazi spies in St. Paul's and getting nothing. Do I have to know exactly what I'm looking for before I can remember it? What good does that do me?

Maybe Langby is not a Nazi spy. Then what is he? An arsonist? A madman? The crypt is hardly conducive to thought, being not at all as silent as a tomb. The chars talk most of the night and the sound of the bombs is muffled, which somehow makes it worse. I find myself straining to hear them. When I did get to sleep this morning, I dreamed about one of the tube shelters being hit, broken mains, drowning people.

October 4—I tried to catch the cat today. I had some idea of persuading it to dispatch the mouse that has been terrifying the chars. I also wanted to see one up close. I took the water bucket I had used with the stirrup pump last night to put out some burning shrapnel from one of the anti-aircraft guns. It still had a bit of water in it, but not enough to drown the cat, and my plan was to clamp the bucket over him, reach under, and pick him up, then carry him down to the crypt and point him at the mouse. I did not even come close to him.

I swung the bucket, and as I did so, perhaps an inch of water splashed out. I thought I remembered that the cat was a domesticated animal, but I must have been wrong about that. The cat's wide complacent face pulled back into a skull-like mask that was absolutely terrifying, vicious claws extended from what I had thought were harmless paws, and the cat let out a sound to top the chars.

In my surprise I dropped the bucket and it rolled against one of

FIREWATCH

the pillars. The cat disappeared. Behind me, Langby said, "That's no way to catch a cat."

"Obviously," I said, and bent to retrieve the bucket.

"Cats hate water," he said, still in that expressionless voice.

"Oh," I said, and started in front of him to take the bucket back to the choir. "I didn't know that."

"Everybody knows it. Even the stupid Welsh."

October 8—We have been standing double watches for a week—bomber's moon. Langby didn't show up on the roofs, so I went looking for him in the church. I found him standing by the west doors talking to an old man. The man had a newspaper tucked under his arm and he handed it to Langby, but Langby gave it back to him. When the man saw me, he ducked out. Langby said, "Tourist. Wanted to know where the Windmill Theater is. Read in the paper the girls are starkers."

I know I looked as if I didn't believe him because he said, "You look rotten, old man. Not getting enough sleep, are you? I'll get somebody to take the first watch for you tonight."

"No," I said coldly. "I'll stand my own watch. I like being on the roofs," and added silently, *where I can watch you.*

He shrugged and said, "I suppose it's better than being down in the crypt. At least on the roofs you can hear the one that gets you."

October 10—I thought the double watches might be good for me, take my mind off my inability to retrieve. The watched pot idea. Actually, it sometimes works. A few hours of thinking about something else, or a good night's sleep, and the fact pops forward without any prompting, without any artificials.

The good night's sleep is out of the question. Not only do the chars talk constantly, but the cat has moved into the crypt and sidles up to everyone, making siren noises and begging for kippers. I am moving my cot out of the transept and over by Nelson before I go on watch. He may be pickled, but he keeps his mouth shut.

October 11—I dreamed Trafalgar, ships' guns and smoke and falling plaster and Langby shouting my name. My first waking thought was that the folding chairs had gone off. I could not see for all the smoke.

"I'm coming," I said, limping toward Langby and pulling on my boots. There was a heap of plaster and tangled folding chairs in the transept. Langby was digging in it. "Bartholomew!" he shouted,

CONNIE WILLIS

flinging a chunk of plaster aside. "Bartholomew!"

I still had the idea it was smoke. I ran back for the stirrup pump and then knelt beside him and began pulling on a splintered chair back. It resisted, and it came to me suddenly, There is a body under here. I will reach for a piece of the ceiling and find it is a hand. I leaned back on my heels, determined not to be sick, then went at the pile again.

Langby was going far too fast, jabbing with a chair leg. I grabbed his hand to stop him, and he struggled against me as if I were a piece of rubble to be thrown aside. He picked up a large flat square of plaster, and under it was the floor. I turned and looked behind me. Both chars huddled in the recess by the altar. "Who are you looking for?" I said, keeping hold of Langby's arm.

"Bartholomew," he said, and swept the rubble aside, his hands bleeding through the coating of smoky dust.

"I'm here," I said. "I'm all right." I choked on the white dust. "I moved my cot out of the transept."

He turned sharply to the chars and then said quite calmly, "What's under here?"

"Only the gas ring," one of them said timidly from the shadowed recess, "and Mrs. Galbraith's pocketbook." He dug through the mess until he had found them both. The gas ring was leaking at a merry rate, though the flame had gone out.

"You've saved St. Paul's and me after all," I said, standing there in my underwear and boots, holding the useless stirrup pump. "We might all have been asphyxiated."

He stood up. "I shouldn't have saved you," he said.

Stage one: shock, stupefaction, unawareness of injuries, words may not make sense except to victim. He would not know his hand was bleeding yet. He would not remember what he had said. He had said he shouldn't have saved my life.

"I shouldn't have saved you," he repeated. "I have my duty to think of."

"You're bleeding," I said sharply. "You'd better lie down." I sounded just like Langby in the Gallery.

October 13—It was a high explosive bomb. It blew a hole in the choir roof; and some of the marble statuary is broken; but the ceiling of the crypt did not collapse, which is what I thought at first. It only jarred some plaster loose.

I do not think Langby has any idea what he said. That should give me some sort of advantage, now that I am sure where the danger lies, now that I am sure it will not come crashing down from some other direction. But what good is all this knowing, when I do not know what he will do? Or when?

Surely I have the facts of yesterday's bomb in long-term, but even falling plaster did not jar them loose this time. I am not even trying for retrieval now. I lie in the darkness waiting for the roof to fall in on me. And remembering how Langby saved my life.

October 15—The girl came in again today. She still has the cold, but she has gotten her paying position. It was a joy to see her. She was wearing a smart uniform and open-toed shoes, and her hair was in an elaborate frizz around her face. We are still cleaning up the mess from the bomb, and Langby was out with Allen getting wood to board up the choir, so I let the girl chatter at me while I swept. The dust made her sneeze, but at least this time I knew what she was doing.

She told me her name is Enola and that she's working for the WVS, running one of the mobile canteens that are sent to the fires. She came, of all things, to thank me for the job. She said that after she told the WVS that there was no proper shelter with a canteen for St. Paul's, they gave her a run in the City. "So I'll just pop in when I'm close and let you know how I'm making out, won't I just?"

She and her brother Tom are still sleeping in the tubes. I asked her if that was safe and she said probably not, but at least down there you couldn't hear the one that got you and that was a blessing.

October 18—I am so tired I can hardly write this. Nine incendiaries tonight and a land mine that looked as though it was going to catch on the dome till the wind drifted its parachute away from the church. I put out two of the incendiaries. I have done that at least twenty times since I got here and helped with dozens of others, and still it is not enough. One incendiary, one moment of not watching Langby, could undo it all.

I know that is partly why I feel so tired. I wear myself out every night trying to do my job and watch Langby, making sure none of the incendiaries falls without my seeing it. Then I go back to the crypt and wear myself out trying to retrieve something, anything, about spies, fires, St. Paul's in the fall of 1940, anything. It haunts me that I am not doing enough, but I do not know what else to do. Without the retrieval, I am as helpless as these poor people here, with no idea what will happen tomorrow.

If I have to, I will go on doing this till I am called home. He cannot

CONNIE WILLIS

burn down St. Paul's so long as I am here to put out the incendiaries. "I have my duty," Langby said in the crypt.

And I have mine.

October 21—It's been nearly two weeks since the blast and I just now realized we haven't seen the cat since. He wasn't in the mess in the crypt. Even after Langby and I were sure there was no one in there, we sifted through the stuff twice more. He could have been in the choir, though.

Old Bence-Jones says not to worry. "He's all right," he said. "The jerries could bomb London right down to the ground and the cats would waltz out to greet them. You know why? They don't love anybody. That's what gets half of us killed. Old lady out in Stepney got killed the other night trying to save her cat. Bloody cat was in the Anderson."

"Then where is he?"

"Someplace safe, you can bet on that. If he's not around St. Paul's, it means we're for it. That old saw about the rats deserting a sinking ship, that's a mistake, that is. It's cats, not rats."

October 25—Langby's tourist showed up again. He cannot still be looking for the Windmill Theatre. He had a newspaper under his arm again today, and he asked for Langby, but Langby was across town with Allen, trying to get the asbestos firemen's coats. I saw the name of the paper. It was *The Worker*. A Nazi newspaper?

November 2—I've been up on the roofs for a week straight, helping some incompetent workmen patch the hole the bomb made. They're doing a terrible job. There's still a great gap on one side a man could fall into, but they insist it'll be all right because, after all, you wouldn't fall clear through but only as far as the ceiling, and "the fall can't kill you." They don't seem to understand it's a perfect hiding place for an incendiary.

And that is all Langby needs. He does not even have to set a fire to destroy St. Paul's. All he needs to do is let one burn uncaught until it is too late.

I could not get anywhere with the workmen. I went down into the church to complain to Matthews, and saw Langby and his tourist behind a pillar, close to one of the windows. Langby was holding a newspaper and talking to the man. When I came down from the library an hour later, they were still there. So is the gap. Matthews says we'll put planks across it and hope for the best.

November 5—I have given up trying to retrieve. I am so far behind on my sleep I can't even retrieve information on a newspaper whose name I already know. Double watches the permanent thing now. Our chars have abandoned us altogether (like the cat), so the crypt is quiet, but I cannot sleep.

If I do manage to doze off, I dream. Yesterday I dreamed Kivrin was on the roofs, dressed like a saint. "What was the secret of your practicum?" I said. "What were you supposed to find out?"

She wiped her nose with a handkerchief and said, "Two things. One, that silence and humility are the sacred burdens of the historian. Two," she stopped and sneezed into the handkerchief. "Don't sleep in the tubes."

My only hope is to get hold of an artificial and induce a trance. That's a problem. I'm positive it's too early for chemical endorphins and probably hallucinogens. Alcohol is definitely available, but I need something more concentrated than ale, the only alcohol I know by name. I do not dare ask the watch. Langby is suspicious enough of me already. It's back to the *OED,* to look up a word I don't know.

November 11—The cat's back. Langby was out with Allen again, still trying for the asbestos coats, so I thought it was safe to leave St. Paul's. I went to the grocer's for supplies and hopefully, an artificial. It was late, and the sirens sounded before I had even gotten to Cheapside, but the raids do not usually start until after dark. It took awhile to get all the groceries and to get up my courage to ask whether he had any alcohol—he told me to go to a pub—and when I came out of the shop, it was as if I had pitched suddenly into a hole.

I had no idea where St. Paul's lay, or the street, or the shop I had just come from. I stood on what was no longer the sidewalk, clutching my brown-paper parcel of kippers and bread with a hand I could not have seen if I held it up before my face. I reached up to wrap my muffler closer about my neck and prayed for my eyes to adjust, but there was no reduced light to adjust to. I would have been glad of the moon, for all St. Paul's watch curses it and calls it a fifth columnist. Or a bus, with its shuttered headlights giving just enough light to orient myself by. Or a searchlight. Or the kickback flare of an ack-ack gun. Anything.

Just then I did see a bus, two narrow yellow slits a long way off. I started toward it and nearly pitched off the curb. Which meant the bus was sideways in the street, which meant it was not a bus. A cat meowed, quite near, and rubbed against my leg. I looked down into

CONNIE WILLIS

the yellow lights I had thought belonged to the bus. His eyes were picking up light from somewhere, though I would have sworn there was not a light for miles, and reflecting it flatly up at me.

"A warden'll get you for those lights, old tom," I said, and then as a plane droned overhead, "Or a jerry."

The world exploded suddenly into light, the searchlights and a glow along the Thames seeming to happen almost simultaneously, lighting my way home.

"Come to fetch me, did you, old tom?" I said gaily. "Where've you been? Knew we were out of kippers, didn't you? I call that loyalty." I talked to him all the way home and gave him half a tin of the kippers for saving my life. Bence-Jones said he smelled the milk at the grocer's.

November 13—I dreamed I was lost in the blackout. I could not see my hands in front of my face, and Dunworthy came and shone a pocket torch at me, but I could only see where I had come from and not where I was going.

"What good is that to them?" I said. "They need a light to show them where they're going."

"Even the light from the Thames? Even the light from the fires and the ack-ack guns?" Dunworthy said.

"Yes. Anything is better than this awful darkness." So he came closer to give me the pocket torch. It was not a pocket torch, after all, but Christ's lantern from the Hunt picture in the south nave. I shone it on the curb before me so I could find my way home, but it shone instead on the firewatch stone and I hastily put the light out.

November 20—I tried to talk to Langby today. "I've seen you talking to the old gentleman," I said. It sounded like an accusation. I meant it to. I wanted him to think it was and stop whatever he was planning.

"Reading," he said. "Not talking." He was putting things in order in the choir, piling up sandbags.

"I've seen you reading then," I said belligerently, and he dropped a sandbag and straightened.

"What of it?" he said. "It's a free country. I can read to an old man if I want, same as you can talk to that little WVS tart."

"What do you read?" I said.

"Whatever he wants. He's an old man. He used to come home from his job, have a bit of brandy and listen to his wife read the papers to him. She got killed in one of the raids. Now I read to him. I don't see what business it is of yours."

It sounded true. It didn't have the careful casualness of a lie, and I almost believed him, except that I had heard the tone of truth from him before. In the crypt. After the bomb.

"I thought he was a tourist looking for the Windmill," I said.

He looked blank only a second, and then he said, "Oh, yes, that. He came in with the paper and asked me to tell him where it was. I looked it up to find the address. Clever, that. I didn't guess he couldn't read it for himself." But it was enough. I knew that he was lying.

He heaved a sandbag almost at my feet. "Of course you wouldn't understand a thing like that, would you? A simple act of human kindness?"

"No," I said coldly. "I wouldn't."

None of this proves anything. He gave away nothing, except perhaps the name of an artificial, and I can hardly go to Dean Matthews and accuse Langby of reading aloud.

I waited till he had finished in the choir and gone down to the crypt. Then I lugged one of the sandbags up to the roof and over to the chasm. The planking has held so far, but everyone walks gingerly around it, as if it were a grave. I cut the sandbag open and spilled the loose sand into the bottom. If it has occurred to Langby that this is the perfect spot for an incendiary, perhaps the sand will smother it.

November 21—I gave Enola some of "uncle's" money today and asked her to get me the brandy. She was more reluctant than I thought she'd be so there must be societal complications I am not aware of, but she agreed.

I don't know what she came for. She started to tell me about her brother and some prank he'd pulled in the tubes that got him in trouble with the guard, but after I asked her about the brandy, she left without finishing the story.

November 25—Enola came today, but without bringing the brandy. She is going to Bath for the holidays to see her aunt. At least she will be away from the raids for awhile. I will not have to worry about her. She finished the story of her brother and told me she hopes to persuade this aunt to take Tom for the duration of the Blitz but is not at all sure the aunt will be willing.

Young Tom is apparently not so much an engaging scapegrace as a near-criminal. He has been caught twice picking pockets in the Bank tube shelter, and they have had to go back to Marble Arch. I comforted her as best I could, told her all boys were bad at one time or another. What I really wanted to say was that she needn't worry at all, that young Tom strikes me as a true survivor type, like my own tom, like Langby, totally unconcerned with anybody but himself, well-equipped to survive the Blitz and rise to prominence in the future.

Then I asked her whether she had gotten the brandy.

She looked down at her open-toed shoes and muttered unhappily, "I thought you'd forgotten all about that."

I made up some story about the watch taking turns buying a bottle, and she seemed less unhappy, but I am not convinced she will not use this trip to Bath as an excuse to do nothing. I will have to leave St. Paul's and buy it myself, and I don't dare leave Langby alone in the church. I made her promise to bring the brandy today before she leaves. But she is still not back, and the sirens have already gone.

November 26—No Enola, and she said their train left at noon. I suppose I should be grateful that at least she is safely out of London. Maybe in Bath she will be able to get over her cold.

Tonight one of the ARP girls breezed in to borrow half our cots and tell us about a mess over in the East End where a surface shelter was hit. Four dead, twelve wounded. "At least it wasn't one of the tube shelters!" she said. "Then you'd see a real mess, wouldn't you?"

November 30—I dreamed I took the cat to St. John's Wood.

"Is this a rescue mission?" Dunworthy said.

"No, sir," I said proudly. "I know what I was supposed to find in my practicum. The perfect survivor. Tough and resourceful and selfish. This is the only one I could find. I had to kill Langby, you know, to keep him from burning down St. Paul's. Enola's brother has gone to Bath, and the others will never make it. Enola wears open-toed shoes in the winter and sleeps in the tubes and puts her hair up on metal pins so it will curl. She cannot possibly survive the Blitz."

Dunworthy said, "Perhaps you should have rescued her instead. What did you say her name was?"

"Kivrin," I said, and woke up cold and shivering.

December 5—I dreamed Langby had the pinpoint bomb. He carried it under his arm like a brown-paper parcel, coming out of St.

Paul's Station and up Ludgate Hill to the west doors.

"This is not fair," I said, barring his way with my arm. "There is no fire watch on duty."

He clutched the bomb to his chest like a pillow. "That is your fault," he said, and before I could get to my stirrup pump and bucket, he tossed it in the door.

The pinpoint was not even invented until the end of the twentieth century, and it was another ten years before the dispossessed Communists got hold of it and turned it into something that could be carried under your arm. A parcel that could blow a quarter-mile of the City into oblivion. Thank God that is one dream that cannot come true.

It was a sunlit morning in the dream, and this morning when I came off watch the sun was shining for the first time in weeks. I went down to the crypt and then came up again, making the rounds of the roofs twice more, then the steps and the grounds and all the treacherous alleyways between where an incendiary could be missed. I felt better after that, but when I got to sleep I dreamed again, this time of fire and Langby watching it, smiling.

December 15—I found the cat this morning. Heavy raids last night, but most of them over towards Canning Town and nothing on the roofs to speak of. Nevertheless the cat was quite dead. I found him lying on the steps this morning when I made my own, private rounds. Concussion. There was not a mark on him anywhere except the white blackout patch on his throat, but when I picked him up, he was all jelly under the skin.

I could not think what to do with him. I thought for one mad moment of asking Matthews if I could bury him in the crypt. Honorable death in war or something. Trafalgar, Waterloo, London, died in battle. I ended by wrapping him in my muffler and taking him down Ludgate Hill to a building that had been bombed out and burying him in the rubble. It will do no good. The rubble will be no protection from dogs or rats, and I shall never get another muffler. I have gone through nearly all of uncle's money.

I should not be sitting here. I haven't checked the alleyways or the rest of the steps, and there might be a dud or a delayed incendiary or something that I missed.

When I came here, I thought of myself as the noble rescuer, the savior of the past. I am not doing very well at the job. At least Enola is out of it. I wish there were some way I could send St. Paul's to Bath for safekeeping. There were hardly any raids last night. Bence-

Jones said cats can survive anything. What if he was coming to get me, to show me the way home? All the bombs were over Canning Town.

December 16—Enola has been back a week. Seeing her, standing on the west steps where I found the cat, sleeping in Marble Arch and not safe at all, was more than I could absorb. "I thought you were in Bath," I said stupidly.

"My aunt said she'd take Tom but not me as well. She's got a houseful of evacuation children, and what a noisy lot. Where is your muffler?" she said. "It's dreadful cold up here on the hill."

"I . . ." I said, unable to answer, "I lost it."

"You'll never get another one," she said. "They're going to start rationing clothes. And wool, too. You'll never get another one like that."

"I know," I said, blinking at her.

"Good things just thrown away," she said. "It's absolutely criminal, that's what it is."

I don't think I said anything to that, just turned and walked away with my head down, looking for bombs and dead animals.

December 20—Langby isn't a Nazi. He's a Communist. I can hardly write this. A Communist.

One of the chars found *The Worker* wedged behind a pillar and brought it down to the crypt as we were coming off the first watch.

"Bloody Communists," Bence-Jones said. "Helping Hitler, they are. Talking against the king, stirring up trouble in the shelters. Traitors, that's what they are."

"They love England same as you," the char said.

"They don't love nobody but themselves, bloody selfish lot. I wouldn't be surprised to hear they were ringing Hitler up on the telephone," Bence-Jones said. " ' 'Ello, Adolf, here's where to drop the bombs.' "

The kettle on the gas ring whistled. The char stood up and poured the hot water into a chipped tea pot, then sat back down. "Just because they speak their minds don't mean they'd burn down old St. Paul's, does it now?"

"Of course not," Langby said, coming down the stairs. He sat down and pulled off his boots, stretching his feet in their wool socks. "Who wouldn't burn down St. Paul's?"

"The Communists," Bence-Jones said, looking straight at him, and I wondered if he suspected Langby, too.

Langby never batted an eye. "I wouldn't worry about them if I were you," he said. "It's the jerries that are doing their bloody best to burn her down tonight. Six incendiaries so far, and one almost went into that great hole over the choir." He held out his cup to the char, and she poured him a cup of tea.

I wanted to kill him, smashing him to dust and rubble on the floor of the crypt while Bence-Jones and the char looked on in helpless surprise, shouting warnings to them and the rest of the watch. "Do you know what the Communists did?" I wanted to shout. "Do you? We have to stop him." I even stood up and started toward him as he sat with his feet stretched out before him and his asbestos coat still over his shoulders.

And then the thought of the Gallery drenched in gold, the Communist coming out of the tube station with the package so casually under his arm, made me sick with the same staggering vertigo of guilt and helplessness, and I sat back down on the edge of my cot and tried to think what to do.

They do not realize the danger. Even Bence-Jones, for all his talk of traitors, thinks they are capable only of talking against the king. They do not know, cannot know, what the Communists will become. Stalin is an ally. Communists mean Russia. They have never heard of Karinsky or the New Russia or any of the things that will make "Communist" into a synonym for "monster." They will never know it. By the time the Communists become what they became, there will be no fire watch. Only I know what it means to hear the name "Communist" uttered here, so carelessly, in St. Paul's.

A Communist. I should have known. I should have known.

December 22—Double watches again. I have not had any sleep, and I am getting very unsteady on my feet. I nearly pitched into the chasm this morning, only saved myself by dropping to my knees. My endorphin levels are fluctuating wildly, and I know I must get some sleep soon or I will become one of Langby's walking dead; but I am afraid to leave him alone on the roofs, alone in the church with his Communist party leader, alone anywhere. I have taken to watching him when he sleeps.

If I could just get hold of an artificial, I think I could induce a trance, in spite of my poor condition. But I cannot even go out to a pub. Langby is on the roofs constantly, waiting for his chance. When Enola comes again, I must convince her to get the brandy for me. There are only a few days left.

December 28—Enola came this morning while I was on the west porch, picking up the Christmas tree. It has been knocked over three nights running by concussion. I righted the tree and was bending down to pick up the scattered tinsel when Enola appeared suddenly out of the fog like some cheerful saint. She stooped quickly and kissed me on the cheek. Then she straightened up, her nose red from her perennial cold, and handed me a box wrapped in colored paper.

"Merry Christmas," she said. "Go on then, open it. It's a gift."

My reflexes are almost totally gone. I knew the box was far too shallow for a bottle of brandy. Nevertheless, I believed she had remembered, had brought me my salvation. "You darling," I said, and tore it open.

It was a muffler. Gray wool. I stared at it for fully half a minute without realizing what it was. "Where's the brandy?" I said.

She looked shocked. Her nose got redder and her eyes started to blur. "You need this more. You haven't any clothing coupons and you have to be outside all the time. It's been so dreadful cold."

"I *needed* the brandy," I said angrily.

"I was only trying to be kind," she started, and I cut her off.

"Kind?" I said. "I asked you for brandy. I don't recall ever saying I needed a muffler." I shoved it back at her and began untangling a string of colored lights that had shattered when the tree fell.

She got that same holy martyr look Kivrin is so wonderful at. "I worry about you all the time up here," she said in a rush. "They're *trying* for St. Paul's, you know. And it's so close to the river. I didn't think you should be drinking. I . . . it's a crime when they're trying so hard to kill us all that you won't take care of yourself. It's like you're in it with them. I worry someday I'll come up to St. Paul's and you won't be here."

"Well, and what exactly am I supposed to do with a muffler? Hold it over my head when they drop the bombs?"

She turned and ran, disappearing into the gray fog before she had gone down two steps. I started after her, still holding the string of broken lights, tripped over it, and fell almost all the way to the bottom of the steps.

Langby picked me up. "You're off watches," he said grimly.

"You can't do that," I said.

"Oh, yes, I can. I don't want any walking dead on the roofs with me."

I let him lead me down here to the crypt, make me a cup of tea, put me to bed, all very solicitous. No indication that this is what he has been waiting for. I will lie here till the sirens go. Once I am on the roofs he will not be able to send me back without seeming suspicious. Do you know what he said before he left, asbestos coat and rubber boots, the dedicated fire watcher? "I want you to get some sleep." As if I could sleep with Langby on the roofs. I would be burned alive.

December 30—The sirens woke me, and old Bence-Jones said, "That should have done you some good. You've slept the clock round."

"What day is it?" I said, going for my boots.

"The twenty-ninth," he said, and as I dived for the door, "No need to hurry. They're late tonight. Maybe they won't come at all. That'd be a blessing, that would. The tide's out."

I stopped by the door to the stairs, holding onto the cool stone. "Is St. Paul's all right?"

"She's still standing," he said. "Have a bad dream?"

"Yes," I said, remembering the bad dreams of all the past

CONNIE WILLIS

weeks—the dead cat in my arms in St. John's Wood, Langby with his parcel and his *Worker* under his arm, the fire-watch stone garishly lit by Christ's lantern. Then I remembered I had not dreamed at all. I had slept the kind of sleep I had prayed for, the kind of sleep that would help me remember.

Then I remembered. Not St. Paul's, burned to the ground by the Communists. A headline from the dailies. "Marble Arch hit. Eighteen killed by blast." The date was not clear except for the year. 1940. There were exactly two more days left in 1940. I grabbed my coat and muffler and ran up the stairs and across the marble floor.

"Where the hell do you think you're going?" Langby shouted to me. I couldn't see him.

"I have to save Enola," I said, and my voice echoed in the dark sanctuary. "They're going to bomb Marble Arch."

"You can't leave now," he shouted after me, standing where the firewatch stone would be. "The tide's out. You dirty . . ."

I didn't hear the rest of it. I had already flung myself down the steps and into a taxi. It took almost all the money I had, the money I had so carefully hoarded for the trip back to St. John's Wood. Shelling started while we were still in Oxford Street, and the driver refused to go any farther. He let me out into pitch blackness, and I saw I would never make it in time.

Blast. Enola crumpled on the stairway down to the tube, her open-toed shoes still on her feet, not a mark on her. And when I try to lift her, jelly under the skin. I would have to wrap her in the muffler she gave me, because I was too late. I had gone back a hundred years to be too late to save her.

I ran the last blocks, guided by the gun emplacement that had to be in Hyde Park, and skidded down the steps into Marble Arch. The woman in the ticket booth took my last shilling for a ticket to St. Paul's Station. I stuck it in my pocket and raced toward the stairs.

"No running," she said placidly. "To your left, please." The door to the right was blocked off by wooden barricades, the metal gates beyond pulled to and chained. The board with names on it for the stations was X-ed with tape, and a new sign that read, "All trains," was nailed to the barricade, pointing left.

Enola was not on the stopped escalators or sitting against the wall in the hallway. I came to the first stairway and could not get through. A family had set out, just where I wanted to step, a communal tea of bread and butter, a little pot of jam sealed with waxed paper, and a kettle on a ring like the one Langby and I had rescued out of the rubble, all of it spread on a cloth embroidered at the corners with flowers. I stood staring down at the layered tea, spread like a waterfall down the steps.

"I . . . Marble Arch . . ." I said. Another twenty killed by flying tiles. "You shouldn't be here."

"We've as much right as anyone," the man said belligerently, "and who are you to tell us to move on?"

A woman lifting saucers out of a cardboard box looked up at me, frightened. The kettle began to whistle.

"It's you that should move on," the man said. "Go on then." He stood off to one side so I could pass. I edged past the embroidered cloth apologetically.

"I'm sorry," I said. "I'm looking for someone. On the platform."

"You'll never find her in there, mate," the man said, thumbing in that direction. I hurried past him, nearly stepping on the teacloth, and rounded the corner into hell.

It was not hell. Shopgirls folded coats and leaned back against them, cheerful or sullen or disagreeable, but certainly not damned. Two boys scuffled for a shilling and lost it on the tracks. They bent over the edge, debating whether to go after it, and the station guard yelled to them to back away. A train rumbled through, full of people. A mosquito landed on the guard's hand and he reached out to slap it and missed. The boys laughed. And behind and before them, stretching in all directions down the deadly tile curves of the tunnel like casualties, backed into the entrance-ways and onto the stairs, were people. Hundreds and hundreds of people.

I stumbled back into the hall, knocking over a teacup. It spilled like a flood across the cloth.

"I told you, mate," the man said cheerfully. "It's Hell in there, ain't it? And worse below."

"Hell," I said. "Yes." I would never find her. I would never save her. I looked at the woman mopping up the tea, and it came to me that I could not save her either. Enola or the cat or any of them, lost here in the endless stairways and cul-de-sacs of time. They were already dead a hundred years, past saving. The past is beyond saving. Surely that was the lesson the history department sent me all this way to learn. Well, fine, I've learned it. Can I go home now?

Of course not, dear boy. You have foolishly spent all your money on taxicabs and brandy, and tonight is the night the Germans burn the City. (Now it is too late, I remember it all. Twenty-eight incendiaries on the roofs.) Langby must have his chance, and you must learn the hardest lesson of all and the one you should have known from the beginning. You cannot save St. Paul's.

I went back out onto the platform and stood behind the yellow line until a train pulled up. I took my ticket out and held it in my hand all the way to St. Paul's Station. When I got there, smoke billowed toward me like an easy spray of water. I could not see St. Paul's.

"The tide's out," a woman said in a voice devoid of hope, and I went down in a snake pit of limp cloth hoses. My hands came up covered with rank-smelling mud, and I understood finally (and too late) the significance of the tide. There was no water to fight the fires.

A policeman barred my way and I stood helplessly before him with no idea what to say. "No civilians allowed up there," he said. "St. Paul's is for it." The smoke billowed like a thundercloud, alive with sparks, and the dome rose golden above it.

"I'm fire watch," I said, and his arm fell away, and then I was on the roofs.

My endorphin levels must have been going up and down like an air raid siren. I do not have any short-term from then on, just moments that do not fit together: the people in the church when we brought Langby down, huddled in a corner playing cards, the whirlwind of burning scraps of wood in the dome, the ambulance driver who wore open-toed shoes like Enola and smeared salve on my burned hands. And in the center, the one clear moment when I went after Langby on a rope and saved his life.

I stood by the dome, blinking against the smoke. The City was on fire and it seemed as if St. Paul's would ignite from the heat, would crumble from the noise alone. Bence-Jones was by the northwest tower, hitting at an incendiary with a spade. Langby was too close to the patched place where the bomb had gone through, looking toward me. An incendiary clattered behind him. I turned to grab a shovel, and when I turned back, he was gone.

"Langby!" I shouted, and could not hear my own voice. He had fallen into the chasm and nobody saw him or the incendiary. Except me. I do not remember how I got across the roof. I think I called for a rope. I got a rope. I tied it around my waist, gave the ends of it into the hands of the fire watch, and went over the side. The fires lit the walls of the hole almost all the way to the bottom. Below me I could see a pile of whitish rubble. He's under there, I thought, and jumped free of the wall. The space was so narrow there was nowhere to throw the rubble. I was afraid I would inadvertently stone him, and I tried to toss the pieces of planking and plaster over my shoulder, but there was barely room to turn. For one awful moment I thought he might not be there at all, that the pieces of splintered wood would brush away to reveal empty pavement, as they had in the crypt.

I was numbed by the indignity of crawling over him. If he was dead I did not think I could bear the shame of stepping on his helpless body. Then his hand came up like a ghost's and grabbed my ankle, and within seconds I had whirled and had his head free.

He was the ghastly white that no longer frightens me. "I put the bomb out," he said. I stared at him, so overwhelmed with relief I could not speak. For one hysterical moment I thought I would even laugh, I was so glad to see him. I finally realized what it was I was supposed to say.

"Are you all right?" I said.

"Yes," he said, and tried to raise himself on one elbow. "So much the worse for you."

He could not get up. He grunted with pain when he tried to shift his weight to his right side and lay back, the uneven rubble crunching sickeningly under him. I tried to lift him gently so I could see where he was hurt. He must have fallen on something.

"It's no use," he said, breathing hard. "I put it out."

I spared him a startled glance, afraid that he was delirious, and went back to rolling him onto his side.

"I know you were counting on this one," he went on, not resisting me at all. "It was bound to happen sooner or later with all these roofs. Only I went after it. What'll you tell your friends?"

His asbestos coat was torn down the back in a long gash. Under it his back was charred and smoking. He had fallen on the incendiary. "Oh, my God," I said, trying frantically to see how badly he was burned without touching him. I had no way of knowing how deep the burns went, but they seemed to extend only in the narrow space where the coat had torn. I tried to pull the bomb out from under him, but the casing was as hot as a stove. It was not melting, though. My sand and Langby's body had smothered it. I had no idea if it would start up again when it was exposed to the air. I looked around, a little wildly, for the bucket and stirrup pump Langby must have dropped when he fell.

"Looking for a weapon?" Langby said, so clearly it was hard to believe he was hurt at all. "Why not just leave me here? A bit of overexposure and I'd be done for by morning. Or would you rather do your dirty work in private?"

I stood up and yelled to the men on the roof above us. One of them shone a pocket torch down at us, but its light didn't reach.

CONNIE WILLIS

"Is he dead?" somebody shouted down to me.

"Send for an ambulance," I said. "He's been burned."

I helped Langby up, trying to support his back without touching the burn. He staggered a little and then leaned against the wall, watching me as I tried to bury the incendiary, using a piece of the planking as a scoop. The rope came down and I tied Langby to it. He had not spoken since I helped him up. He let me tie the rope around his waist, still looking steadily at me. "I should have let you smother in the crypt," he said.

He stood leaning easily, almost relaxed against the wood supports, his hands holding him up. I put his hands on the slack rope and wrapped it once around them for the grip I knew he didn't have. "I've been onto you since that day in the Gallery. I knew you weren't afraid of heights. You came down here without any fear of heights when you thought I'd ruined your precious plans. What was it? An attack of conscience? Kneeling there like a baby, whining, 'What have we done? What have we done?' You made me sick. But you know what gave you away first? The cat. Everybody knows cats hate water. Everybody but a dirty Nazi spy."

There was a tug on the rope. "Come ahead," I said, and the rope tautened.

"That WVS tart? Was she a spy, too? Supposed to meet you in Marble Arch? Telling me it was going to be bombed. You're a rotten spy, Bartholomew. Your friends already blew it up in September. It's open again."

The rope jerked suddenly and began to lift Langby. He twisted his hands to get a better grip. His right shoulder scraped the wall. I put up my hands and pushed him gently so that his left side was to the wall. "You're making a big mistake, you know," he said. "You should have killed me. I'll tell."

I stood in the darkness, waiting for the rope. Langby was unconscious when he reached the roof. I walked past the fire watch to the dome and down to the crypt.

This morning the letter from my uncle came and with it a ten-pound note.

December 31—Two of Dunworthy's flunkies met me in St. John's Wood to tell me I was late for my exams. I did not even protest. I shuffled obediently after them without even considering how unfair it was to give an exam to one of the walking dead. I had not slept in—how long? Since yesterday when I went to find Enola. I had not slept in a hundred years.

Dunworthy was at his desk, blinking at me. One of the flunkies handed me a test paper and the other one called time. I turned the paper over and left an oily smudge from the ointment on my burns. I stared uncomprehendingly at them. I had grabbed at the incendiary when I turned Langby over, but these burns were on the backs of my hands. The answer came to me suddenly in Langby's unyielding voice. "They're rope burns, you fool. Don't they teach you Nazi spies the proper way to come up a rope?"

I looked down at the test. It read, "Number of incendiaries that fell on St. Paul's. Number of land mines. Number of high explosive bombs. Method most commonly used for extinguishing incendiaries. Land mines. High explosive bombs. Number of volunteers on first watch. Second watch. Casualties. Fatalities." The questions made no sense. There was only a short space, long enough for the writing of a number, after any of the questions. Method most commonly used for extinguishing incendiaries. How would I ever fit what I knew into that narrow space? Where were the questions about Enola and Langby and the cat?

I went up to Dunworthy's desk. "St. Paul's almost burned down last night," I said. "What kind of questions are these?"

"You should be answering questions, Mr. Bartholomew, not asking them."

"There aren't any questions about the people," I said. The outer casing of my anger began to melt.

"Of course there are," Dunworthy said, flipping to the second page of the test. "Number of casualties, 1940. Blast, shrapnel, other."

"Other?" I said. At any moment the roof would collapse on me in a shower of plaster dust and fury. "Other? Langby put out a fire with his own body. Enola has a cold that keeps getting worse. The cat . . ." I snatched the paper back from him and scrawled "one cat" in the narrow space next to "blast." "Don't you care about them at all?"

"They're important from a statistical point of view," he said, "but as individuals, they are hardly relevant to the course of history."

My reflexes were shot. It was amazing to me that Dunworthy's were almost as slow. I grazed the side of his jaw and knocked his glasses off. "Of course they're relevant!" I shouted. "They *are* the history, not all these bloody numbers!"

The reflexes of the flunkies were very fast. They did not let me start another swing at him before they had me by both arms and were hauling me out of the room.

"They're back there in the past with nobody to save them. They

CONNIE WILLIS

can't see their hands in front of their faces and there are bombs falling down on them and you tell me they aren't important? You call that being an historian?"

The flunkies dragged me out the door and down the hall. "Langby saved St. Paul's. How much more important can a person get? You're no historian! You're nothing but a . . ." I wanted to call him a terrible name, but the only curses I could summon up were Langby's. "You're nothing but a dirty Nazi spy!" I bellowed. "You're nothing but a lazy bourgeois tart!"

They dumped me on my hands and knees outside the door and slammed it in my face. "I wouldn't be an historian if you paid me!" I shouted, and went to see the firewatch stone.

December 31—I am having to write this in bits and pieces. My hands are in pretty bad shape, and Dunworthy's boys didn't help matters much. Kivrin comes in periodically, wearing her St. Joan look, and smears so much salve on my hands that I can't hold a pencil.

St. Paul's Station is not there, of course, so I got out at Holborn and walked, thinking about my last meeting with Dean Matthews on the morning after the burning of the City. This morning.

"I understand you saved Langby's life," he said. "I also understand that between you, you saved St. Paul's last night."

I showed him the letter from my uncle and he stared at it as if he could not think what it was. "Nothing stays saved forever," he said, and for a terrible moment I thought he was going to tell me Langby had died. "We shall have to keep on saving St. Paul's until Hitler decides to bomb the countryside."

The raids on London are almost over, I wanted to tell him. He'll start bombing the countryside in a matter of weeks. Canterbury, Bath, aiming always at the cathedrals. You and St. Paul's will both outlast the war and live to dedicate the firewatch stone.

"I am hopeful, though," he said. "I think the worst is over."

"Yes, sir." I thought of the stone, its letters still readable after all this time. No, sir, the worst is not over.

I managed to keep my bearings almost to the top of Ludgate Hill. Then I lost my way completely, wandering about like a man in a graveyard. I had not remembered that the rubble looked so much like the white plaster dust Langby had tried to dig me out of. I could not find the stone anywhere. In the end I nearly fell over it, jumping back as if I had stepped on a grave.

It is all that's left. Hiroshima is supposed to have had a handful of untouched trees at ground zero, Denver the capitol steps. Neither of them says, "Remember the men and women of St. Paul's Watch who by the grace of God saved this cathedral." The grace of God.

Part of the stone is sheared off. Historians argue there was another line that said, "for all time", but I do not believe that, not if Dean Matthews had anything to do with it. And none of the watch it was dedicated to would have believed it for a minute. We saved St. Paul's every time we put out an incendiary, and only until the next one fell. Keeping watch on the danger spots, putting out the little fires with sand and stirrup pumps, the big ones with our bodies, in order to keep the whole vast complex structure from burning down. Which sounds to me like a course description for History Practicum 401. What a fine time to discover what historians are for when I have tossed my chance for being one out the windows as easily as they tossed the pinpoint bomb in! No, sir, the worst is not over.

There are flash burns on the stone, where legend says the Dean of St. Paul's was kneeling when the bomb went off. Totally apocryphal, of course, since the front door is hardly an appropriate place for prayers. It is more likely the shadow of a tourist who wandered in to ask the whereabouts of the Windmill Theatre, or the imprint of a girl bringing a volunteer his muffler. Or a cat.

Nothing is saved forever, Dean Matthews; and I knew that when I walked in the west doors that first day, blinking into the gloom, but it is pretty bad nevertheless. Standing here knee-deep in rubble out of which I will not be able to dig any folding chairs or friends, knowing that Langby died thinking I was a Nazi spy, knowing that Enola came one day and I wasn't there. It's pretty bad.

But it is not as bad as it could be. They are both dead, and Dean Matthews too; but they died without knowing what I knew all along, what sent me to my knees in the Whispering Gallery, sick with grief and guilt: that in the end none of us saved St. Paul's. And Langby cannot turn to me, stunned and sick at heart, and say, "Who did this? Your friends the Nazis?" And I would have to say, "No. The Communists." That would be the worst.

I have come back to the room and let Kivrin smear more salve on my hands. She wants me to get some sleep. I know I should pack and get gone. It will be humiliating to have them come and throw me out, but I do not have the strength to fight her. She looks so much like Enola.

January 1—I have apparently slept not only through the night, but through the morning mail drop as well. When I woke up just now, I found Kivrin sitting on the end of the bed holding an envelope. "Your grades came," she said.

I put my arm over my eyes. "They can be marvelously efficient when they want to, can't they?"

"Yes," Kivrin said.

"Well, let's see it," I said, sitting up. "How long do I have before they come and throw me out?"

She handed the flimsy computer envelope to me. I tore it along the perforation. "Wait," she said. "Before you open it, I want to say something." She put her hand gently on my burns. "You're wrong about the history department. They're very good."

It was not exactly what I expected her to say. "Good is not the word I'd use to describe Dunworthy," I said and yanked the inside slip free.

Kivrin's look did not change, not even when I sat there with the printout on my knees where she could surely see it.

"Well," I said.

The slip was hand-signed by the esteemed Dunworthy. I have taken a first. With honors.

January 2—Two things came in the mail today. One was Kivrin's assignment. The history department thinks of everything—even to keeping her here long enough to nursemaid me, even to coming up with a prefabricated trial by fire to send their history majors through.

I think I wanted to believe that was what they had done, Enola and Langby only hired actors, the cat a clever android with its clockwork innards taken out for the final effect, not so much because I wanted to believe Dunworthy was not good at all, but because then I would not have this nagging pain at not knowing what had happened to them.

"You said your practicum was England in 1300?" I said, watching her as suspiciously as I had watched Langby.

"1349," she said, and her face went slack with memory. "The plague year."

"My God," I said. "How could they do that? The plague's a ten."

"I have a natural immunity," she said, and looked at her hands.

Because I could not think of anything to say, I opened the other piece of mail. It was a report on Enola. Computer-printed, facts and dates and statistics, all the numbers the history department so dearly loves, but it told me what I thought I would have to go without knowing: that she had gotten over her cold and survived the Blitz.

Young Tom had been killed in the Baedaker raids on Bath, but Enola had lived until 2006, the year before they blew up St. Paul's.

I don't know whether I believe the report or not, but it does not matter. It is, like Langby's reading aloud to the old man, a simple act of human kindness. They think of everything.

Not quite. They did not tell me what happened to Langby. But I find as I write this that I already know: I saved his life. It does not seem to matter that he might have died in hospital next day; and I find, in spite of all the hard lessons the history department has tried to teach me, I do not quite believe this one: that nothing is saved forever. It seems to me that perhaps Langby is.

January 3—I went to see Dunworthy today. I don't know what I intended to say—some pompous drivel about my willingness to serve in the firewatch of history, standing guard against the falling incendiaries of the human heart, silent and saintly.

But he blinked at me nearsightedly across his desk, and it seemed to me that he was blinking at that last bright image of St. Paul's in sunlight before it was gone forever and that he knew better than anyone that the past cannot be saved, and I said instead, "I'm sorry that I broke your glasses, sir."

"How did you like St. Paul's?" he said, and like my first meeting with Enola, I felt I must be somehow reading the signals all wrong, that he was not feeling loss, but something quite different.

"I loved it, sir," I said.

"Yes," he said. "So do I."

Dean Matthews is wrong. I have fought with memory my whole practicum only to find that it is not the enemy at all, and being an historian is not some saintly burden after all. Because Dunworthy is not blinking against the fatal sunlight of the last morning, but into the gloom of that first afternoon, looking in the great west doors of St. Paul's at what is, like Langby, like all of it, every moment, in us, saved forever.

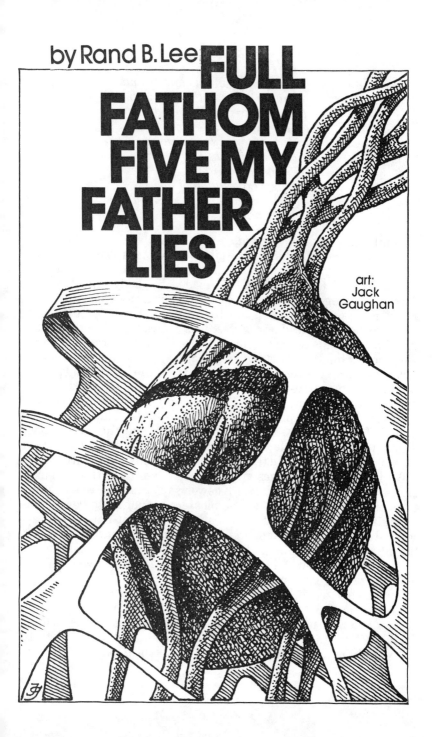

by Rand B. Lee

FULL FATHOM FIVE MY FATHER LIES

art:
Jack
Gaughan

Mr. Lee is 31 and lives in Key West,
where he sponges off his family and
grows tomatoes organically in containers.
His father, Manfred B. Lee, co-authored
the Ellery Queen detective novels
with Frederick Dannay. The author wrote
this story on a dull office day
in St. Louis; he did not have the
slightest expectation of it ever
seeing print. It was his first SF sale.

I buried my father at dawn, in the deep place beyond the reef, where the water sinks down until its blue becomes so black that the creatures living there have no word for light within them. My son Porran helped me bury him. We loaded his body onto the boat, Porran weeping, I not. We pushed the boat away from the shore. We paddled with our hands until we reached the hole in the grey reef's girdle, then used our staves. It is difficult to pass the reef at any time, but it is especially difficult in the early morning. Porran used the flat blade of his stave, *slap, slap!*, against the somber water, *slap, slap!* like Greeter's hands at the Gate of the Newborn. I pushed against the guardian-weed with my stave. For a moment the green tubes resisted. Porran slapped the harder, crying, "Would you hinder the dead?" in his deep voice. The watchers on the shore heard and sighed. The weed heard as well. It relaxed, and the boat slipped through the sudden hole in the girdle and out the other side, where the water lay bloody with the early morning and underneath, black.

We laid down our staves and resumed paddling with our hands. There was no more weed. Sea-Knower says that the weed cannot grow outside the reef just as the ploaters cannot mate beyond the springtime. It was because Sea-Father and Plant-Father had appointed the weed guardian, and a guardian does not leave its post. I think rather it may be that the water is too deep beyond the reef for the weed to grow; I do not say this. I am Plant-Knower, but the sea changes things. Perhaps Sea-Knower is right.

My father's grave is eighty strokes of the arm straight out from the reef-hole, fourteen strokes of the arm to the right of the reef-hole as a man's back is turned. I counted aloud, which is the custom. Porran, whose task it was to witness the counting so proper testimony could be given Death-Knower later, kept making small suppressed weeping sounds which distracted me. Once I nearly lost count. When we reached the place I stopped counting.

We worked quickly, for it is cold outside the reef in Ploatermonth and of course we wore no clothing. Porran handed to me my father's stave. Our hands met briefly on its smoothness, its wood that does not grow. It looked different in the dawn. Before this morning, I had seen it only once in the open, away from the shadows of the lodge-wall where it had always hung. I took it from Porran and raised it high, resting its base between my thighs and pointing its shaft toward the low red sun. I thought as I noticed the sun, *Bad weather today.* It is strange what people think when they are drowning.

To my father I said, "To Sky-Father, O my father, to Earth-Father, O my father, to Sea-Father, O my father, to these make your way."

"Through the dark make your way," said Porran at my side.

That is all there is. I wished for more as I sat there with my father's stave between my thighs, but I could think of nothing more, and after a time Porran whispered, "Hurry," so I lowered the stave and placed it in the boat. My own stave I took and placed upon my father's chest and belly. Porran tied it to him with ropes. I looked upon his face and the need to say something pressed against my temples. Instead I took his head and kissed his eyes and then his mouth.

"Hurry," whispered Porran.

Hating him, I put my hands under my father's shoulders. Porran had already grasped his legs. Slowly we lowered him over the side of the boat. The water touched his buttocks, pooled at his groin. He was bone against it. We let go of him and he sank. At once we turned away our eyes, for it is not lucky to view the beginnings of another's journey, especially the journey that is the last. We waited until we were certain that enough time had passed for him to have journeyed beyond reach of the light; then I glanced at the grave. Its surface was a lodge-wall, and there was nothing in its depths.

We paddled back to the shore. Again the slap of the paddle, only this time it was I who beat the guardians, to let them know that the stave of my father had returned as the stave of his son. The weed resisted us only a little, the warming sun having softened it. By noon it would be flaccid as the brittle-leaf we use to scour our pots. We passed through the reef-hole and made our way in the red dawn toward the ones who waited on the bank.

I did not behave well. I walked past Death-Knower's comfort, past all the faces and the hands, with Porran at my heels urging me to stop. My father's stave I held on my shoulder, and it was as heavy as Earth-Father on Sky-Father's back. Not only did I not speak, I did not weep. When I came to the lodge I replaced my father's stave in its cleft, and I stood gazing upon it. Porran stood dark in the doorway.

"You are a shame to me," he said.

"I am sorry," I said. I did not turn to him. His feet scratched on the floor. He pressed his body against mine, from behind. He did not dare to place his hands upon me, but rested his chin on my shoulder. We stood in this way while I gazed upon my father's stave until something that had curled up within me uncurled. I found myself weak as a ploater-chick, weak as drizzle. I sat down on the floor of the lodge and beat my head against the hearth-stone and shrieked.

My father had told me what it had been like for him to lose his father, in the landslide before I had outgrown the Pool. In the worst agonies of my nights I had never imagined it to be as difficult as it was for me that morning. I heard the others enter the lodge, their hard feet; I heard them settle, and knew that they were seating themselves in semi-circle behind me; I heard my voice, rising and breaking and falling and rising; I even heard the ploaters calling to one another outside. I saw nothing and felt nothing but anger. I had never been so angry. My father had described it as a burning. It was worse, for a flame burns until its fuel is consumed. This needed no fuel.

It was loathsome. I thought it would not end. It did, of course. It ebbed, then withdrew in a rush, like the tide. I felt myself, like the sands uncovered by the tide, littered with stinking, detestable things. So close as to have been at my side, a ploater scolded his child. I began to weep. A glad sound passed through the others, a breaking of tension. My weeping was quiet. Porran came over and knelt directly behind me. He put his arms around me and laid his chin on my hair. I reached up and gripped his hands. "Now you are not a shame to me," he whispered.

Death-Knower was before me in the dimness. I let go of Porran's hands; he kept his arms around me. I looked up at Death-Knower. Above his sandy flank, beyond the farrow-hide skirt and the necklace of ploater-skulls, above his pale beard, his eyes stood. I felt fear. "Forgive me," I said. He spoke not to me but to Porran.

"Was the grave well-found?" he asked. His voice was the voice of the lightless shoals. Porran's arms tightened.

"It was well-found," he said. "Eighty strokes and fourteen."

Death-Knower grunted. His eyes held mine. I became aware of

RAND B. LEE

the closeness of his body. The smell of him, old, and the small brown smell of the farrow skins, came to me. All at once I knew he would not curse me. My father and he had been young together. I said to him, "It was well-found." He held my gaze a moment longer, then blinked, then nodded. Squatting, he reached for me; Porran nearly fell in his haste to escape Death-Knower's touch. The old one embraced me, very strong. We swayed, and the semi-circle of watchers swayed also.

Song-Knower began to sing a song of Fathers. We joined our voices to his, filling the lodge. It is strange, this song; it is the most strange to me of all their songs. Perhaps it is how the voice must form the tune, how it must pace like an old man restless for death-journey. Song-Knower, who knows as much about the hidden things of the First Fathers as Pool-Knower, says that this song is the only song that remains from the time before the Exile, when the First Fathers began their long crawl up Sky-Father's spine. It is a song a son sings sitting in his boat near his father's grave.

> "Full fathom five my father lies," sang Song-Knower,
> "Of his bones are coral made;
> Those are pearls that were his eyes,
> Nothing of him that doth fade
>   but doth suffer a sea-change
> Into something rich and strange.
> Sea-bells hourly ring his knell;
> Hark, now I hear them; hark, now I hear them;
> Ding, dong, bell."

And we sang:

> "Ding dong, ding, dong, bell;
> Ding dong, ding, dong, bell;
> Ding, dong, ding, dong, bell."

There are many words in the songs we do not understand, but we understand *sea,* and how it changes those who descend into it.

Afterward we all sat together, under my father's stave, only it was not my father's stave any longer; it was mine. I talked of how my father had lived and how he had died. The others said the usual things. Porran sat close, thinking of my death. When it came his turn to speak, he said, "He-who-journeys planted for me a scion of the blue earlyvine that bloomed near the cave. Today it flowers for the first time near our lodge."

They murmured and nodded: *A smile from Plant-Father.* I was not grateful. The anger had left, and the weeping had cleansed me of the stinking things, and the song of Fathers had steadied me, but still there was a wrongness. Outside, the wind had changed, and there was a warning note in the calls of the ploaters.

Finally Death-Knower said, "It is well." He rose; we all looked up at him. "He-who-journeys is far beyond the reach of evil. As yet we are not. The storm that comes must be prepared for." Alone, for of course the Death-Knower has no son, he passed from among us and the lodge door opened. We did not turn until we heard the door close. Immediately the others rose, some stretching, some conversing. They were kind. They spoke to me and to Porran, each of them, Sea-Knower and his son; Sand-Knower and his son; Net-Knower and his son who had lost an eye, and all the rest. Some touched me on the shoulder as they departed. I smiled but I did not rise, nor did Porran. When all of them had gone, still we sat.

My father's stave hung in silence. I looked at my son: he was tense; his shoulders bunched in little hills. My father and he had been close. I said, "I know. It is as though someone had stolen the hearth from the lodge. Though it were summer, and there were no need for fire to warm us, still we would feel robbed."

"Yes," he said, deep in his throat like me.

"It is as hard for me, my son."

"I understand," he said. Of course he did not understand. He will not understand until he and his son lower me into the darkness beyond the reef with his stave strapped to my chest and belly.

I said, "We must go now to the Pool."

I took his hand and rose; his arm went with me, his body did not. Then it did. We walked outside. There were many clouds, and a wet smell to the air. Although the morning had far advanced, it was as dark as it had been at dawn. My stave I carried on my shoulder. Those who saw us glanced away, obeying the custom. It is said that the gods hid their faces and wept when the First Fathers turned their backs toward Exile, and that is why we do not look upon the faces of those who journey. We walked over the sand between the lodges and out of the village.

The Pool lies in the white lodge at the edge of the inlet. Porran tensed when we came within sight of it, for of course he had never been there. I had been there, once. It looked the same. Ploaters shrilled, and farrows scattered at the sound of our feet on the hard path. Pool-Knower Morras and his son Yavan were waiting for us at the entrance to the lodge. Morras raised his stave. "Who are you that approach?" he demanded.

When I had last been to the lodge, it had been his father who had challenged my father, and he who had stood to his father's left, watching politely.

"It is Jun Plant-Knower," I replied formally, "with Porran his son."

"Proffer your staves." We did this. Morras made a show of examining them, although he could tell at a glance by the symbols painted on them to whom they belonged. I grew impatient; the wind was rising, tossing Porran's black hair. Finally he said, "Pool-Knower greets Plant-Knower and his son. The Pool is prepared. It is well?"

"It is," I said.

"It is," said Porran, slowly. I glanced at him. His face was guarded. Morras's son Yavan was looking at him. I remembered how nervous I had felt with my father. Morras stepped aside, clearing the entrance to the lodge. I stepped forward, Porran trailing. The door to the lodge moved aside. I entered; Porran followed. I turned to help him, to guide him before me; I saw Yavan's expression, like disease. Morras came after us and closed the door behind him, shutting out his son.

It was exactly the same. The Pool lay in the white glow as though it were expecting something. The time-weed had not grown, or perhaps it had been trimmed; the Pool-Knowers do not tell. We passed the high banks and the god-letters only Pool-Knowers can read. We came to the edge. The clear shell that protected the surface of the Pool was open. We stood together as fathers and sons have always stood. I squatted and touched the surface of the Pool with my stave. Ripples sprang out. The time-weed reacted instantly, opening its scores of little mouths. I laughed and looked up at my son. He was not laughing. "It is not a deep pool," I said.

"It is there I will lie?"

"Yes," I said. "There is nothing to fear." I lifted my stave and touched his chest with its dripping end. His chest was hard, like the stalks of the guardian-weed at night when the reef cannot be passed. His skin shivered as the liquid from the Pool dripped upon it. "We are the same," I said. It was foolish, like saying that ploaters fly, but it meant a great deal to me then to say it. "Like my father and I, we are the same, you and I; and we belong the one to the other."

Behind us, Morras moved swiftly, doing things among the banks and god-letters. He moved like his father.

"Always the same," said Porran. He squatted. He placed his hand on my knee. I reached over and placed my palm full on his chest to feel the heart beating. His eyes were intent, serious. "Why are we always the same?"

I thought of my father's heart, buried in the dark. "Ask rather," I answered softly, "why the scion of the earlyvine is the same as the plant from which it is cut."

"The ploaters are not always the same," Porran said. "A ploater comes from the egg. The egg comes from the body of his father. Yet he has two fathers, and he is not like the father from whom the egg comes, nor is he like the other father, but he is like both of them. Why?"

It was the time for such discussions. I said, "The ploaters have no Pool. For the ploater-father to make a son he needs more strength than is in himself alone, so he must seek out another ploater, and together they are strong enough. It is not so with us. People have the Pool. It takes a man's strength and his flesh and from it gives him a son in his likeness."

Porran stared at the surface of the Pool, as though it were an enemy, as though he had not come from it in his little sack, dripping and squalling in the grasp of Pool-Knower. Among the time-weed there was a movement. I pointed. "See," I said, "the time-weed has woven already the birth-sack for your son." Longing for my father came sharp as an arrow. I put aside the stave and gripped Porran's shoulders with my hands and closed my eyes. He put his hand on my head and stroked my hair, hesitantly. I thought of Song-Knower's song, and the water invading my father's groin. I stood up, pulling him.

It was time. I placed my hand at the small of my son's back and ran my fingers up his spine. He shivered; his grip on my hair tightened. It is where the two of us like to be touched. I held him against me, his thighs inside mine. I rubbed my beard against his. The hair of our chests mingled, and his breath came quickly. I dropped my hands to his buttocks and touched where a father may not touch a son until Poolday, and as I touched him I felt my father's touch again, and passion awoke within me.

Then he pulled away. "Father," he said. Behind him, near the god-lettered wall, Morras stood motionless, his back to us. "Father, stop."

"Do not be afraid, Porran," I said. "I will be kind, and the pain is quickly forgotten. Then you will go into the Pool and sleep. Come." I reached for him. He drew away.

"Father," Porran said, "I do not wish this."

"What?" I said. I do not know what was in my face, but it unnerved him. He took a stop toward me.

"I do not wish to lie with you in this way."

"But it is your Poolday," I said. "Are you afraid? The pain is for a moment, and there is much pleasure; we are one, and afterwards I will put you into the Pool, where you will sleep. The Pool is kind: it feeds you. You awaken to the face of Pool-Knower, to my face, to the walls of your lodge. The Pool will have made your son; it will guard him; he will grow; Pool-Knower will come to us on the day and say, 'He is born.' "

"I did not wish to say it at the lodge, with the others near." I glanced for Morras; I could not find him. "Father, listen. It is another I wish to be united with me. It is another I wish to have with me, to lower me into the Pool for the making of my son."

Clearly I heard his words and did not want them. "What is the matter with you?" I said. "My father is dead; you have no son; you have me. With whom could you wish to lie if not with your father? We are the same." I spoke as an adult to a child. When he spoke, his tone was the same.

"Try to understand," he said. "I have already lain with another in the Poolday way, and it was good."

I could not bear it. I retched, moving quickly so as not to foul the Pool. When I see Death-Father I will not be more filled with horror than I was at that moment. I wiped my mouth with the back of my hand, twin to my son's hand, twin to my father's hand, twin to his father's hand. Morras had moved; I heard a noise behind me, and seeing Porran's eyes, I turned. Yavan son of Morras stood near the entrance to the lodge, watching. The secret times came back to me then, my glimpses of Porran and Yavan, running out of the forest, sitting down at the shore the both of them, close and talking low. "Are you a farrow, which spreads its legs for any creature?" I said. Porran said nothing. I struck him across the mouth. His head snapped to one side; he held it there.

I reached and took hold of his chin and turned his face toward mine. "We are the same," I said. It was all I could do to touch him. "You cannot lie with another. I alone have the right of lowering you into the Pool. It is for fathers and sons. Would you break the stave of he-who-journeys?"

"I love you," Porran said. "You pleasure me. You care for me. But it is Yavan I want." He said it, and his eyes were the eyes of another.

I snatched up my stave and turned toward the son of Morras. He disappeared. His father stood where he had stood, backed by the god-letters. I raised my arms and shook them, helpless. There had been other instances, a very few. I turned back to Porran. "I will lower you into the Pool," I said. "If you do not go of your own will, I will make you go. Otherwise our sameness will be a lie, and our house will be filthied, and I will have no one to send me out on the long journey."

"That is all that concerns you," Porran said, with contempt.

"My father lowered me into the Pool," I said desperately. "Together we went to the white lodge when the tide was out. We lay together and united. He sang to me the Song of the Time. He lowered me with his strength into the Pool, and the time-weed bore me up; the dreams came, and then you." I was shaking, as was my son, both of us in the paleness with the storm, I realized, shaking the trees outside. The Pool's water was unruffled.

"You are selfish," said my son, "and you are old in your spirit." He pointed to Pool-Knower. "Ask Morras. Ask Yavan. They know. Sons should not have to stay with fathers, and fathers with sons. It is a custom that means nothing. The Pool does the begetting; it does not need two, only one it needs. Each may be joined to whom he wishes, and sons will be made all the same."

But we are the same, I said, only I did not say it. It was no longer light in the lodge. It seemed as black as the dark below the reef. Porran stood as tall as I. His voice was triumphant, and sad. He turned and walked past me and joined Yavan and Morras; together the three of them left the lodge. I stayed where I was. The storm roared. The rain came, and tapped the walls and ceiling.

My father was there, his stave weighing down my shoulder. He looked at me, his mouth open, shouting. I heard nothing. There was sea-weed in his beard.

I went out into the rain. It was like night. People scurried about, driving workbeasts and children to shelter. This surprised me; I had thought the storm to have been raging for many hours. I stopped the first man who came close, Tom son of Tom. "Have you seen my son?" I asked him. Thunder struck us. He shook his head; I moved on. I questioned each person I met, and each time the answer was the same. I began to feel that they were not speaking the truth, that the whole village knew and was glad. I continued, fighting the wind. I was still naked from the burial. The rain gathered on my chest and sluiced down my abdomen.

I had reached the lodge of Pool-Knower before I realized that that was where I had been heading. The door was shut tightly, as of course it ought to have been, given the storm. I hammered upon it with my fist. It slid open. Morras stood before me with the light of a fire behind him. In his hand he held his stave, pointed at me as though it were a knife that could cut me. His face was dead. He said, "Go away. Your son is not here."

"Fathers belong to sons, sons to fathers," I said to him. "Always. Always. Your father said this to me before my father lowered me into the Pool. It is a good teaching. With it, each one has another; there is meaning to our sameness, and no sorrow."

"Go away," Morras said.

"Where are they?" I asked.

"They have gone," he said. He was weeping. "My son also is gone, not yours alone."

"Where have they gone?" I asked.

"Jun," said Morras. He spread his hands, stave resting on the palms. "Have you never wished for any but your son?"

"It is one thing to wish," I said. "Where have they gone?"

The storm bellowed. A gust of wind blew rain against my back and spattered it on the floor about Morras' feet. Morras looked at me and said, "It is true, what Porran said. You are old in spirit. Go away." The door slid shut.

I turned from the lodge and held my stave close to me. The wood of it was hard and old, like the wood of which the lodges are fashioned, wood that does not burn and has no grain. Where it is found and how it is fashioned no man knows; this is wisdom of the First Fathers, and dead along the way. Unlike a lodge, a stave may be lost; therefore we hold them rarely, and rarely take them from the lodges. From the First Fathers the staves have been handed down, from father to son. On the day a son is taken from the Pool his father cuts for him from the forest a stave of common wood. It is his stave until his father dies; then he straps it to his father's body and takes his father's stave for his own.

Now Porran and Yavan will act as father and son, I thought, *and all will change.*

Therefore I knew I would have to kill Yavan son of Morras. I stumbled in the rain and wind, moving for my lodge. The killing of a person is something that only Death-Knower may do, and that only when no healing may be found, as when a man must burn a whiteberry bush that has the rot. In the time of the Sixth Fathers, the son of Sand-Knower and the son of Beast-Knower had sought a joining. When this was discovered, the Fathers had gathered, pronounced them diseased, and when they had refused to turn from their way, Death-Knower had drowned them. They are buried in the earth under the green mound at the western edge of the forest, out of sight of the sea. Now I thought, *I must go to Death-Knower; I must go to the Fathers.* But another thought came to me, that with Pool-Knower's word against me, vengeance would not be taken.

I see now that a madness was upon me, come of sorrow and pain. I could not reason, and I moved again to the lodge of Morras.

When he opened the door I hit him with my stave. He was surprised; he fell, and his cry was lost in the storm. I closed the door and sat on him. With my stave I pressed upon his neck until his face grew red. Then I said, "You will tell me where your son has gone."

"First Place," he said. He pulled at my arms, but I am stronger than Morras.

"By which path?" I asked.

"The oldest path," he said.

I must have struck him, for when I next knew reason I was standing with blood on my stave and Morras limp on the floor. His breathing was sure and the bleeding spare; I turned and left the lodge, closing the door. My mind was clear. I ran to my lodge. Everything was as I had left it when I had set out with Porran for the Pool. *He has been planning this,* I thought, *else the stores would have been lessened.* I took some of the dry pulse and the fish-chew, placed it in my bag, strapped my stave to my back, and set out into the rain. The oldest path lies to the west, and leads past the green mound. It is not forbidden, but it is avoided, as it is unlike all other paths, as the Place is unlike all other places. Neither is sought often. So I knew that was indeed where Porran and Yavan had gone.

I turned my back on the sea and the wind pushed me out of the village.

My father visited me three times that day and night. I am not given to visions; that is for Song-Knower. Yet I do not doubt that it was my father who came to me, and not merely memory made wild-edged by grief, as in the white lodge. The first time he came to me it was as I toiled over the roughs, above the thornfruit plantings. The paths begins there, marked with a post of the wood that does not burn. I had had the post in view for some time, but the wind had shifted, and I was fighting it again. I caught a gleam of white in the rocks; I bent to it. It was a shell, marked with the mark of the Pool-Knowers, a talisman or a keepsake of the son of Morras. I put it in my bag; I do not know why. When I looked for the post again I saw my father. He was huge and young, as I remember him from my childhood, and there was a light about him. In his hand he carried a bunch of earlyvine, flower, tendril, and root whipping

RAND B. LEE

in the wind. He was naked. "He said, "My son, do not forget the law of the scion." He vanished, as visions do. I continued, reached the post, and climbed up a boulder to the oldest path.

The oldest path is fashioned of the same wood as the lodges, and like the lodges it does not weather. It stands above the ground the height of a man, and walking upon it one may look down at the land divided on either side. Fence-Knower says that it is not a path, but a wall, yet it has always been called a path, and it could be a barrier only to children and farrows. It is cool to the feet. I began to run, crouching nearly so as less to catch the wind; I moved in this way until the roughs smoothed out and fieldgrass lapped the base of the path. I stopped to rest, lying prone in the middle of the path. The storm roared around me like a father-beast protecting me, his son. I realized that my madness was passing; I no longer felt the village and the storm to be my enemies. But there was Yavan, and his father Morras; so I got up and went on.

I do not know how long I traveled before my father came to me again, but it must have been no little time, for dark not of the storm had begun to come into the sky. The path makes a wide curve toward the forest, not a straight line, so the grassland was still about me when I stopped. My father was standing in the path, like any man. The light was gone. He came up to me and put his arms around me. Our nakednesses met. I put my head on his chest; he held me. The storm continued, but it seemed not to reach us. I felt his hand on my hair, stroking it as Porran strokes it. "Father," I said. He raised my chin and kissed me; then he looked into my eyes. I could not bear his gaze; I lowered my head and clung to him, fiercely. He kissed my cheek, and his breath warmed my ear.

He said, "Jun, it is not Yavan you must kill."

Then he was gone, as before. I stood trembling. The storm had lessened in intensity, but still I stumbled as I walked on.

I reached the green mound about the middle of the first part of the night. By that time the storm had subsided, leaving wet sighing grass and a clear breeze behind it. The sky was yet overcast, and the moons were veiled. The mound rose to the left in a sudden hump. It seemed too old to be repulsive; its owners too long dead to inspire scorn. I wondered at the change in my feelings. I remembered, as a boy, calling Ren son of the old Net-Knower "stupid as a Mounder," and stinging him to tears. My father had punished me. Now I looked at the mound and felt ashamed. *They wished one another, those two,* I thought. *Surely they could not have wished to wish. Surely they were ashamed, but could not leave off. Not even while they breathed in the sea.* I thought of Porran, loving me and wanting Yavan. *What lack of care did you find with me, my son?* I thought, as fathers always think when their children betray them. Then I saw what I had been seeing and not recognizing: two figures, flat in the grass against the top of the mound.

At first I did not know it was a vision. I saw Yavan and Porran, lying together in the grass of the mound. I shouted and brandished my stave. They did not look up, and then I knew it to be a vision, for it was as though I were with them on the mound, watching a short way off. They were united, limbs strong in the patched dark of the afterstorm; I heard Porran gasp, and Yavan groan. They shifted, bending grass, turning their faces to the sky in joy. They were no longer Porran and Yavan. They were my father and the father of Morras. In horror I cried out, reaching; I saw my arm grown pale, and felt the touch of farrow-skulls at my chest. I moved forward; they did not know that I was there. I came up behind them and caught them by the hair of their heads. I yanked, forcing their gazes to meet mine. They lay frozen, coupled, terrified, my father and the father of Morras.

The grass moved and flowed, like water. I took them and pushed them beneath it and held them. They struggled, but they were caught in their coupling. I saw my father's face shining pale, his mouth open, tongue distended; I laughed, and pushed him further down into the deep grass. The grass sucked at my wrists; I withdrew them, emptyhanded. They had disappeared, the two, and I stood on the oldest path, sick.

At dawn I came to the First Place, and found my son.

It is in the woods and it is surrounded by a wall that is made of stones. The path stops a distance from the wall, which is broken in many places and overgrown with forest things. Newborns are taken here. Pool-Knower stands within the circle of the walls and the father stands outside the circle of the walls. Song-Knower sings, and the child is handed through the wall to the father. One of the people, close friend to the father, acts as Greeter, and claps his hands, *clap, clap!* while the child is passed through. It is the only time the First Place is used for anything by people, unless they are fleeing. Why the First Place is not forbidden I do not know, for it is a holy place, the very oldest. It is here that the First Fathers came to rest when Sky-Father set them down. But there is nothing remarkable here, save for the ruined wall, which is not as old as the Place or the path, and within the wall, forest litter.

I dropped from the wall to the forest floor and immediately caught sight of Yavan. He was standing like his father at the Gate of the Newborn. The early light caught his hair, making it soft in the shadow. I could not see his face clearly. He said, "Porran," without turning, and in a moment my son joined him at the Gate. They stood together, so different. I thought of the two I had drowned. I said, "Why have you done this? Why have you gone the way of the Mounders when you have your fathers?"

"It is the way it should be," said Yavan.

"No," I said, gripping my stave. "Never has it been this way. You break the staves of your fathers and tread them into the mud."

"Do you hear him?" the son of Morras said to my son. "Tell him."

And Porran said, "You are wrong, Father. Your way is false. The way of the First Fathers was ours."

I stood stunned. "That is not true," I said.

"It is true," said the son of Morras. "I know. We found it written in the god-letters."

"The god-letters," I said. "The letters in the white lodge?"

"You know nothing," Yavan said. "You do not even know that there are other letters, many of them, carved into wood that does not burn, in the secret places beneath the Pool."

"It is true, Father," Porran said. "Yavan has showed me."

"He is lying about what he reads," I said. My son stood, staunch. "He is lying. The father of Morras himself told me that fathers and sons are meant for one another, and that any other way is diseased. Why would Pool-Knower say this if it were false?"

"He did not know," Yavan said. "My father found them."

"Found them?"

"Pool-Knowers are men only, Plant-Knower," said the son of Morras scornfully. "They do not see all or understand all. The First Fathers made the white lodge the strongest of all the lodges. The Pool is our life; without it, we could have no sons. So it is well-protected. Therefore within the lodge the Fathers placed that which they did not wish lost to time or accident. Among these things were the writings that Morras my father found."

"Mounder writings!" I spat in the shadow. Porran looked stricken, which pleased me.

Yavan shook his fist. "Mounder writings, then, yes!" To Porran he said, "I told you. It is no use. He will never believe us."

"He is my father, Yavan," Porran snapped. Yavan thrust my son behind him and stepped closer to me, large in his anger.

"Listen, Plant-Knower," he said. "Time passes. Things are forgotten. What the First Fathers made and understood, the Third

Fathers made and did not understand. Things were written, so people would not forget, but letters do not cry out with voices; they can be shut away where none may read. My father and I, we do what must be done in the white lodge to keep the time-weed from failing and the Pool from drying, but we do not understand what we do, Plant-Knower. We do what we are told. In the god-letters."

I could not reply. I heard Yavan say, "Pool-Father knew his sons' sons would forget, so you see that he was wise to have had written for us the things we need to know for our lives. And among these things is the truth about fathers and sons."

"And what is your truth?" I asked.

Porran answered, stepping forward again, his words an eager rush, eyes glinting. "They came from far away," he said. "The gods exiled them. They were like the workbeasts, Father. They had no strength to make sons alone. They joined with others. Some gave strength, others received strength, and adding to it their own strength bore sons within them."

"Like ploaters," I said. "Laying eggs."

"The bearing-Fathers were lost on the journey. The others were alone in the sea of the sky. Without the bearers, there could be no sons. It was then that they built the Pool."

"In the sea of the sky they built a Pool?" I asked. I laughed. Porran's face darkened.

"It is true," said Yavan. "There were Pools already, for small beasts they had taken with them into exile. They changed the Pools for people. They found this place, our home, and found the sea, found that it was much like the water in their Pools. They saw that they could make new Pools, here. They came. They made the oldest path, and built the lodges. They brought their staves with them. They made the white lodge and the Pool. They planted in the way of the sea's flow the guardian-weed, which cleanses the waters and makes them fit for the Pool." He stopped for breath. "Do you see? Do you hear? Once it was not fathers and sons, always together, only fathers and sons. Once there were others, like the farrows and the ploaters. *They* are proof! *They are from the old home!*" He spoke like Morras, strong, sure. "A Pool-Knower came who must have hated the old way. He taught lies. Men feared that the old wisdoms would be lost without strictures. Fathers were bound to sons. But the First Fathers wished us to be with whomever we chose. The Pool begets all the same, and no one is unhappy." He stopped. His voice softened. "Do you see, Jun?"

"They built the Pool," I said, stupidly, "so that sons could be made

168   RAND B. LEE

from fathers without these others."

"Without these others," said Porran softly. "And such odd others, more different still from us than Morras is from you. So you see, Father, how can it be wrong for Yavan to lower me into the Pool?"

I did not intend to do then what I did. I took my stave and hurled it, and it struck Yavan son of Morras on the side of the head as my clod of mud had struck Ren Sand-Knower's son on the day my father punished me. He fell, with blood. Porran cried out, and went to him. I strode forward and gripped Porran by the hair. I pulled him from Yavan and cast him to the ground. I took Yavan by the throat and I squeezed his throat until he was dead. Porran tried to stop me; but I was strength, and blood, and fire. At night my head rings from the beating he gave it.

When Yavan was dead I dropped him and Porran left off striking me. I thought that he would fall to his knees and weep over Yavan as I had wept over my father's body; he did not. He had no tears. He looked at me, merely. He has my father's face, as have I. "Porran," I said. I could think of nothing more to say.

I slept. In my sleep I felt the scar in my side where the Pool had taken flesh from which to grow Porran. I felt it grow large, and ugly. The Pool gave it hands, and a knife, and it cut itself from my side where it had grown. And it sang, *"Full fathom five my father lies,"* with the voice of Morras.

I came to myself in the close gloom of my lodge. My father's stave was beside me. Porran was there, sponging my face, making no sound. At the back of the lodge, Death-Knower's form was an aged calm. Porran must have noticed the wits returning to me, for he uttered a cry and came close. There was no warmth in his eyes.

"We are the same," I said. He merely looked.

"The son of Morras is dead," said Death-Knower. "The Fathers have met. It is as it should be; you are released from bloodguilt. Porran your son has admitted his wrong in wishing Yavan for his father; he has asked to be cleansed."

"What of Morras?" I asked.

"He grieves," said Death-Knower. "We are satisfied that all that was done by Yavan was done without Pool-Knower's knowledge. He will give to the Pool something more of his flesh so that he may have another son to raise in the ways of Pool-Father. The wisdom will not be lost."

I glanced at my son, and knew that Death-Knower knew nothing, and knew that Morras had told nothing of the hidden god-letters or the Pool in the middle of the sea of the sky. "Porran," I said, and reached for his hand. He did not move. Like my father he sat, like me he sat, crushing the sponge in his fist. After a moment he turned to me.

"Father," said Porran, and the way he said it touched me cold like the current off the deep beyond the reef. There was a weight about his shoulders. Suddenly he did not look like me at all. "You may lower me into the Pool when you wish, that I may get a son for you." He said it as though he were building a wall with the words. Then he leaned over me, close, as though to kiss me on the mouth. Instead he whispered, so low not even Death-Knower could have heard him. "Do not expect me to look upon your face," he said.

Then he turned away, averting his eyes, and I knew what my father had tried to tell me, that it was not Yavan who had been my enemy after all. I cried out, and would have touched him again; but he sat, and the stillness of the way he sat told me that I would never be able to touch him any more. I knew why he had averted his eyes. It is unlucky to view the beginning of a journey, especially that which is the last. And as I watched him, sitting like one who sits in his boat while his father sinks down into the blackness of his grave, I realized that although it would be many years before my journey's end, it had begun.

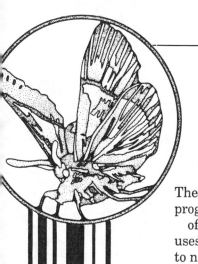

THE MOON & THE MOTH

Peter Payack

The moth
programmed by untold eons
   of evolution
uses the Moon as a beacon
to navigate its flight.

But how has the Moon
fallen from the nighttime sky,
   and become attached
to this post on the porch?

Thus this white-winged lunar explorer
using all the bug logic
   at her dutiful disposal
frantically orbits the porch light
   like a crazed Apollo astronaut
on an endless excursion
ιo oblivion.

As a *deus ex machina* of sorts
in this little insect drama
   I mercifully
switch off the light.

Now free
from the mesmerizing pull
   of the Moon,
the moth breaks out of orbit
   and flutters
safely back to Earth.

On this flight
   at least,
the gods flew with her.

Trial Sample
by Ted Reynolds
art: Tim Kirk

With this printing, Mr. Reynolds has had
as many reprints in anthologies as he has had stories
in print (15), and is wondering if that means anything.

Paul hated sleeptime worse than anything, even meals. His head swam with dizziness, his biceps ached abominably, and his hip-joints felt on the verge of parting. He couldn't even balance his weight with his hands, as the family were still in halfsleep; if they opened their eyes and saw him clutching the sleeping bar, it would hardly bode well for trade and diplomatic prospects.

He'd just have to hold out for another half-hour till the others had entered deepsleep; then he could clamber down from the perch and spread out on the rocky cave floor for a couple of hours. Just as long as he was back suspended from the sleeping bar by his knees when the family woke up.

Sure enough, Pommop opened one eye and looked at Paul lazily. "We got the Morks corraled just fine, didn't we, son?"

"Sure, Pamma," squeaked Paul, strumming his translation voder in affection mode.

Pommop closed his eye contentedly and remained swinging slowly back and forth, head downwards on his own bar.

Halfsleep was always an oscillating time with the Shecklites, entering and leaving. A fair amount of conversation went on, an almost mindless recapitulation of the past day's activities, forecasts of the coming one, and general expressions of mutual esteem and satisfaction.

Now Yoouwee, hanging on the far side of the cave, rustled his (and/or) her batlike wings, muttering somnolently, "Did I tell you today that you're a great sibling, Wayuueo? One of the best."

"You, too, Yoouwee," answered Paul, trying to sound asleep.

There was a short spell of silence. Paul decided it was his turn. "Mappa? Can we have Kabisco for mornmeal tomorrow? I just love your Kabisco." He detested it.

"Mmmmmmm," drowsed Moppom. It sounded gratefully like she, or perhaps he, at least, was nearing deepsleep.

Gradually the talk died away, and the family faded into deepsleep. Paul waited in agony until he was sure they were all quite beyond rewaking. Then he reached up to clutch the perch, painfully brought his legs out from over the sleeping bar, and let himself down to the floor of the cave. Every muscle ached, and he was exhausted. He stretched out his limbs one at a time, working the kinks out of them.

If only sleeping on the floor were an acceptably deviant form of

TED REYNOLDS

behavior among the Shecklites, Paul wouldn't mind being thought strange. But in the minds of the family, a member who refused to sleep in a properly inverted manner from the sleeping bar would be showing signs of incipient madness, possibly of a homicidal variety. With the best will in the world, such a tendency in one of their children must raise strong instinctive anxiety. After the first few nights on Sheckley, Paul had realized this was one of the activities too close to the border of social acceptance to indulge in.

Paul moved wearily to the far end of the cave, where the Mestoiwe family kept its ancestral altars and computer linkups. He lay down on the floor, straddling as few rocks as possible. He'd have about three and a half hours of sleep before the family rose to midsleep again. They'd better find him swinging from his perch, cozy and content, or there'd be diplomatic trouble.

Paul hated sleeptime with a passion!

And now, to top it all, he couldn't get to sleep at once. His mind kept casting up the same old futile question: *Why me?* With four and a half billion humans to choose from, why couldn't the lottery have fallen on someone else; anyone else? He'd like to see his wife, Marilyn, handle this, for instance.

Not for the first time, he cursed the dumb way the Galactic races had of arranging inter-species relationships. Surely humans could have worked out a less ridiculous method. But when Earth joined the Galactic community, the scheme had been a set tradition for millions of years; man could join it, or retreat home and sulk, but there was no changing or circumventing it.

Paul knew the technique was necessary. Species across the Galaxy were too diverse, too varied, to expect each of them to get along with all the others. Some were baby-eaters, some held very firm religious convictions. Each new species that entered Earth's purview was a potential diplomatic ally, trade partner, friend—or perhaps far too different, physically, mentally, socially, morally, for humans ever to get along with.

The lottery was the established way to make or break relationships. Paul knew, intellectually, that it made more sense than wars, for example. But for someone forced to carry it out in a given instance, it sure seemed dumb.

The human representative on the planet Sheckley sank into an uneasy doze.

The family squatted on the ledge outside the cave mouth, shuffling tine-loads of morkmeat into their mouths. Paul could be grateful Moppom hadn't come up with the Kabisco, but mork wasn't much more appetizing.

The sky arched pale yellow overhead, flecked by bilious green cloudlets, the corralled Morks shuffled and boomed softly from their pens upslope, and the birdlets flittered busily across the morning sun. Pommop came stretching out of the cave mouth and stood looking out over Kooluuwe Ravine. Ponderously he shook out his delicately ribbed wings and then his long limbs, rubbing the sleep out of them.

"Beautiful day, a really gorgeous day," he said at last, joining the family at their mornmeal. "Isn't it your turn to flap over to Youoory for eggs, Wayuu?" He beamed affectionately at Paul.

A bit of underdone mork caught in Paul's throat and he coughed helplessly. From where he sat, on the rim of the cliff, he could see the tops of the higher planted houses poking over the flametrees. A mere half mile as the bat flies, he thought. Two hours climbing for me, first down and then up. If I make it.

I'm not *one of you,* he thought desperately at the squatting family. *I don't have wings, I can't fly, I* hate *breeir eggs. You know that, why do you pretend?*

It was no use. They were letting Paul know that he was one of them, that they still accepted him. He should feel relieved and flattered. If they ever started coddling him, then he could really start to worry. It was just that all the members of the Mestoiwe family took their turns in shopping at Youoory village, and now it was his turn. As simple as that.

"Sure, Pamma," he squeaked as expected, his fingers racing over the voder keys. "Oh, boy. Can I stay to see a flooel show?" He couldn't abide the local entertainment, but the original Wayuueo, who loved flooel animations, would certainly have asked. Besides, it would give an easily accepted excuse for the extended time he would have to be gone from the family homestead.

"Well, now . . ." drew out Pommop, in his standard role of not-coddling-the-kids, but Moppom broke in at that point. "I don't see any harm in that, Poms. Wayuu's been a good boy for a long time now. He never molts in the cave," she added approvingly. "Not like Yoouwee."

"I'll start right away, then," said Paul, leaping to his feet in haste.

"You sit right down and finish your mork," said Pommop sternly. "No child of mine is going to visit the village in a vitiated condition. What would the olders think?"

"It's not my fault," said Moppom. "That child just picks at his food.

TED REYNOLDS

I swear, sometimes I don't know what's wrong with him. It must be the mildew itch."

Finally the mornmeal ordeal was over. The family all bid him safe day, Pommop passed him some cash (the dried iridescent underwings of the rock scarab), and then they all assiduously turned to praise the colors of the morning sky to one another. That way they wouldn't have to take notice of the highly unorthodox mode of his departure. When they were all looking upwards, Paul gaily cried out, "Wings up; off, off, and away!" and quietly clambered over the edge of the precipice.

As he cautiously descended from one handhold to another, Paul found himself muttering, "Twenty-seven days of Hell to go, twenty-seven days of Hell. If one of those days should happen to fall . . ."

He stopped humming. He didn't like to think about falling. It was still a long way to the bottom.

Actually, by Earth count it was only twelve days to go, with four hundred twenty passed. Sheckley days were short, though standard galactic years were much too long. It was one of those years he had to hold out.

If he did fall and get killed, would relationships between Earth and Sheckley be established anyway, he wondered. If the Shecklites returned his body to Earth, he supposed not; if they buried him in the family plot and mourned it as one of their own, then everything would be all right. Assuming the real Wayuueo, in his place on Earth, also made out all right.

The walls of the ravine rose higher above him as he descended into the depths. He tried to concentrate on finding firm grasps, and ignoring the sweat that rolled down his neck and soaked the back of his jumper. "I'll bet the real Wayuueo isn't having as much trouble as this," he decided bitterly. A series of rapid visions passed before him; Wayuueo flying to the plant in the morning, working the assembly line, drinking beer at Rod's Grill after work, playing touch football with Paul's sons. Surely he wouldn't find any of that too irksome.

Paul wondered if Wayuueo had to sleep in the same bed with Marilyn. After Paul's wife was asleep, Wayuueo probably crept out of bed and hung upside down from the coat-rack. Paul felt an abrupt surge of sympathy for his distant counterpart.

Finally he reached the bottom of the crevice. Far overhead, the narrow sliver of warm lemon sky beamed down upon him. The hollow was full of tangled mockbush and wildweed and cracklethorn; down it ran Kooluuwe Creek, twenty yards across, three deep, and full of mangleworms. He had to plunge through the bushes downstream ten minutes before he found a fallen flametree that bridged the creek.

The fallen log was thick enough, but slippery with oozing sap, and Paul had to inch his way across it sitting down. Half way across it, he came upon a rogerian. The lizard lay lethargically half out of the water, its long tail streaming in the rapid current. Its tongue flicked meditatively as Paul approached.

"Care to tell me about your problem?" said the rogerian.

"I doubt you'd be any help," said Paul.

"Oh, you doubt I'd be any help?" said the rogerian. "Why is that?"

"Because," answered Paul caustically, "you have about as much intelligence as a tree toad, and you don't understand a word you are saying." He had reached the point where the lizard squatted, and remained straddling the log, waiting for the creature to move.

The rogerian lizard blinked sleepy eyes and regarded Paul steadily. "Is it because I have about as much intelligence as a tree toad, or because I do not understand a word I am saying, that you doubt I would be of any help?" it asked.

"Oh, lord, not another therapy session," said Paul. He drew up his right leg and began to massage the knots out of it. "Your so-called conversation is nothing but a series of evolved tropisms, an eidetic memory and mimic ability. It looks clever, but there's not a thought in your alligator head."

"How do you see this as tying in with your problem?" asked the rogerian.

Paul paused in the midst of switching legs. "You know, that's a good question. If it weren't for you empathic lizards, the pressure on me to hold out the full year wouldn't be nearly so great. Earth dearly wants to be able to import shiploads of you. You may not have an intelligent thought of your own, but you certainly help people solve their own problems. Now move aside."

"Don't you think I could help you solve your own problem?"

Sometimes it was hard to realize that it was a mere tropism.

"No," said Paul.

"Aren't you being a bit negative?"

Paul groaned. "Look, Elijah, or whatever your name is, my problems aren't psychological, they're *real*. If I can't put up with the Shecklites for a full standard year . . . or if they can't put up with me, and kick me out . . . then my name back on Earth is mud. There was a Hungarian a few years back who blew the whole Quatrary

TED REYNOLDS

exchange within a week of the end of the period, when he refused to impregnate a nubile Quatrary prawn. The Quatrary were vastly disturbed at his dereliction, and expelled him. So now the Quatrarian mungo mines and the sciences of Uxode are closed to humans forever; we will never be able to deal with the Quatrary race. And that man was a social leper on Earth till he blew his brains out last year. I don't want to end up like that!"

"You don't want to end up like that?" the lizard suggested quietly.

"You're damn right I don't. But I also don't want to end up like that Ruwandan who clinched the relation with the Humdingers by serving out his whole term to perfection . . . and then died right after of acute radiation poisoning. He's a human hero now, but he's just as dead . . . a martyr to human desire for Humding microfabrics and the electromagnetic dramas of Cliklick! All I want is to get out of here—" Paul broke off suddenly, drew his legs high out of the water, and said, "I think you should consider your own problem first. There's a mangleworm working his way upstream behind you."

"We were discussing you, not me. What does the mangleworm working his way upstream behind me suggest about your prob——"

Paul sighed and continued along the fallen trunk, carefully keeping his legs well out of the water until he was past the point where small fragments of rogerian spun on the current. *Less* intelligent than a tree toad, he decided. Still, a pleasant break in an otherwise tedious day.

He reached the opposite edge and pushed his way through dried crackelthorn to the facing edge of Kooluuwe Ravine. After one disgusted glance up the vertical face of the cliff, he commenced his climb.

Twelve Earth days, he thought; *only a mere twelve days. If I just can hold out . . . and not make any really deadly faux pas . . . I've got it made. It may not be comfortable, but the Shecklites seem to be as eager to make it work out as I am. I wonder,* he thought, not for the first time, *what in the world they see available from Earth that helps them to put up with me. They're not interested in gold or physics or Beethoven. It all seems to be centered around radishes and tiddlywinks and the works of Phillip James Bailey. That gets them all excited. Now who on Earth was Phillip James Bailey?*

By persistent climbing, and refusal to stop to discuss his problem with three other rogerians, Paul neared the top by midmorn. During the last ten meters, he heard voices from above him; they held a sneering quality not at all to his liking. He looked up. Outlined against the yellow sky stood several Shecklites looking down at him.

He clambered up over the lip of the ravine and sat puffing. The Shecklites moved to encircle him. They were mid-adolescents, six of them, and he began to feel nervous. When he recognized one of them as Noowiioy, the mayor's offspring, he felt really depressed. There was a real bully for you.

Despite his exhaustion, he managed to regain his feet. "Got to get to the village," he said. "Eggs. Can't play now." He took a step towards the flametrees bordering the ravine.

Noowiioy took a sidewise step, blocking Paul's escape. "We saw you climbing," he said nastily, his face scrooching up in gray crinkles. "You want to know something? You're not a Shecklite after all." The other five laughed mockingly.

Paul froze in shock. No one was ever supposed to say that; it could be the sign of the end. The adolescents had been taunting from the beginning, even cruel, but none of them had stepped across that line before.

Noowiioy's face wrinkled again, with the humor of what he was about to say. "You're no Shecklite," he said again. "You're some kind of rockcrab."

Paul's heart picked up where it had left off. He had heard that phrase before among the youthful toughs. It was not a reference to his humanity, but a challenge to his Shecklite manhood . . . or perhaps (Paul had given up trying to differentiate in this area) his womanhood.

"I'm a better Shecklite than you, Noowiioy," he played out on his voder. "Now move aside and let me pass."

Noowiioy looked at his cronies. He raised his wings in a large shrug and let them drop again. "Hear that, guys?" he chewed. "Says he's better than we are! Shall we let him prove it?"

The others chortled unpleasantly and moved the ring in closer.

Oh, my God! Not another stupid challenge.

"Some other time," Paul played desperately, "I would be more than delighted to show up your snotty arrogance." He tried, while not cringing utterly, to choose his words carefully from the less provocative ones in use among the youthful gangs. "But as I am on an important mission to Youoory, I cannot pause to engage in your infantile . . ."

Noowiioy bent slowly forward from his upper waist until his beak-nose brushed Paul's snub one. "Little rockcrab gotta do what his Mops says; little rockcrab run to store to get eggs; scared to show what a rockcrab he really is."

Paul sighed. He saw no way out. Noowiioy had chosen firm ground.

TED REYNOLDS

The values were clearly marked; no real Shecklite youth would put parental instructions over a test of 'hoodness; the parents would be ashamed themselves in such a case.

"What did you have in mind, brain-molt?" he asked wearily.

"Rockcrab care to groundplunge?" the other asked bluntly.

Oh, Lord. Scratch one human being.

"Why not?" bluffed Paul. "If it's the only way to stop your asinine yappings."

"Okay. Here and now. I've been waiting months for this. Off the ravine right here, and the last one to lift wing wins."

Paul walked to the edge of Kooluuwe Ravine, the others following. He looked down the sheer drop. Not a chance. He looked at Noowiioy's five cohorts. They seemed nervous, uncertain. But not to the extent they were going to step in and stop this idiocy. His thoughts were running as fast as they ever had before.

"You *are* a cowardly mudworm, Noowiioy," he suggested mildly.

Noowiioy's face blued in rage. "You dare say that!"

Paul pointed down the cliff. "Why lift wing at all? We'll jump together from right here and go all the way to the bottom. If either of us lifts wing before striking bottom, that's being a rockcrab *and* a mudworm."

Noowiioy looked confused. "That's ridiculous. I'll go within ten lengths of the ground before I pull out. Bet you can't do that!"

Paul shook his head disgustedly. "Noowiioy, you're a bully and a boaster, but you just don't have it when it counts. I'm sick of all your ten lengths, five lengths, three, half a length. If you can't face going all the way, then stop bragging about your so-called guts. Put up or shut up."

"But you gotta pull out sometime," choked Noowiioy, not quite getting it even yet. "Or you'll be smeared all over the bottom!"

"Right. You can't face it, can you?" pressed Paul. *"I'm* willing. It might be fun." He looked at the others. "I'd like to show up this creep for the crabworm he is. If he won't jump with me, let's push him over, and watch him cop out."

"Hey, wait a minute!" Noowiioy was scrabbling rapidly back from the edge. He looked about at his compatriots, but the current of mockery had shifted. They were all in glee at seeing the tables so deftly turned. "Don't you see, he's bluffing—"

"Then call his bluff," said one of his friends mockingly.

"Yeah, Noowy, afraid to go all the way to the ground? Looks like *you're* the rockcrab."

They all chortled.

Noowiioy stared wildly about. "But it's not fair," he said, his voice wobbling. "Don't you see? He's actually trying to *kill* me."

"He's willing to do it," said Geeyuuo. "And you're not."

"But *he's* not . . . I mean, he's not really a . . ." There was a sudden hush as all stared at him, wondering if he would actually break the unspoken taboo.

"Radishes," Paul played rapidly in minor key. "Tiddlywinks. Phillip James Bailey."

Noowiioy glared at him, and suddenly lifted wing. With a downrush of air on their upturned faces, he mounted to circle above them. "My father the mayor will hear about this," he flung down, and then was rising up towards the pole-mounted houses visible beyond the treetops.

The other youths crowded about Paul, clapping him on the thighs in friendly fashion. "That was beautiful," said Geeyuuo. "Noowy's been flapping for a fall a long time now. Say, would you really have gone through with it?"

Paul shrugged. "Why not?" he said indifferently. "What have I got to lose?"

He started walking towards Youoory village.

The village of Youoory tottered at the top of its tall poles in the wide clearing just west of the ravine. The poles were not intended for climbing, but they could serve the purpose. Paul crossed to the base of the one holding, among other establishments, the Aoweeyo Eggery.

Something massive, floppy, and quite unfamiliar lay sprawled at the base of the pole. As Paul approached, it raised an ursine head above flat flippers, and spoke to him.

" 'Oo 'r 'oo?" A gruff voice, squeezed out between rollers.

"I am Wayuueo of the Mestoiwe lineage," said Paul. "And you?"

" 'M 'oo'a'ee uv 'e 'ee'i'aa 'inea'," said the other.

"Oh," said Paul uncertainly. He had heard that there was another galactic exchange representative in the area, but this was their first encounter. He felt a surge of companionship for the alien. Perhaps here was someone who could feel for his own difficulties; he wondered if he dared venture on a little frank conversation.

A small voice piped from behind him. "Look, Mops; look at those two *funny* animals!"

"Hush, Uyee," answered a female-priority voice. "That is just two Shecklites talking together. They're just like anybody else. Remember that! Animals indeed!"

TED REYNOLDS

Paul resignedly smiled at the other alien, and began to climb the post. He couldn't risk bringing trouble to three worlds. He wondered what the temporary 'oo'a'ee of the ee'i'aa would bring to the Shecklites in trade if he managed to fulfill his standard year.

The rough knotted wood, warm in the midday sun, offered good handholds for his climb. Weary as he was, Paul had soon attained the lowest level of Youoory, and paused to rest. The eggery was still five levels above him; this level was crammed with the apparatus servicing the eyrie—power, sewage, computer, and interplanetary teleport equipment. The Shecklites might be simple in their lives, and untechnological in their abilities, but they had very solid trade and diplomatic relations with the rest of the galaxy; they weren't primitives.

Paul crossed to the struts supporting the upper levels, took one glance up at the homes and shops dangling from the second level above him, and began to ascend. The Shecklites wouldn't have done so well in making and keeping Galactic contacts, he thought, if they hadn't been very tolerant of differences. Perhaps he was worrying too much; they wanted him to get through the next few days as badly as he did. Surely, even that idiot Noowiioy couldn't manage to mess up an important interracial relationship. He hoped.

Clutching his embryo sack of breeir eggs, Paul turned from the counter of the Aoweeyo Eggery, and stopped short. Above him towered the tall gray form of Mayor Bleewooe of Youoory.

Mayor Bleewooe looked down thoughtfully at Paul, who gulped helplessly. The mayor's puckered lips chewed slowly sideways in his leathery face—the smooth, lineless face of old age. The wide beak opened and words fell from the heights upon Paul's unwilling ears.

"If it is convenient for you, and no imposition, small one, perhaps you would honor me with a slight conversation. But if it is any trouble, then perhaps some other time."

As on Earth, the elected officials of Sheckley called themselves 'public servants.' Unlike Earth, they behaved as such.

Paul gulped again and managed to respond, in a combination of vocal and voder, "When I'm good and ready, you lump of obsequiousness." This also was standard format.

Formalities over, the mayor got to the point. "Young one, we have a problem, and I do hope you can spare the time to hear me out. When I speak of a problem, I do not mean only you and I, but the whole village of Youoory. More, this effects the entire province of

Iewaooe. In fact, the continent of Eewayow is not exempt from interest in this affair. I dare say that the whole planet—"

"I'm listening," said Paul sullenly. "Spit it out."

Mayor Bleewooe nodded his head wisely for a moment, scratched his left shoulder blade with the tip of his right wing, and then enunciated solemnly:

"Small one, you must be aware of the method by which sentient races make, or fail to make, viable relationships with one another. I refer, of course, to the lottery system, by means of which one randomly chosen individual from a given species is selected to live a standard year as a citizen of another world. . . ."

Paul could say nothing. The mayor's roundabout words certainly sounded like the whiplash of descending doom.

Mayor Bleewooe was methodically continuing. ". . . so if the representative individual and the society he has joined can mutually tolerate each other for one standard year, then trade and diplomatic relationships can be entered into between the two species in question. But . . ." and the mayor drew himself up austerely, "if for any reason, *not,* then . . . not!"

Paul could not passively wait for the final blow without a last attempt to assert himself. "Sir," he frantically stumbled over his voder keys, "I mean, you bureaucratic underling, servant of the people, what has all this to do with me? No, rather, I do not care to know! I am . . ." He drew himself erect, and glared up at the mayor, "I am Wayuueo of the Mestoiwe lineage, son and daughter of Oyeuuwa and Jooweyu, of the Niiweyoi clan. Do you intend . . . can you possibly dare . . . to impugn my parentage? To cast doubt on my pedigree as a true Shecklite of the Shecklites, a child of my own peoples?"

Mayor Bleewooe gazed down at him for a long, heart-stopping moment, eye-hoods slowly descending over his white orbits, and then snapping up again like a released window shade.

"No," he said mildly at last. "I am sure you are a credit to your Mops and Poms, Wayuueo of the Mestoiwe. A good Shecklite," he muttered, turning away slowly, his aged face shaking as in disbelief. "A fine young Shecklite."

Paul exhaled, and gradually stilled the shaking of his whole body. Carefully planting each foot as he moved, he crossed to the eggery exit.

From behind him came the voice of the mayor. "Please be at home at sunset this evening, young one. You may expect a visit from the Council of Olders."

TED REYNOLDS

Paul considered jumping and ending the whole mess at once. But even that would have taken too much effort. He began the long crawl home, his mouth filled with the bilious taste of futility.

"Care to tell me about your problem?" said the rogerian.

Paul slumped weariedly on the ledge and carefully cached the embryo sack of breeir eggs in a safe niche. He looked down into Kooluuwe Ravine. The sun had long passed beyond the rim above him, and the bottom of the cleft was filling with late afternoon shadow. Another twenty minutes' climb should bring him back to the homestead.

"Not particularly," he told the lizard.

"You don't particularly want to tell me about your problem?" the lizard prompted.

Paul rested his chin in his cupped hands. "Don't ask questions," he said. "Give me an answer."

"You want me to give you an answer?"

"Yes," said Paul.

The rogerian was silent a moment. "Why do you want me to give you an answer?"

Paul was silent.

The lizard blinked its large azure eyes, and tried again. "What does your wanting me to give you an answer tell you about your problem?"

Paul was silent.

The lizard twitched nervously. "Why does your problem bother you so, *really?*" it said.

Paul collected his eggs and stood up, thinking. "I think what *really* bothers me most," he said at last, "is that Poms and Mops will be so disappointed in me."

He resumed his climb.

Shortly afterwards he heard the slow beat of wings above him, and saw the full Council of Olders flapping their way across the ravine from the direction of Youoory Village. They circled once above him and passed out of sight in the direction of the Mestoiwe cave. By the time Paul had crawled over the rim to the ledge fronting his home, the whole delegation was squatting in a wide semi-circle, delicately nibbling the Kabisco bars Mops saved for special occasions.

None of them looked in his direction until he crawled drearily up to them and handed the embryo sack to Moppom.

"They have come to talk to you, Wayuueo," Mops told him nervously. "It sounds like it's very important. I'm afraid that . . ." She couldn't finish.

Paul turned to the silent crescent of Olders. He could feel the nails of his hands biting into his palms. This wasn't going to be easy. He took three steps forward and halted, his eyes downcast.

Mayor Bleewooe slowly rose to his feet and stared at Paul a long moment. He scuffed his feet on the ground, kicked at an embedded rock, frowned ponderously.

"I have an official announcement to make," he said. "It is not an easy thing to tell, it is a difficult matter to broach. But it must be said, it cannot be otherwise."

Paul felt a sudden urge to push the garrulous mayor off the cliff, but that would solve nothing. He waited.

Eventually the mayor continued. "It is a very important matter, the lottery system," he said bluntly. "It is at the base of the life of all of us here on Sheckley. Without the economies and arts and sciences we have gained from Galactic contacts, our lives would still be short and narrow and miserable as they were before we reached the stars and joined the lottery exchange system." He looked steadily at Paul. "If it is at all possible, if there is any hope at all, we shall do all in our power to make and keep relationships with the other creatures in the Galaxy. Every Shecklite knows the importance of this." He cleared his throat, looking deeply embarrassed.

Paul considered saving everybody further embarrassment by two steps and a jump into the ravine. But the Shecklites would just catch him on the way down. It was useless.

Slowly the Mayor stretched out his leathery wings. "I know you will do well for us, Wayuueo of the Mestoiwe," he was saying huskily. "Tomorrow you will be taken by webship to the world of the Dreffitti. You have been chosen by lottery as Sheckley's representative to those beings."

As the whole delegation and then his family stroked and hugged and ogled him, Paul could hear the mayor's voice ricocheting on: ". . . live in chlorine bubbles under the waters of the muddy estuaries . . . gourmet delicacies and temperature control techniques of huge value to our world . . . far the greatest honor that can befall a Shecklite."

And, oh, were his Poms and Mops proud of him!

A little later, during the formal speeches, Paul *did* step off into the ravine, but they caught him before he fell fifteen feet. Nobody remarked on his awkwardness at such a moment.

After all, such an honor would fluster anybody.

ELEMENTARY DECISION

The quark and the lepton went to see
"If matter could ever conceivably be
Composed of components more element'ry
Than we."

"Between us," the quark said, "we two constitute
The essence of matter, the crux; and to boot,
Besides being, both of us, *ne plus minute*—
We're cute."

"Take care," said the lepton, "although that sounds fine,
They once thought the *atom* the end of the line;
If they found they could parse us, your star would decline.
And mine."

So the quark threw a tantrum. The lepton, on cue,
Snarled scurrilous threats, then, pouting, withdrew.
The quark, in retort, filed complaints for review.
(None true.)

It worked. Their carefully
choreographed "unrehearsed" squall
Shows all sub-atomics in peril of recall
A surefire technique for forestalling the call:
Act small.

—Don Anderson

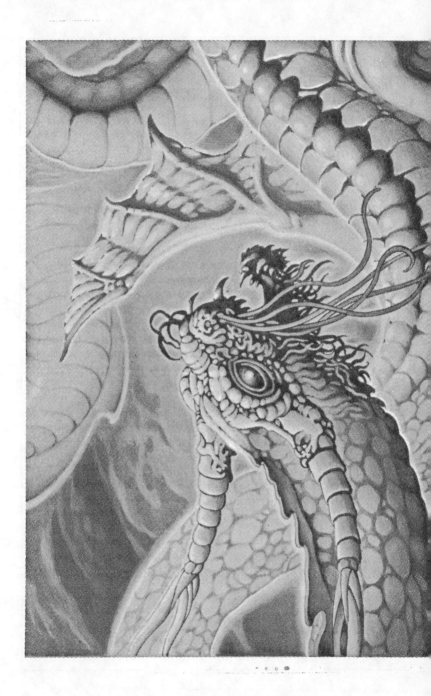

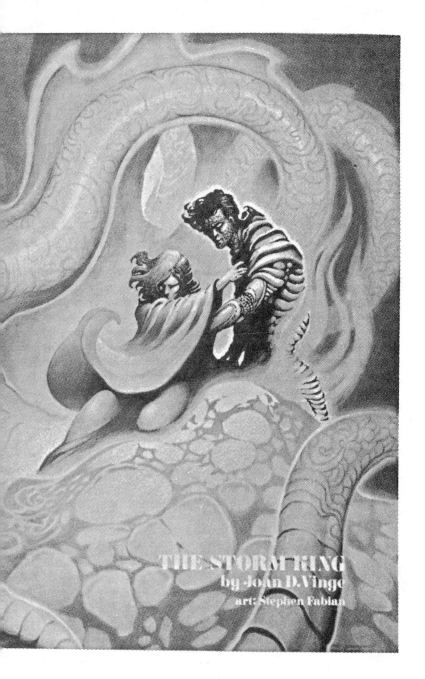

THE STORM KING
by Joan D. Vinge
art: Stephen Fabian

*Originally the author wanted to be
an artist but she somehow ended
up with a degree in anthropology.
Her story "Eyes of Amber" won
the 1977 Hugo Award for Best Novelette,
and* The Snow Queen *won the 1981 Hugo Award for Best Novel.
She is currently working on a
sequel to* The Snow Queen, *and has a
new novel* Psion *out from Delacorte Press.
She lives in Chappaqua, NY
with her husband and daughter Jessica.*

They said that in those days the lands were cursed that lay in the shadow of the Storm King. The peak thrust up from the gently rolling hills and fertile farmlands like an impossible wave cresting on the open sea, a brooding finger probing the secrets of heaven. Once it had vomited fire and fumes; ash and molten stone had poured from its throat; the distant ancestors of the people who lived beneath it now had died of its wrath. But the Earth had spent Her fury in one final cataclysm, and now the mountain lay quiet, dark, and cold, its mouth choked with congealed stone.

And yet still the people lived in fear. No one among them remembered having seen its summit, which was always crowned by cloud; lightning played in the purple, shrouding robes; and distant thunder filled the dreams of the folk who slept below with the roaring of dragons.

For it was a dragon who had come to dwell among the crags: that elemental focus of all storm and fire carried on the wind, drawn to a place where the Earth's fire had died, a place still haunted by ancient grief. And sharing the spirit of fire, the dragon knew no law and obeyed no power except its own. By day or night it would rise on furious wings of wind and sweep over the land, inundating the crops with rain, blasting trees with its lightning, battering walls

JOAN D. VINGE

and tearing away rooftops; terrifying rich and poor, man and beast, for the sheer pleasure of destruction, the exaltation of uncontrolled power. The people had prayed to the new gods who had replaced their worship of the Earth to deliver them; but the new gods made Their home in the sky, and seemed to be beyond hearing.

By now the people had made Their names into curses, as they pried their oxcarts from the mud or looked out over fields of broken grain and felt their bellies and their children's bellies tighten with hunger. And they would look toward the distant peak and curse the Storm King, naming the peak and the dragon both; but always in whispers and mutters, for fear the wind would hear them, and bring the dark storm sweeping down on them again.

The storm-wracked town of Wyddon and its people looked up only briefly in their sullen shaking-off and shoveling-out of mud as a stranger picked his way among them. He wore the woven leather of a common soldier, his cloak and leggings were coarse and ragged, and he walked the planks laid down in the stinking street as though determination alone kept him on his feet. A woman picking through baskets of stunted leeks in the marketplace saw with vague surprise that he had entered the tiny village temple; a man putting fresh thatch on a torn-open roof saw him come out again, propelled by the indignant, orange-robed priest.

"If you want witchery, find yourself a witch! This is a holy place; the gods don't meddle in vulgar magic!"

"I can see that," the stranger muttered, staggering in ankle-deep mud. He climbed back onto the boards with some difficulty and obvious disgust. "Maybe if they did you'd have streets and not rivers of muck in this town." He turned away in anger, almost stumbled over a mud-colored girl blocking his forward progress on the board-walk.

"You priests should bow down to the Storm King!" The girl postured insolently, looking toward the priest. "The dragon can change all our lives more in one night than your gods have done in a life-time."

"Slut!" The priest shook his carven staff at her; its necklace of golden bells chimed like absurd laughter. "There's a witch for you, beggar. If you think she can teach you to tame the dragon, then go with her!" He turned away, disappearing into the temple. The stranger's body jerked, as though it strained against his control, wanting to strike at the priest's retreating back.

"You're a witch?" The stranger turned and glared down at the bony figure standing in his way, found her studying him back with obvious skepticism. He imagined what she saw—a foreigner, his straight black hair whacked off like a serf's, his clothes crawling with filth, his face grimed and gaunt and set in a bitter grimace. He frowned more deeply.

The girl shook her head. "No. I'm just bound to her. You have business to take up with her, I see—about the Storm King." She smirked, expecting him to believe she was privy to secret knowledge.

"As you doubtless overheard, yes." He shifted his weight from one leg to the other, trying fruitlessly to ease the pain in his back.

She shrugged, pushing her own tangled brown hair back from her face. "Well, you'd better be able to pay for it, or you've come a long way from Kwansai for nothing."

He started, before he realized that his coloring and his eyes gave that much away. "I can pay." He drew his dagger from its hidden sheath, the only weapon he had left, and the only thing of value. He let her glimpse the jeweled hilt before he pushed it back out of sight.

Her gray eyes widened briefly. "What do I call you, Prince of Thieves?" with another glance at his rags.

"Call me Your Highness," not lying, and not quite joking.

She looked up into his face again, and away. "Call me Nothing, Your Highness. Because I am nothing." She twitched a shoulder at him. "And follow me."

They passed the last houses of the village without further speech, and followed the mucky track on into the dark, dripping forest that lay at the mountain's feet. The girl stepped off the road and into the trees without warning; he followed her recklessly, half angry and half afraid that she was abandoning him. But she danced ahead of him through the pines, staying always in sight, although she was plainly impatient with his own lagging pace. The dank chill of the sunless wood gnawed his aching back and swarms of stinging gnats feasted on his exposed skin; the bare-armed girl seemed as oblivious to the insects as she was to the cold.

He pushed on grimly, as he had pushed on until now, having no choice but to keep on or die. And at last his persistence was rewarded; he saw the forest rise ahead, and buried in the flank of the hillside among the trees was a mossy hut linteled by immense stones.

The girl disappeared into the hut as he entered the clearing before it. He slowed, looking around him at the clusters of carven images

JOAN D. VINGE

pushing up like unnatural growths from the spongy ground, or dangling from tree limbs. Most of the images were subtly or blatantly obscene. He averted his eyes and limped between them to the hut's entrance.

He stepped through the doorway without waiting for an invitation, to find the girl crouched by the hearth in the hut's cramped interior, wearing the secret smile of a cat. Beside her an incredibly wrinkled, ancient woman sat on a three-legged stool. The legs were carved into shapes that made him look away again, back at the wrinkled face and the black, buried eyes that regarded him with flinty bemusement. He noticed abruptly that there was no wall behind her: the far side of the hut melted into the black volcanic stone, a natural fissure opening into the mountain's side.

"So, Your Highness, you've come all the way from Kwansai seeking the Storm King, and a way to tame its power?"

He wrapped his cloak closely about him and grimaced, the nearest thing to a smile of scorn that he could manage. "Your girl has a quick tongue. But I've come to the wrong place, it seems, for real power."

"Don't be so sure!" The old woman leaned toward him, shrill and spiteful. "You can't afford to be too sure of anything, Lassan-din. You were prince of Kwansai; you should have been king there when your father died, and overlord of these lands as well. And now you're nobody and you have no home, no friends, barely even your life. Nothing is what it seems to be . . . it never is."

Lassan-din's mouth went slack; he closed it, speechless at last. *Nothing is what it seems.* The girl called Nothing grinned up at him from the floor. He took a deep breath, shifting to ease his back again. "Then you know what I've come for, if you already know that much, witch."

The hag half-rose from her obscene stool; he glimpsed a flash of color, a brighter, finer garment hidden beneath the drab outer robe she wore—the way the inner woman still burned fiercely bright in her eyes, showing through the wasted flesh of her ancient body. "Call me no names, you prince of beggars! I am the Earth's Own. Your puny Kwansai priests, who call my sisterhood 'witch', who destroyed our holy places and drove us into hiding, know nothing of power. They're fools; they don't believe in power and they are powerless, charlatans. You know it or you wouldn't be here!" She settled back, wheezing. "Yes, I could tell you what you want; but suppose you tell me."

"I want what's mine! I want my kingdom." He paced restlessly, two steps and then back. "I know of elementals, all the old legends. My people say that dragons are stormbringers, born from a joining of Fire and Water and Air, three of the four Primes of Existence. Nothing but the Earth can defy their fury. And I know that if I can hold a dragon in its lair with the right spells, it must give me what I want, like the heroes of the Golden Time. I want to use its power to take back my lands."

"You don't want much, do you?" The old woman rose from her seat and turned her back on him, throwing a surreptitious handful of something into the fire, making it flare up balefully. She stirred the pot that hung from a hook above it, spitting five times into the noxious brew as she stirred. Lassan-din felt his empty stomach turn over. "If you want to challenge the Storm King, you should be out there climbing, not here holding your hand out to me."

"Damn you!" His exasperation broke loose, and his hand wrenched her around to face him. "I need some spell, some magic, some way to pen a dragon up. I can't do it with my bare hands!"

She shook her head, unintimidated, and leered toothlessly at him. "My power comes to me through my body, up from the Earth Our Mother. She won't listen to a man—especially one who would destroy Her worship. Ask your priests who worship the air to teach you their empty prayers."

He saw the hatred rising in her, and felt it answered: The dagger was out of its hidden sheath and in his hand before he knew it, pressing the soft folds of her neck. "I don't believe you, witch. See this dagger—" quietly, deadly. "If you give me what I want, you'll have the jewels in its hilt. If you don't, you'll feel its blade cut your throat."

"All right, all right!" She strained back as the blade's tip began to bite. He let her go. She felt her neck; the girl sat perfectly still at their feet, watching. "I can give you something—a spell. I can't guarantee She'll listen. But you have enough hatred in you for ten men—and maybe that will make your man's voice loud enough to penetrate Her skin. This mountain is sacred to Her. She still listens through its ears, even if She no longer breathes here."

"Never mind the superstitious drivel. Just tell me how I can keep the dragon in without it striking me dead with its lightning. How I can fight fire with fire—"

"You don't fight fire with fire. You fight fire with water."

He stared at her; at the obviousness of it, and the absurdity—"The dragon is the creator of storm. How can mere water—?"

"A dragon is anathema. Remember that, prince who would be

194   JOAN D. VINGE

king. It is chaos, power uncontrolled; and power always has a price. That's the key to everything. I can teach you the spell for controlling the waters of the Earth; but you're the one who must use it."

He stayed with the women through the day, and learned as the hours passed to believe in the mysteries of the Earth. The crone spoke words that brought water fountaining up from the well outside her door while he looked on in amazement, his weariness and pain forgotten. As he watched she made a brook flow upstream; made crystal droplets beading the forest pines join in a diadem to crown his head, and then with a word released them to run cold and helpless as tears into the collar of his ragged tunic.

She seized the fury that rose up in him at her insolence, and challenged him to do the same. He repeated the ungainly, ancient spellwords defiantly, arrogantly, and nothing happened. She scoffed, his anger grew; she jeered and it grew stronger. He repeated the spell again, and again, and again . . . until at last he felt the terrifying presence of an alien power rise in his body, answering the call of his blood. The droplets on the trees began to shiver and commingle; he watched an eddy form in the swift clear water of the stream— The Earth had answered him.

His anger failed him at the unbelievable sight of his success . . . and the power failed him too. Dazed and strengthless, at last he knew his anger for the only emotion with the depth or urgency to move the body of the Earth, or even his own. But he had done the impossible—made the Earth move to a man's bidding. He had proved his right to be a king, proved that he could force the dragon to serve him as well. He laughed out loud. The old woman moaned and spat, twisting her hands that were like gnarled roots, mumbling curses. She shuffled away toward the woods as though she were in a trance; turned back abruptly as she reached the trees, pointing past him at the girl standing like a ghost in the hut's doorway. "You think you've known the Earth; that you own Her, now. You think you can take anything and make it yours. But you're as empty as that one, and as powerless!" And she was gone.

Night had fallen through the dreary wood without his realizing it. The girl Nothing led him back into the hut, shared a bowl of thick, strangely herbed soup and a piece of stale bread with him. He ate gratefully but numbly, the first warm meal he had eaten in weeks; his mind drifted into waking dreams of banqueting until dawn in royal halls.

When he had eaten his share, wiping the bowl shamelessly with a crust, he stood and walked the few paces to the hut's furthest corner. He lay down on the hard stone by the cave mouth, wrapping his cloak around him, and closed his eyes. Sleep's darker cloak settled over him.

And then, dimly, he became aware that the girl had followed him, stood above him looking down. He opened his eyes unwillingly, to see her unbelt her tunic and pull it off, kneel down naked at his side. A piece of rock crystal, perfectly transparent, perfectly formed, hung glittering coldly against her chest. He kept his eyes open, saying nothing.

"The Old One won't be back until you're gone; the sight of a man calling on the Earth was too strong for her." Her hand moved insinuatingly along his thigh.

He rolled away from her, choking on a curse as his back hurt him sharply. "I'm tired. Let me sleep."

"I can help you. She could have told you more. I'll help you tomorrow . . . if you lie with me tonight."

He looked up at her, suddenly despairing. "Take my body, then; but it won't give you much pleasure." He pulled up the back of his tunic, baring the livid scar low on his spine. "My uncle didn't make a cripple of me—but he might as well have." When he even thought of a woman there was only pain, only rage . . . only that.

She put her hand on the scar with surprising gentleness. "I can help that too . . . for tonight." She went away, returned with a small jar of ointment and rubbed the salve slowly into his scarred back. A strange, cold heat sank through him; a sensuous tingling swept away the grinding ache that had been his only companion through these long months of exile. He let his breath out in an astonished sigh, and the girl lay down beside him, pulling at his clothes.

Her thin body was as hard and bony as a boy's, but she made him forget that. She made him forget everything, except that tonight he was free from pain and sorrow; tonight he lay with a woman who desired him, no matter what her reason. He remembered lost pleasure, lost joy, lost youth, only yesterday . . . until yesterday became tomorrow.

In the morning he woke, in pain, alone and fully clothed, aching on the hard ground. *Nothing.* . . . He opened his eyes and saw her standing at the fire, stirring a kettle. *A dream—?* The cruel betrayal that was reality returned tenfold.

They ate together in a silence that was sullen on his part and inscrutable on hers. After last night it seemed obvious to him that

196   JOAN D. VINGE

she was older than she looked—as obvious as the way he himself had changed from boy to old man in a span of months. And he felt an insubstantiality about her that he had not noticed before, an elusiveness that might only have been an echo of his dream. "I dreamed, last night . . ."

"I know." She climbed to her feet, cutting him off, combing her snarled hair back with her fingers. "You dream loudly." Her face was closed.

He felt a frown settle between his eyes again. "I have a long climb. I'd better get started." He pushed himself up and moved stiffly toward the doorway. The old hag still had not returned.

"Not that way," the girl said abruptly. "This way." She pointed as he turned back, toward the cleft in the rock.

He stood still. "That will take me to the dragon?"

"Only part way. But it's easier by half. I'll show you." She jerked a brand out of the fire and started into the maw of darkness.

He went after her with only a moment's uncertainty. He had lived in fear for too long; if he was afraid to follow this witch-girl into her Goddess's womb, then he would never have the courage to challenge the Storm King.

The low-ceilinged cleft angled steeply upward, a natural tube formed millennia ago by congealing lava. The girl began to climb confidently, as though she trusted some guardian power to place her hands and feet surely—a power he could not depend on as he followed her up the shaft. The dim light of day snuffed out behind him, leaving only her torch to guide them through utter blackness, over rock that was alternately rough enough to flay the skin from his hands and slick enough to give him no purchase at all. The tunnel twisted like a worm, widening, narrowing, steepening, folding back on itself in an agony of contortion. His body protested its own agony as he dragged it up handholds in a sheer rock face, twisted it, wrenched it, battered it against the unyielding stone. The acrid smoke from the girl's torch stung his eyes and clogged his lungs; but it never seemed to slow her own tireless motion, and she took no pity on his weakness. Only the knowledge of the distance he had come kept him from demanding that they turn back; he could not believe that this could possibly be an easier way than climbing the outside of the mountain. It began to seem to him that he had been climbing through this foul blackness for all of eternity, that this was another dream like his dream last night, but one that would never end.

The girl chanted softly to herself now; he could just hear her above his own labored breathing. He wondered jealously if she was drawing strength from the very stone around them, the body of the Earth. He could feel no pulse in the cold heart of the rock; and yet after yesterday he did not doubt its presence, even wondering if the Earth sapped his own strength with preternatural malevolence. *I am a man, I will be a king!* he thought defiantly. And the way grew steeper, and his hands bled.

"Wait—!" He gasped out the word at last, as his feet went out from under him again and he barely saved himself from sliding back down the tunnel. "I can't go on."

The girl, crouched on a level spot above him, looked back and down at him and ground out the torch. His grunt of protest became a grunt of surprise as he saw her silhouetted against a growing gray-brightness. She disappeared from his view; the brightness dimmed and then strengthened.

He heaved himself up and over the final bend in the wormhole, into a space large enough to stand in if he had had the strength. He crawled forward hungrily into the brightness at the cave mouth, found the girl kneeling there, her face raised to the light. He welcomed the fresh air into his lungs, cold and cleansing; looked past her—and down.

They were dizzyingly high on the mountain's side, above the treeline, above a sheer, unscalable face of stone. A fast-falling torrent of water roared on their left, plunging out and down the cliff-face. The sun winked at him from the cloud-wreathed heights; its angle told him they had climbed for the better part of the day. He looked over at the girl.

"You're lucky," she said, without looking back at him. Before he could even laugh at the grotesque irony of the statement she raised her hand, pointing on up the mountainside. "The Storm King sleeps—another storm is past. I saw the rainbow break this sunrise."

He felt a surge of strength and hope, absorbed the indifferent blessing of the Holy Sun. "How long will it sleep?"

"Two more days, perhaps. You won't reach its den before night. Sleep here, and climb again tomorrow."

"And then?" He looked toward her expectantly.

She shrugged.

"I paid you well," not certain in what coin, anymore. "I want a fair return! How do I pen the beast?"

Her hand tightened around the crystal pendant hanging against her tunic. She glanced back into the cave mouth. "There are many waters flowing from the heights. One of them might be diverted to

JOAN D. VINGE

fall past the entrance of its lair."

"A waterfall? I might as well hold up a rose and expect it to cower!"

"Power always has its price; as the Old One said." She looked directly at him at last. "The storm rests here in mortal form—the form of the dragon. And like all mortals, it suffers. Its strength lies in the scales that cover its skin. The rain washes them away—the storm is agony to the stormbringer. They fall like jewels, they catch the light as they fall, like a trail of rainbow. It's the only rainbow anyone here has ever seen . . . a sign of hope, because it means an end to the storm; but a curse, too, because the storm will always return, endlessly."

"Then I could have it at my mercy. . . . " He heard nothing else.

"Yes. If you can make the Earth move to your will." Her voice was flat.

His hands tightened. "I have enough hate in me for that."

"And what will you demand, to ease it?" She glanced at him again, and back at the sky. "The dragon is defiling this sacred place; it should be driven out. You could become a hero to my people, if you forced the dragon to go away. A god. They need a god who can do them some good. . . . "

He felt her somehow still watching him, measuring his response, even though she had looked away. "I came here to solve my problem, not yours. I want my own kingdom, not a kingdom of mud-men. I need the dragon's power—I didn't come here to drive that away."

The girl said nothing, still staring at the sky.

"It's a simple thing for you to move the waters—why haven't you driven the dragon away yourself, then?" His voice rasped in his parched throat, sharp with unrecognized guilt.

"I'm Nothing. I have no power—the Old One holds my soul." She looked down at the crystal.

"Then why won't the Old One do it?"

"She hates, too. She hates what our people have become under the new gods, your gods. That's why she won't."

"I'd think it would give her great pleasure to prove the impotence of the new gods." His mouth stretched sourly.

"She wants to die in the Earth's time, not tomorrow." The girl folded her arms, and her own mouth twisted.

He shook his head. "I don't understand that . . . why didn't you destroy our soldiers, our priests, with your magic?"

"The Earth moves slowly to our bidding, because She is eternal. An arrow is small—but it moves swiftly."

He laughed once, appreciatively. "I understand."

"There's a cairn of stones over there." She nodded back into the darkness. "Food is under it." He realized that this must have been a place of refuge for the women in times of persecution. "The rest is up to you." She turned, merging abruptly into the shadows.

"Wait!" he called, surprising himself. "You must be tired."

She shook her head, a deeper shadow against darkness.

"Stay with me—until morning." It was not quite a demand, not quite a question.

"Why?" He thought he saw her eyes catch light and reflect it back at him, like a wild thing's.

Because I had a dream. He did not say it, did not say anything else.

"Our debts have balanced." She moved slightly, and something landed on the ground at his feet: his dagger. The hilt was pockmarked with empty jewel settings; stripped clean. He leaned down to pick it up. When he straightened again she was gone.

"You need a light—!" He called after her again.

Her voice came back to him, from a great distance: "May you get what you deserve!" And then silence, except for the roaring of the falls.

He ate, wondering whether her last words were a benediction or a curse. He slept, and the dreams that came to him were filled with the roaring of dragons.

With the light of a new day he began to climb again, following the urgent river upward toward its source that lay hidden in the waiting crown of clouds. He remembered his own crown, and lost himself in memories of the past and future, hardly aware of the harsh sobbing of his breath, of flesh and sinew strained past a sane man's endurance. Once he had been the spoiled child of privilege, his father's only son—living in the world's eye, his every whim a command. Now he was as much Nothing as the witchgirl far down the mountain. But he would live the way he had again, his every wish granted, his power absolute—he would live that way again, if he had to climb to the gates of Heaven to win back his birthright.

The hours passed endlessly, inevitably, and all he knew was that slowly, slowly, the sky lowered above him. At last the cold, moist edge of clouds enfolded his burning body, drawing him into another world of gray mist and gray silences; black, glistening surfaces of rock; the white sound of the cataract rushing down from even higher above. Drizzling fog shrouded the distances any way he turned, and he realized that he did not know where in this layer of cloud the dragon's den lay. He had assumed that it would be obvious, he had

JOAN D. VINGE

trusted the girl to tell him all he needed to know. . . . Why had he trusted her? That pagan slut—his hand gripped the rough hilt of his dagger; dropped away, trembling with fatigue. He began to climb again, keeping the sound of falling water nearby for want of any other guide. The light grew vaguer and more diffuse, until the darkness falling in the outer world penetrated the fog world and the haze of his exhaustion. He lay down at last, unable to go on, and slept beneath the shelter of an overhang of rock.

He woke stupefied by daylight. The air held a strange acridness that hurt his throat, that he could not identify. The air seemed almost to crackle; his hair ruffled, although there was no wind. He pushed himself up. He knew this feeling now: a storm was coming. A storm coming . . . a storm, here? Suddenly, fully awake, he turned on his knees, peering deeper beneath the overhang that sheltered him. And in the light of dawn he could see that it was not a simple overhang, but another opening into the mountain's side—a wider, greater one, whose depths the day could not fathom. But far down in the blackness a flickering of unnatural light showed. His hair rose in the electric breeze, he felt his skin prickle. *Yes . . . yes!* A small cry escaped him. He had found it! Without even knowing it, he had slept in the mouth of the dragon's lair all night. Habit brought a thanks to the gods to his lips, until he remembered— He muttered a *thank you* to the Earth beneath him before he climbed to his feet. A brilliant flash silhouetted him; a rumble like distant thunder made the ground vibrate, and he froze. Was the dragon waking—?

But there was no further disturbance, and he breathed again. Two days, the girl had told him, the dragon might sleep. And now he had reached his final trial, the penning of the beast. Away to his right he could hear the cataract's endless song. But would there be enough water in it to block the dragon's exit? Would that be enough to keep it prisoner, or would it strike him down in lightning and thunder, and sweep his body from the heights with torrents of rain? . . . Could he even move one droplet of water, here and now? Or would he find that all the thousand doubts that gnawed inside him were not only useless but pointless?

He shook it off, moving out and down the mist-dim slope to view the cave mouth and the river tumbling past it. A thin stream of water already trickled down the face of the opening, but the main flow was diverted by a folded knot of lava. If he could twist the water's course and hold it, for just long enough . . .

He climbed the barren face of stone at the far side of the cave mouth until he stood above it, confronting the sinuous steel and flashing white of the thing he must move. It seemed almost alive, and he felt weary, defeated, utterly insignificant at the sight of it. But the mountain on which he stood was a greater thing than even the river, and he knew that within it lay power great enough to change the water's course. But he was the conduit, his will must tap and bend the force that he had felt stir in him two days ago.

He braced his legs apart, gathered strength into himself, trying to recall the feel of magic moving in him. He recited the spell-words, the focus for the willing of power—and felt nothing. He recited the words again, putting all his concentration behind them. Again nothing. The Earth lay silent and inert beneath his feet.

Anger rose in him, at the Earth's disdain, and against the strange women who served Her—the jealous, demanding anger that had opened him to power before. And this time he did feel the power stir in him, sluggishly, feebly. But there was no sign of any change in the water's course. He threw all his conscious will toward change, *change, change*—but still the Earth's power faltered and mocked him. He let go of the ritual words at last, felt the tingling promise of energy die, having burned away all his own strength.

He sat down on the wet stone, listened to the river roar with laughter. He had been so sure that when he got here the force of his need would be strong enough. . . . *I have enough hate in me*, he had told the girl. But he wasn't reaching it now. Not the real hatred, that had carried him so far beyond the limits of his strength and experience. He began to concentrate on that hatred, and the reasons behind it: the loss, the pain, the hardship and fear. . . .

His father had been a great ruler over the lands that his ancestors had conquered. And he had loved his queen, Lassan-din's mother. But when she died, his unhealing grief had turned him ruthless and iron-willed. He had become a despot, capricious, cruel, never giving an inch of his power to another man—even his spoiled and insecure son. Disease had left him wasted and witless in the end. And Lassan-din, barely come to manhood, had been helpless, unable to block his jealous uncle's treachery. He had been attacked by his own guard as he prayed in the temple (*In the temple*— his mouth pulled back), and maimed, barely escaping with his life, to find that his entire world had come to an end. He had become a hunted fugitive in his own land, friendless, trusting no one—forced to lie and steal and grovel to survive. He had eaten scraps thrown out to dogs and lain on hard stones in the rain, while the festering wound in his back

JOAN D. VINGE

kept him from any rest. . . .

Reliving each day, each moment, of his suffering and humiliation, he felt his rage and his hunger for revenge grow hotter. The Earth hated this usurper of Her holy place, the girl had said . . . but no more than he hated the usurper of his throne. He climbed to his feet again, every muscle on fire, and held out his hands. He shouted the incantation aloud, as though it could carry all the way to his homeland. *His homeland*: he would see it again, make it his own again—

The power entered him as the final word left his mouth, paralyzing every nerve, stopping even the breath in his throat. Fear and elation were swept up together into the maelstrom of his emotions, and power exploded like a sun behind his eyes. But through the fiery haze that blinded him, he could still see the water heaved up from its bed, a steely wall crowned with white, crumbling over and down on itself. It swept toward him, a terrifying cataclysm, until he thought that he would be drowned in the rushing flood. But it passed him by where he stood, plunging on over the outcropping roof of the cave below. Eddies of foam swirled around his feet, soaking his stained leggings.

The power left him like the water's surge falling away. He took a deep breath, and another, backing out of the flood. His body moved sluggishly, drained, abandoned, an empty husk. But his mind was full with triumph and rejoicing.

The ground beneath his feet shuddered, jarring his elation, dropping him giddily back into reality. He pressed his head with his hands as pain filled his senses, a madness crowding out coherent thought—a pain that was not his own.

(Water. . . !) Not a plea, but outrage and confusion, a horror of being trapped in a flood of molten fire. *The dragon.* He realized suddenly what had invaded his mind; realized that he had never stopped to wonder how a storm might communicate with a man: Not by human speech, but by stranger, more elemental means. Water from the fall he had created must be seeping into its lair. . . . His face twisted with satisfaction. "Dragon!" He called it with his mind and his voice together.

(Who calls? Who tortures me? Who fouls my lair? Show yourself, slave!)

"Show yourself to me, Storm King! Come out of your cave and destroy me—if you can!" The wildness of his challenge was tinged with terror.

The dragon's fury filled his head until he thought that it would burst; the ground shook beneath his feet. But the rage turned to frustration and died, as though the gates of liquid iron had bottled it up with its possessor. He gulped air, holding his body together with an effort of will. The voice of the dragon pushed aside his thoughts again, trampled them underfoot; but he knew that it could not reach him, and he endured without weakening.

(Who are you, and why have you come?)

He sensed a grudging resignation in the formless words, the feel of a ritual as eternal as the rain.

"I am a man who should have been a king. I've come to you, who are King of Storms, for help in regaining my own kingdom."

(You ask me for that? Your needs mean nothing, human. You were born to misery, born to crawl, born to struggle and be defeated by the powers of Air and Fire and Water. You are meaningless, you are less than nothing to me!)

Lassan-din felt the truth of his own insignificance, the weight of the dragon's disdain. "That may be," he said sourly. "But this insignificant human has penned you up with the Earth's blessing, and I have no reason to ever let you go unless you pledge me your aid."

The rage of the storm beast welled up in him again, so like his own rage; it rumbled and thundered in the hollow of the mountain. But again a profound agony broke its fury, and the raging storm subsided. He caught phantom images of stone walls lit by shifting light, the smell of water.

(If you have the strength of the Earth with you, why bother me for mine?)

"The Earth moves too slowly," *and too uncertainly*, but he did not say that. "I need a fury to match my own."

(Arrogant fool,) the voice whispered, (you have no measure of my fury.)

"Your fury can crumble walls and blast towers. You can destroy a fortress castle—and the men who defend it. I know what you can do," refusing to be cowed. "And if you swear to do it for me, I'll set you free."

(You want a castle ruined. Is that all?) A tone of false reason crept into the intruding thoughts.

"No. I also want for myself a share of your strength—protection from my enemies." He had spent half a hundred cold, sleepless nights planning these words; searching his memory for pieces of dragon-lore, trying to guess the limits of its power.

(How can I give you that? I do not share my power, unless I strike you dead with it.)

"My people say that in the Golden Time the heroes wore mail

JOAN D. VINGE

made from dragon scales, and were invincible. Can you give me that?" He asked the question directly, knowing that the dragon might evade the truth, but that it was bound by immutable natural law and could not lie.

(I can give you that,) grudgingly. (Is that all you ask of me?)

Lassan-din hesitated. "No. One more thing." His father had taught him caution, if nothing else. "One request to be granted at some future time—a request within your power, but one you must obey."

The dragon muttered, deep within the mountainside, and Lassan-din sensed its growing distress as the water poured into the cave. (If it is within my power, then, yes!) Dark clouds of anger filled his mind. (Free me, and you will have everything you ask!) *And more*— Did he hear that last, or was it only the echoing of his own mind? (Free me, and enter my den.)

"What I undo, I can do again." He spoke the warning more to reassure himself than to remind the dragon. He gathered himself mentally, knowing this time what he was reaching toward with all his strength, made confident by his success. And the Earth answered him once more. He saw the river shift and heave again like a glistening serpent, cascading back into its original bed; opening the cave mouth to his sight, fanged and dripping. He stood alone on the hillside, deafened by his heartbeat and the crashing absence of the river's voice. And then, calling his own strength back, he slid and clambered down the hillside to the mouth of the dragon's cave.

The flickering illumination of the dragon's fire led him deep into a maze of stone passageways, his boots slipping on the wet rock. His hair stood on end and his fingertips tingled with static charge; the air reeked of ozone. The light grew stronger as he rounded a final corner of rock; blazed up, echoing and reechoing from the walls. He shouted in protest as it pinned him like a creeping insect against the cave wall.

The light faded gradually to a tolerable level, letting him observe as he was observed, taking in the towering, twisted, black-tar formations of congealed magma that walled this cavern . . . the sudden, heart-stopping vision they enclosed. He looked on the Storm King in silence for a time that seemed endless.

A glistening layer of cast-off scales was its bed, and he could scarcely tell where the mound ceased and the dragon's own body began. The dragon looked nothing like the legends described, and yet just as he had expected it to (and somehow he did not find that strange): Great mailed claws like crystal kneaded the shifting opalescence of its bed; its forelegs shimmered with the flexing of its muscles. It had no hindquarters, its body tapered into the fluid coils of a snake's form woven through the glistening pile. Immense segmented wings, as leathery as a bat's, as fragile as a butterfly's, cloaked its monstrous strength. A long, sinuous neck stretched toward him; red faceted eyes shone with inner light from a face that was closest to a cat's face of all the things he knew, but fiercely fanged and grotesquely distorted. The horns of a stag sprouted from its forehead, and foxfire danced among the spines. The dragon's size was a thing that he could have described easily, and yet it was somehow immeasurable, beyond his comprehension.

This was the creature he had challenged and brought to bay with his feeble spell-casting . . . this boundless, pitiless, infinite demon of the air. His body began to tremble, having more sense than he did. But he *had* brought it to bay, taken its word-bond, and it had not blasted him the moment he entered its den. He forced his quavering voice to carry boldly, "I'm here. Where is my armor?"

(Leave your useless garments and come forward. My scales are my strength. Lie among them and cover yourself with them. But remember when you do that if you wear my mail, and share my power, you may find them hard to put off again. Do you accept that?)

"Why would I ever want to get rid of power? I accept it! Power is the center of everything."

(But power has its price, and we do not always know how high it will be.) The dragon stirred restlessly, remembering the price of power as the water still pooling on the cavern's floor seeped up through its shifting bed.

Lassan-din frowned, hearing a deceit because he expected one. He stripped off his clothing without hesitation and crossed the vast, shadow-haunted chamber to the gleaming mound. He lay down below the dragon's baleful gaze and buried himself in the cool, scintillating flecks of scale. They were damp and surprisingly light under his touch, adhering to his body like the dust rubbed from a moth's wing. When he had covered himself completely, until even his hair glistened with myriad infinitesimal lights, the dragon bent its head until the horrible mockery of a cat's face loomed above him. He cringed back as it opened its mouth, showing him row behind row of inward-turning teeth, and a glowing forge of light. It let its breath out upon him, and his sudden scream rang darkly in the chamber as lightning wrapped his unprotected body.

But the crippling lash of pain was gone as quickly as it had come, and looking at himself he found the coating of scales fused into a film of armor as supple as his own skin, and as much a part of him now. His scale-gloved hands met one another in wonder, the hands of an alien creature.

(Now come.) A great glittering wing extended, inviting him to climb. (Cling to me as your armor clings to you, and let me do your bidding and be done with it.)

He mounted the wing with elaborate caution, and at last sat astride the reptilian neck, clinging to it with an uncertainty that did not fully acknowledge its reality.

The dragon moved under him without ceremony or sign, slithering down from its dais of scales with a hiss and rumble that trembled the closed space. A wind rose around them with the movement; Lassan-din felt himself swallowed into a vortex of cold, terrifying force that took his breath away, blinding and deafening him as he was sucked out of the cave-darkness and into the outer air.

Lightning cracked and shuddered, penetrating his closed lids, splitting apart his consciousness; thunder clogged his chest, reverberating through his flesh and bones like the crashing fall of an avalanche. Rain lashed him, driving into his eyes, swallowing him whole but not dissolving or dissipating his armor of scales.

In the first wild moments of storm he had been piercingly aware of an agony that was not his own, a part of the dragon's being tied into his consciousness, while the fury of rain and storm fed back on their creator. But now there was no pain, no awareness of anything tangible; even the substantiality of the dragon's existence beneath him had faded. The elemental storm was all that existed now, he was aware only of its raw, unrelenting power surrounding him, sweeping him on to his destiny.

After an eternity lost in the storm he found his sight again, felt the dragon's rippling motion beneath his hands. The clouds parted and as his vision cleared he saw, ahead and below, the gray stone battlements of the castle fortress that had once been his . . . and was about to become his again. He shouted in half-mad exultation, feeling the dragon's surging, unconquerable strength become his own. He saw from his incredible height the tiny, terrified forms of those men who had defeated and tormented him, saw them cowering like worms before the doom descending upon them. And then the vision was torn apart again in a blinding explosion of energy, as lightning struck the stone towers again and again, and the screams of the fortress's defenders were lost in the avalanche of thunder. His own senses reeled, and he felt the dragon's solidity dissolve beneath him once more; with utter disbelief felt himself falling, like the rain. . . . "No! No—!"

But his reeling senses righted abruptly, and he found himself standing solidly on his own feet, on the smoking battlements of his castle. Storm and flame and tumbled stone were all around him, but the blackened, fear-filled faces of the beaten defenders turned as one to look up at his; their arms rose, pointing, their cries reached him dimly. An arrow struck his chest, and another struck his shoulder, staggering him; but they fell away, rattling harmlessly down his scaled body to his feet. A shaft of sunlight broke the clouds, setting afire the glittering carapace of his armor. Already the storm was beginning to dissipate; above him the dragon's retreat stained the sky with a band of rainbow scales falling. The voice of the storm touched his mind a final time, (You have what you desire. May it bring you the pleasure you deserve.)

The survivors began, one by one, to fall to their knees below him.

Lassan-din had ridden out of exile on the back of the whirlwind, and his people bowed down before him, not in welcome but in awe and terror. He reclaimed his birthright and his throne, purging his realm of those who had overthrown it with vengeful thoroughness, but never able to purge himself of the memories of what they had done to him. His treacherous uncle had been killed in the dragon's attack, robbing Lassan-din of his longed-for retribution, the payment in kind for his own crippling wound. He wore his bitterness like the glittering dragonskin, and he found that like the dragonskin it could not be cast off again. His people hated and feared him for his shining alienness; hated him all the more for his attempts to secure his place as their ruler, seeing in him the living symbol of his uncle's inhumanity, and his father's. But he knew no other way to rule them; he could only go on, as his father had done before him, proving again and again to his people that there was no escaping what he had become. Not for them, not for himself.

They called him the Storm King, and he had all the power he had ever dreamed of—but it brought him no pleasure or ease, no escape from the knowledge that he was hated or from the chronic pain of his maimed back. He was both more and less than a man, but he was no longer a man. He was only the king. His comfort and happiness mattered to no one, except that his comfort reflected their own. No thought, no word, no act affected him that was not performed out of selfishness; and more and more he withdrew from any contact with that imitation of intimacy.

He lay alone again in his chambers on a night that was black and formless, like all his nights. Lying between silken sheets he dreamed that he was starving and slept on stones.

Pain woke him. He drank port wine (as lately he drank it too often) until he slept again, and entered the dream he had had long ago in a witch's hut, a dream that might have been something more. . . . But he woke from that dream too; and waking, he remembered the witch-girl's last words to him, echoed by the storm's roaring—"May you get what you deserve."

That same day he left his fortress castle, where the new stone of its mending showed whitely against the old; left his rule in the hands of advisors cowed by threats of the dragon's return; left his homeland again on a journey to the dreary, gray-clad land of his exile.

He did not come to the village of Wydden as a hunted exile this time, but as a conqueror gathering tribute from his subject lands. No one there recognized the one in the other, or knew why he ordered the village priest thrown bodily out of his wretched temple into the muddy street. But on the dreary day when Lassan-din made his way at last into the dripping woods beneath the ancient volcanic peak, he made the final secret journey not as a conqueror. He came alone to the ragged hut pressed up against the brooding mountain wall, suffering the wet and cold like a friendless stranger.

He came upon the clearing between the trees with an unnatural suddenness, to find a figure in mud-stained, earth-brown robes standing by the well, waiting, without surprise. He knew instantly that it was not the old hag; but it took him a longer moment to realize who it was: The girl called Nothing stood before him, dressed as a woman now, her brown hair neatly plaited on top of her head and bearing herself with a woman's dignity. He stopped, throwing back the hood of his cloak to let her see his own glittering face—though he was certain she already knew him, had expected him.

She bowed to him with seeming formality. "The Storm King honors my humble shrine." Her voice was not humble in the least.

"Your shrine?" He moved forward. "Where's the old bitch?"

She folded her arms as though to ward him off. "Gone forever. As I thought you were. But I'm still here, and I serve in her place; I am Fallatha, the Earth's Own, now. And your namesake still dwells in the mountain, bringing grief to all who live in its cloud-shadow. . . . I thought you'd taken all you could from us, and gained everything you wanted. Why have you come back, and come like a beggar?"

His mouth thinned. But this once he stopped the arrogant response that came too easily to his lips—remembering that he had come here the way he had to remind himself that he must ask, and not demand. "I came because I need your help again."

"What could I possibly have to offer our great ruler? My spells are nothing compared to the storm's wrath. And you have no use for my poor body—"

He jerked at the mocking echo of his own thoughts. "Once I had, on that night we both remember—that night you gave me back the use of mine." He gambled with the words. His eyes sought the curve of her breasts, not quite hidden beneath her loose outer robe.

"It was a dream, a wish; no more. It never happened." She shook her head, her face still expressionless. But in the silence that fell between them he heard a small, uncanny sound that chilled him: Somewhere in the woods a baby was crying.

Fallatha glanced unthinkingly over her shoulder, toward the hut, and he knew then that it was her child. She made a move to stop him as he started past her; let him go, and followed resignedly. He found the child inside, an infant squalling in a blanket on a bed of fragrant pine boughs. Its hair was midnight black, its eyes were dark, its skin dusky; his own child, he knew with a certainty that went beyond simply what his eyes showed him. He knelt, unwrapping the blanket—let it drop back as he saw the baby's form. "A girl-child." His voice was dull with disappointment.

Fallatha's eyes said that she understood the implications. "Of course. I have no more use for a boy-child than you have for this one. Had it been a male child, I would have left it in the woods."

His head came up angrily, and her gaze slapped him with his own scorn. He looked down again at his infant daughter, feeling ashamed. "Then it did happen. . . ." His hands tightened by his knees. "Why?" Looking up at her again.

"Many reasons, and many you couldn't understand. . . . But one was to win my freedom from the Old One. She stole my soul, and hid it in a tree to keep me her slave. She might have died without telling me where it was. Without a soul I had no center, no strength, no reality. So I brought a new soul into myself—this one's," smiling suddenly at the wailing baby, "and used its focus to make her give me back my own. And then with two souls," the smile hardened, "I took hers away. She wanders the forest now searching for it. But she won't find it." Fallatha touched the pendant of rock crystal that hung against her breast; what had been ice-clear before was now a deep, smoky gray color.

Lassan-din suppressed a shudder. "But why *my* child?" *My child.*

His own gaze would not stay away from the baby for long. "Surely any village lout would have been glad to do you the service."

"Because you have royal blood, you were a king's son—you are a king."

"That's not necessarily proof of good breeding." He surprised himself with his own honesty.

"But you called on the Earth, and She answered you. I have never seen Her answer a man before . . . and because you were in need." Her voice softened unexpectedly. "An act of kindness begets a kind soul, they say."

"And now you hope to beget some reward for it, no doubt." He spoke the words with automatic harshness. "Greed and pity—a fitting set of god-parents, to match her real ones."

She shrugged. "You will see what you want to see, I suppose. But even a blind man could see more clearly." A frown pinched her forehead. "You've come here to me for help, Lassan-din; I didn't come to you."

He rubbed his scale-bright hands together, a motion that had become a habit long since; they clicked faintly. "Does—does the baby have a name?"

"Not yet. It is not our custom to name a child before its first year. Too often they die. Especially in these times."

He looked away from her eyes. "What will you do with—our child?" Realizing suddenly that it mattered a great deal to him.

"Keep her with me, and raise her to serve the Earth, as I do."

"If you help me again, I'll take you both back to my own lands, and give you anything you desire." He searched her face for a response.

"I desire to be left in peace with my child and my goddess." She leaned down to pick the baby up, let it seek her breast.

His inspiration crystallized: "Damn it, I'll throw my own priests out, I'll make your goddess the only one and you Her high priestess!"

Her eyes brightened, and faded. "A promise easily spoken, and difficult to keep."

"What do you want, then?" He got to his feet, exasperated.

"You have a boon left with the dragon, I know. Make it leave the mountain. Send it away."

He ran his hands through his glittering hair. "No. I need it. I came here seeking help for myself, not your people."

"They're your people now—they *are* you. Help them and you help yourself! Is that so impossible for you to see?" Her own anger blazed white, incandescent with frustration.

"If you want to be rid of the dragon so much, why haven't you sent it away yourself, witch?"

"I would have." She touched the baby's tiny hand, its soft black hair. "Long ago. But until the little one no longer suckles my strength away, I lack the power to call the Earth to my purpose."

"Then you can't help me, either." His voice was flat and hopeless.

"I still have the salve that eased your back. But it won't help you now, it won't melt away your dragon's skin. . . . I couldn't help your real needs, even if I had all my power."

"What do you mean?" He thrust his face at her. "You think that's why I've come to you—to be rid of this skin? What makes you think I'd ever want to give up *my* power, my protection?" He clawed at his arms.

"It's not a man's skin that makes him a god—or a monster," Fallatha said quietly. "It's what lies beneath the skin, behind the eyes. You've lost your soul, as I lost mine; and only you know where to find it. . . . But perhaps it would do you good to shed that skin that keeps you safe from hatred; and from love and joy and mercy, all the other feelings that might pass between human beings, between your people and their king."

"Yes! Yes, I want to be free of it, by the Holy Sun!" His defiance collapsed under the weight of the truth: He saw at last that he had come here this time to rid himself of the same things he had come to rid himself of—and to find—before. "I have a last boon due me from the dragon. It made me as I am; it can unmake me." He ran his hands down his chest, feeling the slippery, unyielding scales hidden beneath the rich cloth of his shirt.

"You mean to seek it out again, then?"

He nodded, and his hands made fists.

She carried the baby with her to the shelf above the crooked window, took down a small earthenware pot. She opened it and held it close to the child's face still buried at her breast; the baby sagged into sleep in the crook of her arm. She turned back to his uncomprehending face. "The little one will sleep now until I wake her. We can take the inner way, as we did before."

"You're coming? Why?"

"You didn't ask me that before. Why ask it now?"

He wasn't sure whether it was a question or an answer. Feeling as though not only his body but his mind was an empty shell, he shrugged and kept silent.

They made the nightmare climb into blackness again, worming their way upward through the mountain's entrails; but this time

JOAN D. VINGE

she did not leave him where the mountain spewed them out, close under the weeping lid of the sky. He rested the night with the mother of his child, the two of them lying together but apart. At dawn they pushed on, Lassan-din leading now, following the river's rushing torrent upward into the past.

They came to the dragon's cave at last, gazed on it for a long while in silence, having no strength left for speech.

"Storm King!" Lassan-din gathered the rags of his voice and his concentration for a shout. "Hear me! I have come for my last request!"

There was an alien stirring inside his mind; the charge in the air and the dim, flickering light deep within the cave seemed to intensify.

(So you have returned to plague me.) The voice inside his head cursed him, with the weariness of the ages. He felt the stretch and play of storm-sinews rousing; remembered suddenly, dizzily, the feel of his ride on the whirlwind.

(Show yourself to me.)

They followed the winding tunnel as he had done before to an audience in the black hall radiant with the dust of rainbows. The dragon crouched on its scaly bed, its glowering ruby eye fixed on them. Lassan-din stopped, trying to keep a semblance of self-possession. Fallatha drew her robes close together at her throat and murmured something unintelligible.

(I see that this time you have the wisdom to bring your true source of power with you . . . though she has no power in her now. Why have you come to me again? Haven't I given you all that you asked for?)

"All that and more," he said heavily. "You've doubled the weight of the griefs I brought with me before."

(I?) The dragon bent its head; its horns raked them with claw-fingered shadows in the sudden, swelling brightness. (I did nothing to you. Whatever consequences you've suffered are no concern of mine.)

Lassan-din bit back a stinging retort; said, calmly, "But you remember that you owe me one final boon. You know that I've come to collect it."

(Anything within my power.) The huge cat-face bowed ill-humoredly; Lassan-din felt his skin prickle with the static energy of the moment.

"Then take away these scales you fixed on me, that make me invulnerable to everything human!" He pulled off his drab, dark cloak and the rich, royal clothing of red and blue beneath it, so that his body shone like an echo of the dragon's own.

The dragon's faceted eyes regarded him without feeling. (I cannot.)

Lassan-din froze as the words out of his blackest nightmares turned him to stone. "What—what do you mean, you cannot? You did this to me—you can undo it!"

(I cannot. I can give you invulnerability, but I cannot take it away from you. I cannot make your scales dissolve and fall away with a breath any more than I can keep the rain from dissolving mine, or causing me exquisite pain. It is in the nature of power that those who wield it must suffer from it, even as their victims suffer. This is power's price—I tried to warn you. But you didn't listen . . . none of them have ever listened.) Lassan-din felt the sting of venom, and the ache of an ageless empathy.

He struggled to grasp the truth, knowing that the dragon could not lie. He swayed as belief struck him at last, like a blow. "Am I . . . am I to go through the rest of my life like this, then? Like a monster?" He rubbed his hands together, a useless, mindless washing motion.

(I only know that it is not in my power to give you freedom from yourself.) The dragon wagged its head, its face swelling with light, dazzling him. (Go away, then,) the thought struck him fiercely, (and suffer elsewhere!)

Lassan-din turned away, stumbling, like a beaten dog. But Fallatha caught at his glittering, naked shoulder, shook him roughly. "Your boon! It still owes you one—ask it!"

"Ask for what?" he mumbled, barely aware of her. "There's nothing I want."

"There is! Something for your people, for your child—even for you. Ask for it! Ask!"

He stared at her, saw her pale, pinched face straining with suppressed urgency and desire. He saw in her eyes the endless sunless days, the ruined crops, the sodden fields—the mud and hunger and misery the Storm King had brought to the lands below for three times her lifetime. And the realization came to him that even now, when he had lost control of his own life, he still had the power to end this land's misery.

He turned back into the sight of the dragon's hypnotically swaying head. "My last boon, then, is something else; something I know to be within your power, stormbringer. I want you to leave this mountain, leave these lands, and never return. I want you to travel seven days on your way before you seek a new settling place, if you ever

JOAN D. VINGE

do. Travel as fast as you can, and as far, without taking retribution from the lands below. That is the final thing I ask of you."

The dragon spat in blinding fury. Lassan-din shut his eyes, felt the ground shudder and roll beneath him. (You dare to command me to leave my chosen lands? You dare?)

"I claim my right!" He shouted it, his voice breaking. "Leave these lands alone—take your grief elsewhere and be done with them, and me!"

(As you wish, then—) The Storm King swelled above them until it filled the cave-space, its eyes a garish hellshine fading into the night-blackness of storm. Lightning sheeted the closing walls, thunder rumbled through the rock, a screaming whirlwind battered them down against the cavern floor. Rain poured over them until there was no breathing space, and the Storm King roared its agony inside their skulls as it suffered retribution for its vengeance. Lassan-din felt his senses leave him; knowing the storm's revenge would be the last thing he ever knew, the end of the world. . . .

But he woke again, to silence. He stirred sluggishly on the wet stone floor, filling his lungs again and again with clear air, filling his empty mind with the awareness that all was quiet now, that no storm raged for his destruction. He heard a moan, not his own, and coughing echoed hollowly in the silence. He raised his head, reached out in the darkness, groping, until he found her arm. "Fallatha—?"

"Alive . . . praise the Earth."

He felt her move, sitting up, dragging herself toward him. The Earth, the cave in which they lay, had endured the storm's rage with sublime indifference. They helped each other up, stumbled along the wall to the entrance tunnel, made their way out through the blackness onto the mountainside.

They stood together, clinging to each other for support and reassurance, blinking painfully in the glaring light of early evening. It took him long moments to realize that there was more light than he remembered, not less.

"Look!" Fallatha raised her arm, pointing. Water dripped in a silver line from the sleeve of her robe. "The sky! The sky—" She laughed, a sound that was almost a sob.

He looked up into the aching glare, saw patches that he took at first for blackness, until his eyes knew them finally for blue. It was still raining lightly, but the clouds were parting; the tyranny of gray was broken at last. For a moment he felt her joy as his own, a fleeting, wild triumph—until, looking down, he saw his hands

again, and his shimmering body still scaled, monstrous, untrans-
formed. . . . "Oh, gods—!" His fists clenched at the sound of his own
curse, a useless plea to useless deities.

Fallatha turned to him, her arm still around his shoulder, her
face sharing his despair. "Lassan-din, remember that my people will
love you for your sacrifice. In time, even your own people may come
to love you for it. . . ." She touched his scaled cheek hesitantly, a
promise.

"But all they'll ever see is how I look! And no matter what I do
from now on, when they see the mark of damnation on me, they'll
only remember why they hated me." He caught her arms in a bruis-
ing grip. "Fallatha, help me, please—I'll give you anything you ask!"

She shook her head, biting her lips, "I can't, Lassan-din. No more
than the dragon could. You must help yourself, change yourself—I
can't do that for you."

"How? How can I change this if all the magic of Earth and Sky
can't do it?" He sank to his knees, feeling the rain strike the opal-
escent scales and trickle down—feeling it dimly, barely, as though
the rain fell on someone else. . . . Through all of his life, the rain
had never fallen unless it fell on him; the wind had never stirred
the trees, a child had never cried in hunger, unless it was his hunger.
And yet he had never truly felt any of those things—never even
been aware of his own loss. . . . Until now, looking up at the mother
of his only child, whose strength of feeling had forced him to drive
out the dragon, the one unselfish thing he had ever done. Remorse
and resolution filled the emptiness in him, as rage had filled him
on this spot once before. Tears welled in his eyes and spilled over,
in answer to the calling-spell of grief; ran down his face, mingling
with the rain. He put up his hands, sobbing uncontrollably, un-
selfconsciously, as though he were the last man alive in the world,
and alone forever.

And as he wept he felt a change begin in the flesh that met there,
face against hands. A tingling and burning, the feel of skin sleep-
deadened coming alive again. He lowered his hands wonderingly,
saw the scales that covered them dissolving, the skin beneath them
his own olive-brown, supple and smooth. He shouted in amazement,
and wept harder, pain and joy intermingled, like the tears and rain
that melted the cursed scales from his body and washed them away.

He went on weeping until he had cleansed himself in body and
spirit; set himself free from the prison of his own making. And then,
exhausted and uncertain, he climbed to his feet again, meeting the
calm, gray gaze of the Earth's gratitude in Fallatha's eyes. He smiled

and she smiled; the unexpectedness of the expression, and the sight of it, resonated in him.

Sunlight was spreading across the patchwork land far below, dressing the mountain slope in royal greens, although the rain still fell around them. He looked up almost unthinkingly, searching—found what he had not realized he sought. Fallatha followed his glance and found it with him. Her smile widened at the arching band of colors, the rainbow; not a curse any longer, or a mark of pain, but once again a promise of better days to come.

THE REGULARS
by Robert Silverberg
art: Jack Gaughan

Robert Silverberg is the author
of Lord Valentine's Castle *and*
Majipoor Chronicles. *He lives in California.*

It was the proverbial night not fit for man nor beast, black and grim and howling, with the rain coming on in sidewise sheets. But in Charley Sullivan's place everything was as cozy as an old boot, the lights dim, the heat turned up, the neon beer signs sputtering pleasantly, Charley behind the bar filling them beyond the Plimsoll line, and all the regulars in their regular places. What a comfort a tavern like Charley Sullivan's can be on a night that's black and grim and howling!

"It was a night like this," said The Pope to Karl Marx, "that you changed your mind about blowing up the stock exchange, as I recall. Eh?"

Karl Marx nodded moodily. "It was the beginning of the end for me as a true revolutionary, it was." He isn't Irish, but in Charley Sullivan's everybody picks up the rhythm of it soon enough. "When you get too fond of your comforts to be willing to go out into a foul gale to attack the enemies of the proletariat, it's the end of your vocation, sure enough." He sighed and peered into his glass. It held nothing but suds, and he sighed again.

"Can I buy you another?" asked The Pope. "In memory of your vocation."

"You may indeed," said Karl Marx.

The Pope looked around. "And who else is needy? My turn to set them up!"

The Leading Man tapped the rim of his glass. So did Ms. Bewley and Mors Longa. I smiled and shook my head, and The Ingenue passed also, but Toulouse-Lautrec, down at the end of the bar, looked away from the television set long enough to give the signal. Charley efficiently handed out the refills—beer for the apostle of the class struggle, Jack Daniels for Mors Longa, Valpolicella for The Pope, Scotch-and-water for The Leading Man, white wine for Ms. Bewley, Perrier with slice of lemon for Toulouse-Lautrec, since he had had the cognac the last time and claimed to be tapering off. And for me, Myers on the rocks. Charley never needs to ask. Of course, he knows us all very well.

"Cheers," said The Leading Man, and we drank up, and then an angel passed by, and the long silence ended only when a nasty rumble of thunder went through the place at about 6.3 on the Richter scale.

"Nasty night," The Ingenue said. "Imagine trying to elope in a downpour like this! I can see it now, Harry and myself at the boathouse, and the car—"

"Harry and *I*," said Mors Longa. " 'Myself' is reflexive. As you well know, sweet."

The Ingenue blinked sweetly. "I always forget. Anyway, there was Harry and I at the boathouse, and the car was waiting, my cousin's old Pierce-Arrow with the—"

—bar in the back seat that was always stocked with the best imported liqueurs, I went on silently just a fraction of a second ahead of her clear high voice, *and all we had to do was drive 90 miles across the state line to the place where the justice of the peace was waiting—*

I worked on my rum. The Leading Man, moving a little closer to The Ingenue, tenderly took her hand as the nasty parts of the story began to unfold. The Pope wheezed sympathetically into his wine, and Karl Marx scowled and pounded one fist against the other, and even Ms. Bewley, who had very little tolerance for The Ingenue's silliness, managed a bright smile in the name of sisterhood.

"—the rain, you see, had done something awful to the car's wiring, and there we were, Harry on his knees in the mud trying to fix it, and me half crazy with excitement and impatience, and the night getting worse and worse, when we heard dogs barking and—"

—my guardian and two of his men appeared out of the night—

We had heard it all fifty times before. She tells it every horrid rainy night. From no one else do we tolerate any such repetition—we have our sensibilities, and it would be cruel and unusual to be forced to listen to the same fol-de-rol over and over and over—but The Ingenue is a dear sweet young thing, and her special foible it is to repeat herself, and she and she alone gets away with it among the regulars at Charley Sullivan's. We followed along, nodding and sighing and shaking our heads at all the appropriate places, the way you do when you're hearing Beethoven's Fifth or Schubert's Unfinished, and she was just getting around to the tempestuous climax, her fiance and her guardian in a fight to the death illuminated by baleful flashes of lightning, when there was a crack of real lightning outside, followed almost instantly by a blast of thunder that made the last one seem like the sniffle of a mosquito. The vibrations shook three glasses off the bar and stood Charley Sullivan's framed photos of President Kennedy and Pope John XXIII on their corners.

The next thing that happened was the door opened and a new customer walked in. And you can imagine that we all sat to attention at that, because you would expect only the regulars to be populating Charley's place in such weather, and it was a genuine novelty to have a stranger materialize. Well timed, too, because without him we'd have had fifteen minutes more of the tale of The Ingenue's bungled elopement.

He was maybe 32 or a little less, roughly dressed in heavy-duty Levi's, a thick black cardigan, and a ragged pea-jacket. His dark unruly hair was soaked and matted. On no particular evidence I decided he was a merchant sailor who had just jumped ship. For a moment he stood a little way within the door, eyeing us all with that cautious look a bar-going man has when he comes to a new place where everyone else is obviously a long-time regular; and then he smiled, a little shyly at first, more warmly as he saw some of us smiling back. He took off his jacket, hung it on the rack above the jukebox, shook himself like a drenched dog, and seated himself at the bar between The Pope and Mors Longa. "Jesus," he said, "what a stinking night! I can't tell you how glad I was to see a light burning at the end of the block."

"You'll like it here, brother," said The Pope. "Charley, let me buy this young man his first."

"You took the last round," Mors Longa pointed out. "May I, Your Holiness?"

The Pope shrugged. "Why not?"

"My pleasure," said Mors Longa to the newcomer. "What will it be?"

"Do they have Old Bushmill here?"

"They have everything here," said Mors Longa. "*Charley* has everything. Our host. Bushmill for the lad, Charley, and a double, I think. And is anyone else ready?"

"A sweetener here," said The Leading Man. Toulouse-Lautrec opted for his next cognac. The Ingenue, who seemed to have forgotten that she hadn't finished telling her story, waved for her customary rye-and-ginger. The rest of us stood pat.

"What's your ship?" I asked.

The stranger gave me a startled look. "*Pequod Maru,* Liberian flag. How'd you know?"

"Good guesser. Where bound? D'ye mind?"

He took a long pull of his whiskey. "Maracaibo, they said. Not a

ROBERT SILVERBERG

tanker. Coffee and cacao. But I'm not going. I—ah—resigned my commission. This afternoon, very suddenly. Jesus, this tastes good. What a fine warm place this is!"

"And glad we are to see you," said Charley Sullivan. "We'll call you Ishmael, eh?"

"Ishmael?"

"We all need names here," said Mors Longa. "This gentleman we call Karl Marx, for example. He's socially conscious. That's Toulouse-Lautrec down there by the tube. And you can think of me as Mors Longa."

Ishmael frowned. "Is that an Italian name?"

"Latin, actually. Not a name, a sort of a phrase. *Mors longa, vita brevis.* My motto. And that's The Ingenue, who needs a lot of love and protection, and this is Ms. Bewley, who can look after herself, and—"

He went all around the room. Ishmael appeared to be working hard at remembering the names. He repeated them until he had them straight, but he still looked a little puzzled. "Bars I've been in," he said, "it isn't the custom to make introductions like this. Makes it seem more like a private party than a bar."

"A family gathering, more like," said Ms. Bewley.

Karl Marx said, "We constitute a society here. It is not the consciousness of men that determines their existence, but on the contrary their social existence determines their consciousness. We look after one another in this place."

"You'll like it here," said The Pope.

"I do. I'm amazed how much I like it." The sailor grinned. "This may be the bar I've been looking for all my life."

"No doubt but that it is," said Charley Sullivan. "And a Bushmill's on me, lad?"

Shyly Ishmael pushed his glass forward, and Charley topped it off.

"So friendly here," Ishmael said. "Almost like—home."

"Like one's club, perhaps," said The Leading Man.

"A club, a home, yes," said Mors Longa, signalling Charley for another bourbon. "Karl Marx tells it truly: we care for each other here. We are friends, and we strive constantly to amuse one another and protect one another, which are the two chief duties of friends. We buy each other drinks, we talk, we tell stories to while away the darkness."

"Do you come here every night?"

"We never miss a one," Mors Longa said.

"You must know each other very well by this time."

"Very well. Very very well."

"The kind of place I've always dreamed of," Ishmael said wonderingly. "The kind of place I'd never want to leave." He let his eyes pan in a slow arc around the whole room, past the jukebox, the pool table, the dart board, the television screen, the tattered 1934 calendar that had never been changed, the fireplace, the piano. He was glowing, and not just from the whiskey. "Why would anyone ever want to leave a place like this?"

"It is a very good place," said Karl Marx.

Mors Longa said, "And when you find a very good place, it's the place where you want to remain. Of course. It becomes your club, as our friend says. Your home away from home. But that reminds me of a story, young man. Have you ever heard about the bar that nobody actually ever does leave? The bar where everyone stays forever, because they couldn't leave even if they wanted to? Do you know that one?"

"Never heard it," said Ishmael.

But the rest of us had. In Charley Sullivan's place we try never to tell the same story twice, in order to spare each other's sensibilities, for boredom is the deadliest of afflictions here. Only The Ingenue is exempt from that rule, because it is her nature to tell her stories again and again, and we love her all the same. Nevertheless it sometimes happens that one of us must tell an old and familiar story to a newcomer; but though at other times we give each other full attention, it is not required at a time such as that. So The Leading Man and The Ingenue wandered off for a tete-a-tete by the fireplace; and Karl Marx challenged The Pope to a round of darts; and the others drifted off to this corner or that, until only Mors Longa and the sailor and I were still at the bar, I drowsing over my rum and Mors Longa getting that far-away look and Ishmael, leaning intently forward, saying, "A bar where nobody can ever leave? What a strange sort of place!"

"Yes," said Mors Longa.

"Where is there such a place?"

"In no particular part of the Universe. By which I mean it lies somewhere outside of space and time as we understand those concepts, everywhere and nowhere at once, although it looks not at all alien or strange apart from its timelessness and its spacelessness. In fact, it looks, I'm told, like every bar you've ever been in in your life, only more so. The proprietor's a big man with black Irish in him, a lot like Charley Sullivan here; and he doesn't mind setting

ROBERT SILVERBERG

one up for the regulars now and then on the house; and he always gives good measure and keeps the heat turned up nicely. And the wood is dark and mellow and well polished, and the railing is the familiar brass, and there are the usual two hanging ferns and the usual aspidistra in the corner next to the spittoon, and there's a dart board and a pool table and all those other things that you find in bars of the kind that this one is. You understand me? This is *a perfectly standard sort of bar*, but it doesn't happen to be in New York City or San Francisco or Hamburg or Rangoon, or in any other city you're likely to have visited, though the moment you walk into this place you feel right at home in it."

"Just like here."

"Very much like here," said Mors Longa.

"But people never leave?" Ishmael's brows furrowed. "*Never?*"

"Well, actually, some of them do," Mors Longa said. "But let me talk about the other ones first, all right? The regulars, the ones who are there *all the time*. You know, there are certain people who absolutely never go into bars, the ones who prefer to do their drinking at home, or in restaurants before dinner, or not at all. But then there are the bar-going sorts. Some of them are folks who just like to drink, you know, and find a bar a convenient place to get their whistles wetted when they're en route from somewhere to somewhere else. And there are some who think drinking's a social act, eh? But you also find people in bars, a lot of them, who go to the place because there's an emptiness in them that needs to be filled, a dark cold hollow space, to be filled not just with good warm bourbon, you understand, but a mystic and invisible substance that emanates from others who are in the same way, people who somehow have had a bit of their souls leak away from them by accident, and need the comfort of being among their own kind. Say, a priest who's lost his calling, or a writer who's forgotten the joy of putting stories down on paper, or a painter to whom all colors have become shades of gray, or a surgeon whose scalpel hand has picked up a bit of a tremor, or a photographer whose eyes don't quite focus right any more. You know the sort, don't you? You find a lot of that sort in bars. Something in their eyes tells you what they are. But in this particular bar that I'm talking about, you find *only* that sort, good people, decent people, but people with that empty zone inside them. Which makes it even more like all the other bars there are, in fact the Platonic ideal of a bar, if you follow me, a kind of three-dimensional stereotype populated by flesh-and-blood clichés, a sort of perpetual stage set, do you see? Hearing about a place like that where

THE REGULARS 225

everybody's a little tragic, everybody's a bit on the broken side, everyone is a perfect bar type, you'd laugh, you'd say it's unreal, it's too much like everybody's idea of what such a place ought to be like to be convincing. Eh? But all stereotypes are rooted firmly in reality, you know. That's what makes them stereotypes, because they're exactly like reality, only more so. And to the people who do their drinking in the bar I'm talking about, it isn't any stereotype and they aren't cliches. It's the only reality they have, the realest reality there is, for them, and it's no good sneering at it, because it's their own little world, the world of the archetypical saloon, the world of the bar regulars."

"Who never leave the place," said Ishmael.

"How can they? Where would they go? What would they do on a day off? They have no identity except inside the bar. The bar is their life. The bar is their universe. They have no business going elsewhere. They simply stay where they are. They tell each other stories and they work hard to keep each other happy, *and for them there is no world outside*. That's what it means to be a regular, to be a Platonic ideal. Every night the bar and everything in it vanishes into a kind of inchoate gray mist at closing time, and every morning when it's legal to open, the bar comes back, and meanwhile the regulars don't go anywhere except into the mist, because that's all there is, mist and then bar, bar and then mist. Platonic ideals don't have daytime jobs and they don't go to Atlantic City on the weekend and they don't decide to go bowling one night instead of to their bar. Do you follow me? They stay there the way the dummies in a store window stay in the store window. Only they can walk and talk and feel and drink and do everything else that window dummies can't do. And that's their whole life, night after night, month after month, year after year, century after century—maybe till the end of time."

"Spooky place," said Ishmael with a little shudder.

"The people who are in that bar are happier than they could possibly be anywhere else."

"But they never leave it. Except you said some of them do, and you'd be telling me about those people later."

Mors Longa finished his bourbon and, unbidden, Charley Sullivan gave him one more, and set another rum in front of me, and an Irish for the sailor. For a long while Mors Longa studied his drink. Then he said, "I can't really tell you much about the ones who leave, because I don't know much about them. I intuit their existence logically, is all. You see, from time to time there's a newcomer in this bar that's outside of space and time. Somebody comes wandering

ROBERT SILVERBERG

in out of the night the way you did here tonight, and sits down and joins the regular crowd, and bit by bit fits right in. Now, obviously, if every once in a while somebody new drops in, and nobody ever leaves, then it wouldn't take more than a little while for the whole place to get terribly crowded, like Grand Central at commuter time, and what kind of a happy scene would that make? So I conclude that sooner or later each of the regulars very quietly must disappear, must just vanish without anybody's knowing it, maybe go into the john and never come out, something like that. And not only does no one ever notice that someone's missing, but *no one remembers that that person was ever there.* Do you follow? That way the place never gets too full."

"But where do they go, once they disappear from the bar that nobody ever leaves, the bar that's outside of space and time?"

"I don't know," said Mors Longa quietly. "I don't have the foggiest idea." After a moment he added, "There's a theory, though. Mind you, only a theory. It's that the people in the bar are really doing time in a kind of halfway house, a sort of purgatory, you understand, between one world and another. And they stay there a long, long time, however long a time it is until their time is up, and then they leave, but they can only leave when their replacement arrives. And immediately they're forgotten. The fabric of the place closes around them, and nobody among the regulars remembers that once there used to be a doctor with the d.t.'s here, say, or a politician who got caught on the take, or a little guy who sat in front of the piano for hours and never played a note. But everybody has a hunch that that's how the system works. And so it's a big thing when somebody new comes in. Every regular starts secretly wondering, Is it I who's going to go? And wondering too, Where am I going to go, if I'm the one?"

Ishmael worked on his drink in a meditative way. "Are they afraid to go, or afraid that they won't?"

"What do you think?"

"I'm not sure. But I guess most of them would be afraid to go. The bar's such a warm and cozy and comforting place. It's their whole world and has been for a million years. And now maybe they're going to go somewhere horrible—who knows? —but for certain they're going to go somewhere *different.* I'd be afraid of that. Of course, maybe if I'd been stuck in the same place for a million years, no matter how cozy, I'd be ready to move along when the chance came. Which would you want?"

"I don't have the foggiest," said Mors Longa. "But that's the story of the bar where nobody leaves."

"Spooky," said Ishmael.

He finished his drink, pushed the glass away, shook his head to Charley Sullivan, and sat in silence. We all sat in silence. The rain drummed miserably against the side of the building. I looked over at The Leading Man and the Ingenue. He was holding her hand and staring meaningfully into her eyes. The Pope, hefting a dart, was toeing the line and licking his lips to sharpen his aim. Ms. Bewley and Toulouse-Lautrec were playing chess. It was the quiet part of the evening, suddenly.

Slowly the sailor rose, and took his jacket from the hook. He turned, smiled uncertainly, and said, "Getting late. I better be going." He nodded to the three of us at the bar and said, "Thanks for the drinks. I needed those. And thanks for the story, Mr. Longa. That was one strange story, you know?"

We said nothing. The sailor opened the door, wincing as cold sheets of rain lashed at him. He pulled his jacket tight around him and, shivering a little, stepped out in the darkness. But he was gone only a moment. Hardly had the door closed behind him but it opened again and he stumbled back in, drenched.

"Jesus," he said, "it's raining worse than ever. What a stinking night! I'm not going out into that!"

"No," I said. "Not fit for man nor beast."

"You don't mind if I stay here until it slackens off some, then?"

"Mind? Mind?" I laughed. "This is a public house, my friend. You've got as much right as anyone. Here. Sit down. Make yourself to home."

"Plenty of Bushmill's left in the bottle, lad," said Charley Sullivan.

"I'm a little low on cash," Ishmael muttered.

Mors Longa said, "That's all right. Money's not the only coin of the realm around here. We can use some stories we haven't heard before. Let's hear the strangest story you can tell us, for openers, and I'll undertake to keep you in Irish while you talk. Eh?"

"Fair enough," said Ishmael. He thought a moment. "All right. I have a good one for you. I have a really good one, if you don't mind them weird. It's about my uncle Timothy and his tiny twin brother, that he carried around under his arm all his life. Does that interest you?"

"Most assuredly it does," I said.

"Seconded," said Mors Longa. He grinned with a warmth I had not seen on his face for a long time. "Set them up," he said to Charley Sullivan. "On me. For the house."

MEMO
by Frank Ward

The author is a 30-year-old English teacher at an all-boys high school. He has two previous fiction sales to semi-professional magazines; this is his first to an SF magazine

September 24, 2010
To: Harvey Richards
     Project Supervisor—Div 1985
     T.T. Inc.
Subject: Comments covered in your recent memo to this office,
     No. 249.

Harvey,

I swear to god, this is the last time I intend to go through this with you. Everything about T.T. Inc. is aboveboard and legitimate. I should know, for Christ's sake! We are not "perpetrating a fraud," as you so quaintly put it, on anybody. Just because you haven't developed the product yet doesn't mean that there aren't thousands of satisfied customers here who have used and enjoyed it thoroughly. God damn it! You're even more cautious than I remember. You will build a time machine, now that I'm supplying the necessary capital to overcome the hardware problem; that's always been the biggest snag. So have some trust, will you? If you can't trust *me,* who can you trust?

Look, how else could I have sold a dozen premier excursions to Caligula's A.D. 40 New Year's Eve party? This week alone? How else could those platinum bars (not to mention this memo) arrive on your desk to keep financing the work unless I were flitting back twenty-five years into my past to keep all this straight? And by the way, stop lurking around in your office closet trying to catch me at it. You're as bad as you were as a kid at Christmas and it's just as futile. Yes, we have to go on not meeting like this. That's final.

Please, relax and get back to the lab. There is nothing wrong—not now, not ever. Just keep saying to yourself, "I'm on schedule, I'm on schedule."

P.S. Your lack of faith in me is what really hurts!

                    Ever yours,
                    Harvey Richards
           Executive Director—2010 Div
                    T.T. Inc.

ENEMY
MINE

Mr. Longyear has recently completed and delivered to Berkley the manuscript for The Tomorrow Testament, a novel based on the "Enemy Mine" universe. He is currently at work on a historical novel set during the Civil War.

by Barry B. Longyear

art: Vincent Di Fate

The Dracon's three-fingered hands flexed. In the thing's yellow eyes I could read the desire to either have those fingers around a weapon or my throat. As I flexed my own fingers, I knew it read the same in my eyes.

"Irkmaan!" the thing spat.

"You piece of Drac slime." I brought my hands up in front of my chest and waved the thing on. "Come on, Drac; come and get it."

"Irkmaan vaa, koruum su!"

"Are you going to talk, or fight? Come on!" I could feel the spray from the sea behind me—a boiling madhouse of white-capped breakers that threatened to swallow me as it had my fighter. I had ridden my ship in. The Drac had ejected when its own fighter had caught one in the upper atmosphere, but not before crippling my power plant. I was exhausted from swimming to the grey, rocky beach and pulling myself to safety. Behind the Drac, among the rocks on the otherwise barren hill, I could see its ejection capsule. Far above us, its people and mine were still at it, slugging out the possession of an uninhabited corner of nowhere. The Drac just stood there and I went over the phrase taught us in training—a phrase calculated to drive any Drac into a frenzy. *"Kiz da yuomeen, Shizumaat!"* Meaning: Shizumaat, the most revered Drac philosopher, eats kiz excrement. Something on the level of stuffing a Moslem full of pork.

The Drac opened its mouth in horror, then closed it as anger literally changed its color from yellow to reddish-brown. *"Irkmann, yaa stupid Mickey Mouse is!"*

I had taken an oath to fight and die over many things, but that venerable rodent didn't happen to be one of them. I laughed, and continued laughing until the guffaws in combination with my exhaustion forced me to my knees. I forced open my eyes to keep track of my enemy. The Drac was running toward the high ground, away from me and the sea. I half-turned toward the sea and caught a glimpse of a million tons of water just before they fell on me, knocking me unconscious.

"Kiz da yuomeen, Irkmaan, ne?"

My eyes were gritty with sand and stung with salt, but some part of my awareness pointed out: "Hey, you're alive." I reached to wipe the sand from my eyes and found my hands bound. A straight metal rod had been run through my sleeves and my wrists tied to it. As my tears cleared the sand from my eyes, I could see the Drac sitting on a smooth black boulder looking at me. It must have pulled me out of the drink. "Thanks, toad face. What's with the bondage?"

"Ess?"

I tried waving my arms and wound up giving an impression of an atmospheric fighter dipping its wings. "Untie me, you Drac slime!" I was seated on the sand, my back against a rock.

The Drac smiled, exposing the upper and lower mandibles that looked human—except that instead of separate teeth, they were solid. *"Eh, ne, Irkmaan."* It stood, walked over to me and checked my bonds.

"Untie me!"

The smile disappeared. *"Ne!"* It pointed at me with a yellow finger. *"Kos son va?"*

"I don't speak Drac, toad face. You speak Esper or English?"

The Drac delivered a very human-looking shrug, then pointed at its own chest. *"Kos va son Jeriba Shigan."* It pointed again at me. *"Kos son va?"*

"Davidge. My name is Willis E. Davidge."

"Ess?"

I tried my tongue on the unfamiliar syllables. *"Kos va son Willis Davidge."*

"Eh." Jeriba Shigan nodded, then motioned with its fingers. *"Dasu, Davidge."*

"Same to you, Jerry."

"Dasu, dasu!" Jeriba began sounding a little impatient. I shrugged as best I could. The Drac bent over and grabbed the front of my jump suit with both hands and pulled me to my feet. *"Dasu, dasu, kizlode!"*

"All right! So *dasu* is 'get up.' What's a *kizlode*?"

Jerry laughed. *"Gavey 'kiz'?"*

"Yeah, I *gavey*."

Jerry pointed at its head. *"Lode."* It pointed at my head. *"Kizlode, gavey?"*

I got it, then swung my arms around, catching Jerry upside its head with the metal rod. The Drac stumbled back against a rock, looking surprised. It raised a hand to its head and withdrew it covered with that pale pus that Dracs think is blood. It looked at me with murder in its eyes. *"Gefh! Nu Gefh, Davidge!"*

"Come and get it, Jerry, you *kizlode* sonafabitch!"

Jerry dived at me and I tried to catch it again with the rod, but the Drac caught my right wrist in both hands and, using the momentum of my swing, whirled me around, slamming my back against another rock. Just as I was getting back my breath, Jerry picked up a small boulder and came at me with every intention of turning my melon into pulp. With my back against the rock, I lifted a foot and kicked the Drac in the midsection, knocking it to the sand. I ran up, ready to stomp Jerry's melon, but he pointed behind me. I turned and saw another tidal wave gathering steam, and heading our way. *"Kiz!"* Jerry got to its feet and scampered for the high ground with me following close behind.

With the roar of the wave at our backs, we weaved among the water- and sand-ground black boulders, until we reached Jerry's ejection capsule. The Drac stopped, put its shoulder to the egg-shaped contraption, and began rolling it uphill. I could see Jerry's point. The capsule contained all of the survival equipment and food either of us knew about. "Jerry!" I shouted above the rumble of the fast approaching wave. "Pull out this damn rod and I'll help!" The Drac frowned at me. "The rod, *kizlode*, pull it out!" I cocked my head toward my outstretched arm.

Jerry placed a rock beneath the capsule to keep it from rolling back, then quickly untied my wrists and pulled out the rod. Both of us put our shoulders to the capsule, and we quickly rolled it to higher ground. The wave hit and climbed rapidly up the slope until it came up to our chests. The capsule bobbed like a cork, and it was all we could do to keep control of the thing until the water receded, wedging the capsule between three big boulders. I stood there, puffing.

Jerry dropped to the sand, its back against one of the boulders, and watched the water rush back out to sea. *"Magasienna!"*

"You said it, brother." I sank down next to the Drac; we agreed by eye to a temporary truce, and promptly passed out.

My eyes opened on a sky boiling with blacks and greys. Letting my head loll over on my left shoulder, I checked out the Drac. It was still out. First, I thought that this would be the perfect time to get the drop on Jerry. Second, I thought about how silly our insignificant scrap seemed compared to the insanity of the sea that surrounded us. Why hadn't the rescue team come? Did the Dracon fleet wipe us out? Why hadn't the Dracs come to pick up Jerry? Did they wipe out each other? I didn't even know where I was. An island. I had seen that much coming in, but where and in relation to what? Fyrine IV: the planet didn't even rate a name, but was important enough to die over.

With an effort, I struggled to my feet. Jerry opened its eyes and quickly pushed itself to a defensive crouching position. I waved my hand and shook my head. "Ease off, Jerry. I'm just going to look around." I turned my back on it and trudged off between the boulders. I walked uphill for a few minutes until I reached level ground.

BARRY B. LONGYEAR

It was an island, all right, and not a very big one. By eyeball estimation, height from sea level was only eighty meters, while the island itself was about two kilometers long and less than half that wide. The wind whipping my jump suit against my body was at least drying it out, but as I looked around at the smooth-ground boulders on top of the rise, I realized that Jerry and I could expect bigger waves than the few puny ones we had seen.

A rock clattered behind me and I turned to see Jerry climbing up the slope. When it reached the top, the Drac looked around. I squatted next to one of the boulders and passed my hand over it to indicate the smoothness, then I pointed toward the sea. Jerry nodded. *"Ae, Gavey."* It pointed downhill toward the capsule, then to where we stood. *"Echey masu, nasesay."*

I frowned, then pointed at the capsule. *"Nasesay?* The capsule?"

"Ae, capsule *nasesay. Echey masu."* Jerry pointed at its feet.

I shook my head. "Jerry, if you *gavey* how these rocks got smooth," I pointed at one, "then you *gavey* that *masu*ing the *nasesay* up here isn't going to do a damned bit of good." I made a sweeping up and down movement with my hands. "Waves." I pointed at the sea below. "Waves, up here"; I pointed to where we stood. "Waves, *echey."*

"Ae, gavey." Jerry looked around the top of the rise, then rubbed the side of its face. The Drac squatted next to some small rocks and began piling one on top of another. *"Viga, Davidge."*

I squatted next to it and watched while its nimble fingers constructed a circle of stones that quickly grew into a doll-house-sized arena. Jerry stuck one of its fingers in the center of the circle. *"Echey, nasesay."*

The days on Fyrine IV seemed to be three times longer than any I had seen on any other habitable planet. I use the designation 'habitable' with reservations. It took us most of the first day to painfully roll Jerry's *nasesay* up to the top of the rise. The night was too black to work and was bone-cracking cold. We removed the couch from the capsule, which made just enough room for both of us to fit inside. The body heat warmed things up a bit; and we killed time between sleeping, nibbling on Jerry's supply of ration bars (they taste a bit like fish mixed with cheddar cheese), and trying to come to some agreement about language.

"Eye."

"Thuyo."

"Finger."

"Zurath."

"Head."

The Drac laughed. *"Lode."*

"Ho, ho, very funny."

"Ho, ho."

At dawn on the second day, we rolled and pushed the capsule into the center of the rise and wedged it between two large rocks, one of which had an overhang that we hoped would hold down the capsule when one of those big soakers hit. Around the rocks and capsule, we laid a foundation of large stones and filled in the cracks with smaller stones. By the time the wall was knee high, we discovered that building with those smooth, round stones and no mortar wasn't going to work. After some experimentation, we figured out how to break the stones to give us flat sides with which to work. It's done by picking up one stone and slamming it down on top of another. We took turns, one slamming and one building. The stone was almost a volcanic glass, and we also took turns extracting rock splinters from each other. It took nine of those endless days and nights to complete the walls, during which waves came close many times and once washed us ankle deep. For six of those nine days, it rained. The capsule's survival equipment included a plastic blanket, and that became our roof. It sagged in at the center, and the hole we put in it there allowed the water to run out, keeping us almost dry and giving us a supply of fresh water. If a wave of any determination came along, we could kiss the roof goodbye; but we both had confidence in the walls, which were almost two meters thick at the bottom and at least a meter thick at the top.

After we finished, we sat inside and admired our work for about an hour, until it dawned on us that we had just worked ourselves out of jobs. "What now, Jerry?"

"Ess?"

"What do we do now?"

"Now wait, we." The Drac shrugged. "Else what, *ne?*"

I nodded. *"Gavey."* I got to my feet and walked to the passageway we had built. With no wood for a door, where the walls would have met, we bent one out and extended it about three meters around the other wall with the opening away from the prevailing winds. The never-ending winds were still at it, but the rain had stopped. The shack wasn't much to look at, but looking at it stuck there in the center of that deserted island made me feel good. As Shizumaat observed: "Intelligent life making its stand against the universe." Or, at least, that's the sense I could make out of Jerry's hamburger of English. I shrugged and picked up a sharp splinter of stone and made another mark in the large standing rock that served as my log. Ten scratches in all, and under the seventh, a small 'x' to indicate the big wave that just covered the top of the island.

I threw down the splinter. "Damn, I hate this place!"

"Ess?" Jerry's head poked around the edge of the opening. "Who talking at, Davidge?"

I glared at the Drac, then waved my hand at it. "Nobody."

"Ess va, 'nobody'?"

"Nobody. Nothing."

"Ne gavey, Davidge."

I poked at my chest with my finger. "Me! I'm talking to myself! You *gavey* that stuff, toad face!"

Jerry shook its head. "Davidge, now I sleep. Talk not so much nobody, *ne?"* It disappeared back into the opening.

"And so's your mother!" I turned and walked down the slope. *Except, strictly speaking, toad face, you don't have a mother—or father. "If you had your choice, who would you like to be trapped on a desert island with?"* I wondered if anyone ever picked a wet freezing corner of Hell shacked up with a hermaphrodite.

Half of the way down the slope, I followed the path I had marked with rocks until I came to my tidal pool, that I had named "Rancho Sluggo." Around the pool were many of the water worn rocks, and underneath those rocks below the pool's waterline, lived the fattest orange slugs either of us had ever seen. I made the discovery during a break from house building and showed them to Jerry.

Jerry shrugged. "And so?"

"And so what? Look, Jerry, those ration bars aren't going to last forever. What are we going to eat when they're all gone?"

"Eat?" Jerry looked at the wriggling pocket of insect life and grimaced. *"Ne,* Davidge. Before then pickup. Search us find, then pickup."

"What if they don't find us? What then?"

Jerry grimaced again and turned back to the half-completed house. "Water we drink, then until pickup." He had muttered something about kiz excrement and my tastebuds, then walked out of sight.

Since then I had built up the pool's walls, hoping the increased protection from the harsh environment would increase the herd. I looked under several rocks, but no increase was apparent. And, again, I couldn't bring myself to swallow one of the things. I replaced the rock I was looking under, stood and looked out to the sea. Al-

ENEMY MINE

though the eternal cloud cover still denied the surface the drying rays of Fyrine, there was no rain and the usual haze had lifted.

In the direction past where I had pulled myself up on the beach, the sea continued to the horizon. In the spaces between the white-caps, the water was as grey as a loan officer's heart. Parallel lines of rollers formed approximately five kilometers from the island. The center, from where I was standing, would smash on the island, while the remainder steamed on. To my right, in line with the breakers, I could just make out another small island perhaps ten kilometers away. Following the path of the rollers, I looked far to my right, and where the grey-white of the sea should have met the lighter grey of the sky, there was a black line on the horizon.

The harder I tried to remember the briefing charts on Fyrine IV's land masses, the less clear it became. Jerry couldn't remember anything either—at least nothing it would tell me. Why should we remember? The battle was supposed to be in space, each one trying to deny the other an orbital staging area in the Fyrine system. Neither side wanted to set foot on Fyrine, much less fight a battle there. Still, whatever it was called, it was land and considerably larger than the sand and rock bar we were occupying.

How to get there was the problem. Without wood, fire, leaves, or animal skins, Jerry and I were destitute compared to the average poverty-stricken caveman. The only thing we had that would float was the *nasesay*. The capsule. Why not? The only real problem to overcome was getting Jerry to go along with it.

That evening, while the greyness made its slow transition to black, Jerry and I sat outside the shack nibbling our quarter portions of ration bars. The Drac's yellow eyes studied the dark line on the horizon, then it shook its head. "*Ne,* Davidge. Dangerous is."

I popped the rest of my ration bar into my mouth and talked around it. "Any more dangerous than staying here?"

"Soon pickup, *ne?*"

I studied those yellow eyes. "Jerry, you don't believe that any more than I do." I leaned forward on the rock and held out my hands. "Look, our chances will be a lot better on a larger land mass. Protection from the big waves, maybe food. . . ."

"Not maybe, *ne?*" Jerry pointed at the water. "How *nasesay* steer, Davidge? In that, how steer? *Ess eh* soakers, waves, beyond land take, *gavey? Bresha,*" Jerry's hand slapped together. "*Ess eh breahs* rocks on, *ne?* Then we death."

I scratched my head. "The waves are going in that direction from here, and so is the wind. If the land mass is large enough, we don't have to steer, *gavey?*"

Jerry snorted. "*Ne* large enough; then?"

"I didn't say it was a sure thing."

"*Ess?*"

"A sure thing; certain, *gavey?*" Jerry nodded. "And for smashing up on the rocks, it probably has a beach like this one."

"Sure thing, *ne?*"

I shrugged. "No, it's not a sure thing, but, what about staying here? We don't know how big those waves can get. What if one just comes along and washes us off the island? What then?"

Jerry looked at me, its eyes narrowed. "What there, Davidge? *Irkmaan* base, *ne?*"

I laughed. "I told you, we don't have any bases on Fyrine IV."

"Why want go, then?"

"Just what I said, Jerry. I think our chances would be better."

"Ummm." The Drac folded its arms. "*Viga,* Davidge, *nasesay* stay. I know."

"Know what?"

Jerry smirked, then stood and went into the shack. After a moment it returned and threw a two-meter long metal rod at my feet. It was the one Drac had used to bind my arms. "Davidge, I know."

I raised my eyebrows and shrugged. "What are you talking about? Didn't that come from your capsule?"

"*Ne, Irkmaan.*"

I bent down and picked up the rod. Its surface was uncorroded and at one end were arabic numerals—a part number. For a moment a flood of hope washed over me, but it drained away when I realized it was a civilian part number. I threw the rod on the sand. "There's no telling how long that's been here, Jerry. It's a civilian part number and no civilian missions have been in this part of the galaxy since the war. Might be left over from an old seeding operation or exploratory mission. . . ."

The Drac nudged it with the toe of his boot. "New, *gavey?*"

I looked up at it. "You *gavey* stainless steel?"

Jerry snorted and turned back toward the shack. "I stay, *nasesay* stay; where you want, you go, Davidge!"

With the black of the long night firmly bolted down on us, the wind picked up, shrieking and whistling in and through the holes in the walls. The plastic roof flapped, pushed in and sucked out with such violence it threatened to either tear or sail off into the night.

Jerry sat on the sand floor, its back leaning against the *nasesay* as if to make clear both Drac and capsule were staying put, although the way the sea was picking up seemed to weaken Jerry's argument

"Sea rough now is, Davidge, *ne?*"

"It's too dark to see, but with this wind. . . ." I shrugged more for my own benefit than the Drac's, since the only thing visible inside the shack was the pale light coming through the roof. Any minute we could be washed off that sandbar. "Jerry, you're being silly about that rod. You know that."

"*Surda.*" The Drac sounded contrite if not altogether miserable.

"*Ess?*"

"*Ess eh 'Surda'?*"

"*Ae.*"

Jerry remained silent for a moment. "Davidge, *gavey* 'not certain not is'?"

I sorted out the negatives. "You mean 'possible,' 'maybe,' 'perhaps'?"

"*Ae*, possiblemaybeperhaps. Dracon fleet Irkmaan ships have. Before war buy; after war capture. Rod possiblemaybeperhaps Dracon is."

"So, if there's a secret base on the big island, *surda* it's a Dracon base?"

"Possiblemaybeperhaps, Davidge."

"Jerry, does that mean you want to try it? The *nasesay?*"

"*Ne.*"

"*Ne?* Why, Jerry? If it might be a Drac base—"

"*Ne! Ne* talk!" The Drac seemed to choke on the words.

"Jerry, we talk, and you better *believe* we talk! If I'm going to death it on this island, I have a right to know why."

The Drac was quiet for a long time. "Davidge."

"*Ess?*"

"*Nasesay*, you take. Half ration bars you leave. I stay."

I shook my head to clear it. "You want me to take the capsule alone?"

"What you want is, *ne?*"

"*Ae*, but why? You must realize there won't be any pickup."

"Possiblemaybeperhaps."

"*Surda*, nothing. You know there isn't going to be a pickup. What is it? You afraid of the water? If that's it, we have a better chance—"

"Davidge, up your mouth shut. *Nasesay* you have. Me *ne* you need, *gavey?*"

I nodded in the dark. The capsule was mine for the taking; what

did I need a grumpy Drac along for—especially since our truce could expire at any moment? The answer made me feel a little silly—human. Perhaps it's the same thing. The Drac was all that stood between me and utter aloneness. Still, there was the small matter of staying alive. "We should go together, Jerry."

"Why?"

I felt myself blush. If humans have this need for companionship, why are they also ashamed to admit it? "We just should. Our chances would be better."

"Alone your chances better are, Davidge. Your enemy I am."

I nodded again and grimaced in the dark. "Jerry, you *gavey* 'loneliness'?"

"Ne gavey."

"Lonely. Being alone, by myself."

"Gavey you alone. Take *nasesay*; I stay."

"That's it . . . see, *viga,* I don't want to."

"You want together go?" A low, dirty chuckle came from the other side of the shack. "You Dracon like? You me death, *Irkmaan."* Jerry chuckled some more. *"Irkmaan poorzhab* in head, *poorzhab."*

"Forget it!" I slid down from the wall, smoothed out the sand and curled up with my back toward the Drac. The wind seemed to die down a bit and I closed my eyes to try and sleep. In a bit, the snap, crack of the plastic roof blended in with the background of shrieks and whistles and I felt myself drifting off, when my eyes opened wide at the sound of footsteps in the sand. I tensed, ready to spring.

"Davidge?" Jerry's voice was very quiet.

"What?"

I heard the Drac sit on the sand next to me. "You loneliness, Davidge. About it hard you talk, *ne?"*

"So what?" The Drac mumbled something that was lost in the wind. "What?" I turned over and saw Jerry looking through a hole in the wall.

"Why I stay. Now, you I tell, *ne?"*

I shrugged. "Okay; why not?"

Jerry seemed to struggle with the words, then opened its mouth to speak. Its eyes opened wide. *"Magasienna!"*

I sat up. *"Ess?"*

Jerry pointed at the hole. "Soaker!"

I pushed it out of the way and looked through the hole. Steaming toward our island was an insane mountainous fury of whitecapped rollers. It was hard to tell in the dark, but the one in front looked taller than the one that had wet our feet a few days before. The ones following it were bigger. Jerry put a hand on my shoulder and I looked into the Drac's eyes. We broke and ran for the capsule. We heard the first wave rumbling up the slope as we felt around in the dark for the recessed doorlatch. I just got my finger on it when the wave smashed against the shack, collapsing the roof. In half a second we were under water, the currents inside the shack agitating us like socks in a washing machine.

The water receded, and as I cleared my eyes, I saw that the windward wall of the shack had caved in. "Jerry!"

Through the collapsed wall, I saw the Drac staggering around outside. *"Irkmaan?"* Behind him I could see the second roller gathering speed.

"Kizlode, what'n the Hell you doing out there? Get in here!"

I turned to the capsule, still lodged firmly between the two rocks, and found the handle. As I opened the door, Jerry stumbled through the missing wall and fell against me. "Davidge . . . forever soakers go on! Forever!"

"Get in!" I helped the Drac through the door and didn't wait for it to get out of the way. I piled in on top of Jerry and latched the door just as the second wave hit. I could feel the capsule lift a bit and rattle against the overhang of the one rock.

"Davidge, we float?"

"No. The rocks are holding us. We'll be all right once the breakers stop."

"Over you move."

"Oh." I got off Jerry's chest and braced myself against one end of the capsule. After a bit, the capsule came to rest and we waited for the next one. "Jerry?"

"Ess?"

"What was it that you were about to say?"

"Why I stay?"

"Yeah."

"About it hard me talk, *gavey?"*

"I know, I know."

The next breaker hit and I could feel the capsule rise and rattle against the rock. "Davidge, *gavey 'vi nessa'?"*

"Ne gavey."

"Vi nessa . . . little me, *gavey?"*

The capsule bumped down the rock and came to rest. "What about little you?"

"Little me . . . little Drac. From me, *gavey?"*

"Are you telling me you're *pregnant?"*

"Possiblemaybeperhaps."

I shook my head. "Hold on, Jerry. I don't want any misunder-standings. Pregnant . . . are you going to be a parent?"

"*Ae*, parent, two-zero-zero in line, very important is, *ne?*"

"Terrific. What's this got to do with you not wanting to go to the other island?"

"Before, me *vi nessa, gavey? Tean* death."

"Your child, it died?"

"*Ae!*" The Drac's sob was torn from the lips of the universal mother. "I in fall hurt. *Tean* death. *Nasesay* in sea us bang. *Tean* hurt, *gavey?*"

"*Ae*, I *gavey*." So, Jerry was afraid of losing another child. It was almost certain that the capsule trip would bang us around a lot, but staying on the sandbar didn't appear to be improving our chances. The capsule had been at rest for quite a while, and I decided to risk a peek outside. The small canopy windows seemed to be covered with sand, and I opened the door. I looked around, and all of the walls had been smashed flat. I looked toward the sea, but could see nothing. "It looks safe, Jerry . . ." I looked up, toward the blackish sky, and above me toward the white plume of a descending breaker. "*Maga* damn *sienna!*" I slammed the hatch door.

"*Ess,* Davidge?"

"Hang on, Jerry!"

The sound of the water hitting the capsule was beyond hearing. We banged once, twice against the rock, then we could feel ourselves twisting, shooting upward. I made a grab to hang on, but missed as the capsule took a sickening lurch downward. I fell into Jerry, then was flung to the opposite wall where I struck my head. Before I went blank, I heard Jerry cry "*Tean! Vi tean!*"

. . . . . *the lieutenant pressed his hand control and a figure—tall, humanoid, yellow—appeared on the screen.*

"*Dracslime!*" *shouted the auditorium of seated recruits.*

The lieutenant faced the recruits. "Correct. This is a Drac. Note that the Drac race is uniform as to color; they are all yellow." The recruits chuckled politely. The officer preened a bit, then with a light wand began pointing out various features. "The three-fingered hands are distinctive, of course, as is the almost noseless face, which gives the Drac a toad-like appearance. On average, eyesight is slightly better than human, hearing about the same, and smell . . ." The lieutenant paused. "The smell is terrible!" The officer beamed at the uproar from the recruits. When the auditorium quieted down, he pointed his light wand at a fold in the figure's belly. "This is where the Drac keeps its family jewels—all of them." Another chuckle. "That's right, Dracs are hermaphrodites, with both male and female reproductive organs contained in the same individual." The lieutenant faced the recruits. "You go tell a Drac to go boff himself, then watch out, because he can!" The laughter died down, and the lieutenant held out a hand toward the screen. "You see one of these things, what do you do?"

"KILL IT. . . ."

. . . . I cleared the screen and computer sighted on the next Drac fighter, looking like a double x in the screen's display. The Drac shifted hard to the left, then right again. I felt the autopilot pull my ship after the fighter, sorting out and ignoring the false images, trying to lock its electronic crosshairs on the Drac. "Come on, toad face . . . a little bit to the left. . . ." The double cross image moved into the ranging rings on the display and I felt the missile attached to the belly of my fighter take off. "Gotcha!" Through my canopy I saw the flash as the missile detonated. My screen showed the Drac fighter out of control, spinning toward Fyrine IV's cloud-shrouded surface. I dived after it to confirm the kill . . . skin temperature increasing as my ship brushed the upper atmosphere. "Come on, dammit, blow!" I shifted the ship's systems over for atmospheric flight when it became obvious that I'd have to follow the Drac right to the ground. Still above the clouds, the Drac stopped spinning and turned. I hit the auto override and pulled the stick into my lap. The fighter wallowed as it tried to pull up. Everyone knows the Drac ships work better in atmosphere . . . heading toward me on an interception course . . . why doesn't the slime fire . . . just before the collision, the Drac ejects . . . power gone; have to deadstick it in. I track the capsule as it falls through the muck intending to find that Dracslime and finish the job. . . .

It could have been for seconds or years that I groped into the darkness around me. I felt touching, but the parts of me being touched seemed far, far away. First chills, then fever, then chills again, my head being cooled by a gentle hand. I opened my eyes to narrow slits and saw Jerry hovering over me, blotting my forehead with something cool. I managed a whisper. "Jerry."

The Drac looked into my eyes and smiled. "Good is, Davidge. Good is."

The light on Jerry's face flickered and I smelled smoke. "Fire."

ENEMY MINE

Jerry got out of the way and pointed toward the center of the room's sandy floor. I let my head roll over and realized that I was lying on a bed of soft, springy branches. Opposite my bed was another bed, and between them crackled a cheery campfire. "Fire now we have, Davidge. And wood." Jerry pointed toward the roof made of wooden poles thatched with broad leaves.

I turned and looked around, then let my throbbing head sink down and closed my eyes. "Where are we?"

"Big island, Davidge. Soaker off sandbar us washed. Wind and waves us here took. Right you were."

"I . . . I don't understand; *ne gavey*. It'd take days to get to the big island from the sandbar."

Jerry nodded and dropped what looked like a sponge into a shell of some sort filled with water. "Nine days. You I strap to *nasesay*, then here on beach we land."

"Nine days? I've been out for nine days?"

Jerry shook his head. "Seventeen. Here we land eight days . . ." The Drac waved its hand behind itself.

"Ago . . . eight days ago."

"*Ae.*"

Seventeen days on Fyrine IV was better than a month on Earth. I opened my eyes again and looked at Jerry. The Drac was almost bubbling with excitement. "What about *tean,* your child?"

Jerry patted its swollen middle. "Good is, Davidge. You more *nasesay* hurt."

I overcame an urge to nod. "I'm happy for you." I closed my eyes and turned my face toward the wall, a combination of wood poles and leaves. "Jerry?"

"*Ess?*"

"You saved my life."

"*Ae.*"

"Why?"

Jerry sat quietly for a long time. "Davidge. On sandbar you talk. Loneliness now *gavey*." The Drac shook my arm. "Here, now you eat."

I turned and looked into a shell filled with a steaming liquid. "What is it; chicken soup?"

"*Ess?*"

"*Ess va?*" I pointed at the bowl, realizing for the first time how weak I was.

Jerry frowned. "Like slug, but long."

"An eel?"

"Ae, but eel on land, *gavey?"*

"You mean 'snake'?"

"Possiblemaybeperhaps."

I nodded and put my lips to the edge of the shell. I sipped some of the broth, swallowed and let the broth's healing warmth seep through my body. "Good."

"You *custa* want?"

"Ess?"

"Custa." Jerry reached next to the fire and picked up a squareish chunk of clear rock, I looked at it, scratched it with my thumbnail, then touched it with my tongue.

"Halite! Salt!"

Jerry smiled. *"Custa* you want?"

I laughed. "All the comforts. By all means, let's have *custa."*

Jerry took the halite, knocked off a corner with a small stone, then used the stone to grind the pieces against another stone. He held out the palm of his hand with a tiny mountain of white granules in the center. I took two pinches, dropped them into my snake soup and stirred it with my finger. Then I took a long swallow of the delicious broth. I smacked my lips. "Fantastic."

"Good, *ne?"*

"Better than good; fantastic." I took another swallow making a big show of smacking my lips and rolling my eyes.

"Fantastic, Davidge, *ne?"*

"Ae." I nodded at the Drac. "I think that's enough. I want to sleep."

"Ae, Davidge, *gavey."* Jerry took the bowl and put it beside the fire. The Drac stood, walked to the door and turned back. Its yellow eyes studied me for an instant, then it nodded, turned and went outside. I closed my eyes and let the heat from the campfire coax the sleep over me.

In two days I was up in the shack trying my legs, and in two more days, Jerry helped me outside. The shack was located at the top of a long, gentle rise in a scrub forest; none of the trees were any taller than five or six meters. At the bottom of the slope, better than eight kilometers from the shack, was the still-rolling sea. The Drac had carried me. Our trusty *nasesay* had filled with water and had been dragged back into the sea soon after Jerry pulled me to dry land. With it went the remainder of the ration bars. Dracs are very fussy about what they eat, but hunger finally drove Jerry to sample some of the local flora and fauna—hunger and the human lump that was rapidly drifting away from lack of nourishment. The Drac had settled on a bland, starchy type of root, a green bushberry that when dried made an acceptable tea, and snakemeat. Exploring, Jerry had found a partly eroded salt dome. In the days that followed, I grew stronger and added to our diet with several types of sea mollusk and a fruit resembling a cross between a pear and a plum.

As the days grew colder, the Drac and I were forced to realize that Fyrine IV had a winter. Given that, we had to face the possibility that the winter would be severe enough to prevent the gathering of food—and wood. When dried next to the fire, the berrybush and roots kept well, and we tried both salting and smoking snakemeat. With strips of fiber from the berrybush for thread, Jerry and I pieced together the snake skins for winter clothing. The design we settled on involved two layers of skins with the down from berrybush seed pods stuffed between and then held in place by quilting the layers. We agreed that the house would never do. It took three days of searching to find our first cave, and another three days before we found one that suited us. The mouth opened onto a view of the eternally tormented sea, but was set in the face of a low cliff well above sea level. Around the cave's entrance we found great quantities of dead wood and loose stone. The wood we gathered for heat; and the stone we used to wall up the entrance, leaving only space enough for a hinged door. The hinges were made of snake leather and the door of wooden poles tied together with berrybush fibre. The first night after completing the door, the sea winds blew it to pieces; and we decided to go back to the original door design we had used on the sandbar.

Deep inside the cave, we made our living quarters in a chamber with a wide, sandy floor. Still deeper, the cave had natural pools of water, which were fine for drinking but too cold for bathing. We used the pool chamber for our supply room. We lined the walls of our living quarters with piles of wood and made new beds out of snakeskins and seed pod down. In the center of the chamber we built a respectable fireplace with a large, flat stone over the coals for a griddle. The first night we spent in our new home, I discovered that, for the first time since ditching on that damned planet, I couldn't hear the wind.

During the long nights, we would sit at the fireplace making things—gloves, hats, packbags—out of snake leather, and we would talk. To break the monotony, we alternated days between speaking Drac and English, and by the time the winter hit with its first ice storm, each of us was comfortable in the other's language.

We talked of Jerry's coming child:

"What are you going to name it, Jerry?"

"It already has a name. See, the Jeriba line has five names. My name is Shigan; before me came my parent, Gothig; before Gothig was Haesni; before Haesni was Ty, and before Ty was Zammis. The child is named Jeriba Zammis."

"Why only the five names? A human child can have just about any name its parents pick for it. In fact, once a human becomes an adult, he or she can pick any name he or she wants."

The Drac looked at me, its eyes filled with pity. "Davidge, how lost you must feel. You humans—how lost you must feel."

"Lost?"

Jerry nodded. "Where do you come from, Davidge?"

"You mean my parents?"

"Yes."

I shrugged. "I remember my parents."

"And their parents?"

"I remember my mother's father. When I was young we used to visit him."

"Davidge, what do you know about this grandparent?"

I rubbed my chin. "It's kind of vague . . . I think he was in some kind of agriculture—I don't know."

"And his parents?"

I shook my head. "The only thing I remember is that somewhere along the line, English and Germans figured. *Gavey* Germans and English?"

Jerry nodded. "Davidge, I can recite the history of my line back to the founding of my planet by Jeriba Ty, one of the original settlers, one hundred and ninety-nine generations ago. At our line's archives on Draco, there are the records that trace the line across space to the racehome planet, Sindie, and there back seventy generations to Jeriba Ty, the founder of the Jeriba line."

"How does one become a founder?"

"Only the firstborn carries the line. Products of second, third, or fourth births must found their own lines."

I nodded, impressed. "Why only the five names? Just to make it easier to remember them?"

Jerry shook its head. "No. The names are things to which we add distinction; they are the same, commonplace five so that they do not overshadow the events that distinguish their bearers. The name I carry, Shigan, has been served by great soldiers, scholars, students of philosophy, and several priests. The name my child will carry has been served by scientists, teachers, and explorers."

"You remember all of your ancestors' occupations?"

Jerry nodded. "Yes, and what they each did and where they did it. You must recite your line before the line's archives to be admitted into adulthood as I was twenty-two of my years ago. Zammis will do the same, except the child must begin its recitation . . ." Jerry smiled, "with my name, Jeriba Shigan."

"You can recite almost two hundred biographies from memory?"

"Yes."

I went over to my bed and stretched out. As I stared up at the smoke being sucked through the crack in the chamber's ceiling, I began to understand what Jerry meant by feeling lost. A Drac with several dozens of generations under its belt knew who it was and what it had to live up to. "Jerry?"

"Yes, Davidge?"

"Will you recite them for me?" I turned my head and looked at the Drac in time to see an expression of utter surprise melt into joy. It was only after many years had passed that I learned I had done Jerry a great honor in requesting his line. Among the Dracs, it is a rare expression of respect, not only of the individual, but of the line.

Jerry placed the hat he was sewing on the sand, stood and began.

"Before you here I stand, Shigan of the line of Jeriba, born of Gothig, the teacher of music. A musician of high merit, the students of Gothig included Datzizh of the Nem line, Perravane of the Tuscor line, and many lesser musicians. Trained in music at the Shimuram, Gothig stood before the archives in the year 11,051 and spoke of its parent Haesni, the manufacturer of ships. . . ."

As I listened to Jerry's singsong of formal Dracon, the backward biographies—beginning with death and ending with adulthood—I experienced a sense of time-binding, of being able to know and touch the past. Battles, empires built and destroyed, discoveries made, great things done—a tour through twelve thousand years of history, but perceived as a well-defined, living continuum.

Against this: I Willis of the Davidge line stand before you, born of Sybil the housewife and Nathan the second-rate civil engineer, one of them born of Grandpop, who probably had something to do with agriculture, born of nobody in particular. . . . Hell, I wasn't even that! My older brother carried the line; not me. I listened and made up my mind to memorize the line of Jeriba.

We talked of war:

"That was a pretty neat trick, suckering me into the atmosphere, then ramming me."

Jerry shrugged. "Dracon fleet pilots are best; this is well known."

I raised my eyebrows. "That's why I shot your tail feathers off, huh?"

Jerry shrugged, frowned, and continued sewing on the scraps of snake leather. "Why do the Earthmen invade this part of the Galaxy, Davidge? We had thousands of years of peace before you came."

"Hah! Why do the Dracs invade? We were at peace, too. What are you doing here?"

"We settle these planets. It is the Drac tradition. We are explorers and founders."

"Well, toad face, what do you think we are, a bunch of homebodies? Humans have had space travel for less than two hundred years, but we've settled almost twice as many planets as the Dracs—"

Jerry held up a finger. "Exactly! You humans spread like a disease. Enough! We don't want you here!"

"Well, we're here, and here to stay. Now, what are you going to do about it?"

"You see what we do, *Irkmaan,* we fight!"

"Phooey! You call that little scrap we were in a fight? Hell, Jerry, we were kicking you junk jocks out of the sky—"

"Haw, Davidge! That's why you sit here sucking on smoked snake-meat!"

I pulled the little rascal out of my mouth and pointed it at the Drac. "I notice your breath has a snake flavor too, Drac!"

Jerry snorted and turned away from the fire. I felt stupid, first because we weren't going to settle an argument that had plagued a hundred worlds for over a century. Second, I wanted to have Jerry check my recitation. I had over a hundred generations memorized. The Drac's side was toward the fire leaving enough light falling on its lap to see its sewing.

"Jerry, what are you working on?"

"We have nothing to talk about, Davidge."

"Come on, what is it?"

Jerry turned its head toward me, then looked back into its lap and picked up a tiny snakeskin suit. "For Zammis." Jerry smiled and I shook my head, then laughed.

We talked of philosophy:

"You studied Shizumaat, Jerry; why won't you tell me about its teachings?"

Jerry frowned. "No, Davidge."

"Are Shizumaat's teachings secret or something?"

Jerry shook its head. "No. But we honor Shizumaat too much for talk."

I rubbed my chin. "Do you mean too much to talk about it, or to talk about it with a human?"

"Not with humans, Davidge; just not with you."

"Why?"

Jerry lifted its head and narrowed its yellow eyes. "You know what you said . . . on the sandbar."

I scratched my head and vaguely recalled the curse I laid on the Drac about Shizumaat eating it. I held out my hands. "But, Jerry, I was mad, angry. You can't hold me accountable for what I said then."

"I do."

"Will it change anything if I apologize?"

"Not a thing."

I stopped myself from saying something nasty and thought back to that moment when Jerry and I stood ready to strangle each other. I remembered something about that meeting and screwed the corners of my mouth in place to keep from smiling. "Will you tell me Shizumaat's teachings if I forgive you . . . for what you said about Mickey Mouse?" I bowed my head in an appearance of reverence, although its chief purpose was to suppress a cackle.

Jerry looked up at me, its face pained with guilt. "I have felt bad about that, Davidge. If you forgive me, I will talk about Shizumaat."

"Then, I forgive you, Jerry."

"One more thing."

"What?"

"You must tell me of the teachings of Mickey Mouse."

"I'll . . . uh, do my best."

We talked of Zammis:

"Jerry, what do you want little Zammy to be?"

The Drac shrugged. "Zammis must live up to its own name. I want it to do that with honor. If Zammis does that, it is all I can ask."

"Zammy will pick its own trade?"

"Yes."

"Isn't there anything special you want, though?"

Jerry nodded. "Yes, there is."

"What's that?"

"That Zammis will, one day, find itself off this miserable planet."

I nodded. "Amen."

"Amen."

The winter dragged on until Jerry and I began wondering if we had gotten in on the beginning of an ice age. Outside the cave, everything was coated with a thick layer of ice, and the low temperature combined with the steady winds made venturing outside a temptation of death by falls or freezing. Still, by mutual agreement, we both went outside to relieve ourselves. There were several isolated chambers deep in the cave; but we feared polluting our water supply, not to mention the air inside the cave. The main risk outside was dropping one's drawers at a wind chill factor that froze breath vapor before it could be blown through the thin face muffs we had made out of our flight suits. We learned not to dawdle.

One morning, Jerry was outside answering the call, while I stayed by the fire mashing up dried roots with water for griddle cakes. I heard Jerry call from the mouth of the cave. "Davidge!"

"What?"

"Davidge, come quick!"

A ship! It had to be! I put the shell bowl on the sand, put on my hat and gloves, and ran through the passage. As I came close to the door, I untied the muff from around my neck and tied it over my mouth and nose to protect my lungs. Jerry, its head bundled in a similar manner, was looking through the door, waving me on. "What is it?"

Jerry stepped away from the door to let me through. "Come, look!"

Sunlight. Blue sky and sunlight. In the distance, over the sea, new clouds were piling up; but above us the sky was clear. Neither of us could look at the sun directly, but we turned our faces to it and felt the rays of Fyrine on our skins. The light glared and sparkled off the ice-covered rocks and trees. "Beautiful."

"Yes." Jerry grabbed my sleeve with a gloved hand. "Davidge, you know what this means?"

"What?"

"Signal fires at night. On a clear night, a large fire could be seen from orbit, *ne?*"

I looked at Jerry, then back at the sky. "I don't know. If the fire were big enough, and we get a clear night, and if anybody picks that moment to look . . ." I let my head hang down. "That's always supposing that there's someone in orbit up there to do the looking." I felt the pain begin in my fingers. "We better go back in."

"Davidge, it's a chance!"

"What are we going to use for wood, Jerry?" I held out an arm toward the trees above and around the cave. "Everything that can burn has at least fifteen centimeters of ice on it."

"In the cave—"

"Our firewood?" I shook my head. "How long is this winter going to last? Can you be sure that we have enough wood to waste on signal fires?"

"It's a chance, Davidge. It's a chance!"

Our survival riding on a toss of the dice. I shrugged. "Why not?"

We spent the next few hours hauling a quarter of our carefully gathered firewood and dumping it outside the mouth of the cave. By the time we were finished and long before night came, the sky was again a solid blanket of grey. Several times each night, we would check the sky, waiting for stars to appear. During the days, we would frequently have to spend several hours beating the ice off the wood pile. Still, it gave both of us hope, until the wood in the cave ran out and we had to start borrowing from the signal pile.

That night, for the first time, the Drac looked absolutely defeated. Jerry sat at the fireplace, staring at the flames. Its hand reached inside its snakeskin jacket through the neck and pulled out a small golden cube suspended on a chain. Jerry held the cube clasped in both hands, shut its eyes and began mumbling in Drac. I watched from my bed until Jerry finished. The Drac sighed, nodded and replaced the object within its jacket.

"What's that thing?"

Jerry looked up at me, frowned, then touched the front of its jacket. "This? It is my *Talman*—what you call a Bible."

"A Bible is a book. You know, with pages that you read."

Jerry pulled the thing from its jacket, mumbled a phrase in Drac, then worked a small catch. Another gold cube dropped from the first and the Drac held it out to me. "Be very careful with it, Davidge."

I sat up, took the object and examined it in the light of the fire. Three hinged pieces of the golden metal formed the binding of a book two-and-a-half centimeters on an edge. I opened the book in the middle and looked over the double columns of dots, lines, and squiggles. "It's in Drac."

"Of course."

"But I can't read it."

Jerry's eyebrows went up. "You speak Drac so well, I didn't remember . . . would you like me to teach you?"

"To read this?"

"Why not? You have an appointment you have to keep?"

I shrugged. "No." I touched my finger to the book and tried to turn

BARRY B. LONGYEAR

one of the tiny pages. Perhaps fifty pages went at once. "I can't separate the pages."

Jerry pointed at a small bump at the top of the spine. "Pull out the pin. It's for turning the pages."

I pulled out the short needle, touched it against a page and it slid loose of its companion and flipped. "Who wrote your *Talman*, Jerry?"

"Many. All great teachers."

"Shizumaat?"

Jerry nodded. "Shizumaat is one of them."

I closed the book and held it in the palm of my hand. "Jerry, why did you bring this out now?"

"I needed its comfort." The Drac held out its arms. "This place. Maybe we will grow old here and die. Maybe we will never be found. I see this today as we brought in the signal fire wood." Jerry placed its hands on its belly. "Zammis will be born here. The *Talman* helps me to accept what I cannot change."

"Zammis; how much longer?"

Jerry smiled. "Soon."

I looked at the tiny book. "I would like you to teach me to read this, Jerry."

The Drac took the chain and case from around its neck and handed it to me. "You must keep the *Talman* in this."

I held it for a moment, then shook my head. "I can't keep this, Jerry. It's obviously of great value to you. What if I lost it?"

"You won't. Keep it while you learn. The student must do this."

I put the chain around my neck. "This is quite an honor you do me."

Jerry shrugged. "Much less than the honor you do me by memorizing the Jeriba line. Your recitations have been accurate and moving." Jerry took some charcoal from the fire, stood and walked to the wall of the chamber. That night I learned the thirty-one letters and sounds of the Drac alphabet, as well as the additional nine sounds and letters used in formal Drac writings.

The wood eventually ran out. Jerry was very heavy and very, very sick as Zammis prepared to make its appearance, and it was all the Drac could do to waddle outside with my help to relieve itself. Hence, woodgathering, which involved taking our remaining stick and beating the ice off the dead standing trees, fell to me, as did cooking.

On a particularly blustery day, I noticed that the ice on the trees was thinner. Somewhere we had turned winter's corner and were heading for spring. I spent my ice-pounding time feeling great at the thought of spring, and I knew Jerry would pick up some at the news. The winter was really getting the Drac down. I was working the woods above the cave, taking armloads of gathered wood and dropping them down below, when I heard a scream. I froze, then looked around. I could see nothing but the sea and the ice around me. Then, the scream again. "Davidge!" It was Jerry. I dropped the load I was carrying and ran to the cleft in the cliff's face that served as a path to the upper woods. Jerry screamed again; and I slipped, then rolled until I came to the shelf level with the cave's mouth. I rushed through the entrance, down the passage way until I came to the chamber. Jerry writhed on its bed, digging its fingers into the sand.

I dropped on my knees next to the Drac. "I'm here, Jerry. What is it? What's wrong?"

"Davidge!" The Drac rolled its eyes, seeing nothing, its mouth worked silently, then exploded with another scream.

"Jerry, it's me!" I shook the Drac's shoulder. "It's me, Jerry. Davidge!"

Jerry turned its head toward me, grimaced, then clasped the fingers of one hand around my left wrist with the strength of pain. "Davidge! Zammis . . . something's gone wrong!"

"What? What can I do?"

Jerry screamed again, then its head fell back to the bed in a half-faint. The Drac fought back to consciousness and pulled my head down to its lips. "Davidge, you must swear."

"What, Jerry? Swear what?"

"Zammis . . . on Draco. To stand before the line's archives. Do this."

"What do you mean? You talk like you're dying."

"I am, Davidge. Zammis two hundredth generation . . . very important. Present my child, Davidge. Swear!"

I wiped the sweat from my face with my free hand. "You're not going to die, Jerry. Hang on!"

"Enough! Face truth, Davidge! I die! You must teach the line of Jeriba to Zammis . . . and the book, the *Talman, gavey?*"

"Stop it!" Panic stood over me almost as a physical presence. "Stop talking like that! You aren't going to die, Jerry. Come on; fight, you *kizlode* sonofabitch. . . ."

Jerry screamed. Its breathing was weak and the Drac drifted in and out of consciousness. "Davidge."

"What?" I realized I was sobbing like a kid.

"Davidge, you must help Zammis come out."

"What . . . how? What in the Hell are you talking about?"

Jerry turned its face to the wall of the cave. "Lift my jacket."

"What?"

"Lift my jacket, Davidge. Now!"

I pulled up the snakeskin jacket exposing Jerry's swollen belly. The fold down the center was bright red and seeping a clear liquid. "What . . . what should I do?"

Jerry breathed rapidly, then held its breath. "Tear it open! You must tear it open, Davidge!"

"No!"

"Do it! Do it, or Zammis dies!"

"What do I care about your goddamn child, Jerry? What do I have to do to save you?"

"Tear it open . . ." whispered the Drac. "Take care of my child, *Irkmaan*. Present Zammis before the Jeriba archives. Swear this to me."

"Oh, Jerry . . ."

"Swear this!"

I nodded, hot fat tears dribbling down my cheeks. "I swear it. . . ." Jerry relaxed its grip on my wrist and closed its eyes. I knelt next to the Drac, stunned. "No. No, no, no, no."

Tear it open! You must tear it open, Davidge!

I reached up a hand and gingerly touched the fold on Jerry's belly. I could feel life struggling beneath it, trying to escape the airless confines of the Drac's womb. I hated it; I hated the damned thing as I never hated anything before. Its struggles grew weaker, then stopped.

Present Zammis before the Jeriba archives. Swear this to me. . . .

I swear it. . . .

I lifted my other hand and inserted my thumbs into the fold and tugged gently. I increased the amount of force, then tore at Jerry's belly like a madman. The fold burst open, soaking the front of my jacket with the clear fluid. Holding the fold open, I could see the still form of Zammis huddled in a well of the fluid, motionless.

I vomited. When I had nothing more to throw up, I reached into the fluid and put my hands under the Drac infant. I lifted it, wiped my mouth on my upper left sleeve, and closed my mouth over Zammis's and pulled the child's mouth open with my right hand. Three times, four times, I inflated the child's lungs, then it coughed. Then it cried. I tied off the two umbilicals with berrybush fibre, then cut them. Jeriba Zammis was freed of the dead flesh of its parent.

I held the rock over my head, then brought it down with all of my force upon the ice. Shards splashed away from the point of impact, exposing the dark green beneath. Again, I lifted the rock and brought it down, knocking loose another rock. I picked it up, stood and carried it to the half-covered corpse of the Drac. "The Drac," I whispered. *Good. Just call it 'the Drac.' Toadface. Dragger.*

The enemy. Call it anything to insulate those feelings against the pain.

I looked at the pile of rocks I had gathered, decided it was sufficient to finish the job, then knelt next to the grave. As I placed the rocks on the pile, unmindful of the gale-blown sleet freezing on my snakeskins, I fought back the tears. I smacked my hands together to help restore the circulation. Spring was coming, but it was still dangerous to stay outside too long. And I had been a long time building the Drac's grave. I picked up another rock and placed it into position. As the rock's weight leaned against the snakeskin mattress cover, I realized that the Drac was already frozen. I quickly placed the remainder of the rocks, then stood.

The wind rocked me and I almost lost my footing on the ice next to the grave. I looked toward the boiling sea, pulled my snakeskins around myself more tightly, then looked down at the pile of rocks. *There should be words. You don't just cover up the dead, then go to dinner. There should be words.* But what words? I was no religionist, and neither was the Drac. Its formal philosophy on the matter of death was the same as my informal rejection of Islamic delights, pagan Valhallas, and Judeo-Christian pies in the sky. Death is death; *finis*; the end; the worms crawl in, the worms crawl out ... *Still, there should be words.*

I reached beneath my snakeskins and clasped my gloved hand around the golden cube of the *Talman*. I felt the sharp corners of the cube through my glove, closed my eyes and ran through the words of the great Drac philosophers. But there was nothing they had written for this moment.

The *Talman* was a book on life. *Talma* means life, and this occupies Drac philosophy. They spare nothing for death. Death is a fact; the end of life. The *Talman* had no words for me to say. The wind knifed through me, causing me to shiver. Already my fingers were numb and pains were beginning in my feet. Still, there should be words. But the only words I could think of would open the gate, flooding my being with pain—with the realization that the Drac was gone. *Still ... still, there should be words.*

"Jerry, I . . ." I had no words. I turned from the grave, my tears mixing with the sleet.

With the warmth and silence of the cave around me, I sat on my mattress, my back against the wall of the cave. I tried to lose myself in the shadows and flickers of light cast on the opposite wall by the fire. Images would half-form, then dance away before I could move my mind to see something in them. As a child I used to watch clouds, and in them, see faces, castles, animals, dragons and giants. It was a world of escape—fantasy; something to inject wonder and adventure into the mundane, regulated life of a middle-class boy leading a middle-class life. All I could see on the wall of the cave was a representation of Hell: flames licking at twisted, grotesque representations of condemned souls. I laughed at the thought. We think of Hell as fire, supervised by a cackling sadist in a red union suit. Fyrine IV had taught me this much: Hell is loneliness, hunger, and endless cold.

I heard a whimper, and I looked into the shadows toward the small mattress at the back of the cave. Jerry had made the snakeskin sack filled with seed pod down for Zammis. It whimpered again, and I leaned forward, wondering if there was something it needed. A pang of fear tickled my guts. What does a Drac infant eat? Dracs aren't mammals. All they ever taught us in training was how to recognize Dracs—that, and how to kill them. Then real fear began working on me. "What in the hell am I going to use for diapers?"

It whimpered again. I pushed myself to my feet, walked the sandy floor to the infant's side, then knelt beside it. Out of the bundle that was Jerry's old flight suit, two chubby three-fingered arms waved. I picked up the bundle, carried it next to the fire, and sat on a rock. Balancing the bundle on my lap, I carefully unwrapped it. I could see the yellow glitter of Zammis's eyes beneath yellow, sleep-heavy lids. From the almost noseless face and solid teeth to its deep yellow color, Zammis was every bit a miniature of Jerry, except for the fat. Zammis fairly wallowed in rolls of fat. I looked, and was grateful to find that there was no mess.

I looked into Zammis' face. "You want something to eat?"

"Guh."

Its jaws were ready for business, and I assumed that Dracs must chew solid food from day one. I reached over the fire and picked up a twist of dried snake, then touched it against the infant's lips. Zammis turned its head. "C'mon, eat. You're not going to find anything better around here."

I pushed the snake against its lips again, and Zammis pulled back a chubby arm and pushed it away. I shrugged. "Well, whenever you get hungry enough, it's there."

"Guh meh!" Its head rocked back and forth on my lap, a tiny, three-fingered hand closed around my finger, and it whimpered again.

"You don't want to eat, you don't need to be cleaned up, so what do you want? *Kos va nu?*"

Zammis's face wrinkled, and its hand pulled at my finger. Its other hand waved in the direction of my chest. I picked Zammis up to arrange the flight suit, and the tiny hands reached out, grasped the front of my snakeskins, and held on as the chubby arms pulled the child next to my chest. I held it close, it placed its cheek against my chest, and promptly fell asleep. "Well . . . I'll be damned."

Until the Drac was gone, I never realized how closely I had stood near the edge of madness. My loneliness was a cancer—a growth that I fed with hate: hate for the planet with its endless cold, endless winds, and endless isolation; hate for the helpless yellow child with its clawing need for care, food, and an affection that I couldn't give; and hate for myself. I found myself doing things that frightened and disgusted me. To break my solid wall of being alone, I would talk, shout, and sing to myself—uttering curses, nonsense, or meaningless croaks.

Its eyes were open, and it waved a chubby arm and cooed. I picked up a large rock, staggered over to the child's side, and held the weight over the tiny body. "I could drop this thing, kid. Where would you be then?" I felt laughter coming from my lips. I threw the rock aside. "Why should I mess up the cave? Outside. Put you outside for a minute, and you die! You hear me? Die!"

The child worked its three-fingered hands at the empty air, shut its eyes, and cried. "Why don't you eat? Why don't you crap? Why don't you do anything right, but cry?" The child cried more loudly. "Bah! I ought to pick up that rock and finish it! That's what I ought . . ." A wave of revulsion stopped my words, and I went to my mattress, picked up my cap, gloves, and muff, then headed outside.

Before I came to the rocked-in entrance to the cave, I felt the bite of the wind. Outside I stopped and looked at the sea and sky—a roiling panorama in glorious black and white, grey and grey. A gust of wind slapped against me, rocking me back toward the entrance. I regained my balance, walked to the edge of the cliff and shook my fist at the sea. "Go ahead! Go ahead and blow, you *kizlode* sonofa-bitch! You haven't killed me yet!"

I squeezed the windburned lids of my eyes shut, then opened them and looked down. A forty-meter drop to the next ledge, but if I took a running jump, I could clear it. Then it would be a hundred and fifty meters to the rocks below. *Jump.* I backed away from the cliff's edge. "Jump! Sure, jump!" I shook my head at the sea. "I'm not going to do your job for you! You want me dead, you're going to have to do it yourself!"

I looked back and up, above the entrance to the cave. The sky was darkening and in a few hours, night would shroud the landscape. I turned toward the cleft in the rock that led to the scrub forest above the cave.

I squatted next to the Drac's grave and studied the rocks I had placed there, already fused together with a layer of ice. "Jerry. What am I going to do?"

The Drac would sit by the fire, both of us sewing. And we talked.

"You know, Jerry, all this," I held up the Talman, *"I have heard it all before. I expected something different."*

The Drac lowered its sewing to its lap and studied me for an instant. Then it shook its head and resumed its sewing. "You are not a terribly profound creature, Davidge."

"What's that supposed to mean?"

Jerry held out a three-fingered hand. "A universe, Davidge—there is a universe out there, a universe of life, objects, and events. There are differences, but it is all the same universe, and we all must obey the same universal laws. Did you ever think of that?"

"No."

"That is what I mean, Davidge. Not terribly profound."

I snorted. "I told you, I'd heard this stuff before. So I imagine that shows humans to be just as profound as Dracs."

Jerry laughed. "You always insist on making something racial out of my observations. What I said applied to you, not to the race of humans. . . ."

I spat on the frozen ground. "You Dracs think you're so damned smart." The wind picked up, and I could taste the sea salt in it. One of the big blows was coming. The sky was changing to that curious darkness that tricked me into thinking it was midnight blue, rather than black. A trickle of ice found its way under my collar.

"What's wrong with me just being me? Everybody in the universe doesn't have to be a damned philosopher, toadface!" There were millions—billions—like me. More maybe. "What difference does it make to anything whether I ponder existence or not? It's here; that's all I have to know."

"Davidge, you don't even know your family line beyond your parents, and now you say you refuse to know that of your universe that you can know. How will you know your place in this existence, Davidge? Where are you? Who are you?"

I shook my head and stared at the grave, then I turned and faced the sea. In another hour, or less, it would be too dark to see the whitecaps. "I'm me, that's who." But was that 'me' who held the rock over Zammis, threatening a helpless infant with death? I felt my guts curdle as the loneliness I thought I felt grew claws and fangs and began gnawing and slashing at the remains of my sanity. I turned back to the grave, closed my eyes, then opened them. "I'm a fighter pilot, Jerry. Isn't that something?"

"That is what you do, Davidge; that is not who nor what you are."

I knelt next to the grave and clawed at the ice-sheathed rocks with my hands. "You don't talk to me now, Drac! *You're dead!"* I stopped, realizing that the words I had heard were from the *Talman,* processed into my own context. I slumped against the rocks, felt the wind, then pushed myself to my feet. "Jerry, Zammis won't eat. It's been three days. What do I do? Why didn't you tell me anything about Drac brats before you . . ." I held my hands to my face. "Steady, boy. Keep it up, and they'll stick you in a home." The wind pressed against my back, I lowered my hands, then walked from the grave.

I sat in the cave, staring at the fire. I couldn't hear the wind through the rock, and the wood was dry, making the fire hot and quiet. I tapped my fingers against my knees, then began humming. Noise, any kind, helped to drive off the oppressive loneliness. "Sonofabitch." I laughed and nodded. "Yea, verily, and *kizlode va nu, dutschaat.*" I chuckled, trying to think of all the curses and obscenities in Drac that I had learned from Jerry. There were quite a few. My toe tapped against the sand and my humming started up again. I stopped, frowned, then remembered the song.

"Highty tighty Christ almighty,
Who the Hell are we?
Zim zam, Gawd Damn,
We're in Squadron B."

I leaned back against the wall of the cave, trying to remember another verse. *A pilot's got a rotten life/no crumpets with our tea/ we have to service the general's wife/ and pick fleas from her knee.*

"Damn!" I slapped my knee, trying to see the faces of the other pilots in the squadron lounge. I could almost feel the whiskey fumes tickling the inside of my nose. Vadik, Wooster, Arnold . . . the one with the broken nose—Demerest, Kadz. I hummed again, swinging an imaginary mug of issue grog by its imaginary handle.

"And if he doesn't like it,
I'll tell you what we'll do:
We'll fill his ass with broken glass,
and seal it up with glue."

The cave echoed with the song. I stood, threw up my arms and screamed "Yaaaaahooooooo!"

Zammis began crying. I bit my lip and walked over to the bundle on the mattress. "Well? You ready to eat?"

"Unh, unh, weh." The infant rocked its head back and forth. I went to the fire, picked up a twist of snake, then returned. I knelt next to Zammis and held the snake to its lips. Again, the child pushed it away. "Come on, you. You have to eat." I tried again with the same results. I took the wraps off the child and looked at its body. I could tell it was losing weight, although Zammis didn't appear to be getting weak. I shrugged, wrapped it up again, stood and began walking back to my mattress.

"Guh, weh."

I turned. "What?"

"Ah, guh, guh."

I went back, stooped over and picked the child up. Its eyes were open and it looked into my face, then smiled.

"What're you laughing at, ugly? You should get a load of your own face."

Zammis barked out a short laugh, then gurgled. I went to my mattress, sat down and arranged Zammis in my lap. "Gumma, buh, buh." Its hand grabbed a loose flap of snakeskin on my shirt and pulled on it.

"Gumma buh buh to you, too. So, what do we do now? How about I start teaching you the line of Jeriban? You're going to have to learn it sometime, and it might as well be now." The Jeriban line. My recitations of the line were the only things Jerry ever complimented me about. I looked into Zammis' eyes. "When I bring you to stand before the Jeriba archives, you will say this: 'Before you here I stand, Zammis of the line of Jeriba, born of Shigan, the fighter pilot.'" I smiled, thinking of the upraised yellow brows if Zammis continued: *"and, by damn, Shigan was a Helluva good pilot, too. Why, I was once told he took a smart round in his tail feathers, then pulled around and rammed the* kizlode *sonofabitch, known to one and all as Willis E. Davidge . . ."* I shook my head. "You're not going to get your wings by doing the line in English, Zammis." I began again:

"Naatha nu enta va Zammis zea does Jeriba, estay va Shigan, asaam naa denvadar. . . ."

For eight of those long days and nights, I feared the child would die. I tried everything—roots, dried berries, dried plumfruit, snake-meat dried, boiled, chewed, and ground. Zammis refused it all. I checked frequently, but each time I looked through the child's wraps, they were as clean as when I had put them on. Zammis lost weight, but seemed to grow stronger. By the ninth day it was crawling the floor of the cave. Even with the fire, the cave wasn't really warm. I feared that the kid would get sick crawling around naked, and I dressed it in the tiny snakeskin suit and cap Jerry had made for it. After dressing it, I stood Zammis up and looked at it. The kid had already developed a smile full of mischief that, combined with the twinkle in its yellow eyes and its suit and cap, made it look like an elf. I was holding Zammis up in a standing position. The kid seemed pretty steady on its legs, and I let go. Zammis smiled, waved its thinning arms about, then laughed and took a faltering step toward me. I caught it as it fell, and the little Drac squealed.

In two more days Zammis was walking and getting into everything that could be gotten into. I spent many an anxious moment searching the chambers at the back of the cave for the kid after coming in from outside. Finally, when I caught him at the mouth of the cave heading full steam for the outside, I had had enough. I made a harness out of snakeskin, attached it to a snake-leather leash, and tied the other end to a projection of rock above my head. Zammis still got into everything, but at least I could find it.

Four days after it learned to walk, it wanted to eat. Drac babies are probably the most convenient and considerate infants in the universe. They live off their fat for about three or four Earth weeks, and can therefore make it to a mutually agreed upon spot, then they want food and begin discharging wastes. I showed the kid once how to use the litter box I had made, and never had to again. After five or six lessons, Zammis was handling its own drawers. Watching the little Drac learn and grow, I began to understand those pilots in my squadron who used to bore each other—and everyone else—with countless pictures of ugly children, accompanied by thirty-minute narratives for each snapshot. Before the ice melted, Zammis was talking. I taught it to call me "Uncle."

For lack of a better term, I called the ice-melting season "spring." It would be a long time before the scrub forest showed any green or the snakes ventured forth from their icy holes. The sky maintained its eternal cover of dark, angry clouds, and still the sleet would come and coat everything with a hard, slippery glaze. But the next day the glaze would melt, and the warmer air would push another millimeter into the soil.

I realized that this was the time to be gathering wood. Before the winter hit, Jerry and I working together hadn't gathered enough wood. The short summer would have to be spent putting up for food for the next winter. I was hoping to build a tighter door over the mouth of the cave, and I swore that I would figure out some kind of indoor plumbing. Dropping your drawers outside in the middle of winter was dangerous. My mind was full of these things as I stretched out on my mattress watching the smoke curl through a crack in the roof of the cave. Zammis was off in the back of the cave playing with some rocks that it had found, and I must have fallen asleep. I awoke with the kid shaking my arm.

"Uncle?"

"Huh? Zammis?"

"Uncle. Look."

I rolled over on my left and faced the Drac. Zammis was holding up his right hand, fingers spread out. "What is it, Zammis?"

"Look." It pointed at each of its three fingers in turn. "One, two, three."

"So?"

"Look." Zammis grabbed my right hand and spread out the fingers. "One, two, three, *four, five!*"

I nodded. "So you can count to five."

The Drac frowned and made an impatient gesture with its tiny fists. "Look." It took my outstretched hand and placed its own on top of it. With its other hand, Zammis pointed first at one of its own fingers, then at one of mine. "One, one." The child's yellow eyes studied me to see if I understood.

"Yes."

The child pointed again. "Two, two." It looked at me, then looked back at my hand and pointed. "Three, three." Then he grabbed my two remaining fingers. *"Four, five!"* It dropped my hand, then pointed to the side of its own hand. "Four, five?"

I shook my head. Zammis, at less than four Earth months old, had detected part of the difference between Dracs and humans. A human child would be—what—five, six, or seven years old before asking questions like that. I sighed. "Zammis."

"Yes, Uncle?"

"Zammis, you are a Drac. Dracs only have three fingers on a hand." I held up my right hand and wiggled the fingers. "I'm a human. I have five."

I swear that tears welled in the child's eyes. Zammis held out its hands, looked at them, then shook its head. "Grow four, five?"

I sat up and faced the kid. Zammis was wondering where its other four fingers had gone. "Look, Zammis. You and I are different . . . different kinds of beings, understand?"

Zammis shook its head. "Grow four, five?"

"You won't. You're a Drac." I pointed at my chest. "I'm a human." This was getting me nowhere. "Your parent, where you came from, was a Drac. Do you understand?"

Zammis frowned. "Drac. What Drac?"

The urge to resort to the timeless standby of "you'll understand when you get older" pounded at the back of my mind. I shook my head. "Dracs have three fingers on each hand. Your parent had three fingers on each hand." I rubbed my beard. "My parent was a human and had five fingers on each hand. That's why I have five fingers on each hand."

Zammis knelt on the sand and studied its fingers. It looked up at me, back to its hands, then back to me. "What parent?"

I studied the kid. It must be having an identity crisis of some kind. I was the only person it had ever seen, and I had five fingers per hand. "A parent is . . . the thing . . ." I scratched my beard again. "Look . . . we all come from someplace. I had a mother and father—two different kinds of humans—that gave me life; that made me, understand?"

Zammis gave me a look that could be interpreted as "Mac, you are full of it." I shrugged. "I don't know if I can explain it."

Zammis pointed at its own chest. "My mother? My father?"

I held out my hands, dropped them into my lap, pursed my lips, scratched my beard, and generally stalled for time. Zammis held an unblinking gaze on me the entire time. "Look, Zammis. You don't have a mother and father. I'm a human, so I have them; you're a Drac. You have a parent—just one, see?"

Zammis shook its head. It looked at me, then pointed at its own chest. "Drac."

BARRY B. LONGYEAR

"Right."

Zammis pointed at my chest. "Human."

"Right again."

Zammis removed its hand and dropped it in its lap. "Where Drac come from?"

Sweet Jesus! Trying to explain hermaphroditic reproduction to a kid who shouldn't even be crawling yet! "Zammis . . . " I held up my hands, then dropped them into my lap. "Look. You see how much bigger I am than you?"

"Yes, Uncle."

"Good." I ran my fingers through my hair, fighting for time and inspiration. "Your parent was big, like me. Its name was . . . Jeriba Shigan." Funny how just saying the name was painful. "Jeriba Shigan was like you. It only had three fingers on each hand. It grew you in its tummy." I poked Zammis's middle. "Understand?"

Zammis giggled and held its hands over its stomach. "Uncle, how Dracs grow there?"

I lifted my legs onto the mattress and stretched out. Where do little Dracs come from? I looked over to Zammis and saw the child hanging upon my every word. I grimaced and told the truth. "Damned if I know, Zammis. Damned if I know." Thirty seconds later, Zammis was back playing with its rocks.

Summer, and I taught Zammis how to capture and skin the long grey snakes, and then how to smoke the meat. The child would squat on the shallow bank above a mudpool, its yellow eyes fixed on the snake holes in the bank, waiting for one of the occupants to poke out its head. The wind would blow, but Zammis wouldn't move. Then a flat, triangular head set with tiny blue eyes would appear. The snake would check the pool, turn and check the bank, then check the sky. It would advance out of the hole a bit, then check it all again. Often the snakes would look directly at Zammis, but the Drac could have been carved from rock. Zammis wouldn't move until the snake was too far out of the hole to pull itself back in tail first. Then Zammis would strike, grabbing the snake with both hands just behind the head. The snakes had no fangs and weren't poisonous, but they were lively enough to toss Zammis into the mudpool on occasion.

The skins were spread and wrapped around tree trunks and pegged in place to dry. The tree trunks were kept in an open place near the entrance to the cave, but under an overhang that faced away from the ocean. About two thirds of the skins put up in this manner cured; the remaining third would rot.

Beyond the skin room was the smokehouse: a rock-walled chamber that we would hang with rows of snakemeat. A greenwood fire would be set in a pit in the chamber's floor, then we would fill in the small opening with rocks and dirt.

"Uncle, why doesn't the meat rot after it's smoked?"

I thought upon it. "I'm not sure; I just know it doesn't."

"Why do you know?"

I shrugged. "I just do. I read about it, probably."

"What's read?"

"Reading. Like when I sit down and read the *Talman*."

"Does the *Talman* say why the meat doesn't rot?"

"No. I meant that I probably read it in another book."

"Do we have more books?"

I shook my head. "I meant before I came to this planet."

"Why did you come to this planet?"

"I told you. Your parent and I were stranded here during the battle."

"Why do the humans and Dracs fight?"

"It's very complicated." I waved my hands about for a bit. The human line was that the Dracs were aggressors invading our space. The Drac line was that the humans were aggressors invading their space. The truth? "Zammis, it has to do with the colonization of new planets. Both races are expanding and both races have a tradition of exploring and colonizing new planets. I guess we just expanded into each other. Understand?"

Zammis nodded, then became mercifully silent as it fell into deep thought. The main thing I learned from the Drac child was all of the questions I didn't have answers to. I was feeling very smug, however, at having gotten Zammis to understand about the war, thereby avoiding my ignorance on the subject of preserving meat. "Uncle?"

"Yes, Zammis?"

"What's a planet?"

As the cold, wet summer came to an end, we had the cave jammed with firewood and preserved food. With that out of the way, I concentrated my efforts on making some kind of indoor plumbing out of the natural pools in the chambers deep within the cave. The bathtub was no problem. By dropping heated rocks into one of the pools, the water could be brought up to a bearable—even comfortable—temperature. After bathing, the hollow stems of a bamboo-like plant could be used to siphon out the dirty water. The tub could then be refilled from the pool above. The problem was where to siphon the water. Several of the chambers had holes in their floors. The first three holes we tried drained into our main chamber, wetting the low edge near the entrance. The previous winter, Jerry and I had considered using one of those holes for a toilet that we would flush with water from the pools. Since we didn't know where the goodies would come out, we decided against it.

The fourth hole Zammis and I tried drained out below the entrance to the cave in the face of the cliff. Not ideal, but better than answering the call of nature in the middle of a combination ice-storm and blizzard. We rigged up the hole as a drain for both the tub and toilet. As Zammis and I prepared to enjoy our first hot bath, I removed my snakeskins, tested the water with my toe, then stepped in. "Great!" I turned to Zammis, the child still half dressed. "Come on in, Zammis. The water's fine." Zammis was staring at me, its mouth hanging open. "What's the matter?"

The child stared wide-eyed, then pointed at me with a three-fingered hand. "Uncle . . . what's that?"

I looked down. "Oh." I shook my head, then looked up at the child. "Zammis, I explained all that, remember? I'm a human."

"But what's it *for?*"

I sat down in the warm water, removing the object of discussion from sight. "It's for the elimination of liquid wastes . . . among other things. Now, hop in and get washed."

Zammis shucked its snakeskins, looked down at its own smooth-surfaced, combined system, then climbed into the tub. The child settled into the water up to its neck, its yellow eyes studying me. "Uncle?"

"Yes?"

"What *other things?*"

Well, I told Zammis. For the first time, the Drac appeared to be trying to decide whether my response was truthful or not, rather than its usual acceptance of my every assertion. In fact, I was convinced that Zammis thought I was lying—probably because I was.

Winter began with a sprinkle of snowflakes carried on a gentle breeze. I took Zammis above the cave to the scrub forest. I held the child's hand as we stood before the pile of rocks that served as Jerry's grave. Zammis pulled its snakeskins against the wind, bowed its head, then turned and looked up into my face. "Uncle, this is the grave of my parent?"

I nodded. "Yes."

Zammis turned back to the grave, then shook its head. "Uncle, how should I feel?"

"I don't understand, Zammis."

The child nodded at the grave. "I can see that you are sad being here. I think you want me to feel the same. Do you?"

I frowned, then shook my head. "No. I don't want you to be sad. I just wanted you to know where it is."

"May I go now?"

"Sure. Are you certain you know the way back to the cave?"

"Yes. I just want to make sure my soap doesn't burn again."

I watched as the child turned and scurried off into the naked trees, then I turned back to the grave. "Well, Jerry, what do you think of your kid? Zammis was using wood ashes to clean the grease off the shells, then it put a shell back on the fire and put water in it to boil off the burnt-on food: Fat and ashes. The next thing, Jerry, we were making soap. Zammis' first batch almost took the hide off us, but the kid's getting better . . ."

I looked up at the clouds, then brought my glance down to the sea. In the distance, low, dark clouds were building up. "See that? You know what that means, don't you? Ice-storm number one." The wind picked up and I squatted next to the grave to replace a rock that had rolled from the pile. "Zammis is a good kid, Jerry. I wanted to hate it . . . after you died. I wanted to hate it." I replaced the rock, then looked back toward the sea.

"I don't know how we're going to make it off planet, Jerry—" I caught a flash of movement out of the corner of my vision. I turned to the right and looked over the tops of the trees. Against the grey sky, a black speck streaked away. I followed it with my eyes until it went above the clouds.

I listened, hoping to hear an exhaust roar, but my heart was pounding so hard, all I could hear was the wind. Was it a ship? I stood, took a few steps in the direction the speck was going, then stopped. Turning my head, I saw that the rocks on Jerry's grave were already capped with thin layers of fine snow. I shrugged and headed for the cave. "Probably just a bird."

Zammis sat on its mattress, stabbing several pieces of snakeskin with a bone needle. I stretched out on my own mattress and watched the smoke curl up toward the crack in the ceiling. Was it a bird? Or was it a ship? Damn, but it worked on me. Escape from the planet had been out of my thoughts, had been buried, hidden for all that summer. But again, it twisted at me. To walk where a sun shined, to wear cloth again, experience central heating, eat food prepared by a chef, to be among . . . people again.

I rolled over on my right side and stared at the wall next to my mattress. People. Human people. I closed my eyes and swallowed. Girl human people. Female persons. Images drifted before my eyes—faces, bodies, laughing couples, the dance after flight training . . . what was her name? Dolora? Dora?

I shook my head, rolled over and sat up, facing the fire. Why did I have to see whatever it was? All those things I had been able to bury—to forget—boiling over.

"Uncle?"

I looked up at Zammis. Yellow skin, yellow eyes, noseless toadface. I shook my head. "What?"

"Is something wrong?"

Is something wrong, hah. "No. I just thought I saw something today. It probably wasn't anything." I reached to the fire and took a piece of dried snake from the griddle. I blew on it, then gnawed on the stringy strip.

"What did it look like?"

"I don't know. The way it moved, I thought it might be a ship. It went away so fast, I couldn't be sure. Might have been a bird."

"Bird?"

I studied Zammis. It'd never seen a bird; neither had I on Fyrine IV. "An animal that flies."

Zammis nodded. "Uncle, when we were gathering wood up in the scrub forest, I saw something fly."

"What? Why didn't you tell me?"

"I meant to, but I forgot."

"Forgot!" I frowned. "In which direction was it going?"

Zammis pointed to the back of the cave. "That way. Away from the sea." Zammis put down its sewing. "Can we go see where it went?"

I shook my head. "The winter is just beginning. You don't know what it's like. We'd die in only a few days."

Zammis went back to poking holes in the snakeskin. To make the trek in the winter would kill us. But spring would be something else. We could survive with double layered snakeskins stuffed with seed pod down, and a tent. We had to have a tent. Zammis and I could spend the winter making it, and packs. Boots. We'd need sturdy walking boots. Have to think on that. . . .

It's strange how a spark of hope can ignite, and spread, until all desperation is consumed. Was it a ship? I didn't know. If it was, was it taking off, or landing? I didn't know. If it was taking off, we'd be heading in the wrong direction. But the opposite direction meant crossing the sea. Whatever. Come spring we would head beyond the scrub forest and see what was there.

The winter seemed to pass quickly, with Zammis occupied with the tent and my time devoted to rediscovering the art of boot making. I made tracings of both of our feet on snakeskins, and, after some experimentation, I found that boiling the snake leather with plum-fruit made it soft and gummy. By taking several of the gummy layers, weighting them, then setting them aside to dry, the result was a tough, flexible sole. By the time I finished Zammis's boots, the Drac needed a new pair.

"They're too small, Uncle."

"Waddaya mean, too small?"

Zammis pointed down. "They hurt. My toes are all crippled up."

I squatted down and felt the tops over the child's toes. "I don't understand. It's only been twenty, twenty-five days since I made the tracings. You sure you didn't move when I made them?"

Zammis shook its head. "I didn't move."

I frowned, then stood. "Stand up, Zammis." The Drac stood and I moved next to it. The top of Zammis's head came to the middle of my chest. Another sixty centimeters and it'd be as tall as Jerry. "Take them off, Zammis. I'll make a bigger pair. Try not to grow so fast."

Zammis pitched the tent inside the cave, put glowing coals inside, then rubbed fat into the leather for waterproofing. It had grown taller, and I had held off making the Drac's boots until I could be sure of the size it would need. I tried to do a projection by measuring Zammis's feet every ten days, then extending the curve into spring. According to my figures, the kid would have feet resembling a pair of attack transports by the time the snow melted. By spring, Zammis would be full grown. Jerry's old flight boots had fallen apart before Zammis had been born, but I had saved the pieces. I used the soles to make my tracings and hoped for the best.

I was busy with the new boots and Zammis was keeping an eye on the tent treatment. The Drac looked back at me.

BARRY B. LONGYEAR

"Uncle?"

"What?"

"Existence is the first given?"

I shrugged. "That's what Shizumaat says; I'll buy it."

"But, Uncle, how do we *know* that existence is real?"

I lowered my work, looked at Zammis, shook my head, then resumed stitching the boots. "Take my word for it."

The Drac grimaced. "But, Uncle, that is not knowledge; that is faith."

I sighed, thinking back to my sophomore year at the University of Nations—a bunch of adolescents lounging around a cheap flat experimenting with booze, powders, and philosophy. At a little more than one Earth year old, Zammis was developing into an intellectual bore. "So, what's wrong with faith?"

Zammis snickered. "Come now, Uncle. *Faith?*"

"It helps some of us along this drizzle-soaked coil."

"Coil?"

I scratched my head. "This mortal coil; life. Shakespeare, I think."

Zammis frowned. "It is not in the *Talman*."

"He, not it. Shakespeare was a human."

Zammis stood, walked to the fire and sat across from me. "Was he a philosopher, like Mistan or Shizumaat?"

"No. He wrote plays—like stories, acted out."

Zammis rubbed its chin. "Do you remember any of Shakespeare?"

I held up a finger. " 'To be, or not to be; that is the question.' "

The Drac's mouth dropped open, then it nodded its head. "Yes. Yes! To be or not to be; that *is* the question!" Zammis held out its hands. "How do we *know* the wind blows outside the cave when we are not there to see it? Does the sea still boil if we are not there to feel it?"

I nodded. "Yes."

"But, Uncle, how do we *know?*"

I squinted at the Drac. "Zammis, I have a question for you. Is the following statement true or false: What I am saying right now is false."

Zammis blinked. "If it is false, then the statement is true. But . . . if it's true . . . the statement is false, but . . ." Zammis blinked again, then turned and went back to rubbing fat into the tent. "I'll think upon it, Uncle."

"You do that, Zammis."

The Drac thought upon it for about ten minutes, then turned back. "The statement is false."

I smiled. "But that's what the statement said, hence it is true, but . . ." I let the puzzle trail off. Oh, smugness, thou temptest even saints.

"No, Uncle. The statement is meaningless in its present context." I shrugged. "You see, Uncle, the statement assumes the existence of truth values that can comment upon themselves devoid of any other reference. I think Lurrvena's logic in the *Talman* is clear on this, and if meaninglessness is equated with falsehood . . ."

I sighed. "Yeah, well—"

"You see, Uncle, you must, first, establish a context in which your statement has meaning."

I leaned forward, frowned, and scratched my beard. "I see. You mean I was putting Descartes before the horse?"

Zammis looked at me strangely, and even more so when I collapsed on my mattress cackling like a fool.

"Uncle, why does the line of Jeriba have only five names? You say that human lines have many names."

I nodded. "The five names of the Jeriba line are things to which their bearers must add deeds. The deeds are important—not the names."

"Gothig is Shigan's parent as Shigan is my parent."

"Of course. You know that from your recitations."

Zammis frowned. "Then, I *must* name my child Ty when I become a parent?"

"Yes. And Ty must name its child Haesni. Do you see something wrong with that?"

"I would like to name my child Davidge, after you."

I smiled and shook my head. "The Ty name has been served by great bankers, merchants, inventors, and—well, you know your recitation. The name Davidge hasn't been served by much. Think of what Ty would miss by not being Ty."

Zammis thought awhile, then nodded. "Uncle, do you think Gothig is alive?"

"As far as I know."

"What is Gothig like?"

I thought back to Jerry talking about its parent, Gothig. "It taught music, and is very strong. Jerry . . . Shigan said that its parent could bend metal bars with its fingers. Gothig is also very dignified. I imagine that right now Gothig is also very sad. Gothig must think that the line of Jeriba has ended."

Zammis frowned and its yellow brow furrowed. "Uncle, we must make it to Draco. We must tell Gothig the line continues."

"We will."

The winter's ice began thinning, and boots, tent, and packs were ready. We were putting the finishing touches on our new insulated suits. As Jerry had given the *Talman* to me to learn, the golden cube now hung around Zammis's neck. The Drac would drop the tiny golden book from the cube and study it for hours at a time.

"Uncle?"

"What?"

"Why do Dracs speak and write in one language and the humans in another?"

I laughed. "Zammis, the humans speak and write in many languages. English is just one of them."

"How do the humans speak among themselves?"

I shrugged. "They don't always; when they do, they use interpreters—people who can speak both languages."

"You and I speak both English and Drac; does that make us interpreters?"

"I suppose we could be, if you could ever find a human and a Drac who want to talk to each other. Remember, there's a war going on."

"How will the war stop if they do not talk?"

"I suppose they will talk, eventually."

Zammis smiled. "I think I would like to be an interpreter and help end the war." The Drac put its sewing aside and stretched out on its new mattress. Zammis had outgrown even its old mattress, which it now used for a pillow. "Uncle, do you think that we will find anybody beyond the scrub forest?"

"I hope so."

"If we do, will you go with me to Draco?"

"I promised your parent that I would."

"I mean, after. After I make my recitation, what will you do?"

I stared at the fire. "I don't know." I shrugged. "The war might keep us from getting to Draco for a long time."

"After that, what?"

"I suppose I'll go back into the service."

Zammis propped itself up on an elbow. "Go back to being a fighter pilot?"

"Sure. That's about all I know how to do."

"And kill Dracs?"

I put my own sewing down and studied the Drac. Things had

changed since Jerry and I had slugged it out—more things than I had realized. I shook my head. "No. I probably won't be a pilot—not a service one. Maybe I can land a job flying commercial ships." I shrugged. "Maybe the service won't give me any choice."

Zammis sat up, was still for a moment, then it stood, walked over to my mattress and knelt before me on the sand. "Uncle, I don't want to leave you."

"Don't be silly. You'll have your own kind around you. Your grand-parent, Gothig, Shigan's siblings, their children—you'll forget all about me."

"Will you forget about me?"

I looked into those yellow eyes, then reached out my hand and touched Zammis' cheek. "No. I won't forget about you. But, remember this, Zammis: you're a Drac and I'm a human, and that's how this part of the universe is divided."

Zammis took my hand from his cheek, spread the fingers and studied them. "Whatever happens, Uncle, I will never forget you."

The ice was gone, and the Drac and I stood in the wind-blown drizzle, packs on our backs, before the grave. Zammis was as tall as I was, which made it a little taller than Jerry. To my relief, the boots fit. Zammis hefted its pack up higher on its shoulders, then turned from the grave and looked out at the sea. I followed Zammis' glance and watched the rollers steam in and smash on the rocks. I looked at the Drac. "What are you thinking about?"

Zammis looked down, then turned toward me. "Uncle, I didn't think of it before, but . . . I will miss this place."

I laughed. "Nonsense! This place?" I slapped the Drac on the shoulder. "Why would you miss this place?"

Zammis looked back out to sea. "I have learned many things here. You have taught me many things here, Uncle. My life happened here."

"Only the beginning, Zammis. You have a life ahead of you." I nodded my head at the grave. "Say goodbye."

Zammis turned toward the grave, stood over it, then knelt to one side and began removing the rocks. After a few moments, it had exposed the hand of a skeleton with three fingers. Zammis nodded, then wept. "I am sorry, Uncle, but I had to do that. This has been nothing but a pile of rocks to me. Now it is more." Zammis replaced the rocks, then stood.

I cocked my head toward the scrub forest. "Go on ahead. I'll catch up in a minute."

"Yes, Uncle."

Zammis moved off toward the naked trees, and I looked down at the grave. "What do you think of Zammis, Jerry? It's bigger than you were. I guess snake agrees with the kid." I squatted next to the grave, picked up a small rock and added it to the pile. "I guess this is it. We're either going to make it to Draco, or die trying." I stood and looked at the sea. "Yeah, I guess I learned a few things here. I'll miss it, in a way." I turned back to the grave and hefted my pack up. *"Ehdevva sahn, Jeriba Shigan.* So long, Jerry."

I turned and followed Zammis into the forest.

The days that followed were full of wonder for Zammis. For me, the sky was still the same, dull grey, and the few variations in plant and animal life that we found were nothing remarkable. Once we got beyond the scrub forest, we climbed a gentle rise for a day, and then found ourselves on a wide, flat, endless plain. It was ankle deep in a purple weed that stained our boots the same color. The nights were still too cold for hiking, and we would hole up in the tent. Both the greased tent and suits worked well keeping out the almost constant rain.

We had been out perhaps two of Fyrine IV's long weeks when we saw it. It screamed overhead, then disappeared over the horizon before either of us could say a word. I had no doubt that the craft I had seen was in landing attitude.

"Uncle! Did it see us?"

I shook my head. "No. I doubt it. But it was landing. Do you hear? It was landing somewhere ahead."

"Uncle?"

"Let's get moving! What is it?"

"Was it a Drac ship, or a human ship?"

I cooled in my tracks. I had never stopped to think about it. I waved my hand. "Come on. It doesn't matter. Either way, you go to Draco. You're a noncombatant, so the USE forces couldn't do anything, and if they're Dracs, you're home free."

We began walking. "But, Uncle, if it's a Drac ship, what will happen to you?"

I shrugged. "Prisoner of war. The Dracs say they abide by the interplanetary war accords, so I should be all right." *Fat chance,* said the back of my head to the front of my head. The big question was whether I preferred being a Drac POW or a permanent resident of Fyrine IV. I had figured that out long ago. "Come on, let's pick up the pace. We don't know how long it will take to get there, or how long it will be on the ground."

Pick 'em up; put 'em down. Except for a few breaks, we didn't stop—even when night came. Our exertion kept us warm. The horizon never seemed to grow nearer. The longer we slogged at it, the duller my mind grew. It must have been days, my mind as numb as my feet, when I fell through the purple weed into a hole. Immediately, everything grew dark, and I felt a pain in my right leg. I felt the blackout coming, and I welcomed its warmth, its rest, its peace.

"Uncle? Uncle? Wake up! Please, wake up!"
I felt slapping against my face, although it felt somehow detached. Agony thundered into my brain, bringing me wide awake. Damned if I didn't break my leg. I looked up and saw the weedy edges of the hole. My rear end was seated in a trickle of water. Zammis squatted next to me.
"What happened?"
Zammis motioned upwards. "This hole was only covered by a thin crust of dirt and plants. The water must have taken the ground away. Are you all right?"
"My leg. I think I broke it." I leaned my back against the muddy wall. "Zammis, you're going to have to go on by yourself."
"I can't leave you, Uncle!"
"Look, if you find anyone, you can send them back for me."
"What if the water in here comes up?" Zammis felt along my leg until I winced. "I must carry you out of here. What must I do for the leg?"
The kid had a point. Drowning wasn't in my schedule. "We need something stiff. Bind the leg so it doesn't move."
Zammis pulled off its pack, and kneeling in the water and mud, went through its pack, then through the tent roll. Using the tent poles, it wrapped my leg with snakeskins torn from the tent. Then, using more snakeskins, Zammis made two loops, slipped one over each of my legs, then propped me up and slipped the loops over its shoulders. It lifted, and I blacked out.

On the ground, covered with the remains of the tent, Zammis shaking my arm. "Uncle? Uncle?"
"Yes?" I whispered.
"Uncle, I'm ready to go." It pointed to my side. "Your food is here,

BARRY B. LONGYEAR

and when it rains, just pull the tent over your face. I'll mark the trail I make so I can find my way back."

I nodded. "Take care of yourself."

Zammis shook its head. "Uncle, I can carry you. We shouldn't separate."

I weakly shook my head. "Give me a break, kid. I couldn't make it. Find somebody and bring 'em back." I felt my stomach flip, and cold sweat drenched my snakeskins. "Go on; get going."

Zammis reached out, grabbed its pack and stood. The pack shouldered, Zammis turned and began running in the direction that the craft had been going. I watched until I couldn't see it. I faced up and looked at the clouds. "You almost got me that time, you *kizlode* sonofabitch, but you didn't figure on the Drac . . . you keep forgetting . . . there's two of us. . . ." I drifted in and out of consciousness, felt rain on my face, then pulled up the tent and covered my head. In seconds, the blackout returned.

"Davidge? Lieutenant Davidge?"

I opened my eyes and saw something I hadn't seen for four Earth years: a human face. "Who are you?"

The face, young, long, and capped by short blond hair, smiled. "I'm Captain Steerman, the medical officer. How do you feel?"

I pondered the question and smiled. "Like I've been shot full of very high grade junk."

"You have. You were in pretty bad shape by the time the survey team brought you in."

"Survey team?"

"I guess you don't know. The United States of Earth and the Dracon Chamber have established a joint commission to supervise the colonization of new planets. The war is over."

"Over?"

"Yes."

Something heavy lifted from my chest. "Where's Zammis?"

"Who?"

"Jeriban Zammis; the Drac that I was with."

The doctor shrugged. "I don't know anything about it, but I suppose the Draggers are taking care of it."

Draggers. I'd once used the term myself. As I listened to it coming out of Steerman's mouth, it seemed foreign: alien, repulsive. "Zammis is a Drac, not a Dragger."

The doctor's brows furrowed, then he shrugged. "Of course. Whatever you say. Just you get some rest, and I'll check back on you in a few hours."

"May I see Zammis?"

The doctor smiled. "Dear, no. You're on your way back to the Delphi USEB. The . . . Drac is probably on its way to Draco." He nodded, then turned and left. God, I felt lost. I looked around and saw that I was in the ward of a ship's sick bay. The beds on either side of me were occupied. The man on my right shook his head and went back to reading a magaine. The one on my left looked angry.

"You damned Dragger suck!" He turned on his left side and presented me his back.

Among humans once again, yet more alone than I had ever been. *Misnuuram va siddeth,* as Mistan observed in the Talman from the calm perspective of eight hundred years in the past. Loneliness is a thought—not something done to someone; instead, it is something that someone does to oneself. *Jerry shook its head that one time, then pointed a yellow finger at me as the words it wanted to say came together. "Davidge . . . to me loneliness is a discomfort—a small thing to be avoided if possible, but not feared. I think you would almost prefer death to being alone with yourself."*

Misnuuram yaa va nos misnuuram van dunos. "You who are alone by yourselves will forever be alone with others." Mistan again. On its face, the statement appears to be a contradiction; but the test of reality proves it true. I was a stranger among my own kind because of a hate that I didn't share, and a love that, to them, seemed alien, impossible, perverse. *"Peace of thought with others occurs only in the mind at peace with itself."* Mistan again. Countless times, on the voyage to the Delphi Base, putting in my ward time, then during my processing out of the service, I would reach to my chest to grasp the *Talman* that no longer hung there. What had become of Zammis? The USESF didn't care, and the Drac authorities wouldn't say—none of my affair.

Ex-Force pilots were a drag on the employment market, and there were no commercial positions open—especially not to a pilot who hadn't flown in four years, who had a gimpy leg, and who was a Dragger suck. "Dragger suck" as an invective had the impact of several historical terms—Quisling, heretic, fag, nigger lover—all rolled into one.

I had forty-eight thousand credits in back pay, and so money wasn't a problem. The problem was what to do with myself. After kicking around the Delphi Base, I took transportation to Earth and, for several months, was employed by a small book house translating manuscripts into Drac. It seems that there was a craving among Dracs for Westerns: "Stick 'em up *naagusaat!*"

"*Nu Geph,* lawman." *Thang, thang!* The guns flashed and the *Kizlode shaddsaat* bit the *thessa.*

I quit.

I finally called my parents. *Why didn't you call before, Willy? We've been worried sick . . . Had a few things I had to straighten out, Dad . . . No, not really . . . Well, we understand, son . . . it must have been awful . . . Dad, I'd like to come home for awhile. . . .*

Even before I put down the money on the used Dearman Electric, I knew I was making a mistake going home. I felt the need of a home, but the one I had left at the age of eighteen wasn't it. But I headed there because there was nowhere else to go.

I drove alone in the dark, using only the old roads, the quiet hum of the Dearman's motor the only sound. The December midnight was clear, and I could see the stars through the car's bubble canopy. Fyrine IV drifted into my thoughts, the raging ocean, the endless winds. I pulled off the road onto the shoulder and killed the lights. In a few minutes, my eyes adjusted to the dark and I stepped outside and shut the door. Kansas has a big sky, and the stars seemed close enough to touch. Snow crunched under my feet as I looked up, trying to pick Fyrine out of the thousands of visible stars.

Fyrine is in the constellation Pegasus, but my eyes were not practiced enough to pick the winged horse out from the surrounding stars. I shrugged, felt a chill, and decided to get back in the car. As I put my hand on the doorlatch, I saw a constellation that I did recognize, north, hanging just above the horizon: Draco. The Dragon, its tail twisted around Ursa Minor, hung upside down in the sky. Eltanin, the Dragon's nose, is the homestar of the Dracs. Its second planet, Draco, was Zammis' home.

Headlights from an approaching car blinded me, and I turned toward the car as it pulled to a stop. The window on the driver's side opened and someone spoke from the darkness.

"You need some help?"

I shook my head. "No, thank you." I held up a hand. "I was just looking at the stars."

"Quite a night, isn't it?"

"Sure is."

"Sure you don't need any help?"

I shook my head. "Thanks . . . wait. Where is the nearest commercial spaceport?"

"About an hour ahead in Salina."

"Thanks." I saw a hand wave from the window, then the other car pulled away. I took another look at Eltanin, then got back in my car.

Six months later, I stood in front of an ancient cut-stone gate wondering what in the hell I was doing. The trip to Draco, with nothing but Dracs as companions on the last leg, showed me the truth in Namvaac's words: "Peace is often only war without fighting." The accords, on paper, gave me the right to travel to the planet, but the Drac bureaucrats and their paperwork wizards had perfected the big stall long before the first human step into space. It look threats, bribes, and long days of filling out forms, being checked and re-checked for disease, contraband, reason for visit, filling out more forms, refilling out the forms I had already filled out, more bribes, waiting, waiting, waiting . . .

On the ship, I spent most of my time in my cabin, but since the Drac stewards refused to serve me, I went to the ship's lounge for my meals. I sat alone, listening to the comments about me from other booths. I had figured the path of least resistance was to pretend I didn't understand what they were saying. It is always assumed that humans do not speak Drac.

"Must we eat in the same compartment with the *Irkmaan* slime?"

"Look at it, how its pale skin blotches—and that evil smelling thatch on top. Feh! The smell!"

I ground my teeth a little and kept my glance riveted to my plate.

"It defies the *Talman* that the universe's laws could be so corrupt as to produce a creature such as that."

I turned and faced the three Dracs sitting in the booth across the aisle from mine. In Drac, I replied: "If your line's elders had seen fit to teach the village *kiz* to use contraceptives, you wouldn't even exist." I returned to my food while the two Dracs struggled to hold the third Drac down.

On Draco, it was no problem finding the Jeriba estate. The problem was getting in. A high stone wall enclosed the property, and from the gate, I could see the huge stone mansion that Jerry had described to me. I told the guard at the gate that I wanted to see Jeriba Zammis. The guard stared at me, then went into an alcove behind the gate. In a few moments, another Drac emerged from the mansion and walked quickly across the wide lawn to the gate. The Drac nodded at the guard, then stopped and faced me. It was a dead ringer for Jerry.

"You are the *Irkmaan* that asked to see Jeriba Zammis?"

I nodded. "Zammis must have told you about me. I'm Willis Davidge."

The Drac studied me. "I am Estone Nev, Jeriba Shigan's sibling. My parent, Jeriba Gothig, wishes to see you." The Drac turned abruptly and walked back to the mansion. I followed, feeling heady at the thought of seeing Zammis again. I paid little attention to my surroundings until I was ushered into a large room with a vaulted stone ceiling. Jerry had told me that the house was four thousand years old. I believed it. As I entered, another Drac stood and walked over to me. It was old, but I knew who it was.

"You are Gothig, Shigan's parent."

The yellow eyes studied me. "Who are you, *Irkmaan?*" It held out a wrinkled, three-fingered hand. "What do you know of Jeriba Zammis, and why do you speak the Drac tongue with the style and accent of my child Shigan? What are you here for?"

"I speak Drac in this manner because that is the way Jeriba Shigan taught me to speak it."

The old Drac cocked its head to one side and narrowed its yellow eyes. "You knew my child? How?"

"Didn't the survey commission tell you?"

"It was reported to me that my child, Shigan, was killed in the battle of Fyrine IV. That was over six of our years ago. What is your game, *Irkmaan?*"

I turned from Gothig to Nev. The younger Drac was examining me with the same look of suspicion. I turned back to Gothig. "Shigan wasn't killed in the battle. We were stranded together on the surface of Fyrine IV and lived there for a year. Shigan died giving birth to Jeriba Zammis. A year later the joint survey commission found us and —"

"Enough! Enough of this, *Irkmaan!* Are you here for money, to use my influence for trade concessions—what?"

I frowned. "Where is Zammis?"

Tears of anger came to the old Drac's eyes. "There is no Zammis, *Irkmaan!* The Jeriba line ended with the death of Shigan!"

My eyes grew wide as I shook my head. "That's not true. I know. I took care of Zammis—you heard nothing from the commission?"

"Get to the point of your scheme, *Irkmaan*. I haven't all day."

I studied Gothig. The old Drac had heard nothing from the commission. The Drac authorities took Zammis, and the child had evaporated. Gothig had been told nothing. Why? "I was with Shigan, Gothig. That is how I learned your language. When Shigan died giving birth to Zammis, I—"

"*Irkmaan,* if you cannot get to your scheme, I will have to ask Nev to throw you out. Shigan died in the battle of Fyrine IV. The Drac Fleet notified us only days later."

I nodded. "Then, Gothig, tell me how I came to know the line of Jeriba? Do you wish me to recite it for you?"

Gothig snorted. "You say you know the Jeriba line?"

"Yes."

Gothig flipped a hand at me. "Then, recite."

I took a breath, then began. By the time I had reached the hundred and seventy-third generation, Gothig had knelt on the stone floor next to Nev. The Dracs remained that way for the three hours of the recital. When I concluded, Gothig bowed its head and wept. "Yes, *Irkmaan,* yes. You must have known Shigan. Yes." The old Drac looked up into my face, its eyes wide with hope. "And, you say Shigan continued the line—that Zammis was born?"

I nodded. "I don't know why the commission didn't notify you."

Gothig got to its feet and frowned. "We will find out, *Irkmaan*—what is your name?"

"Davidge. Willis Davidge."

"We will find out, Davidge."

Gothig arranged quarters for me in its house, which was fortunate, since I had little more than eleven hundred credits left. After making a host of inquiries, Gothig sent Nev and me to the Chamber Center in Sendievu, Draco's capital city. The Jeriba line, I found, was influential, and the big stall was held down to a minimum. Eventually, we were directed to the Joint Survey Commission representative, a Drac named Jozzdn Vrule. It looked up from the letter Gothig had given me and frowned. "Where did you get this, *Irkmaan?*"

"I believe the signature is on it."

The Drac looked at the paper, then back at me. "The Jeriba line is one of the most respected on Draco. You say that Jeriba Gothig gave you this?"

"I felt certain I said that; I could feel my lips moving—"

Nev stepped in. "You have the dates and the information concerning the Fyrine IV survey mission. We want to know what happened to Jeriba Zammis."

Jozzdn Vrule frowned and looked back at the paper. "Estone Nev, you are the founder of your line, is this not true?"

"Is it true."

"Would you found your line in shame? Why do I see you with this *Irkmaan?*"

Nev curled its upper lip and folded its arms. "Jozzdn Vrule, if you contemplate walking this planet in the foreseeable future as a free being, it would be to your profit to stop working your mouth and to start finding Jeriba Zammis."

Jozzdn Vrule looked down and studied its fingers, then returned its glance to Nev. "Very well, Estone Nev. You threaten me if I fail to hand you the truth. I think you will find the truth the greater threat." The Drac scribbled on a piece of paper, then handed it to Nev. "You will find Jeriba Zammis at this address, and you will curse the day that I gave you this."

We entered the imbecile colony feeling sick. All around us, Dracs stared with vacant eyes, or screamed, or foamed at the mouth, or behaved as lower-order creatures. After we had arrived, Gothig joined us. The Drac director of the colony frowned at me and shook its head at Gothig. "Turn back now, while it is still possible, Jeriba Gothig. Beyond this room lies nothing but pain and sorrow."

Gothig grabbed the director by the front of its wraps. "Hear me, insect: If Jeriba Zammis is within these walls, bring my grandchild forth! Else, I shall bring the might of the Jeriba line down upon your pointed head!"

The director lifted its head, twitched its lips, then nodded. "Very well. Very well, you pompous *Kazzmidth!* We tried to protect the Jeriba reputation. We tried! But now you shall see." The director nodded and pursed its lips. "Yes, you overwealthy fashion follower, now you shall see." The director scribbled on a piece of paper, then handed it to Nev. "By giving you that, I will lose my position, but take it! Yes, take it! See this being you call Jeriba Zammis. See it, and weep!"

Among trees and grass, Jeriba Zammis sat upon a stone bench, staring at the ground. Its eyes never blinked, its hands never moved. Gothig frowned at me, but I could spare nothing for Shigan's parent.

I walked to Zammis. "Zammis, do you know me?"

The Drac retrieved its thoughts from a million warrens and raised its yellow eyes to me. I saw no sign of recognition. "Who are you?"

I squatted down, placed my hands on its arms and shook them.

"Dammit, Zammis, don't you know me? I'm your Uncle. Remember that? Uncle Davidge?"

The Drac weaved on the bench, then shook its head. It lifted an arm and waved to an orderly. "I want to go to my room. Please, let me go to my room."

I stood and grabbed Zammis by the front of its hospital gown. "Zammis, it's me!"

The yellow eyes, dull and lifeless, stared back at me. The orderly placed a yellow hand upon my shoulder. "Let it go, *Irkmaan*."

"Zammis!" I turned to Nev and Gothig. "Say something!"

The Drac orderly pulled a sap from its pocket, then slapped it suggestively against the palm of its hand. "Let it go, *Irkmaan*."

Gothig stepped forward. "Explain this!"

The orderly looked at Gothig, Nev, me, and then Zammis. "This one—this creature—came to us professing a love, a *love*, mind you, of humans! This is no small perversion, Jeriba Gothig. The government would protect you from this scandal. Would you wish the line of Jeriba dragged into this?"

I looked at Zammis. "What have you done to Zammis, you *kizlode* sonofabitch? A little shock? A little drug? Rot out its mind?"

The orderly sneered at me, then shook its head. "You, *Irkmaan*, do not understand. This one would not be happy as an *Irkmaan vul*—a human lover. We are making it possible for this one to function in Drac society. You think this is wrong?"

I looked at Zammis and shook my head. I remembered too well my treatment at the hands of my fellow humans. "No. I don't think it's wrong . . . I just don't know."

The orderly turned to Gothig. "Please understand, Jeriba Gothig. We could not subject the Jeriba line to this disgrace. Your grandchild is almost well and will soon enter a reeducation program. In no more than two years, you will have a grandchild worthy of carrying on the Jeriba line. Is this wrong?"

Gothig only shook its head. I squatted down in front of Zammis and looked up into its yellow eyes. I reached up and took its right hand in both of mine. "Zammis?"

Zammis looked down, moved its left hand over and picked up my left hand and spread the fingers. One at a time Zammis pointed at the fingers of my hand, then it looked into my eyes, then examined the hand again. "Yes . . ." Zammis pointed again.

"One, two, three, *four five!*" Zammis looked into my eyes. "Four, five!"

I nodded. "Yes. Yes."

Zammis pulled my hand to its cheek and held it close. "Uncle . . . Uncle. I told you I'd never forget you."

I never counted the years that passed. My beard was back, and I knelt in my snakeskins next to the grave of my friend, Jeriba Shigan. Next to the grave was the four-year-old grave of Gothig. I replaced some rocks, then added a few more. Wrapping my snakeskins tightly against the wind, I sat down next to the grave and looked out to sea. Still the rollers steamed in under the grey-black cover of clouds. Soon, the ice would come. I nodded, looked at my scarred, wrinkled hands, then back at the grave.

"I couldn't stay in the settlement with them, Jerry. Don't get me wrong; it's nice. Damned nice. But I kept looking out my window, seeing the ocean, thinking of the cave. I'm alone, in a way. But it's good. I know what and who I am, Jerry, and that's all there is to it, right?"

I heard a noise. I crouched over, placed my hands upon my withered knees, and pushed myself to my feet. The Drac was coming from the settlement compound, a child in its arms.

I rubbed my beard. "Eh, Ty, so that is your first child?"

The Drac nodded. "I would be pleased, Uncle, if you would teach it what it must be taught: the line, the *Talman;* and about life on Fyrine IV, our planet called 'Friendship'."

I took the bundle into my arms. Chubby three-fingered arms waved at the air, then grasped my snakeskins. "Yes, Ty, this one is a Jeriba." I looked up at Ty. "And how is your parent, Zammis?"

Ty shrugged. "It is as well as can be expected. My parent wishes you well."

I nodded. "And the same to it, Ty. Zammis ought to get out of that air-conditioned capsule and come back to live in the cave. It'll do it good."

Ty grinned and nodded its head. "I will tell my parent, Uncle."

I stabbed my thumb into my chest. "Look at me! You don't see me sick, do you?"

"No, Uncle."

"You tell Zammis to kick that doctor out of there and to come back to the cave, hear?"

"Yes, Uncle." Ty smiled. "Is there anything you need?"

I nodded and scratched the back of my neck. "Toilet paper. Just a couple of packs. Maybe a couple of bottles of whiskey—no, forget the whiskey. I'll wait until Haesni, here, puts in its first year. Just the toilet paper."

Ty bowed. "Yes, Uncle, and may the many mornings find you well."

I waved my hand impatiently. "They will, they will. Just don't forget the toilet paper."

Ty bowed again. "I won't, Uncle."

Ty turned and walked through the scrub forest back to the colony. Gothig had put up the cash and moved the entire line, and all the related lines, to Fyrine IV. I lived with them for a year, but I moved out and went back to the cave. I gathered the wood, smoked the snake, and withstood the winter. Zammis gave me the young Ty to rear in the cave, and now Ty had handed me Haesni. I nodded at the child. "Your child will be called Gothig, and then . . ." I looked at the sky and felt the tears drying on my face. ". . . and then, Gothig's child will be called Shigan." I nodded and headed for the cleft that would bring us down to the level of the cave.

BARRY B. LONGYEAR